D0483882

Architects of
Emortality

Tor Books by Brian Stableford

Inherit the Earth
Architects of Emortality

Architects of
Emortality

BRIAN STABLEFORD

A Tom Doherty Associates Book   •   New York

This is a work of fiction. All the characters and events portrayed in this novel are either fictitious or are used fictitiously.

ARCHITECTS OF EMORTALITY

Copyright © 1999 by Brian Stableford

All rights reserved, including the right to reproduce this book, or portions thereof, in any form.

This book is printed on acid-free paper.

Edited by David G. Hartwell

A Tor Book

Published by Tom Doherty Associates, LLC

175 Fifth Avenue

New York, NY 10010

www.tor.com

Tor® is a registered trademark of Tom Doherty Associates, LLC.

ISBN 0-312-87207-0

Printed in the United States of America

For Jane, and all who nourish fond remorse

Acknowledgments

A much shorter and substantially different version of this story was published in the October 1994 issue of *Asimov's Science Fiction*. I owe considerable debts of gratitude to Gardner Dozois, for publishing that novella and reprinting it in his annual collection of the *Year's Best Science Fiction,* and to Charles Baudelaire, Oscar Fingal O'Flahertie Wills Wilde, the original Gustave Moreau, John Milton, and Nathaniel Hawthorne, without whose contributions and general inspiration the story would have been much slighter. I should also like to thank Sonia Feldman for the shamirs, Jane Stableford for proofreading services and helpful commentary, and Andy Robertson for being prepared to claim that he had read *every word*.

A King in His Countinghouse

G abriel King stared out of the window of his thirty-ninth-floor apartment in the Trebizond Tower. He was looking at the island of Manhattan, where the apparatus of civilization was being slowly but surely demolished. The old skyline was decaying; the sharp sharks' teeth of the traditional skyscrapers were collapsing into mere blunted molars. One by one, the oldest buildings in the world were gently folding into themselves, meekly putting themselves away.

The sight made Gabriel feel slightly sad. It should, in theory, have had the opposite effect; he, after all, was the man primarily responsible for the many kinds of rot that had set in and the voracity of their consumption. Every minute diminution of the classic silhouette sent a surge of credit into his multifarious bank accounts. The MegaMall was paying him generously for his efforts, as it always did. Those who had served the MegaMall well—as Gabriel always had, in dealings under the counter as well as above it—were always well served in their turn.

The squat foundations of the new city were already in place behind and among the decaying edifices, and the shamirs were ready to begin the reshaping. They too were Gabriel's slaves, and their labors would maintain the flow of his capital, but contemplation of the endeavors and rewards to come could not lift his mood.

The simple fact was that New York had always stood, in Gabriel's quintessentially American consciousness, for the world, and he could not see a world die without a slight pang of regret. He had not been born in the USNA—his nominal citizenship was Australian—but he had always been a demolition and construction man, a materialist, and an ardent champion of progress. Those were the core values of the real America: the America that knew no geographical boundaries, because it was a dream. To witness the demolition of New York was, for Gabriel, to witness the end of a historical epoch. He had witnessed the ending of mere eras and felt nothing but joy in the contemplation of progress, but this was different. The new dawn which his shamirs were programmed to break for the MegaMall was the dawn of an epoch: the epoch of the New Human Race. It was not merely Old New York that had been declared redundant; it was the people who had lived in it for the last few hundred years.

The personal shamirs that had seen Gabriel's body through two full rejuvenations and countless cosmetic patch-ups had all but exhausted their resources. With luck he might live for another thirty or forty years, but the chances of his mind surviving a third full rejuve were very slim indeed. For the moment, he was compos mentis, with no more holes in his memory than the average one-hundred-and-ninety-four-year-old, but the integrity of his personality had grown perilously brittle; any sudden jolt might shatter it. The shadow of death was hanging over him, ready to descend upon his person as it was now descending upon Old New York.

When he looked upon the rotting of New York, therefore, Gabriel saw the end of *his* world, and everything that it had meant. At long last, progress had outstripped him and all of his kind. Progress would go on, but he and others like him could not. Even if he survived another sixty years, or a hundred, he could make no further progress—and nor could any man of his obsolete kind.

He was what he was; for him, the process of becoming was finished. Any sons born after him would be members of a new species, children of the MegaMall and the Architects of Emortality.

The miracle was, he supposed, that he only felt *slightly* sad. Fortunately, he had led a good and productive life, as a loyal servant of the MegaMall. He had never reached the upper echelons even of its servant class, let alone its Inner Circle, but he had been richly rewarded. Nor was wealth the limit of his good fortune, he told himself; although he could not claim a place in the new world that he was helping to build, he still had pleasures in store. There was much in life that could still be savored. Within the hour, he knew, his sadness would be lifted—for a while.

Gabriel brushed the back of his right hand over his lips, wiping away a trace of moisture which had accumulated in the corner of his mouth. He had no difficulty whatsoever in visualizing the new skyline which would eventually replace the one already decayed. He had seen it often enough in virtual reality, modeled with exquisite care, lit by a sky much brighter than the sullen one which loomed over the city now.

The new edifices would not reach for the heavens in the same thrusting and predatory fashion as the old. Their discreet curves would be the harbingers of a new era of harmony and stability: an era in which the New Human Race would put an end forever to death and its terrible handmaidens, angst and war.

The carefully worded but unvoiced thought brought forth an unexpectedly sour surge of resentment. "The Age of the Human Herbivores," he murmured, speaking loudly enough for the apartment's recorders to catch the words, although he was not entirely sure that he wanted evidence of a childish explosion of envy to remain on the record. "The Cud-Chewing Era."

The wave of resentment died quickly enough, and the manufactured contempt with it. Intellectually, Gabriel did not begrudge the New Human Race its dreams, and he was not a man to let his emotions get the better of his intellect. The judgment of his intellect was—as it had to be—that the demolition of New York was work of which a man of his sort should be proud. It was, after all, a fitting culmination of his career.

Long ago, while Gabriel had been a student at Wollongong, someone—probably Magnus Teidemann—had told him that sharks' teeth were not like the teeth of humans. Sharks' teeth were continually renewed, new ones growing in the rear and migrating forward to replace the old as they were worn down by use. New

York's skyscrapers had followed that pattern for more than five hundred years; whenever one had been removed, another had sprung up to take its place, usually brighter, sharper, and more durable. Despite piecemeal change, the whole ensemble had remained essentially the same. No one had ever taken on the entire island before, let alone the entire city. This was the first time that the whole set of shark's teeth had been swept away, along with the implicit shark. From now on, New York would be the mouth of a very different social organism. Gabriel was proud to have been the man appointed to that task. In fact, he was *very* proud—intellectually speaking, of course.

Gabriel felt perfectly entitled to think of himself as *the* man appointed to the task, although a pedant would have insisted that he was merely one of many, and perhaps not the most important. History would give primary credit to the planners who had pronounced a sentence of death on the old city and the architects who had designed the new. If the engineers who actually carried out the work were to be remembered at all, they would be seen as mere applicants of a suite of technologies that still bore the name of their ancient founder, Leon Gantz, and a nickname borrowed from the legend of Solomon.

Gabriel knew well enough that when the day finally came for the news tapes to record his obituary and commemorate his life, he would be described as a gantzer and a master of shamirs, as if all he had ever done was to use another man's tools—but he also knew that the description would be misleading and unfair. Leon Gantz had only laid the foundations of biological cementation and deconstruction; it was not until the late twenty-second century that the anonymous nanotechnologists of PicoCon had succeeded in forming the first vital partnership between the organic and the inorganic, and not until the mid-twenty-fourth century that the MegaMall had delivered the full spectrum of modern nanomanipulators into the eager hands of ambitious young men like himself.

Leon Gantz, the PicoCon teamworkers, and the MegaMall's

backroom buccaneers had all been scientists, but Gabriel King was a practical man, a materialist through and through. In his own estimation, Gabriel was a *maker,* and an *artist* in the truest sense of the word—a truer sense, at any rate, than the sense in which the word was used by certain people he could name.

"Posturing apes in fancy dress," Gabriel murmured, again speaking loudly enough to impress the words upon the microscopic ears with which all the apartment's rooms save one were liberally supplied. Being a practical man, Gabriel did not approve of the "posturing" by means of which certain *so-called* artists attempted to attract the public eye. Nor did he approve of "apes" who dedicated their lives to making ever more flamboyant versions of entities that were useless in the first place. Nor did he approve of "fancy dress"; his own suitskins were always gray or dark blue, always neatly tailored in such a way as to proclaim that they and he were good utilitarians, with no energy to spare for nonsensical display.

Gabriel knew that there were some who thought that the work in which he was now engaged was an assault on nonsensical display. The would-be prophets of Decivilization had formed a particular hatred for New York and the supposed symbolism of its skyline. It was, in their eyes, the ultimate city, and hence the ultimate symbol of the supposedly decadent past that the Decivilizers desired to obliterate—regardless of the needs and desires of the New Human Race.

Gabriel was prepared to admit that if ever there was a city whose ugliness demanded that it be torn down and built anew, that city was Old New York, but he found talk of "eliminating the display of history" and "shedding the empty cultural heritage of the past" difficult to endure. He had more than a little respect for "the display of history," on the grounds that if mankind's mistakes were not made manifest as well as remembered, they might be repeated, even by a New Human Race engineered in the artificial womb for true emortality. To make this unrepentantly misshapen metropolis a scapegoat for antediluvian folly and greed seemed to him to be foolish and simpleminded.

To Gabriel, as to all Americans in spirit, Manhattan was the last urban wilderness, the last geographically confined space on Earth where so many people so ardently desired to gather that it had been forced to grow further and further upward, extending its magnificently vicious fangs into gleaming blades of crystal and alloy. Given that the island had to be domesticated and made fit for habitation by the ironically titled Naturals, Gabriel would not have wanted the labor of its deconstruction to be entrusted to anyone else—but it was hardly surprising that the job had imported a sadness into his soul that he could not shake off and did not really want to.

It was only natural—was it not?—that he should be unable to take as much delight in contemplation of the raising of the tame city as he was from contemplation of the devastation of the wild.

"The devastation of the wild," he repeated, aloud, in order that he could savor the phrase. Some thoughts were too precious to remain unspoken.

Then the door chime sounded, and his sadness vanished like smoke as he turned away from the window. His heart was already beginning to beat a little faster in anticipation of delight.

Gabriel checked the viewscreen, although he knew perfectly well who it was. As a conscientious utilitarian, he never received personal visitors in the many temporary homes which business forced him to adopt, except for purposes that were strictly personal. He was of the old school, which held that all professional matters should be consigned to virtual environments, where the full panoply of technical support was available—and he was also of the even older school, which held that the pressures of the flesh were best dealt with in the flesh.

He was certain that the woman waiting to be admitted to the apartment was authentically young, not because he had expertise enough to detect a first-rate rejuve, but because the way she talked and the fact that she was here at all smacked of awesome naïveté. At a distance, one might have judged that she looked like thousands of other young women, sculpted to a currently fashionable ideal, but at close quarters her uniqueness became obvious. Her eyes were wonderful, her hair utterly glorious. In an age where only the subtlest nuances could discriminate between the very beautiful and the extremely beautiful, she belonged to the furthest reaches of the extreme category.

"Come in," Gabriel said as he released the locks and slid the door aside.

It seemed that she understood what it meant to belong to a very old school, because she had brought him flowers. "These are for you," she said as she handed them over, smiling broadly. The blooms were like miniature sunflowers, and their densely clustered petals had the color and texture of nascent gold.

"They're beautiful," Gabriel said. "I don't think I've seen their like before."

"They're new," she said, still smiling. "An Oscar Wilde original."

Gabriel could not help falling prey to the slightest hint of a frown, but he turned his head so that his visitor would not see it, and the phrase he murmured—"*That* posturing ape!"—was pronounced too softly for her merely human ears to discern.

Lest she ask him what he had said, and why, he was quick to add: "I have a vase somewhere. Should I put them in water, or do they require something more nourishing?"

"Oh no," she said. "They're self-sufficient, provided that the atmosphere isn't too dry. You can mount them on the wall if you don't want them cluttering up a table." Her gaze traveled around the walls as she spoke, offering silent comment on the fact that the apartment was unfashionably bare of vegetative decoration.

"That's all right," Gabriel replied, a little more stiffly than he would have liked. He handed them back to her while he went to search for the vase.

When they had first met, in the park, the woman had been delighted to find out who he was and what had brought him to the city. She had been fascinated to hear him talk about himself, and he had talked more freely to her than he had to anyone since the ninth and last of his bond marriages had come to the inevitable parting of the ways.

She had told him almost nothing about herself, but that was probably because she had little or nothing to tell. Given the presumable difference in their ages, it was only natural that she should be content to listen and learn. When Gabriel had told her that he had been twice rejuvenated, and how long ago his second rejuvenation had been, her eyes had grown wide.

"You must be one of the oldest men in the world," she had said. "But you seem much better preserved than most others of your generation."

"I suppose so," he had replied. "Many people—men and women alike—seem to come apart quite rapidly once the effects of their second full rejuve wear off, but I've been lucky, at least superficially. Internally, the balance of my organic and inorganic IT is way past critical. If I were to attempt another rejuve I'd very probably end up a vegetable, but if I can stay reasonably fit I can probably keep on getting older for another thirty years, and keep some faint echo of my fading looks until the day I die."

"You look wonderful," she had assured him. "So wonderfully *wise*." When he came back into the reception room the woman was standing at the window, exactly where he had been standing a few moments before. He hoped that she was admiring his handiwork—and that her admiration was not tainted by the slightest sadness. "Let me take the vase," she said.

Gabriel surrendered his find with a vague gesture of apology for its mere adequacy. He had never believed the die-hard psychobiologists who had insisted that the aesthetic judgments which underlay sexual attractiveness were genetically hardwired so that the idea of beauty and the appearance of youth were inextricably tied together. He had scored too many notable successes in pick-up spots far less promising than Central Park to accept the apologetic argument that the attraction which the very young sometimes manifested for the very old was merely a matter of the momentary fascination of the extraordinary.

"It's a fine view," he said, nodding toward the softening skyline.

"It certainly is," she replied. "The outline of the city is changing day by day, and you're the man responsible."

"Only one of many," he said, deeply regretting the duty of false modesty and hoping that she might contradict him.

"Oh no," she said, right on cue. "You're the one who's actually *doing* it. You're the deconstructor, the Decivilizer."

He was determined not to let the final noun distract from the effect of the compliment.

"Would you like a drink?" he asked.

"Oh no," she said again. "I prefer making love without the aid of chemical stimulants—don't you?"

He did, but he knew that she would have assumed as much because of the way he dressed. He knew too that she would never have used a phrase like "making love" when talking to someone of her own generation. For a fleeting moment, he wondered whether she might be making a little *too much* effort, but then he smiled, realizing that she was only trying to make a good impression. Her eyes were wonderful, and the way she brushed her flowing tresses aside so that she could see him more clearly was nothing short of divine. No VE siren could ever replace the quotidian reality of her presence and the naive insouciance of her gesture. She placed the vase on the table in front of the sofa, carefully spreading the blooms. There had been a card hidden among them, and she plucked it out, standing it on its edge against the vase. There was something written on the card, but Gabriel made no attempt to read it. There would be time for that later.

"A long time ago," Gabriel said, making the most of the phrase, "I wrote a thesis for my doctorate on the twenty-first-century Greenhouse Crisis. The rising sea levels forced New York's citizens to fight a fantastic battle to preserve it from the flood, raising the entire island and remodeling the buildings so that the old streets became flood tunnels. In those days, New York was a symbol of United America's defiance of the forces of nature: an embodiment of the determination of the Hundred States to survive the crisis and remake the world. Sometimes I can't help thinking that it's slightly disrespectful to the efforts of those twenty-first-century heroes to renounce the city's heritage—and whatever motivates my paymasters, that's not the spirit in which I'm working. I'm trying to do as they did, to *save* the city and everything it has symbolized." Silently he cursed himself for excessive pomposity, but the young woman seemed to mop it up.

"Yes," she said. "I see. I understand what you're saying—what you're doing."

Gabriel felt a sudden moment of dizziness, which had nothing to do with the elevation of the thirty-ninth floor of the undeconstructed Trebizond Tower.

He realized that he could not now remember what complex chain of accidents and decisions had made him a master of demolition. He must have begun adult life as a historian, if he had indeed written the thesis he had glibly recalled, and must have continued it as a businessman enthusiastic for any opportunity. Deconstruction was the pattern into which his life had eventually fallen, but he no longer knew exactly how or why. It must have been the trail of profit and loss, not any special interest, which had led him into the specific line of business whose master he now was, but he had developed a passion for it nevertheless. He was an engineer, not a scientist, and he still knew next to nothing about the molecular biology of the bacterial agents which were his ultimate minions, but he loved the discretion and the artistry of their work. Felling by artificial decay was neat as well as economical.

"Wouldn't it be more satisfying, Gabriel," one of his aides had recently asked him, "if you made as much money building things as you do tearing them down?"

Would it? he wondered as he stared at his visitor's beautifully guileless eyes. He honestly didn't know.

He rallied himself, blinking away the momentary hint of vertigo and breaking away from his companion's gaze. On the far side of Central Park the rotting teeth were slowly and politely folding themselves away into their internal cavities. He had to remind himself that he was not at all like them; he was no ugly transient, fading into decrepitude for the last time. The presence of the lovely woman was adequate proof of that fact. She was authentically young, perhaps even a Natural, and yet she was here, ready to embrace him, to savor the thrill of being with a man who had done so much: a *complete* man.

"What do you love best in all the world?" the young woman asked Gabriel King as she took his hand and drew him away from the table where she had placed the vase.

It was a strange question, but she asked it as if it were serious—and she was, after all, authentically young. She had come to him in the flesh, seeking enlightenment.

Gabriel had not the slightest idea what he loved best in all the world. Everything he had done—everything, at least, that he *remembered* having done—he had done for money, but he had never been an overdevout worshipper at the shrine of Mammon. He had made money because that was what people of his particular tribe had always done. His foster father and his foster grandfather before him had made money, in the crisis and its aftermath, and six or seven generations of woman-born Kings before them had made money even during the Dark Ages of the unextended life span. Kings had always been the most loyal and best-rewarded servants of the forebears of the MegaMall, even in the dark days before the Pharaohs of Capitalism had formed the Hardinist Cabal and brought a precious world order out of primordial chaos.

Gabriel was sure that those primitive Kings had never been ashamed to make money. Even before the days of Leon Gantz and his marvelous shamirs they had probably made it from decadence, devastation, destruction, decay, dereliction, and decivilization. . . . It had been, he had to suppose, their particular version of divine right. But Gabriel, unlike the worst of them, had never *loved* money. No matter what he had done in the name of progress and the service of the MegaMall, he had severed his connection with that heritage of unalloyed greed.

"I've loved many people and many things at different times," he told the woman, knowing that his answer was a little belated. "Too many, I think, for any one person or any one thing to stand out as the best."

It might even have been true. You've lived too long, his forefathers might have said. You've had three lifetimes instead of one, and no true sons to carry forward the family name. You've betrayed our heritage for your own selfish pleasure. And you never even loved the money you made.

The Kings are dead, he said silently, by way of imaginary reply. Long live the King.

He guided the young woman to the door of the bedroom, which was privacy-screened. Given that the apartment building was so relentlessly respectable, he had every faith in the assurance that the bedroom walls contained neither hidden eyes nor hidden ears.

As the door slid open before them Gabriel increased the length of his stride slightly, but the woman reached out to pull him back, forcing him to hesitate on the threshold.

She turned to look briefly at the golden flowers, as if approving her own excellent taste; then she turned back to him, looking up into his face as if to do exactly the same. She reached up, put her hand at the back of his neck, and eased his face forward and down, so that she could kiss him on the lips.

The kiss was deliberately languorous, as if she were savoring a moment that would remain precious in memory for a long time.

Gabriel felt giddy again. He could not help but wonder why the young woman seemed to like him so much. For a moment, he was half-convinced that her presence—indeed, her very existence—was a mere delusion, a siren unnaturally wrenched by some trick of his failing intellect out of some uniquely seductive virtual environment. He was, however, old enough and wise enough not to question his good fortune too closely.

A man of his age—a member of the last generation which had no alternative but to be mortal—owed it both to himself and his vanishing species to do his utmost to drain the last drop of pleasure from every random whim of happy chance.

Like his as-yet-undiscovered predecessors, Gabriel King did not know that he had already begun to die, and that the murderous shadow would move upon him with remarkable swiftness.

C harlotte had plugged her beltphone into a wall socket so that she could bring up a full-sized image on the screen mounted beside the door of Gabriel King's apartment. Unfortunately, the only image of Walter Czastka she had so far been able to obtain was that of a sim which must have been coded eighty or ninety years ago. It was a very low-grade sim, no more capable than the meanest of modern sloths, and it had obviously been programmed with brutal simplicity.

"Dr. Czastka is unable to take your call at the moment," it said for the fourth time.

"The codes I've just transmitted are empowered to set aside any instruction written into your programming," Charlotte replied, unable to help herself. She was used to dealing with silvers, even when she had to talk to an answerphone. "This is Detective Sergeant Charlotte Holmes of the United Nations police, and your programmer will be guilty of a criminal offense if you do not summon him immediately to take this call in person."

"Dr. Czastka is unable to take your call at the moment," said the missing man's doppelgänger, as it had been programmed to do in response to any and all inquiries. In programming it thus, Walter Czastka was indeed committing a technical offense, given that he was a fully certified expert whose services could be commandeered by any duly authorized agent of the World Government—but he had probably never expected to receive any kind of urgent summons from the police, given that his field of certified expertise was the design and development of flowering plants.

As she broke the connection, temporarily admitting defeat, Charlotte bit her lip. It was bad enough to be assigned as site supervisor to an area which the forensic team had insisted on sealing tight—after rating it a grade A biohazard, thus forcing her to conduct her part of the investigation from the corridor outside—without having expert witnesses ducking out of their duties by assigning obsolete sims to the vital task of answering their phones.

She tried desperately to collect her thoughts. This was by far the biggest case of her fledgling career, and it was certainly the most remarkable. Routine police work was incredibly dull, at least for site-supervision officers, and there had been nothing in her training or experience to prepare her for anything half as bizarre as *this*. When the newscasters got hold of it, it was going to generate a lot of interest—interest which would put immense pressure on Hal Watson and his silver surfers, if they hadn't yet got to the bottom of the affair.

The building supervisor, whose name was Rex Carnevon, handed her a bag full of eyes and ears. He was an unfashionably small man, whose girth suggested that his IT was having difficulty compensating for the effects of his appetites. There wasn't much that could be done to add to his height, but even a building supervisor should be sufficiently well paid to afford regular body-image readjustments.

"That's it," Carnevon said resentfully. "Every last one. The lobby, the elevator, and the corridor are all blind and deaf until I can get the replacements in."

"Thanks," she said dully.

"You're welcome," the supervisor informed her, implying by his tone that she was not at all welcome.

Charlotte was supposed to treat members of the public with politeness and respect at all times, especially when they were co-operating to the best of their ability, but something in the supervisor's manner got right up her nose.

"If anything turns up on the evening news, Mr. Carnevon," she said, in what she hoped was a suitably menacing manner, "I'll make sure that whoever leaked it never holds a position of trust in this city again."

"Oh, sure," Carnevon said. "I really want it broadcast all over the world that the King of Shamirs was murdered in *my* building. I can't *wait* to give them the pictures of the killer riding up in *my* elevator carrying a bunch of fancy flowers. Miss Holmes, if anything leaks, you'd better make sure that your own backyard is clean, because it sure as hell won't have come from me."

"We don't know for certain that anyone has been murdered, Mr. Carnevon," Charlotte informed him with a sigh. "And if, in fact, someone has, we certainly don't know that the young woman who came up in the elevator was responsible."

"Of course not," the supervisor said sarcastically. "I'm only the one who answered the alarm call. If I'd been fool enough to barge in after seeing what I saw through the spy eyes I'd probably be dead too—and there wouldn't be any point in your friends staggering around in those damn moon suits. Believe me, Miss Holmes, that wasn't any accidental death—and he was absolutely fine before that whore called in on him. She was even carrying a bunch of fancy flowers—what more do you want?"

What Charlotte wanted, and what Hal would certainly demand, was *evidence*. Carrying a bunch of flowers—even state-of-the-art flowers formed according to a brand new gentemplate—was not yet illegal, although it might one day become so if the forensic team was right about the biohazard aspect of the case.

"Thank you, Mr. Carnevon," said Charlotte, meaning Go away, you horrid little man. The meaning was clear enough to have the desired effect, although Carnevon might have decided to hang around out of spite if he'd caught the full import of her thought.

As the screen above the elevator began to count down the car's descent, Charlotte turned back to the screen beside the apartment door, which was now occupied by an unsimulated image of her superior officer.

"I've enhanced the audiotapes the team transmitted from the apartment's ears," Hal said laconically. "I'm ninety-nine percent sure that we have all the subvocalized remarks. The first of the three he muttered before the girl came in was 'The age of the human herbivores; the cud-chewing era.' The second was 'Posturing apes in fancy dress.' The third was 'The devastation of the wild.' The one that was an aside to his conversation was 'That posturing ape,' first word stressed—presumably referring to the man she named, Oscar Wilde. It's possible, of course, given that he seems to have had posturing apes on his mind, that the previous reference was to the same person, but the fact that he said 'the wild' makes it unlikely. It's also possible, I suppose, that the three remarks might be symptomatic of a suicidal turn of mind, but all the other evidence I've looked at seems to be against that."

"Do you have Wilde's number?" Charlotte asked.

"Already tried it," Hal told her, in a tone which implied that she should have realized that. "The sim which answered says that he's here in New York, but that he's currently in transit and never takes calls in cabs because it's unaesthetic."

What is it with these flower designers? Charlotte wondered. "I'll bet the sim was a Stone Age sloth, carefully designed for maximum stupidity," she said.

"On the contrary," said Hal. "It was a medium-level silver, as clever as any answering machine I've ever had occasion to speak to, but it's still a slave to its programming, and it hasn't been programmed with the authority to break in while the Young Master is in a cab."

"The Young Master?" Charlotte queried.

"The silver's phrase, not mine," said Hal. "I'll get through to him as soon as I can—and if he still feels like playing the winsome eccentric I'll get tough with him. In the meantime, the public eyes are beginning to turn up a lot of tentative matches to the girl's face—far too many and much too tentative for my liking. It's bad enough that she's been sculpted to a standard model without her having changed key details of her appearance both before and after leaving the building. If she did carry the murder weapon in, she was almost certainly more than a mere mule. With luck, I'll have the case cracked in a matter of hours, once the moonwalkers have run tests on the bedsheets. She can hide her idealized face from the street's eyes, but she can't hide her DNA."

"Great," said Charlotte. "At the pace the boys and girls inside are working, they should be able to get the data to you by the middle of next week."

"Don't worry," Hal said. "It'll all open up once we have the forensics. It's just a matter of starting with the right data—at the moment I'm fiddling around the periphery. With average luck, we'll have it all wrapped up before the story leaks out to the vidveg."

When Hal broke the connection Charlotte went to the window at the end of the corridor in order to look out over the city. She was on the thirty-ninth floor of Trebizond Tower, and there was quite a view.

Central Park looked pretty much the way it must have looked for centuries, carefully restored to its antediluvian glory, but the decaying skyline was very much a product of the moment. She wondered whether the fact that Gabriel King had been in New York to execute the demolition of the old city might have provided the motive for his murder. Some Manhattanites had become very angry indeed when the Decivilizers had finally claimed the jewel in their crown, and murder was said to be the daughter of obsession.

There was a funeral procession making its patient way along the southern flank of the park. The traffic must have been backed up for miles, and anyone in the queue older than a hundred must have been complaining that such a thing would never have been allowed in the old days. Nowadays, deaths were so rare that it was tacitly taken for granted that even the meanest corpse had an inalienable right to hold up traffic for an hour or two, whatever the letter of the law might be.

How long, Charlotte wondered, would Gabriel King's funeral

train be, and how long a standstill would it cause?

The train she was watching was led by six carriages laden with flowers, all of them black, white, or scarlet. Each of the carriages was drawn by four jet-black horses. Behind the carriages came the black-clad mourners. Professionals, friends, and family members were all mingled together, but they were distinguishable even at this distance by the tall stovepipe hats the professionals invariably wore. Charlotte counted thirty-some pros and estimated that there must be about a hundred and forty amateurs. For New York, that was very small-scale. Gabriel King would probably command ten times as many, maybe more; he had, after all, been one of the oldest men in the world. In his time, he must have met—as well as made— *millions*.

Among those millions, it seemed, was one who had found motive enough to kill him, and to kill him in a manner so bizarre as to be utterly without precedent.

Murder was nowadays the rarest of crimes, and such murders which did happen usually occurred when some private tsunami of rage or spite smashed through the barriers erected by years of primary-school biofeedback training. *Planned* murders were virtually unheard-of in these not-yet-decivilized times. Charlotte was very conscious of the fact that such a crime required the maximum of respect and effort from all concerned, even people whose lowly station in life involved visiting crime scenes and threatening building supervisors.

The Decivilization movement, she thought, must have been a great boon to King's business. He must have been very grateful indeed to the city-hating prophets, although the more extreme among them would have detested Gabriel King as thoroughly as they detested all old-fashioned entrepreneurs—especially those who were fabulously wealthy double rejuvenates. King could easily have made enemies even among the people whose crusade he was furthering, and among the business rivals who had competed with him for the contracts—but those who hated him most fervently of all must surely be the New Yorkers whose city he was even now subjecting to unnaturally rapid decay. If she could only figure out which one of them had sent the young woman and armed her with her remarkable murder weapon, she would be famous—at least for a day. Unfortunately, Hal was the one to whom the forensic evidence would be sent, and he was the one who would pull the relevant DNA match from the records. The best Charlotte could hope for was to be part of the team sent to make the arrest.

Charlotte heard the hum of the motor as the elevator became active again, and she glanced back at the screen above the door; it dutifully revealed that the left-hand car was bound for thirty-nine.

Charlotte frowned. It had to be Rex Carnevon—the whole floor had been temporarily quarantined until the forensic team had made a more accurate assessment of the biohazard.

She moved to meet the elevator car, psyching herself up for another confrontation, but when the door opened, it was not the supervisor's elliptical form that emerged but that of a tall young man with perfect blond hair and luminous blue eyes. His suitskin was sober in hue but very delicately fashioned, taking full advantage of the sculpted curves of his elegant frame. Now that cosmetic engineering was available to everyone, it had become exceedingly difficult for its artisans to produce striking individual effects, but this man struck her instantly as a person of exceptional beauty and bearing.

"Sergeant Holmes?" he inquired.

The warmth and politeness of his tone cut right through her intention to say "Who the hell are you?" in a petulant fashion, and all she could contrive was a rather weak "Yes."

"My name is Lowenthal," he said. "Michael Lowenthal."

"You shouldn't be here, Mr. Lowenthal," she said, having recovered her breath and something of her sense of purpose. "This area is under quarantine."

"I know," he said, taking a swipecard from an invisible pocket without disturbing the line of his suitskin. He held the card out to her, and while she took it in order to slot it into her beltphone he added: "I'm a special investigator."

The display on her phone read: FULLY AUTHORIZED. OFFER FULL COOPERATION.

Charlotte, slightly numb with shock, turned around in order to plug her machine into the wall socket again. She summoned Hal's image to the screen beside Gabriel King's door.

"What's this, Hal?" she said.

"Exactly what it says," her superior replied rather brusquely. "The instruction came down from above, presumably from the very top. We're to copy Mr. Lowenthal in on the progress of our investigation. Anything we get, he gets."

Charlotte knew that it would be as useless to express surprise as it would be to object. She had never known that such an instruction was possible, but she was uncomfortably aware that she had not been long in the job. She had only the vaguest idea of what and where the "very top" might be from which this remarkable command had apparently descended. She turned to stare at Michael Lowenthal as if he were some kind of legendary beast.

"I'm sorry," he said. "To tell you the truth, I don't really know what's going on either. The serious investigation is being done by my superiors—Webwalkers working in close collaboration with Inspector Watson, and a pack of silver surfers to join forces with his. Like you, I'm just a . . . what's the term? *Legman*—I'm just a legman."

"You're a *private investigator*?" said Charlotte incredulously.

"Nothing so glamorous, I'm afraid," he replied. "Merely a humble employee, like yourself."

She opened her mouth to say "Employee of what?" but was saved from the verbal infelicity by the opening of the apartment door. It slid back into its bed to reveal a shimmering plane, like the surface of a soap bubble. The first of the protectively clad forensic investigators was already stepping into the bubble. She was carrying a camera in one hand and a bulky plastic bag in the other, but the bubble stretched to accommodate everything and folded around her, equipping her suit and her luggage with yet another monomolecular layer of protection.

Her three companions followed her one by one, each one stepping through the quarantine barrier in careful slow motion, as if fearful of puncturing the surface—although that would, of course, have been impossible.

The team leader looked at Michael Lowenthal with obvious apprehension, unwilling to say anything until the stranger's presence was explained.

"It's okay," Charlotte told her. "This is Michael Lowenthal, special investigator. He's been cleared. Mr. Lowenthal, this is Lieutenant Regina Chai." Lowenthal merely nodded, evidently as eager to hear what the lieutenant had to say as Charlotte was.

"We've stripped the place," Chai reported in her usual businesslike manner. "You can lock the door now. The air's been thoroughly cleaned, but until we get a fix on the agent, the apartment has to stay sealed. Given that the woman walked in and out without a care in the world—and given that you've been standing around out here for the past couple of hours—the surrounds must be safe, and if they aren't it's too damn late to do anything about it, so you can unseal the other apartments and free up the floor.

"We transmitted all the film back to Hal—he should have an edited version ready for briefing purposes in a couple of minutes. The skeleton is definitely King's, but there's nothing on the tapes to indicate how the agent was administered. The bedroom was privacy-sealed, just like the brochure says—classy building! All I can say for sure is that he looked happy enough when he came out. The card that came with the yellow flowers might have given him a clue, if he'd bothered to read it, but he didn't. Died without ever knowing that there was anything really wrong—even his alarm call wasn't panic-stricken. If this thing ever gets loose . . . but I guess that's why *you're* here."

The last remark was addressed to Michael Lowenthal. Chai had obviously assumed that he was from whatever UN department was responsible for maintaining eternal vigilance against the possibility that the specter of plague war might one day return to haunt the world. The blond man didn't make any sign that could be construed as a confirmation or a denial.

"Thanks, Lieutenant," said Charlotte. "Can you get all that stuff down to the van and away without being seen?"

"As long as the supervisor's following instructions. Be seeing you." Chai turned away to join her companions, who were waiting in the elevator car that had brought Lowenthal up to the thirty-ninth floor. There was just about room for her to squeeze in along with all the equipment and the plastic bags. Charlotte watched the door slide shut behind them, and stabbed the button that would summon the second car from the lobby. The display screen informed her that it had not begun to move.

Cursing under her breath, Charlotte punched out Rex Carnevon's number on her beltphone, which was still plugged into the wall socket.

"You can liberate the second elevator car now," she told him. "I'm ready to come down."

"I know," the horrid little man replied smugly, "but I thought I'd better hold it. I was just on the point of calling *you*. There's a man here who says that he's got an appointment with Gabriel King. He's anxious to get up there because he's a little late—his cab got held up by a funeral procession, or so he says. I thought you might want me to bring him up—unless you'd rather talk to him in my office."

Charlotte was uncomfortably aware of Michael Lowenthal's bright blue eyes. She dared not meet his inquisitive stare.

"What's this man's name?" she asked.

The smug expression on Rex Carnevon's face deepened as he relished his petty supremacy. He gave himself the luxury of a three-second pause before he decided that he had drunk his fill of satisfaction and said: "Oscar Wilde."

Charlotte, although slightly stunned by the news, thought fast. Evidently the cab in which the self-styled Young Master had been traveling, unwilling to be disturbed even by the UN police, had been heading for Trebizond Tower—and the Young Master himself had been heading for Gabriel King's apartment, to see the murdered man. Given that the girl who had probably carried out the murder had been carrying a bunch of Oscar Wilde flowers, and given that the murder weapon was also a flower, that put Oscar Wilde at the dead center of the puzzle. Charlotte was very enthusiastic to talk to him—but the last thing she wanted to do was allow Rex Carnevon to eavesdrop on her conversation. It would be bad enough having Lowenthal looking on, even though she'd have had to hand over a tape in any case.

"Send him up," said Charlotte tersely as soon as she had recovered her composure. "Alone."

This, she thought, was a golden opportunity to do some real detective work: to question a witness; to get to grips with a mystery; to play a significant part in cracking a case. Hal was a top-class fisherman—his average time for completing an investigation was two hours, seventeen minutes, and fourteen seconds—but he never had suspects turn up on his doorstep ready for questioning. This case had already lasted longer than Hal's average cracking time, and it seemed highly likely to set a new record. It would be a *very* good case in which to get more deeply involved, and Wilde's unexpected arrival at the crime scene had to be reckoned a godsend to a humble site supervisor.

While the elevator car made its stately ascent, Charlotte tried hard to collect herself and focus her mind. Please let him be guilty! she prayed. If not of the murder, of something—something far more serious than programming his silver to block official phone calls. Beneath the silent prayer, however, was an uncomfortable feeling that she might be out of her depth. She was only what Lowenthal had called a *legman,* after all. She knew that Hal Watson wouldn't like this new turn of events one little bit. Having an expert witness turn up in the flesh before he'd even been contacted by phone added yet another item to a growing list of things that simply didn't make sense.

When the newcomer emerged from the elevator car Charlotte felt a curious sense of déjà vu. He was by no means Michael Lowenthal's twin—his hair was russet brown and flowing, his eyes were green, and his bodily frame was much more abundantly furnished with flesh—but he was exactly the same height, and he had something of the same air about him. Like Lowenthal, he was one of the most beautiful men—handsome would have been the wrong word—Charlotte had ever seen, and like Lowenthal, he was well aware of his beauty. He was wearing a green carnation in the lapel of his neatly tailored jet-black suitskin, whose color was a perfect match for his eyes.

Oscar Wilde bowed to Charlotte with deliberate grace and favored Michael Lowenthal with a slight nod of the head. Then he glanced up, briefly, at the place where a discreet eye would normally have been set in the wall to record the faces of everyone emerging from the lift. The eye in question was in the bag Charlotte was holding, along with all the others, but Wilde couldn't know that.

Charlotte was puzzled by the glance. Public eyes and private bubblebugs were everywhere in a city like New York, and all city dwellers were entirely accustomed to living under observation; those who had grown up with the situation took it completely for granted. In some WG-unintegrated nationettes it still wasn't common for *all* walls to have eyes and ears, but within the compass of the World Government everyone had long since learned to tolerate the ever-presence of the benevolent mechanical observers which guaranteed their safety. Most people ignored them, but Wilde obviously did not belong to the category of "most people." Might his reflexive glance toward the eye be a tacit admission of guilt?

Wilde smiled broadly—and Charlotte realized, belatedly, that she had jumped to the wrong conclusion. Wilde hadn't glanced at the place where the eye should have been because he *resented* its assumed presence, but because he welcomed its attention. He had actually adjusted his stance as he moved out of the elevator so that he might better be observed, not merely by her and Lowenthal but by the cameras he supposed to be recording the encounter.

Posturing ape! Charlotte thought, remembering Gabriel King's muttered aside.

"Mr. Wilde?" she said tentatively. "I'm Detective Sergeant Charlotte Holmes, UN Police Department. This is my, um, colleague, Michael Lowenthal."

"Please call me Oscar," said the beautiful man. "What exactly has happened to poor Gabriel? Something nasty *has* happened, has it not? The orotund gentleman downstairs left me in no doubt of it, but would not tell me what it was."

"He's dead," Charlotte replied shortly. "I understand from Carnevon that you had an appointment with him. Will you tell me what the purpose of the appointment was to have been?" She winced at the unintentionally clumsy phrasing of the question.

"I'm afraid that I can't," Wilde told her smoothly. "The message summoning me here came as text only, with a supplementary fax. I received it about two hours ago. It was an invitation—although it was, I fear, couched more in the manner of a *command*. I suppose that it was sufficiently impolite to warrant disobedience, but sufficiently intriguing to be tempting. Dead, you say?"

"That message wasn't sent from this apartment," Charlotte told him, ignoring his teasing prompt.

"Then you must trace it," Wilde replied affably, "and discover where it did come from. If Gabriel was already dead when it was sent, it would be very interesting to know who sent it in his stead—and why."

Charlotte hesitated. She was not entirely certain what to say next but she wanted to say *something* lest Michael Lowenthal should decide to step into the breach. She was saved from the hazards of improvisation by Hal Watson, whose image reappeared on the screen by the apartment door.

"What's going on, Charlotte?" he asked sharply.

Her heart sank. She felt as if she were at infants' school and had been caught doing something naughty in the playground.

"Oscar Wilde arrived here a few moments ago," she said. "He has an appointment to see Gabriel King. I'm just trying to find out—"

"Of course," Hal said, brusquely cutting her off. "Dr. Wilde?"

Having been effectively instructed to surrender her position in front of the beltpack's camera to Wilde, Charlotte reluctantly handed it over.

"I'm Hal Watson, Dr. Wilde," Hal said politely. "I've been trying to contact you, but your silver refused to interrupt your journey. We need your services as an expert witness. I'm required to inform you that you will henceforth be acting under UN authority, bound by the duty to report honestly and fully on everything you may see, hear, or discover. Will you affirm that you accept that duty and all that is implied thereby?"

That's what I should have done! Charlotte thought, mortified by the error of omission.

"Of course," said Wilde. "I shall be delighted to assist you in any way that I can, and I hereby affirm my willingness and intention to tell the truth, the whole truth, and nothing but the truth. Will that suffice?"

"It will," said Hal grimly. "Now, Dr. Wilde, I'm going to display a videotape on the screen. I'm sorry the picture quality is so poor, but time is of the essence. I want you to look at it carefully, and then I want you to tell me everything you know, or are able to deduce, about the contents of the tape."

Charlotte stood to one side, quietly fuming, as Wilde casually handed back her beltphone and took up his own instead, plugging it in beside hers. The tape began to run, beginning with a pan around the crime scene.

The reception room where Gabriel King had died was furnished in an unusually utilitarian manner; the gantzer's tastes had obviously been rather Spartan. Apart from the food delivery point, the room's main feature was a particularly elaborate array of special-function telescreens. There were VE-mural screens on two of the walls, but they displayed plain shades of pastel blue. There was no decorative plant life integrated into either of the remaining walls, nor was there any kind of inert decoration within the room—except for the vase containing the golden flowers that King's last visitor had given to him, which had been set on a glass-topped table in the center of a three-sided square formed by a sofa and two chairs.

On the sofa lay all that remained of the late Gabriel King. The "corpse" was no more than a skeleton, whose white bones were intricately entwined with gorgeous flowers.

The camera zoomed in on the strange garlands which dressed the reclining skeleton. The stems and leaves of the marvelous plant were green, but the petals of each bloom—which formed a hemispherical bell—were black. The waxy stigma at the center of each flower was dark red and was shaped into a decorated *crux ansata*.

Charlotte watched Oscar Wilde lean forward to inspect the structure and texture of the flowers as closely as the wallscreen permitted. The camera followed the rim of a corolla, then passed along a stem. The stem bore huge curved thorns, paler in color than the flesh from which they sprouted. Each thorn was tipped with red, as if it had drawn blood. There were other embellishments too—bracts of intricate design, like little lace handkerchiefs, arrayed beneath each flower head.

Wilde seemed to Charlotte to be lost in rapt contemplation of the way that the stems wound around the long bones, holding the skeleton together even though every vestige of flesh had been consumed. The plant had no roots but had supportive structures like holdfasts, which maintained the shape of the whole organism and the coherence of the skeleton too.

Charlotte knew that all this could not be mere accident; the winding of the stems had been carefully programmed for exactly this purpose. The skull, in particular, was very strikingly embellished, with a single stem emerging from each of the empty eye sockets. Charlotte knew well enough what level of genius this meticulous design implied—and what level of insanity.

"Can you be certain that it's Gabriel?" asked Oscar finally.

"Absolutely certain." Hal sounded strangely remote; the tape was still playing and he was reduced to the status of a mere voice-over.

"Do you know when he died?"

"Yes—it's all on camera. I suppose we're lucky that he never made it back to the bedroom. The metamorphosis happened very quickly. It appears that the seeds of that plant *devoured* him as they grew, transforming his flesh into its own."

"Quite remarkable," said Oscar Wilde. He said it very lightly, but the understatement must have been carefully calculated. "How did the seeds get into him—or *on*to him?"

"We don't know. We're trying to trace his last visitor, of course, but it's conceivable that the seeds might have been lying dormant in his body for some time."

"Fascinating," Wilde opined, in a tone which seemed to have more admiration in it than horror.

"Fascinating!" Charlotte echoed in exasperation. "Wouldn't you say it was a little more than merely *fascinating,* Dr. Wilde? Can you imagine what an organism like that might do if it ever got loose? We're looking at something that could wipe out the entire human race."

"Perhaps," said Wilde calmly, "but I think not. How long ago did he die?"

"Between two and three days," Hal told him, swiftly excluding Charlotte from the conversation yet again. "He seems to have felt the first symptoms about seventy hours ago; he was incapacitated soon afterward and died a few hours later."

Oscar Wilde licked his full lips, as if to savor his own astonishment. "Those delightful flowers must have a voracious appetite," he said.

Charlotte eyed him carefully, wondering exactly what his reaction might signify.

"I don't have to explain to you how serious this matter is, Dr. Wilde," Hal said. "Quite apart from the fact that the man must have been deliberately infected, the laws regarding the creation of artificial organisms hazardous to human life have clearly been breached. We need your help to find the maker of those flowers. Incidentally, do you happen to recognize the *other* flowers—the ones in the vase?"

"Indeed I do," the designer replied. "They're mine—my newest line. I'm rather proud of them; I never suspected that Gabriel had such good taste. You realize, of course, that the flowers which have replaced poor Gabriel's flesh are similar to mine in that they're single-sexed flowers from a dioecious species? They're all female, incapable of producing fertile seed. Our murderer isn't as reckless as he may seem."

OUR murderer! Charlotte echoed silently. This investigation is becoming ridiculously crowded.

"Could you make plants like those, Dr. Wilde?" Hal asked insouciantly.

Oscar Wilde glanced sideways to meet Charlotte's inquisitive gaze. She was at least six centimeters shorter than he, but she attempted to look at him as if their stares were perfectly level, trying with all her might to deny him the psychological advantage. He frowned slightly as he appeared to consider the question. Then he said: "It all depends what you mean by 'like,' Inspector Watson." He was still looking at Charlotte.

"Don't play games with me, Dr. Wilde," Hal retorted. "Just answer the question."

"I'm sorry," Wilde said silkily, his eyebrows arching slightly as he invited Charlotte to join him in a conspiracy of sympathy. "I meant no offense. I assume that you're asking whether I could make a plant which would do what this one has apparently done—grow in the flesh of a human being, utterly consuming everything but the bones. I believe that I could, although I assure you that I never have and never would."

"And how many other people could do it?" Hal wanted to know.

"You're going too fast, Inspector Watson. I was about to continue by saying that although I—and many other men—could design a plant to do what this one has done, I must confess that I could not have designed *this plant*. I could not have designed an organism to work with such astonishing speed and such amazing precision. Until I saw this marvel I would have judged that no man could. This is work of a quality that the world has never seen before, and I am eaten up by envy of the genius which produced it."

"You're saying that you know of *no one* who could have done this?" Hal said. Although he was invisible, the impatience in his voice made it obvious that he was skeptical.

"Had you asked me yesterday whether this were possible," Wilde stated punctiliously, "I would have said no. Clearly, I have underrated one of my peers."

Charlotte stared hard at the uncannily beautiful Oscar Wilde, trying hard to weigh him up. She wondered whether anyone in the world were capable of committing a crime like this and then turning up in person to confront and mock the officers investigating it. It seemed difficult to believe that anyone who looked so young and so perfect could be guilty of anything, but she knew that his apparent youth and apparent perfection were both products of ingenious technology. Wilde was not a man who could be judged by appearances—and those of his appearances that were entirely under his own control announced clearly enough that he was a man who loved artifice and ostentation.

Charlotte decided that if Oscar Wilde could be guilty of the primary madness of planning and committing a crime such as this, the secondary madness of revisiting the scene while it was still under the supervision of investigating officers might easily be within his compass.

"*Someone* clearly has the required technical expertise to do this, Dr. Wilde," she said stiffly, to lend unnecessary support to Hal's patient inquisition.

Oscar Wilde shook his luxuriantly furnished head slowly. He did seem genuinely perplexed, even though the apparent level of his concern for the victim and for the fact that a serious biohazard had been let loose left much to be desired. "The technical expertise, my dear Charlotte, is only a part of it," he said. "I might be able to cultivate the relevant technical expertise, were I to attempt such a thing. Perhaps a dozen others might have been able to do it, had they been prepared to put in the time and effort. But what kind of man would devote his energies to such a project for months on end? Who has a *reason* for doing this kind of work with this degree of intricacy? I confess that I am deeply intrigued by the sheer demonic artistry of the organism."

"I really don't think that matters of *demonic artistry* are important here, Dr. Wilde," said Charlotte, taking sarcastic advantage of Hal's continued silence. "This is murder."

"True," admitted the green-eyed man. "And yet—a great genetic artist is every bit as distinctive in his work as a great painter. Perhaps we might learn as much from the *style* of the creation as from its evident purpose. My presence here suggests that some such judgment is required. It seems—does it not?—that the UN Police Department was not alone in requiring my presence as an expert witness,"

"What do you mean?" Charlotte asked warily.

"Given that it seems to be impossible that I was summoned

here by the victim," Wilde said, as though it were perfectly obvious, "I can only conclude that I was summoned by the murderer."

As if to provide a dramatic counterpart to this remarkable statement, the tape that was running on the wallscreen was abruptly switched off. Hal Watson's face reappeared in its stead. "I find that hard to believe, Dr. Wilde," Hal said, reclaiming the interrogation.

"It *is* hard to believe," Wilde agreed. "But when we have eliminated the impossible, are we not committed to believing the improbable? Unless, of course, you think that *I* did this to poor Gabriel and have come to gloat over his fate?"

Charlotte had to look away when he said that, and could only hope that she was not blushing too fiercely.

"I can assure you," Wilde continued, still looking at Charlotte with arched eyebrows, "that although I disliked the man as heartily as he disliked me, I did not dislike him as much as *that*—and if I had for some peculiar reason decided to murder him, I certainly would not have revisited the scene of my crime in this reckless fashion. A showman I might be, a madman never."

A posturing ape, Charlotte thought, yet again. "Why should the murderer take the trouble to summon you to the scene of his crime?" she demanded. "We would probably have shown all this material to you anyway, given that Walter Czastka's in the Hawaiian islands and that I couldn't get through to him by phone. Why would the murderer send you a message?"

"I'm deeply offended by the fact that your first choice of expert witness was Walter Czastka," Wilde murmured infuriatingly, "but I suppose that I must forgive you. He has, after all, made so much more money than I have."

"Dr. Wilde—," Hal cut in—and was promptly cut off.

"Yes, of course," said Oscar Wilde. "This is a very serious matter—a murder investigation and a potential biohazard. I'm sorry. At the risk of annoying you further, I think I might be able to guess why a message was sent in order to summon me here. It seems insane, I know, but I suspect that I *might* have been brought to identify the person who made those flowers. As to whether or not he is your murderer, I cannot say, but I believe that I know who forged the weapon."

"How do you know?" Charlotte demanded.

"By virtue of his *demonic artistry*," Wilde replied. "I hesitate to accuse a man of a serious crime on the basis of a purely aesthetic judgment, but in due reflection, I believe that I do recognize his style."

"That's ridiculous," Hal Watson said petulantly. "If the murderer had wanted to identify himself, all he had to do was call us or leave a signed message. How would he know that you would recognize his work—and why, if he knew it, would he want you to do it?"

"Those are interesting questions," admitted Oscar, "to which I have as yet no answers. Nevertheless, I can only suppose that I was sent an invitation to this mysterious event in order that I might play a part in its unraveling. I can see no other possibility—unless, of course, I am mistaken in my judgment, in which case I might have been summoned in order to lay down a false trail. I repeat, however, that I cannot conclusively identify your murderer— merely the maker of his instrument."

"Who?" said Charlotte, more succinctly than she would have preferred.

Oscar Wilde opened his arms wide in a gesture of exaggerated helplessness. "I cannot claim to be *absolutely* certain," he said, "but if appearances and my expert judgment are to be trusted, those flowers are the work of the man who has always been known to me by the pseudonym Rappaccini!"

The name of Rappaccini was perfectly familiar to Charlotte, as it was to everyone who had ever attended a funeral procession or watched one on TV, but she had always assumed that it was the name of a company rather than an individual. The carriages leading the funeral train she had been watching only a few minutes before would undoubtedly have been decked with produce bearing that name, although the actual flowers would have been the handiwork of subcontractors using mass-produced seeds manufactured according to patented gentemplates. No fashionable funeral—and there were no longer many unfashionable ones within the boundaries of the USNA—could be reckoned complete without flowers by Rappaccini Inc. The name would doubtless have been found on every condolence card attached to every wreath.

Charlotte remembered something Regina Chai had said: "The card that came with the yellow flowers might have given him a clue, if he'd bothered to read it, but he didn't."

"I fear," Wilde continued with annoying casualness, "that I never thought to ask Rappaccini's real name in the days when he used to appear in public. Most members of the Institute of Genetic Art preferred to exhibit their work pseudonymously in those days—a hangover from the era when there were too many people still alive who associated genetic engineers with the weapons employed in the plague wars and the chiasmatic transformers which caused the Crash."

"Is Oscar Wilde a pseudonym?" Hal Watson was quick to ask.

Wilde shook his head. "My name was a jest naively bestowed upon me by my parents. I was happy to use it in those days because it *sounded* like a pseudonym—a double bluff encouraged by the delight I took in aping the mannerisms of my ancient namesake."

"Perhaps," Hal said suspiciously, "the message which summoned you here was also a double bluff. Perhaps your identification of the pseudonymous Rappaccini as the person who made the flowers is a double bluff too."

Oscar Wilde shook his head sorrowfully and breathed in deeply, as though to prepare for a huge sigh. "I wish that I could take pride in being a prime suspect," he said dolefully, "but I really *am* aware of the serious implications of this matter. Perhaps I should be flattered that you think me to be capable not only of producing these astounding blooms, but also of returning to the scene of my crime in this cavalier manner; I really must not be tempted to take credit for such daring and arrogance, however. It would only hold up your investigation. I can assure you that I have an ironclad alibi for the time of death. Three days ago I was in a small private hospital, and the flesh of my outer tissues was unbecomingly fluid. I had been there for some time, undergoing rejuvenation treatment."

"That doesn't prove anything," Charlotte put in. She was beginning to think that this facetious poseur might be capable of almost anything. "You might have made the seeds months ago, and you might have taken great care to make sure that they were delivered—or, at least, that they began to take effect—while you were in the hospital."

"I suppose I might have," said the man who had programmed his sim to call him *the Young Master* in anticipation of his re-emergence from the hospital, "but I didn't. If you are determined to ignore my advice there is evidently nothing I can say to change your mind—but I assure you that your investigation will proceed much more smoothly if you forget about me and concentrate on Rappaccini."

Charlotte could not tell whether or not Wilde's manner was calculated to give an impression of arrogant insincerity. It was, she supposed, just about possible that he conducted himself in this florid fashion all the time. She could not help glancing at Michael Lowenthal, as if to inquire what *he* thought of all this, but the blond man was content to watch in fascination; he did not even meet her glance.

"If the murderer wished to be identified," Hal Watson said, "why didn't he simply leave his own name on the screens in King's apartment, with an explanation of his motive?"

"Why did he not simply shoot Gabriel King with a revolver?" countered the geneticist. "Why has he gone to the effort of designing and making this fabulous plant? There is something very strange going on here, no matter how much you might wish that it were

simpler than it seems. We must accept the facts of the matter and
do our best to see the significance within them."

Charlotte noticed Michael Lowenthal nodding his head slightly,
presumably in mute agreement. She wished, belatedly, that she had
had the patience to stand by, as Lowenthal had done, and watch
the farce unfold while wearing an expression of keen concentration.
Unlike Hal and herself, Lowenthal had not yet contrived to make
a fool of himself by dueling verbally with Oscar Wilde.

"Perhaps there is no real significance in the more bizarre facts,"
Hal said, stubbornly plugging on. "As you must have realized, Dr.
Wilde, we're obviously dealing with a mad person: a *very dangerous*
mad person. The method of murder may simply be an expression
of his—or, of course, *her*—madness."

"Perhaps we are dealing with a mad person," Wilde agreed,
refusing to respond to the obvious suggestion that he might be the
mad person in question, "but if this *is* madness, it is very method-
ical madness, and madness with a hint of artistic genius. You must
confess that as crimes go, this qualifies as one of the most unusual
ever devised—highly original, and executed with great care."

"Dr. Wilde," said Hal, his voice weary with tried patience,
"*originality* is not an issue here. This was cold-blooded murder,
and it has to be treated like any other murder."

"I love that phrase," said the geneticist teasingly. "*Cold-
blooded murder*. It's so provocative."

Charlotte stared at him, wondering whether she might indeed
be face-to-face with a uniquely dangerous madman—and whether,
if so, he might still be a murderously inclined madman. She did not
know what to make of the man at all, any more than she knew what
to make of the crazy investigation into which he had so casually
intruded himself. She knew that she was supposed to leave the real
detective work to Hal Watson, but she couldn't help wrestling with
the logic of the affair, trying hard to see some glimmer of sense
somewhere within the absurd pattern.

"Hal," she put in, remembering again what Regina Chai had

said. "Wasn't there a card with the flowers? Have you a still you can put up on the screen?"

Hal apparently had sufficient respect for her judgment not to ask her why—although, for once, he was probably glad of the opportunity to let go of the conversation.

The image on the screen flickered, then shifted to a shot in which the camera was zooming in on something which lay on the glass-topped table, propped up against the vase containing the yellow flowers. It was a small cardboard rectangle. It had already been monomol-sealed as a safety measure, but the transparent film did not obscure the words written on the card.

Charlotte's eyes went directly to the bottom right-hand corner of the card, which bore the legend: *Rappaccini Inc.*

Perhaps he did leave his name after all, Charlotte marveled. If the flowers in the vase are one of Wilde's designs, the card might conceivably refer to the others: the ones which consumed Gabriel King. If Wilde's right, the arrogant swine has actually signed his crime! But what, she quickly wondered, if Wilde were a liar? What if this had been planted purely and simply to back up his story?

Her eyes had reflexively moved from the bottom of the card to the top, so that she could read the message of condolence inscribed there. Unfortunately, she couldn't understand the words; the message was not written in English. It read:

> *La sottise, l'erreur, le péché, la lésine,*
> *Occupent nos esprits et travaillent nos corps,*
> *Et nous alimentons nos amiables remords,*
> *Comme les mendiants nourrissent leur vermine.*

" 'Stupidity, error, sin, and poverty of spirit,' " Oscar Wilde obligingly translated, thoughtfully, " 'possess our hearts and work within our bodies, and we nourish our fond remorse as beggars suckle their parasites.' Hardly an orthodox condolence card—if

Rappaccini mass-produces them, I can't believe that he sells very many."

"Do you recognize the words?" Charlotte asked suspiciously.

"A poem by Charles Baudelaire. 'Au lecteur'—that is, 'To the Reader.' From *Les Fleurs du Mal*. A play on words, I think." The camera's eye had obligingly moved back, to focus once again upon the black flowers which had destroyed Gabriel King. It occurred to Charlotte that Hal must have known about this all along—and in spite of that advantage and all of his experience, he had still allowed Oscar Wilde to rattle him.

"He's right," Hal said, as if on cue. "I checked—that's where the words come from. The book was originally published in eighteen fifty-seven. Dr. Wilde is also an expert of nineteenth- and twentieth-century literature. The condolence card is a fake, though—no such message has ever been commercially released by Rappaccini Inc."

"My expertise does not extend to *all* of nineteenth- and twentieth-century literature," said Oscar Wilde modestly. He was wearing a slight frown, as if he had taken offense at the suggestion that his judgment might have been mistaken. Charlotte wondered how many men there were in the world who could recognize six-hundred-year-old poems written in French. Surely, she thought, Wilde must have made up the card himself. He *must* be the person behind all this. But if so, what monstrous game was he playing?

"What significance do you attach to the poem, Dr. Wilde?" Hal asked, having recovered his most officious manner.

"Assuming that my earlier reasoning was correct, I must suppose that its message is directed to me," replied the imperturbable and ever ingenious Wilde. "Rappaccini—if he is indeed the ultimate author of this affair—seems to have made every effort to ensure that I would be a witness to, and perhaps a partner in, your investigation. I must assume that *all* of this is communication—not merely the card, and the message which summoned me, but the flowers, and the crime itself. The whole affair is to be read, decoded, and understood. I am here because Rappaccini expects me to be able to interpret and comprehend what he is doing. There is more to this, Sergeant Holmes and Inspector Watson, than has yet met our eyes. May I address you as Charlotte and Hal, by the way? If we are to work together in this matter, it will be more convenient—and you, of course, must call me Oscar."

Charlotte tried to remain impassive, but she knew that her amazement must be showing. She was grateful when Michael Lowenthal spoke to Wilde for the first time. "In that case," he said, "you must call me Michael. It seems that we shall *all* be working together."

There was a pause before Hal's voice came back on line. "I'm blocked on Rappaccini for the moment," he said, evidently having turned away to consult one of his many assistant silvers. "Publicly available information regarding the founder of the company gives his real name as Jafri Biasiolo, but there's hardly any official data on Biasiolo at all apart from his date of birth, 2323. It's all old data, of course, and it's possible that it's just sketchy disinformation. I'll have to mount a deep scan into Rappaccini's more recent activities—especially his business interests—but it looks as if that will involve cutting through some very tangled undergrowth."

Charlotte knew what Hal's contemptuous reference to "old data" implied. Old data was incomplete data, often corrupted by all kinds of omissions and errors—although she noticed that Hal had said "disinformation," which meant lies, rather than "misinformation," which meant mistakes. In Hal's view, old data was senile and corrupt data, too decrepit and intrinsically unreliable to be of much use in a slick, modern police inquiry. But Gabriel King had been nearly two hundred years old, and Oscar Wilde—in spite of appearances—might well be over a hundred, given that he had just undergone intensive rejuvenation treatment. If the man who had once called himself Rappaccini really had been born in 2323, the motive for this affair might conceivably date back to the mid-twenty-fourth century.

In theory, the Web had been fully formed as early as the beginning of the twenty-first century, but its checkered history was full of holes. In the wake of the epidemic of sterility that had caused the Crash a century afterward many data stores—including many that had come through the plague wars unscathed—had been irredeemably lost and many others fragmented. The losses had been further compounded by data sabotage, which had itself become epidemic as the twenty-second century gave way to the twenty-third, loudly advertised as "youth's last stand against the empire of the old." Once it had become clear, in the late twenty-third century, that all the miracles of nanotechnology could not give human minds more than two centuries of effective life, the young had realized that they would, after all, inherit the earth if they would only be patient—but the years spanning the birth dates of Gabriel King and Jafri Biasiolo, 2301 and 2323, remained years of acute data blight in the reckoning of perfectionists like Hal Watson. It was an era in which the truth, the whole truth, and nothing but the truth had rarely been recorded, and whose already inefficient records had been markedly eroded in the interim.

Given that the data on file was so old and so sparse, and quite probably misleading, Charlotte knew that it might be very difficult to find—or even reliably to identify—the founder of Rappaccini Inc. It was, alas, easy enough in the late twenty-fifth century to establish electronic identities whose telescreen appearances could be wholly maintained by silver-level sims. Virtual individuals could play so full a role in modern society that their puppet masters could easily remain anonymous and hidden, at least until they came under the intense scrutiny of a highly skilled Webwalker. Hal had the authority to get through any conventional information wall, and he was clever enough to work his way through any data maze, but if the man behind Rappaccini Inc. had gone into hiding, it would take time to winkle him out.

Charlotte still had a gut feeling which told her that the real author of this crazy psychodrama was right in front of her, taunting her with his excessively lovely presence, but she didn't dare say so to Hal. Hal Watson was no respecter of gut feelings.

"Have you traced the call which summoned Dr. Wilde here?" Michael Lowenthal asked Hal Watson. Charlotte heard the hesitation in Hal's voice and knew that natural discretion must be begging him not to lay all his cards on the table where both Lowenthal and Wilde could see them, but he answered the question.

"It was placed some days ago from a blind unit, time-triggered to arrive when it did," Hal reported reluctantly. "Effectively untraceable, I fear—the ticket too. My best surfers are working on it, but they haven't even been able to track the woman to or from the building. I need the DNA analyses before I can take the next step."

The wall unit buzzed as another caller clamored for attention.

"Hold on," Charlotte said to Hal, thumbing the relevant key. Rex Carnevon's face appeared on the screen as the image of the apartment blinked out.

"I have tenants, you know," said the building supervisor rudely. "As long as your quarantine lasts, half of them are trapped inside their apartments and the other half are locked out. Your forensic team drove off thirty minutes ago. What's the holdup?"

"Please be patient, Mr. Carnevon," Charlotte said, painfully aware that she was under observation from all sides. "We're conducting an investigation here."

"I know," Carnevon retorted. "What I want to know is when you're going to conduct it *somewhere else*."

"We'll let you know," Charlotte said brutally, switching back to Hal without further ado.

Hal's face didn't reappear. The tape patched together from the apartment's eyes was playing again. Now there was somebody in the apartment. This section had been recorded several days before. Gabriel King, alive and well, was talking to a young woman.

"Ah," said Oscar Wilde softly. "*Cherchez la femme!* Without a mysterious woman, the puzzle would be lacking its most important piece."

Charlotte studied the woman carefully, although her back was turned to the camera. She seemed to be authentically young—perhaps eighteen or nineteen years of age—with a profusion of lustrous brown hair that she wore unfashionably long. When the tape switched to a different eye, Charlotte saw that the woman had clear blue eyes like Michael Lowenthal's. She also had finely chiseled features—but they had not, of course, been molded in recognition of the same ideal of beauty as Lowenthal's. Psychobiologists had produced seven supposed female archetypes and seven male ones; whereas the woman's flesh had been sculpted into a variant of the most commonplace female archetype, Lowenthal had been modeled on one of the less fashionable male ideals.

Even in this day and age, when cosmetic engineers could so easily remold superficial flesh, the exceptional beauty of Gabriel King's visitor was very evident—but it did not seem to Charlotte to be as striking as the beauty of Michael Lowenthal, or of Oscar Wilde. That, presumably, was a matter of taste and sexual orientation; Hal probably saw things differently.

King and his visitor were speaking to one another, but the sound track had not yet been added to the tape. Charlotte watched as the two of them moved toward the bedroom door, and saw the woman stop the gantzer in his tracks, compelling him to turn and kiss her on the lips before proceeding into the room and closing the door behind them.

The kiss did not seem particularly passionate to Charlotte, but it was definitely tender. It might, she thought, as easily have been a polite greeting between people who had some history of intimacy as a prelude to a first erotic encounter, but it certainly did not have the appearance of a transaction between a prostitute and a client.

The tape ended, and Hal's face returned to the screen.

"She was inside for about half an hour," said Hal, presumably addressing Oscar Wilde. "King was still perfectly healthy when she left, and it wasn't until some twelve or thirteen hours later that he felt sufficient discomfort to call up a diagnostic program. He never had a chance to hit his panic button; the progress of the plant was too swift. The woman might have had nothing to do with it, but she *was* the last person to see him alive. Do you have any idea who she might be?"

"I don't believe that I've ever seen her before," Wilde answered. "I fear that I can only offer the obvious suggestion."

"Which is?" Hal said.

"Rappaccini's daughter."

Hal had nothing to say in reply to that, and neither did Charlotte. They simply waited for clarification.

"It's another echo of the nineteenth century," said Oscar, with a slight sigh. "Rappaccini borrowed his pseudonym from a story by Nathaniel Hawthorne entitled 'Rappaccini's Daughter.' You don't know the period, I take it?"

"Not very well," Charlotte said awkwardly, when it became obvious that Hal wasn't about to reply. "Hardly at all" would have been nearer the truth.

"Then it's as well that I'm here," the beautiful man said in a manner that surely must be calculated to infuriate. "Otherwise, this exotic performance might be entirely wasted."

The wall unit's buzzer sounded again.

Charlotte stabbed at it angrily and didn't give Carnevon the opportunity to open his mouth. *"All right!"* she snapped, no longer caring whether she was under observation or not. "We're *going*. Apart from King's apartment, everything's usable—but you'd better remember what I said about leaks, Carnevon, because if *any* information gets loose from here that might confuse or impede our investigation, *I'll be back.*"

Then she ripped the plug of her beltphone from the wall and said, "We'd better continue this conversation in the elevator and the car. It would probably be better if we were all back at base when that DNA data begins to come in. Then Hal can get to work on tracing the woman and Dr. Wilde can get to work on the gen-template of the killer plant—while you and I, Mr. Lowenthal, can rest our weary feet. With luck, we'll have the killer in custody in time to make the Breakfast News."

"I fear, dear Charlotte," murmured Oscar Wilde as they all moved toward the open elevator car, "that this might be the kind of case in which luck will not be of much assistance."

A Lover in the Mother's Arms

Magnus Teidemann was exhausted by the time he got back to the tent, but it was a good kind of exhaustion: the kind that resulted from a long walk through resentful undergrowth, carrying a heavy pack loaded with specimen jars.

The specimen jars had been carefully dug out of the humus-littered forest floor, where they had served as pitfall traps to capture wandering insects and arachnids. As the director of the Seventh Biodiversity Survey, Magnus had a legion of assistants to carry out such work, but he insisted on taking shifts himself. There was no tokenism about the gesture; the reason he had involved himself with the Natural Biodiversity Movement in the first place was to have the opportunity to work at ground level.

Old though he was, Magnus was not ready to be confined to a laboratory, let alone a desk. A man of his age had to be reckoned to be taking a serious risk if he insisted in isolating himself out here, where help might take ten or twelve hours to reach him if he contrived to send an alarm call and ten or twelve days if he did not, but it was a risk he was prepared to take. Indeed, his dearest and most secret wish was to die in some such place as this, in the humid maternal shadow of the forest giants, where his body would decay in a matter of days into the placental humus so that its atoms could be redistributed within the organisms that collaborated in the constitution of one of the world's new lungs.

Magnus had always worked in the cause of life—the greatest cause there was—and he knew that a man condemned to die, as all men of his misfortunate generation were, ought to make a gift of his body to Mother Earth. He did not want a gaudy funeral in which his coffin would be dragged around the streets of some sterile city, followed by cartloads of Rappaccini flowers purchased from the MegaMall. He would rather die in the sisterly company of sylphs and dryads, surrounded by the flowers of the forest, donating his flesh to the seething cauldron of benign witchery.

The "tent" in which Magnus was temporarily resident was not, of course, an actual tent. It was a bubble dome made out of Life-Simulating Plastic, of a kind originally designed for use on Mars. It was second cousin to those which currently dotted the airless plains of the moon and those which were anchored to the bedrock beneath the snows and glutinous muds of Titan. It was a high-tech product of the MegaMall, and its presence here confirmed that no matter what Magnus's dreams and wishes might be, he was a stranger in an alien environment. *Man* was an alien invader here, as he was everywhere else in the solar system. Man was a product of the savanna, a creator of fields and deserts. The forest was its own world, but the entire ecosphere was part of the human empire now. The forest could not survive without the protection and support of such benevolent invaders as himself, and the LSP dome was the price of his own comfortable survival within it.

The purpose of Magnus's dome, as of its extraterrestrial cousins, was to secure a miniature alien environment and to keep a natural ecosphere at bay. The only difference was that the primary purpose of his dome was to protect the environment without, rather than the environment within. The biospheric fragment in which the dome was set had to be guarded from contamination because it was, in spite of its relative geographical isolation, too near a neighbor that was the most dangerous and malign of all alien environments: the fin de siècle cities of the twenty-fifth century. The humming hives of the MegaMall's customers and sales force were far beyond the horizon, but while they shared the same spherical surface and the same atmosphere they had to be reckoned close neighbors. From the forest's viewpoint, the MegaMall's minions were the neighbors from hell.

Ultimately, of course, it was the MegaMall that paid Magnus

his living wage, just as it paid the wage of every other man and woman living on and beyond Earth, but Magnus always thought of his particular portion of the great capitalist pie as conscience money, or as a tribute to the oldest goddess of them all: the ultimate mother, Gaea the Great.

Tired as he was, Magnus had neither the inclination nor the energy to make an elaborate investigation of his new captives. The most interesting specimens, in any case, would be too small to see without the aid of a magnifying glass, and his eyes, long overdue for replacement, were too weak to take the strain. He took his time decanting the contents of his specimen jars into more economical storage units, and then put the empty jars into the sterilizer, ready to be taken out into the field again tomorrow. They would be alternated with their duplicates for the sixty-third time, with thirty-seven still to go.

When his duty had been adequately done, Magnus used the microwave oven—which had been dutifully storing solar power all day long—to heat up a plastic-wrapped meal. The sole meunière tasted excellent, as was to be expected of one of the finest products of modern food science, but Magnus hardly noticed. In the wilderness, eating was a utilitarian business, a mere matter of fueling the body.

The tropical night arrived with characteristic swiftness, but Magnus did not reach for the wall panel whose virtual control keys were displayed in patterns of red light. He could have instructed the Life-Simulating Plastic to become opaque, but he did not want to do that. Privacy was not an issue hereabouts, and the fact that the discreetly muted lights inside the bubble dome would attract every moth for miles around did not concern him—except, of course, insofar as the moths themselves might be inconvenienced.

Magnus loved wilderness better than anything else in the world. That is to say, he loved *green* wilderness: wilderness the color of the world that men had all but lost. What he hated most in all the world was wasteland: *gray* wasteland, the color of the glutinous organic dust which had consumed the first-generation cities left derelict by the Crash, and the color of the second-generation cities that had been gantzed out of that dust to supply the alleged needs of the multitudinous produce of Conrad Helier's New Reproductive System. Today's third-generation cities were multicolored, and Magnus knew that the fourth-generation complexes which were no longer to be called cities—out of respect for the current fashionability of the absurd philosophy of Decivilization—would take care to mimic the green which had been banished from the ever-extending jet-black SAP fields; to Magnus, however, the underlying color of the human hive and all its honeycombs would always be gray.

Magnus loved to sleep beneath the stars, as if in the open air. Even though the LSP prevented his breathing in the myriad scents of the renewed rain forest while he lay upon his bunk, he felt that he was sharing communion with the benign soul of the world. Thanks to the protective power of the tent, he could lie naked on his bed without the least fear of cold or persecution by predators and parasites.

It was still early when he finished his strictly utilitarian meal, but he was too tired for serious work, and the last thing he wanted was to watch TV. He discarded his beltphone along with his clothes, knowing full well that it would not emit the slightest sound. His answering machine was a low-grade silver, and he had trained it very carefully to be as stubborn as it was clever. It would not break into his communion even to give him news of the end of the world.

He turned the light down to a mere glow. Then he laid himself down on his bed, displaying himself with all due reverence, feeling deliciously humble in the presence of Gaea. In public, he always denied that he was a Gaean Mystic, because two centuries of mockery had contrived to attach a comical significance to the term, but in private he was prepared to admit that Gaea had been the one true love of his life, the core of his spirituality. Her cause was his cause, and would be for as long as he lived.

Sleep did not come to Magnus immediately, but he was unworried by its lack of hurry. He was content to look serenely up at the handful of stars that were visible through the forest canopy.

Darkness had leached all color from the outside world, but it was still green to him. Green was more than mere appearance, after all; it was essence and symbol, belonging at least as much to inner vision as to the deceptive wisdom of the eye.

In the days of his youth, which Magnus could no longer remember with any clarity, there had been such an abundance of gray in the world that he must surely have been filled with anguish by its contemplation. Even then, he had been avid—recklessly avid, on occasion—to work in the cause of life, although he had not had such a clear idea of what the cause of life required of a man. In those days, he had associated freely with the engineers whose cause was to subdue and manipulate life and reduce it to the status of one more MegaMall product; nowadays, he knew better. He had not seen or spoken to Walter Czastka for more than a century.

Now that he was old, Magnus was exceedingly glad that the empire of the gray had been so much reduced. The one good thing to be said for the vast black landscapes of modern agri-industry was that they had liberated space for the limited restoration of the greenery of Ancient Nature. Magnus was now old for the third time, and he knew that this time would be the last. He was glad enough and wise enough to accept that truth; he was not one of those vainglorious individuals who would dare anything and everything in the usually futile pursuit of a fourth youth.

The lessons of the twenty-third and twenty-fourth centuries had been hard, but the limits of inorganic nanotechnology had finally been recognized and admitted by his own generation. Had they been admitted two hundred years earlier, he knew, far more research might have been redirected into pure bioscience, and members of the new generation of Naturals might now be welcoming their second century of hopefully eternal youth instead of climbing out of slightly protracted adolescence. Magnus was not unduly resentful of the fact that he had been born too soon to benefit from Zaman engineering, however; nor did he begrudge the fact that he had lived to see the advent of the New Human Race while still confined to the tattered flesh of the Old, doomed to become a thing of nanotech thread and patches.

Magnus knew that there were many people in the world—most of them younger by far than he—who considered the reborn wilderness to be an artifact of nostalgia, a brief folly of the MegaMall's Dominant Shareholders, but he was convinced that the work he was doing would provide a legacy for which the new inheritors of the earth would be deeply grateful. He would die, and soon, but the work to which he had dedicated his life would go on. The forest would survive. Alien to man it might be, but man would protect it nevertheless. The members of the New Human Race had even elected to call themselves Naturals. Gaean Mystics they were not, but at heart—or so Magnus believed—every *true* human was a Gaean in essence. The inheritors of Earth would guard their heritage far better than his own kind ever had.

As these thoughts wandered across his mind, Magnus had to blink a tear from the corner of his left eye. He immediately suffered a sudden stab of doubt, which was not so easily blinked away. He could not help but recall the fact that many people considered him to be an obsessive fool, not merely a lunatic but—and this was surely the final insult—a *harmless* lunatic.

"In the empire of the ecosphere, Magnus," a once-valued colleague had said to him, only a few weeks before, "everything is controlled. It has to be. What you call 'wilderness' was born from the gene banks which conserved DNA from the world which existed before the ecocatastrophes of the twenty-first and twenty-second centuries. It flourishes by our permission, entirely subject to our guidance. Its freedom is merely the result of our refusal fully to exercise our ecological hegemony. You're fooling yourself if you think that it's Ancient Nature reborn, in any meaningful sense. Ancient Nature began to die with the first discovery of agriculture and ended its long torment in the years before the Crash. Your so-called wilderness is at best a ghost and at worst a mere echo."

"I know and understand all that," Magnus now took leave to reply, exercising his inalienable right to *l'esprit de l'escalier.* "I am not a fool—I merely recognize both the necessity and the propriety of returning these tracts of land to the dominion of natural selection. It is a wholly desirable act of expiation, whose efficacy is clearly displayed by the results of the biodiversity surveys."

"It's a shallow gesture," the colleague had told him, in response to a less carefully formulated reply. "It's a temporary indulgence—a brief guilt trip whose futility will be recognized by the New Human Race as soon as its first generation reaches true adulthood. The time has already arrived when forest green is just as much an artifact as SAP black. You can't halt progress, Magnus. You can't turn back the clock. Your forest is a sham, and a temporary folly."

"I'm trying to turn the clock *forward,*" Magnus had not thought to say at the time. "What I'm doing *is* progress. The forest is forever, and its flesh is as real as its soul."

And yet, he could not deny that all the forest trees whose company he preferred to that of his fellow men had been planted within his own lifetime. The seeds from which they were grown had come from gene banks: the static arks that had been hastily stocked in the twenty-first century, before the Greenhouse Crisis had sent a second Deluge to devastate the lowlands of civilization. The young trees had required careful protection and assiduous nurture for decades before they could be left to fend for themselves. The recreation of wilderness had been, in its fashion, as delicate a task as any exercise in Creation of the kind which hundreds of hubristic engineers were now carrying out in the real and artificial islands of the vast Pacific.

In spite of all this, Magnus knew that he must somehow have

faith in the assertion that what surrounded him, as he slept beneath the stars, really *was* a part of the authentic soul of the world. He had to believe that the gene banks had merely been a phase in an evolutionary story that stretched back from the present to the magical day when life had first ventured forth from the littoral zones of the primordial ocean to embrace the land.

Like all good Gaeans, Magnus preferred to think of that adventure as an "embrace"; he had always hated to hear it described as a "conquest."

Had he not been assailed by such troublesome doubts, Magnus would not have been delighted to receive an unexpected visitor— but it happened that he *was* assailed by doubts on that particular night, and that his visitor brought welcome relief.

When Magnus first heard the noise of the newcomer's approach, he could not help the reflexive twitch of his hand which impelled it toward the place where his dart gun lay hidden, but he suppressed the impulse readily enough. Within the dome, he was invulnerable to attack by any creature which had only teeth and claws to use as weapons. When he saw that the approaching figure was a human woman, however, a different set of reflexes was immediately invoked, and he tumbled from his bed with indecent haste.

By the time the woman had come through the protective undergrowth, Magnus had framed his protests, but they were half-hearted, motivated by shame that she should have come upon him naked in a transparent tent rather than by annoyance at the violation of his privacy.

"You shouldn't have come," he said when he had let her in— having partly clothed himself, although he still felt more than a little exposed. "It's dangerous to walk through the forest by night."

"I was lonely," she said. "My dome's only a couple of kilometers from yours, and it seemed foolish to endure the loneliness when company was so close to hand. By day, the nature of our work confines us to our own tracts, but that's no reason why we can't get together in our own time. There is a track, after all—it's not as if I had to hack my way through thorny bushes and sticky creepers with a machete. I would have called to tell you I was coming, but that damned silver of yours wouldn't let me through. You really should instruct it to allow a few exceptions."

Magnus didn't have the heart to tell her that if he had been disposed to file a list of people exempted from the silver's stalling strategy, her name would not have been among them. She was undeniably lovely—her eyes were perfectly delightful, her flowing hair absolutely magnificent—but he hardly knew her. He had never seen her at the base, nor had he even noticed her name in any of the documents that flitted across his busy screens. Had she not taken it into her head to begin making these mercifully infrequent journeys from her LSP tent to his, he would probably never have become aware of her existence, let alone made love to her. But even in the depths of his beloved forest he could take comfort from genuine human warmth, and she did seem genuine, in that naive fashion that only the authentically young could manifest.

They talked for a while, as they always did. She liked him to talk and never thought him pompous or foolish. She was not a Natural, but she was one of the committed ones, one of those who understood—or was, at least, capable of understanding, given the guidance of a man as wise as himself.

"If you are to understand what you are," he told her, when they had got to the strong meat of the conversation, "you must understand the true history of your own genes. Like everyone else, you were born from an artificial womb, the child of a sperm and an ovum which might well have been stored in the banks for centuries. I'm sure that the resultant egg was carefully screened, before cell division was even allowed to begin, for immunity to those hereditary diseases for which even the best IT cannot compensate— but that doesn't mean that you're a creature of human artifice. No matter how extensively the designers of the New Human Race may tamper with the blueprint which is written in the DNA carried by our kind, the DNA retains a history which extends in an unbroken double helix all the way back to the cradle of life itself. Like the forest, you and I are part of the soul of the world—and so is the legion of Naturals whose privilege it will be to inherit that world."

The woman had always replied to such proud and portentous statements with a welcoming smile, and she did so now. "That's right," she said. "I was born from a Helier womb, like my mother before me, but the essence of my being didn't begin its development in an artificial environment. As it happens, the sperm and egg whose combination formed my own gentemplate *hadn't* been stored in the banks for centuries, and in spite of everything that was done to the embryo, and everything else which separates me from the moment of my first genesis, I feel that I'm less a creature of artifice than many. It's a pity that the Naturals have been allowed to hijack that label. I was educated to believe that I too am a Natural of sorts."

Magnus heard the entire speech as an echo of his own voice. The young woman had never tried to contradict him and always seemed to be genuinely inspired by his vision. Although she would presumably be one of the last-born members of the Old Human Race, her youth allowed her to feel completely at ease with herself and completely at ease with the world. That easefulness was far more precious than her silken hair, her luminous flesh, or her lithe limbs.

Although he was not ungrateful to be old, and not afraid to die, Magnus was still capable of loving youth. He was still capable of loving *her,* even though she really should not have left her own bubble dome to visit him in his. He had to forgive her the breach of protocol. He had forgiven her before, and he did so now.

It was a fine irony, Magnus thought, that the cycle of fashion had come full circle yet again, so that the young people of her generation were once again inclined to favor sexual intercourse with actual human beings over the infinitely more various seductions of intimate technology. The truly young had, of course, always been inclined to such experiments, but the newest generation seemed more fervent than its predecessors in challenging the inherited opinion of their elders that only *virtual* reality could offer ideal partners.

Magnus was old enough and wise enough to have known all along that real partners were better than virtual ones. He had always had faith in the sanctity of true flesh. His love of wilderness and his love of authentic youth were, he supposed, merely different aspects of his faith in the sanctity of flesh. Flesh itself might be seen as a kind of wilderness, and wilderness as a kind of youth.

When the soul of the world was young, Magnus thought as he prepared to lie down upon his bed for a second time, naked and unashamed, and man's ancestors were hairy apes on the point of venturing forth from the forests to the great African plain, everything was wilderness. There was wasteland even then—the slopes of active volcanoes; the polar ice fields; the true deserts—but the latter-day wastelands which men have made by deforestation and civilization and biotech wars had not yet offended the all-embracing empire of flesh and youth. Nothing then had been made by ignorance and stupidity and greed, and we still have the opportunity to recall and recreate that lovely innocence. This too is a sacrament offered to Gaea. This too is worship, and labor in the cause of life. No man or woman has been born from a human womb for nearly two centuries—longer than that if the official records are believable—but the womb is still a temple of life, and its rites of approach are Gaea's rites. This is not merely love but worshipful love, the antithesis of ignorance, stupidity, and greed.

Magnus hated ignorance, stupidity, and greed. All wise men, he supposed, must hate ignorance, stupidity, and greed. Wisdom was love of knowledge, intelligence, and moderation. Wisdom was thinking in terms of embraces, and not in terms of conquests. He did not think of the wondrous woman as a conquest, and he was certain that she did not think of herself as having been conquered.

When he kissed her before lowering her onto the narrow bed, Magnus thought for a fleeting instant that he might have known the young woman before—that somewhen in the mists of time which had clouded his memory over the years, he had caught a glimpse of a supremely beautiful face almost exactly like hers—but he dismissed the thought. She was far too young, and her face had clearly been somatically modified to bring the features into line with one of the so-called seven archetypes of female beauty. He had long grown used to the silly tricks which memory sometimes played, and was too wise to let them bother him unduly.

The kiss was delicious, the taste of it far from merely utilitarian.

Before the sun rose again, Magnus Teidemann was dead.

He had died peacefully, and happily, in the forest which he loved. Because it was wilderness, to which human access was, by necessity, very strictly controlled, no one found his body for a long time. No alarm had been raised, and no one thought it in the least odd that they could not get access to him via his answering machine.

By the time his body was discovered, the cunning flowers which had transmuted his flesh into their own had withered and died. The humus had reclaimed them, and in reclaiming them had reclaimed *him*. He was no longer alien to the forest; he had been assimilated. It was the end for which he had yearned.

Of all the kindly murders which the innocent flowers and their innocent host were to commit, this was both the first and the most generous.

A s soon as the elevator door slid shut, Oscar Wilde seemed to take it for granted that Charlotte's interrogation had been temporarily suspended. Had she been quick enough to seize the initiative, Charlotte might have established that no such suspension had been granted, but she was not. While she paused to collect her thoughts, Wilde turned his attention to Michael Lowenthal.

"I hope you won't think me impolite, Michael," said Wilde, "but I believe you are what common parlance calls a Natural, or a member of the New Human Race."

"Yes, I am," Lowenthal agreed in a slightly surprised tone. "I congratulate you on your perspicacity. Most people can't identify a Zaman transformation by means of superficial appearances."

"I'm something of a connoisseur of authentic youth," Wilde admitted. "Charlotte is, of course, a fine specimen of the Old Race, but I could never doubt that she and I are of the same sad kind. Perhaps you think that I am too old to share her inevitable regret that her foster parents did not seize the opportunity of subjecting her embryo to the Zaman transformation, but I am not. I have been a genetic engineer all my life, you see, born in the days of prejudice. Like others of my kind, I have always known the perversity and tragedy of the folly which long withheld the generosity of the Finest Art from the most precious flower of all: the flower of human youth."

"You are not so very old, Dr. Wilde," said Lowenthal politely.

"Call me Oscar," said Wilde reflexively. "Indeed I am not— but my youth has been hard-won. I have had to renew it three times over. Having been immunized against the ravages of age from the moment of conception, you have every right to expect—or at least to hope—that you will look hardly a day older than you look now when you have lived as many years as I."

A triple rejuvenate! Charlotte thought, knowing that her astonishment must be visible. I never saw a triple rejuvenate who looked like that! Even Gabriel King, who was far better preserved than most, had skin like weathered wood, until he was rudely transformed into flesh of a very different kind.

"The error which our forebears made in concentrating their efforts on the development of cleverer nanotechnologies was understandable," Lowenthal said, his tone relentlessly neutral. "They believed, not unreasonably, in the escalator effect—that true emortality would eventually be bestowed upon them if only they could keep on reaping the rewards of new and better instruments of repair. With the aid of hindsight, we can see that the hope was illusory—but as a triple rejuvenate, you must have believed in your own youth that presently imperfect technologies would nevertheless be adequate to deliver you into a world in which improved nanotechnologies really would give you the means to preserve your body and mind indefinitely."

"I never believed it," Wilde said bluntly. "Even as a child, I could see that the logical end point of excessive reliance on inorganic nanotechnologies would be a dehumanizing robotization—that the only entities which could emerge from an endless process of *repair* would be creatures less human than the cleverest silvers: caricaturish automata. The only respect in which I have been forced to alter my opinion is that I feared such travesties would actually be able to think of themselves as human and even to believe themselves to be the same individuals who had been born into an earlier era. Mercifully, the workings of the Miller effect have spared us *that*. And now, at last, the old folly is over and done with. Now, we have a New Human Race, as artfully created as the best products of my own industry."

"I wish that you could be one of them," said Michael Lowenthal politely as the elevator car came to a halt and the door slid open

again to reveal the modified gloom of the Trebizond Tower's sub-
terranean garage, "since you wish it so fervently."

"Thank you," said Oscar Wilde. "I hope that I shall never grow
used to the cruelties of fate—and I hope that you, dear Charlotte,
will preserve your own resentments as jealously. It will help you to
be a better policeman."

Charlotte nearly fell into the trap of declaring that she had no
such resentments and that she was perfectly content with the decision her eight parents had made to produce and foster a child of
their own kind, but she strangled the impulse. Time was passing,
and there was work to be done.

"My car's over there," she said, extending a finger to indicate
to Wilde the direction he should take. "Will you follow us, Mr.
Lowenthal?"

"I'd rather travel with you, if you don't mind," Lowenthal said.
"My superiors sent me out in person so that I could keep my finger
on the pulse of the investigation, so to speak. There's no purpose
in my actually being here if I have to keep in touch with you by
phone."

"Suit yourself," said Charlotte shortly. "But I'd be obliged if
you could both keep it in mind that this *is* an investigation, not a
dinner party. We're not here to talk about the relative merits of
internal technology and Zaman engineering. We're here to figure
out who killed Gabriel King—preferably before the news tapes get
hold of the grisly details of his demise."

"Of course," said Lowenthal. "With luck, the DNA samples
collected by Lieutenant Chai will lead us to the murderer—and then
we shall only be required to figure out *why*."

He said it in a vaguely admonitory manner—as if he were suggesting that the relative merits of internal nanotech and engineered
emortality might perhaps be the crux of the matter.

For the moment, Charlotte could only wonder whether, perhaps, they might.

•   •   •

Charlotte opened the doors of her car and climbed into the seat which offered primary access to the driver, leaving Wilde and Lowenthal to decide for themselves which seats they would take. As if to emphasize their newly cemented alliance, they both got into the rear of the vehicle, leaving the other front seat vacant.

Having keyed in their destination, Charlotte left the silver to plan and navigate a route. She turned to face her passengers, but she was too late to take control. Oscar Wilde had already begun talking again.

"I fear," he said, addressing himself to Lowenthal, "that it might not be possible to get to the bottom of this affair before the newsmen unleash their electronic bloodhounds. If what I have so far seen is a reliable guide, the puzzle must have been carefully designed so as not to unravel in a hurry."

Lowenthal nodded his head sagely. "It does seem—"

"That's all the more reason to concentrate our efforts on the facts we have," Charlotte cut in rudely. "So will you please tell me what you meant, Dr. Wilde, about the supposedly obvious suggestion that the woman in the tape might be Rappaccini's daughter."

"Ah," said Wilde. "The thickening of the plot. May I tell you a story?"

"If you must," Charlotte said as evenly as she could contrive. It did not help her mood to observe that Michael Lowenthal seemed to be suppressing a smile.

"In an age that was long past even in the nineteenth century," Wilde began, relaxing into the delicate embrace of the car's LSP upholstery, "a young man comes to study at the University of Padua. He takes a small room beneath the eaves of an old house, which looks out upon a walled garden filled with exotic flowers. This garden, he soon learns, is tended by the aged Dr. Rappaccini and his lovely daughter, Beatrice.

"Over a period of weeks, the student watches the delightful Beatrice while she is at work in the garden. Having some knowledge of botany, he soon notices that she can handle with impunity certain plants which he knows to be poisonous to other living things. He is fascinated by this revelation—and, of course, by the lovely girl herself. Eventually, his landlady shows him a secret way into the garden so that he can meet her.

"Beatrice, who has led an extraordinarily secluded life, is as fascinated by the handsome student as he is by her. Innocence and beauty are a fine and deadly combination in a young woman—a combination which ensures that he soon falls in love with her—and she mirrors his infatuation. The student is, however, a very respectable young man, and he is careful to maintain an appropriate distance from his chaste beloved.

"One of Rappaccini's colleagues at the university discovers that the young man has managed to obtain access to the secret garden. He warns the student that he is in great danger, because the plants in the garden—many of which are Rappaccini's own creations—are all poisonous. Beatrice, because she has grown up there, is immune to the poisons; but she has in consequence become poisonous herself. This rival professor, who despises Rappaccini as a 'vile empiric' defiant of tradition, gives the student a vial which, he claims, contains an antidote to the poisons. This, he says, can redeem the unfortunate Beatrice and make her as harmless as other women.

"The student gradually realizes that he too is being polluted by the deadly plants. By virtue of having entered the garden so frequently, he has been infected with the power to blight and kill. He accuses Beatrice of visiting a curse upon him but then proposes that they should both drink the antidote and be cured.

"Rappaccini has by now discovered the intrigue between his daughter and her suitor. He tries to intervene, warning Beatrice not to take the antidote because it will destroy her. He insists that what he has bestowed upon her is a marvelous gift, which makes her powerful while all other women remain weak.

"Beatrice will not listen to her father; she prefers the advice of her young lover. He, being deluded as to the true situation, recklessly urges her to drink the potion, which is to her peculiar nature a poison rather than an antidote. She dies, and in dying, breaks the hearts of her father and lover alike.''

Charlotte had struggled hard to follow the implications of this curious tale while it was being told, trying to figure out how it could possibly have anything to do with the murder of Gabriel King—or why Oscar Wilde might think that it did. In the end, she could only say: "You think that the man you know as Rappaccini might be acting the part of his namesake—much as you make a show of acting the part of yours?''

Wilde shrugged his shoulders. "In the story, it was Rappaccini's jealous colleague who committed murder, if anyone did. But Rappaccini did collect the fatal flowers: *les fleurs du mal*. In today's world, of course, it would be very difficult indeed to raise a child in such perfect seclusion as Beatrice. If the man I knew as Rappaccini had a daughter raised to be immune to poisons, but poisonous herself, we must assume that she would be wiser by far than her predecessor. She would surely know, would she not, that her glamor and her kiss would be poisonous?''

"Her kiss?" Charlotte echoed.

"We saw her kiss poor Gabriel, did we not? Did you not think that it was a very *deliberate* kiss?''

"This is too bizarre," Charlotte complained.

"I quite agree," said Wilde equably. "As lushly extravagant as a poem in prose by Baudelaire himself. But then, we *have* been instructed to expect a Baudelairean dimension to this affair, have we not? I can hardly wait for the next installment of the story.''

"What's that supposed to mean?" asked Charlotte.

"I doubt that the affair is concluded," Wilde replied.

"You think this is going to happen again?''

"I'm almost sure of it," said the beautiful but exceedingly infuriating man, with appalling calmness. "If the author of this mystery intends to present us with a real psychodrama, he will not stop when he has only just begun. The next murder, as your aptly named colleague must by now have deduced, might well be committed in San Francisco."

Charlotte could only look at Oscar Wilde as if he were mad—but she could not quite believe that he was. For a moment, she thought that his reference to her "aptly named colleague" was to Lowenthal, but then she remembered the stale jokes about Holmes and Watson, which had had to be explained to her when she had first been teamed with Hal. She recalled that Wilde considered himself an expert on nineteenth- and twentieth-century literature—or some of it, at least.

"Why San Francisco?" she asked, wishing that she did not have to hold herself in such an awkward position while her car threaded its way through the dense traffic. The funeral was long gone, but its congestive aftereffects still lingered.

"The item which was faxed through to me along with the peremptory summons that took me to the Trebizond Tower here was not a copy of the text which appeared on my screen," Wilde belatedly informed her. "It's a reservation for the midnight maglev to San Francisco. Inspector Watson discovered that when he traced the call."

The flower designer took a sheet of paper from a pocket in his suitskin and held it out for Charlotte's inspection. She took it from him and stared at it dumbly.

"Why didn't you show me this before?" she said.

"I'm sorry," Wilde said, "but my mind was occupied with other things. I do hope that you won't try to prevent me from using the ticket. I realize that Hal took great care to recruit me as an expert witness in order to make sure that I might be kept under close surveillance, but I assure you that I will be of more use to the investigation if I am allowed to follow the trail which the murderer seems to be carefully laying down for me."

"Why should we?" she replied, bitterly aware of the fact that it was entirely Hal's decision. "We're the UN police, after all—and this isn't a game. Whether or not those flowers that killed Gabriel King were capable of producing fertile seeds, they constitute a serious biohazard. If something like that ever got loose . . . why do you think Lowenthal's here?"

"I thought he was with you," said Wilde mildly.

"Well, he's not," Charlotte snapped back. "He's from some mysterious upper stratum of the World Government, intent on making sure that we aren't trembling on the brink of a new plague war."

"I hope you'll forgive the contradiction, Sergeant, but I never said any such thing," said Michael Lowenthal, speaking just as mildly as the man beside him. "You seem to have taken the wrong inference from my declaration that I'm just a humble employee."

This was too much. "Well who the hell *are* you, then?" she retorted.

"I'm not required to divulge that information," Lowenthal countered, apparently having taken it upon himself to see if he could match Oscar Wilde's skill in the art of infuriation. "But I'd rather you weren't laboring under any delusions about my working for the UN. I don't."

Charlotte knew that every word of this conversation would eventually be replayed by Hal Watson, even if he were content for the time being to rely on her summary of its results while he was busy chasing silvers through the dusty backwaters of the Web. She was painfully aware of the fact that the replay wasn't going to make her look good—or even halfway competent.

"What do you think is going to happen in San Francisco, Dr. Wilde?" she asked, taking a firm grip of her temper.

"Call me Oscar," he pleaded. "I fear, dear Charlotte, that it may already have happened. The question is: what am I being sent to San Francisco to *discover*? I daresay that Hal is doing what he can to make the relevant discovery before I get there, and we shall doubtless find out whether he has succeeded in a few minutes' time, but the pieces of the puzzle have so far been placed with the utmost care. There is so much in the unfolding picture that I am able to recognize without having to delve in esoteric databases that I am forced to the conclusion that the whole affair was planned with my role as expert witness very much in mind. I don't know why this ingenious murderer should have taken the trouble to invite me to play detective, but it seems that I may be better equipped to draw inferences from whatever discoveries you may make than anyone else. I hope that you will trust my judgment, allowing me to help you in the way that seems most appropriate to me."

"And if we did that," Charlotte said, "we'd look even more idiotic than the meanest sloth if it eventually turned out that you were the one who had planted all these crazy clues, wouldn't we? If it turned out that you were the architect of the whole affair, and we'd let you lead us halfway around the world while posing as an expert witness, we'd look like the stupidest idiots that ever enlisted in the UN police."

"I suppose you would," said Oscar Wilde. "I fear that I can't offer you any incontrovertible proof that I'm innocent—but you'll seem just as foolish, I fear, if you refuse to avail yourself of my expertise, and it later turns out that I *am* innocent and could have given you significant help in solving the mystery."

Charlotte had to admit, if only silently, that it was true. If Wilde really did have the temerity to have himself summoned to the scene of a crime which he had committed, so that he could savor the frustration of the UN's investigators, the ticket to San Francisco might be a means of escape that he was flaunting in front of her, but if not. . . .

"If you're going to San Francisco," she said, hoping that she could get Hal to back her up, "then I'm going too." On the theory that a reckless gamble shared was an uncomfortable responsibility halved, she added: "How about you, Mr. Lowenthal?"

"I wouldn't miss it for the world," Lowenthal said. "I'll book our tickets now." He unhooked his beltphone and set about doing exactly that.

"We have several hours in hand before midnight," Charlotte said to Oscar Wilde, feeling a little better now that she had actually made an executive decision. "Even if Hal hasn't cracked the case by then, he's sure to have turned up a wealth of useful information. If you really have been invited to the party in order to give us the benefit of your expertise, you'll doubtless be able to give us a better idea of what it might all mean than any impression we can form on our own behalf."

"I certainly hope so," he replied warmly. "You can count on my complete cooperation—and, of course, on my absolute discretion."

And you, Charlotte said silently, can count on being instantly arrested, the moment Hal digs up anything that will stand up in court as evidence of your involvement in this unholy mess. If you're trying to run rings around us, you'd better not count on our getting dizzy.

The "new" UN complex built in 2431 was now under sentence of death, along with every other edifice on Manhattan Island, but it was intended to remain functional for at least another year while its multitudinous departments were relocated on a piecemeal basis. Charlotte thought that its loss would be a pity, given that it had so much history attached to it—the complex embraced the site of the original building, which had been demolished in 2039—but the MegaMall and the Decivilizers both saw the matter in a different light.

Charlotte had only the vaguest notion of how the Decivilization movement had come to be so influential, but she could see perfectly well that it was a matter of fashion rather than ideological commitment. Perhaps people *had* been huddled into the old cities for far too long, and perhaps the populations of the New Human Race ought to be more diffusely distributed if they were really to develop new and better ways of life, but that didn't mean that history ought to be forgotten and all its artifacts rendered down into biotech sludge. What would happen when the fashion passed, and "Decivilization" ceased to be a buzzword? Would the Naturals then begin to restore everything that Gabriel King had demolished?

There had once been talk of the UN taking over the whole of Manhattan, but that had gone the way of most dream schemes during the still-troubled years of the late twenty-second century. Now, an even more grandiose plan to move the core of the UN bureaucracy to Antarctica—the "continent without nations"—was well advanced and seemed likely to proceed to completion. Fortunately, that was unlikely to include the Police Department. Charlotte didn't want to relocate to a penguin-infested wilderness of ice.

Oscar Wilde mentioned to Charlotte as they transferred from her car to the elevator that he had visited the UN complex many times before but had never penetrated into the secret sanctum of the Police Department. He seemed to find the prospect of a visit to Hal's lair rather amusing. Charlotte was confident that he would be disappointed by the clutter; Hal was not a tidy man, and Wilde's manner of dress suggested that he valued neatness.

"How well did you know Gabriel King, Dr. Wilde?" she suddenly asked as they stepped across the threshold of the elevator. Having seen and understood what had happened last time, she was determined to seize the initiative before the ascent commenced.

"We used to meet for business reasons at infrequent intervals," Wilde replied, apparently having given up on his attempt to achieve first-name status, "and we must have been in the same room on numerous social occasions. I think of myself as belonging to a different generation, but the world at large presumably considers us to be of equivalent antiquity. I haven't spoken to Gabriel for more than twenty years, although I would undoubtedly have bumped into him sometime soon had I remained in New York and had he remained alive. I've supplied his company with decorative materials for various building projects, but we were never friends. He was one of the great bores of his era, and not for want of competition, but I had nothing else against him. Even a man of my acute aesthetic sensibilities would not stoop so low as to murder a man merely for being a bore."

"And how well do you know Rappaccini?" she followed up doggedly.

"I haven't seen him in the flesh for more years than I can count. I know the body of his work far better than I know the man behind it, but there was a period immediately before and after the Great Exhibition when we used to meet quite frequently. We were often bracketed together by critics and reporters who observed a kinship in our ideas, methods, and personalities, and tended to oppose us to a more orthodox school headed by Walter Czastka. The reportage created a sense of common cause, although I was never sure how closely akin we really were, aesthetically speaking. Our conversations were never intimate—we discussed art and genetics, never our personal histories and ambitions."

Charlotte would have pursued the line of questioning further, but the elevator had reached its destination.

Oscar Wilde did not seem in the least surprised or reluctant to comply when Charlotte asked her two companions to wait in her office for a few minutes while she consulted her colleague in private, but Michael Lowenthal almost voiced an objection before deciding better of it. She could not tell whether he was being scrupulously polite, or whether he thought that there might be more advantage in remaining with Wilde. As soon as she had shown Wilde and Lowenthal into her room, the two of them fell into earnest conversation again, seemingly losing interest in her before she closed the door on them.

Charlotte made a mental note to review the tape before she went to bed, even if she had to do it in a sleeper on the maglev.

Charlotte saw no point in beating about the bush when she presented herself to her superior officer.

"I brought Wilde with me," she said brusquely. "I think he did it. I think this whole mad scheme is a bizarre game. He may be a victim of mental disruption caused by excessive use of repair nano-tech within the brain. He's older than he looks."

Even in the dim light of Hal's crowded quarters Charlotte was easily able to see the expression of amusement which flitted across the inspector's face, but all he actually said was: "I know how old he is. Less than one-fifty, and already he's risked a third rejuve—but every test they applied at the hospital says that he's still in possession of a *mens sana in corpore sano*. I've checked his records."

"He knows far too much about this business for it to be mere coincidence," Charlotte insisted, wishing that her argument hadn't collapsed quite as feebly on exposure to the oxygen of publicity. "I know it sounds crazy, but I think he set this whole thing up and then turned up in person to watch us wrestle with it."

"So you think his introduction of Rappaccini's name is just a red herring?"

"He's been careful not to say that Rappaccini's guilty of the murder," she pointed out. "When he told us that silly story about Rappaccini's daughter, he pointed out that the murderer, if there was one, was a jealous rival. Wilde's a flower designer, like Rappaccini—and he put on a convincing show of being offended when I told him that our first choice of expert witness was Walter Czastka. If this Biasiolo character hasn't been glimpsed for decades, it's possible that Wilde has actually taken over the Rappaccini pseudonym from its original user."

"It's an interesting hypothesis," said Hal, with an air of affected tolerance that was almost as excruciating as Oscar Wilde's. "But my surfers haven't found a jot of evidence to support it."

Charlotte hesitated but decided that it would be best not to continue. She'd put her suspicions on the record; the best thing to do now was to follow them up herself, as best she could. She figured that it would be sensible to change the subject of the present conversation—and there was a question she had been longing to ask.

"Who the hell is this Lowenthal, Hal? When you said that the order to copy him in came from upstairs I assumed that he came from upstairs too, but he says he didn't. Who's he *really* working for?"

Hal shrugged. "Pick your cliché," he said. "The Secret Masters. The Hardinist Cabal. The Nine Unknown. The Ice-Age Elite. The Knights of the Round Table. The Gods of Olympus. The Heirs Apparent. The Inner Circle. The Dominant Shareholders."

"The *MegaMall*?" Charlotte completed the sequence incredulously. "Why would the MegaMall be interested in this? King's murder can't possibly have any macroeconomic implications."

"Everything has macroeconomic implications," Hal informed her, although—as his recitation of the list of names by which the world's economic elite were mockingly known suggested—he didn't seem to be entirely serious. "This is a very sensitive time, world-supply-and-demand-wise. We're on the hot upslope of the economic cycle, and the Dominant Shareholders have taken what must seem even to them to be a *brave decision* in pandering to the prophets of Decivilization. Clearing out the old cities and changing the lifestyle of the race will certainly generate a lot of *lovely* economic activity, but the Shareholders must be a little nervous about the possibility that it might all boil over. They don't want anything to get out of hand, and the assassination of a man like King—the publicly acknowledged spearhead of the demolition of New York— might be a symptom of something ugly."

"Are you saying that King was part of the Inner Circle?" Charlotte asked incredulously.

"No. But he was a committed servant—close enough to make the real Shareholders think that it might be worthwhile to track my investigation move for move. Lowenthal's just learning the ropes, though. For him, this is schoolwork. Be nice to him—one day, he'll probably be up there on Olympus with the rest of the Heirs Apparent, jockeying for a good seat at the Round Table, at the right hand of the Once and Future Managing Director."

Hal was still taking the trouble to sound nonserious, but Charlotte wondered whether he was only doing it to conceal the true seriousness of what he was saying.

"You really think Lowenthal's going to be a big wheel in the MegaMall one day?" she said, uncertain as to whether it was the sort of question that should even be asked, if it might receive an affirmative answer.

"Him or someone very like him," Hal replied. "Once members of the New Human Race get their bums on the boardroom seats, they're likely to be there forever and a day—unless, of course, Zaman transformations turn out to be a storm in a teacup, just like PicoCon's much-vaunted nanotech escalator. The prophets of Decivilization know that, of course, and they probably understand well enough why the MegaMall is letting them play their games with real cities. If they were to decide not to be content with their concessionary inch, and set out to claim a mile . . . well, some might say that it's a short enough step from being a hard-line Decivilizer to becoming an Eliminator."

"Oh," said Charlotte, recognizing that this line of thought might be the basis of a much more intriguing hypothesis as to the *why* of Gabriel King's murder than her supposition that Oscar Wilde was an insane criminal genius. After a pause she said: "Have you got the DNA analyses from King's apartment yet?"

"Twenty minutes," Hal told her. "Maybe thirty. Better wheel Wilde in anyway, though. My silvers have turned up some other stuff he might be interested to look at—and it really isn't a good idea to appear to be shutting Lowenthal out."

"Wilde wants to go to San Francisco on the midnight maglev," Charlotte reported mechanically. "Lowenthal wants to go with him. So do I."

"I know," said Hal in the infuriating manner he always reserved for her best revelations. "Wilde's got every right to do so, of course, provided that he gives the gentemplate of the killer plant his full and immediate attention once Regina's finished the analysis. What difference does it make? If he *has* done something wrong, we can find him easily enough, whether he's in San Francisco or on the moon. You don't have to go with him."

"Suppose he *were* the murderer and went on to murder some-one else?" Charlotte asked desperately.

"He'll be under close surveillance whether you're with him or not—but if you want to go, you can. I don't need you here. If Low-enthal chooses to go with you instead of sticking with me, it's his choice."

Charlotte had no difficulty at all in deducing that Hal would far rather Lowenthal went with her, especially if she led him off on a wild-goose chase for which she had taken sole responsibility. The simple fact was, however, that Hal *didn't* need her here. Modern police work involved packs of assiduous silver surfers checking ob-jective data, carefully attempting to sort the relevant from the ir-relevant, and the real information from misinformation and disinformation. Talking to people, even on the phone, was a "real-time activity," generally considered by most seasoned policemen to be a terrible imposition and a woefully uneconomic use of precious hours—and if she remained here, talking to people on the phone was exactly what she would be doing.

"I'll go with Wilde," she said. "It's okay—I'll take the blame if it turns out to be a stupid move. I'll just have to hope that Low-enthal will one day find it in his heart to forgive me."

Hal smiled, and his eyes expressed wry gratitude—but what he said aloud, for the sake of listening ears, was: "If you think it's necessary."

Charlotte collected Oscar Wilde and Michael Lowenthal from her office and brought them into Hal's workplace. The space was over-crowded with screens and comcons, and there were trails of print-out hanging down like creepers from every shelf and desktop—Hal had an absurdly anachronistic and altogether unreasonable fond-ness for paper—but there were enough workstations for both of them to sit down in reasonable comfort.

"Oscar Wilde, Michael Lowenthal—Hal Watson," she said with awkward formality.

Hal got up to shake hands with both of them, but he took Lowenthal's hand first. He met the Natural's eyes with an expression of pure professional concern and muttered something about always being appreciative of extra professional help. Charlotte observed that he was careful to put that particular mask away before greeting Wilde.

"Charlotte tells me that your unique insight into the motives and methods of the man behind Rappaccini Inc. might be of considerable help in the investigation, Dr. Wilde," said Hal, implying by his indifferent tone that he shared his assistant's skepticism regarding Wilde's usefulness as an amateur detective.

"Call me Oscar," said Wilde smoothly. "I certainly hope so. There are, I think, times when instant recognition and artistic sensitivity might facilitate more rapid deduction than the most powerful analytical engines. I'm a naive invader in your territory, of course—and I confess, as I contemplate this awesome battery of electronic weaponry, that I feel like one of those mortals of old who fell asleep on a burial mound and woke to find himself in the gloomy land of the fairy folk—but I really do feel that I can help you. I have some time in hand before the midnight maglev leaves, if there's anything you'd like to tell me by way of background."

"As I say, I'm always grateful for any help I can get," said Hal, still feigning casual indifference. "You're welcome to listen in while I fill Mr. Lowenthal in on some relevant details, provided that he has no objection."

"None," said Lowenthal. "I agree that Dr. Wilde's special insights might be valuable. I'm keen to hear what he thinks."

Charlotte was glad, but not surprised, to observe that her colleague seemed equally unimpressed by Oscar Wilde's recently renewed handsomeness and Michael Lowenthal's authentically youthful beauty. Hal, whose machine-assisted perceptions ground up all the richness and complexity of the social world into mere atoms of data, had not the same idea of beauty as common men. In a Webwalker's eyes, the cataract of encoded data which poured through his screens and VE hoods was the only reality. Hal never thought of himself as a man watching a shadow play; he found his aesthetic delights in patterns woven out of information or enigmas smoothed into comprehension, not in the hard and soft sculptures of stone and flesh.

Unfortunately, it seemed that the unshadowy world of hard and superabundant data had yet to be persuaded to explain how it had produced the eccentric masterpiece of mere appearances which was the murder of Gabriel King.

"I'm afraid that the man behind Rappaccini Inc. is proving rather evasive," Hal told his visitors offhandedly, while his eyes continued to scan his screens. "His business dealings are fairly elaborate, but he's been effectively invisible for a long time. Jafri Biasiolo still holds a flag-of-convenience citizenship in the Kalahari Republic, but he has no recorded residency. There's no record of his death, but he seems to have faded out of fleshy existence by degrees. The currently listed telephonic addresses of his pseudonym are black boxes, and all his financial transactions are conducted by silver-level computer-synthesized simulacra; the implication is that Biasiolo has constructed an entirely new identity under a different name. That's not so very unusual these days, of course, especially among those older people whose reflexive response to increasing intensity of observation is to devise ever more elaborate means of hiding. Most of the macabre stories about people dying and nobody finding out for years because their sims keep up a ghostly dialogue with the world are exaggerated, but a man who seriously wants to vanish behind a smoke screen of electronic appearances can produce some very dense smoke. Any who then decide to re-create themselves as someone else can just as easily manufacture a new electronic identity. My surfers will winkle out the truth about Rappaccini eventually, but it all takes time, and time is the great enemy."

"Timing is the essence of any psychodrama," said Oscar Wilde. Michael Lowenthal gave no overt indication that he or his employers felt any particular sense of urgency, but Charlotte knew that he would not be here if they did not.

"The story so far is that Jafri Biasiolo first became manifest as Rappaccini in 2380," Hal continued evenly. "That's when he registered as a member with the Institute of Genetic Art in Sydney. He participated in a number of public exhibitions, including the Great Exhibition of 2405, sometimes putting in personal appearances. Unlike other genetic engineers specializing in flowering plants, Rappaccini never got involved in designing gardens or in the kind of interior decoration that is Dr. Wilde's chief source of income. He appears to have specialized almost exclusively in the design of funeral wreaths, although his unusual patterns of expenditure suggest that he may have been involved in other business activities under other names."

"What unusual patterns of expenditure?" Lowenthal wanted to know.

"He was a heavy investor in encephalic augmentation research. So was Gabriel King, it seems."

It took Charlotte a second or two to realize that "encephalic augmentation" was the polite term for brainfeed technology. "But that's illegal!" she blurted out, knowing as soon as the words had passed her lips that it was a stupid thing to say. Attempts to augment the capabilities of the brain by stimulating the growth of extra neurons which could then be hooked up via synthetic synapses to inorganic electronic equipment were currently hedged around by all manner of legal restrictions, as human genetic engineering had been in the days that Oscar Wilde still remembered less than fondly—but those laws were mostly of recent origin. Gabriel King and Jafri Biasiolo were very old men.

"There's still scope for legitimate inquiry," was all that Hal said in reply. Charlotte frowned, realizing that he was being deliberately terse. Obviously, this was a link he was still chasing hard. Lowenthal's lovely face was impassive, but Charlotte wasn't convinced that he thought the detail insignificant.

"Rappaccini Inc.'s flowers have always been grown under contract by middlemen," Hal continued, evidently more than willing to share this aspect of his inquiry. "Insofar as the corporation can be said to have a home base, it's located in Australia, in a sector of what used to be called the outback that was re-irrigated for conventional use in the days before the advent of Solid Artificial Photosynthesis. We're checking the routes by which seeds used to be delivered to the growing areas, trying to backtrack them to the laboratories of origin. Unfortunately, it seems that Rappaccini Inc. hasn't put anything really new onto the market in forty years, even though the increasing ostentation of funerals has boosted its profits enormously. Nor has Jafri Biasiolo appeared in public during that time. He still has bank accounts drawing royalty credit from the corporation, but nobody within the organization has had any personal contact with him since 2430. It's probable that he's been using at least one other name for at least the last sixty-five years—possibly more than one.

"By virtue of his flag-of-convenience citizenship, Biasiolo avoided inclusion in most official records, but there is a DNA print allegedly taken immediately after birth. It doesn't match any other print registered to any living person, but he evidently made a thorough job of building a new identity; the print attached to his current name is probably fake. Rappaccini continued to maintain a telephone persona until 2460 or thereabouts, but the sim involved was an elementary sloth. I can't tell whether it was taken off-line or simply broke down. There aren't many programs like that still functioning."

"Walter Czastka has one," Charlotte put in.

"The only surprise in that instance," Oscar Wilde adjudged, "is that *Walter* is still functioning."

"Given that he still hasn't returned my call," Charlotte observed, "he might not be."

"Have you turned up anything which might suggest a possible motive for King's murder?" asked Lowenthal, who presumably suspected—as Charlotte did—that Hal's concentration on the mystery of Rappaccini's new identity might be something of a red herring screening the real substance of his investigation.

"We're delving into King's background, of course," Hal assured him. "If there's a motive in his financial affairs, we'll find it. We're examining every conversation he's had since coming to New York, and we're examining all activity in opposition to his demolition work. The truly remarkable thing about the murder is, however, the *method*. If we can understand that, we might be in a better position to understand the motive. Like Sergeant Holmes, I'm disappointed that Walter Czastka hasn't returned our call. If he were to confirm Dr. Wilde's judgment that the flowers were designed by Rappaccini. . . ."

"He won't," said Oscar Wilde airily.

"Why not?" asked Charlotte.

"Because the judgment required a sense of style," Wilde said. "Walter has none. He never had."

"According to our database," Hal observed, "he's the top man in the field of flower design—or was, until he retired to his private island to play the Creationist."

"Databases are incapable of forming opinions," Wilde stated firmly. "The figures presumably show that Walter has made more money than anyone else out of engineered flowers. That is not at all the same thing as being the best designer. Walter was always a mass-producer, not an artist. Ancient Nature provided all his models, and such amendments as he made to the stocks extracted from the arks were mere tinkering. I'm afraid that you will be unable to find anyone capable of reassuring you that my identification of Rappaccini as the designer of Gabriel's executioner was not a self-protective lie. The only man I ever knew with sufficient sense of style to be capable of offering an informed opinion is, I fear, Rappaccini himself."

He might have said more but was interrupted by a quiet beep from one of Hal's comcons. A silver was reporting news that required Hal's immediate attention.

The conversation lapsed while the Webwalker's fingers raced back and forth across the relevant keyboard for a few seconds. The pregnant silence persisted while Hal stared thoughtfully at a screen half-hidden from Charlotte's view. Lowenthal had turned back to Wilde, but his expression did not seem to be redolent with suspicion; Charlotte hoped that her own was equally opaque.

After half a minute or so, Hal said: "You might be interested to see this, Dr. Wilde." He pointed to the biggest of his display screens, which was mounted high on the wall directly in front of them. His fingers danced from one keyboard to another, and then another.

A picture appeared on the left of the screen, covering about a third of the display area. It showed a tall man with silver hair, a dark beard trimmed into a goatee, and a prominent nose.

"Jafri Biasiolo, alias Rappaccini, in 2381," Hal said.

He pressed more keys, and another image appeared in the center of the screen. This one showed two men side by side, apparently posing for the camera. One of them was clearly the same man whose image was on the left of the screen.

"Isn't that . . . ?" Charlotte began as she recognized the other.

"I fear that it is," said Wilde regretfully. "I looked a lot older then, of course. The photograph was taken in 2405, I believe, at the Sydney exhibition."

"It was 2405," agreed Hal. At the command of his fingers a third picture appeared, again showing Biasiolo alone. This time, Charlotte realized why Hal had taken the trouble to display them.

"This is 2430," Hal said. "Rappaccini's last personal appearance in the corridors of his own organization."

There was hardly any difference between the three images of Jafri Biasiolo. The man had evidently not undergone a full rejuvenation between 2381 and 2430, although he must surely have employed conventional methods of light cosmetic reconstruction to maintain the appearance of dignified middle age.

"If he really was born in 2323 he seems to have delayed rejuvenation far longer than was usual," said Lowenthal pensively.

"He must have had a comprehensive rejuve very soon after the last picture was taken," Hal agreed. "He probably came out with a very different appearance as well as a new name—but now we know the approximate date, I can set a silver to trawl all the records."

"On the other hand," Lowenthal suggested, "he *could* have used purely cosmetic somatic engineering to appear older than he actually was in 2381."

"If he was actually born considerably later than 2323 he might have falsely assumed the identity of Jafri Biasiolo," Hal conceded. "It's possible that he always maintained a second identity alongside his manifestations as Rappaccini and merely reverted in 2430 to being the person he's really been all along. It's a pity that picture-search programs are so unreliable—*very* messy data. That's why it's proving so difficult to track the woman who visited Gabriel King's apartment. There are plenty of cameras on those streets, and the silvers which are interrogating them are state-of-the-art, but a little old-fashioned paint and powder and a wig can cause a great deal of confusion when half the people on the street have modified themselves to fit a currently fashionable ideal. We're checking all the passengers who took the maglev to San Francisco during the twenty-four hours after she left the apartment, of course."

There was another beep. Charlotte knew immediately, by virtue of the expression of relief that formed on Hal's face, that it was Regina Chai's forensic report.

Hal immediately began printing out a gentemplate, presumably that of the flowers which had consumed Gabriel King's flesh, but he didn't watch its emergence from the printer's mouth. His fingers were dancing with what seemed to Charlotte to be impossible rapidity, and he was watching a virtual display whose detail she could not make out at all.

"We've got a good DNA print of the woman from the bedsheet detritus," he said eventually, sounding far less enthusiastic than he should have. "Unfortunately, we can't get a match with the print of any living person. Ordinarily, that would imply that she must be *much* older than she seems. . . ."

"But in this case," said Oscar Wilde, "it might mean that I was wrong to suggest that it would be impossible to raise a child in absolute seclusion in today's world."

"What do *you* mean by ordinarily?" Charlotte asked Hal, judging from his expression that he had not even considered Wilde's caveat.

Hal glanced at Michael Lowenthal before replying. "Regina says that the woman's DNA trace also shows evidence of some rather idiosyncratic somatic engineering. It's possible that the tissues which left the traces on King's bedsheets have been deliberately modified to obscure the print—to make sure that it wouldn't match the woman's natal record. We're conducting a more detailed search for near matches, but I don't know how far we can narrow down the field of suspects, or how fast."

Michael Lowenthal nodded, as if the bad news was not unexpected.

"Did you check the print against Rappaccini's?" asked Wilde.

"It's been very carefully checked against Biasiolo's, in toto and piece by piece," said Hal carefully. "The basic similarity index is only forty-one percent, but inspection of individual key sequences suggests that it might well have been fifty percent before the somatic modifications were made. If so, the woman *could* be Biasiolo's daughter, even though there's no official record of his ever having fathered, or even fostered, a child."

Wilde nodded sagely, as if this datum confirmed every impression he had so far formed about the nature and twisted logic of the crime.

Hal handed Wilde the other gentemplate, which had now printed out in full with all its associated annotations. "Your sense of style has taken you as far as it can, Dr. Wilde," he said. "It's time for some hard work now. We need your expert opinion as a genetic engineer—*everything* you can tell us about the nature of the plant and the level of biohazard it poses. Do you want a workstation here, or would you rather use a private cubbyhole?"

"I'll need access to my own records," Wilde said in a thoroughly businesslike manner. "Any VE hood will do; I won't be distracted by conversation."

"I think it's best if you're privacy-screened anyway," said Hal, for reasons which Charlotte was easily able to deduce. "If you'll come this way, I'll get you set up."

Charlotte and Michael Lowenthal looked on as Hal guided the awkwardly oversized Wilde through an inconveniently narrow gap in his labyrinth. Charlotte knew that she ought to say something, if only for the sake of conversation, but she didn't know what, so she kept silent. Lowenthal didn't step in to fill the gap.

Charlotte made herself busy picking up streamers of printout from Hal's machines, scanning the data accumulated by his silvers. She couldn't help nurturing the frail hope that there might be something there which Hal had considered too trivial to mention but which might in the fullness of time prove to be the nub of the case. She looked for a streamer holding data relating to Oscar Wilde, but none came readily to hand. She did, however, pick up a stray sheet which contained cross-correlated data on Gabriel King and Michael Lowenthal—and instantly lowered her head lest her expression attract the interest of her companion.

The page revealed that Lowenthal and King had been simultaneously involved—along with dozens of others—in a series of Web conferences relating to the plans for New York's reconstruction. Lowenthal had been present in the capacity of an observer, allegedly reporting to the boards of eight different corporations.

Five of the names were unfamiliar to Charlotte, but that was irrelevant; the fact that Lowenthal was reporting to all eight implied
that they were mere parts of a greater whole: the huge cartel which
was the engine of the world economy.

The industrial/entertainment complex which most people nowadays referred to as the MegaMall was a constant presence in Charlotte's life, as it was in everyone's, but it had always been a
background, unobtrusive precisely because it was so all-pervasive.
She had learned in school, if not actually at the manifold knees of
her foster mothers, that the MegaMall was a private corporation,
and that effective ownership of the world's entire means of production had long rested in the hands of a few hundred individuals,
but the thought had never crossed her mind that one day she might
actually meet a flesh-and-blood individual who belonged—however
peripherally or provisionally—to that intimate inner circle. Nor had
it occurred to her that the MegaMall's administrators, whether
reckoned as the Hardinist Cabal or any of the ironic alternatives
that Hal had proffered, must already have set plans in place to hand
over their empire to a favored few of the New Human Race. Now,
though, she tried to force her attention away from the infuriating
Oscar Wilde in order to focus her thoughts on the quieter of her
new companions, and the question of exactly what his interest in
this puzzling affair might be.

She had just made up her mind to ask Lowenthal directly when
Hal returned—at which point Lowenthal made his own belated bid
for the center-stage position.

"Is there any sign of a Decivilizationist connection?" he asked
bluntly.

"Not that I can see, as yet," Hal told him. "Do your own investigators have any particular reason to think that there might
be?"

"No, but we're anxious about the possibility. Someone has gone
to a great deal of trouble to make this murder newsworthy—such
gaudy display is an obvious bid for attention. Wilde may well be

right to see it as some kind of theatrical performance."

"I can understand that your employers might be jealous of their monopoly on the art of window dressing," Hal said mildly, "but I can't quite see the prophets of Decivilization as serious rivals."

"Don't mistake my meaning, Inspector Watson," Lowenthal said with equal mildness. "My employers approve of the Decivilization movement. Stability Without Stagnation has always been their motto. They approve wholeheartedly of change, novelty, fashion, and eccentricity. They even approve of social movements opposed to their own ideals, whose leaders disapprove of their very existence. An element of challenge is a healthy thing in a society, always provided that it doesn't get out of hand. It's a thin line that separates challenge from conflict, reform from revolution—and there are a good many people here in New York who wonder whether the Decivilization movement might have been granted too many concessions."

"None of the movement's spokesmen has ever criticized the institution of ownership or the logic of Global Hardinism," Hal pointed out. "Their attacks on the idea of civilization have always been narrowly focused on the supposedly stultifying effects of city life and city landscapes. They're essentially a bunch of aesthetes, not too different in kind from the flamboyant Dr. Wilde. If they did have anything to do with the murder of Gabriel King, they're more likely to have done it because he was a crude utilitarian than because he was an accessory to the supposed tyranny of the MegaMall. If you have any evidence that the Decivilization movement is fostering a revival of the Eliminators, or the Robot Assassins, I'd very much like to see it—but if not, I think you might be wasting your time chasing that particular hare."

"Not if that plant's as dangerous as your Dr. Chai thinks it might be," Lowenthal countered. "That could be a powerful agent of Decivilization."

"Dr. Chai's paid to be supremely cautious," Hal retorted. "We'll know more when we get Wilde's report, but my guess is that there's no danger of an epidemic. If the people who designed and deployed it wanted to start a new plague war, they would have gone about the work in a very different way."

"And if they only wanted to *threaten* to start a new plague war?" Lowenthal asked.

Hal laughed. "I thought that the MegaMall never gave in to blackmail," he said. "According to history, it never has—but I suppose history would say that, given that it's just as much a MegaMall product as Solid Artificial Photosynthesis." Charlotte was surprised by the provocatively naked cynicism of the comment, although she had heard Hal express similarly skeptical opinions before, when he had occasion to despair of the quality of old data. If the Web's vast tree of knowledge really was infested with disinformation, it was more likely to have been placed there by its owners than its detractors. She realized that Hal must be more resentful of Lowenthal's intrusion than she had supposed.

"No one sensible ever gives in to blackmail," Lowenthal replied lightly. "Capitulation gives out the wrong signals. It's difficult enough coping with hobbyist vandals and software saboteurs without fostering the illusion that there's profit in malevolence. I don't suppose, by any chance, that your industrious silvers have turned up any connection between Rappaccini Inc. and any eccentric political organizations?"

"Not unless the organizations sponsoring encephalic augmentation count as political," said Hal. "Have yours?"

Lowenthal merely smiled at that, as if to say that if they had, he wouldn't have bothered to ask.

Charlotte didn't imagine for a moment that she understood all the implications of Lowenthal's involvement in the investigation, but she was beginning to see some of them.

Perhaps it was the fact that politically motivated murders had become so very rare since the demise of the Robot Assassins that was causing the Natural's employers to examine the possibility so carefully. If King's murder turned out to be merely personal, there was no need for the MegaMall to be concerned about it, but if it was not—and now she came to think about it, Gabriel King might be exactly the kind of person that the ancient Eliminators might have regarded as "unworthy of immortality"—then the killing might be an early warning of far worse to come. The Decivilization movement's front men were harmless enough, but every such movement had its lunatic fringe—and the encouragement that had been given to the movement's official agenda might well have enthused those with more radical ideas.

The biohazard aspect of the case was especially worrying, if it was indeed the opening shot of some kind of campaign. The apparent use of an untraceable assassin, whose DNA print could not be matched to that of any living person, also seemed ominous. If someone else was already dead in San Francisco, awaiting discovery by Oscar Wilde, this affair was likely to escalate—and whether Rex Carnevon tipped anyone the wink or not, the newscasters would catch hold of it soon enough. If the assassin *had* gone to San Francisco immediately after killing King, she might already have left, continuing westward. If any more bodies were to turn up, she might soon qualify as a terrorist.

"I think we should send someone out to Walter Czastka's island," she said, on a sudden impulse. "I'm worried about the fact that he never returned my call."

Hal turned to look at her. "Old men are often fiercely jealous of their privacy," he said. "Creationists especially. Designing an entire self-enclosed ecosystem is an intricate business, and they're all desperately secretive about it because they all feel that they're involved in a competition. Every islet in those parts, natural or engineered, has been taken over by some semiretired engineer avid to turn it into his own little Garden of Eden. It's a large-scale replay of the run-up to the Great Exhibition, when every genetic engineer in the world was paranoid about his best ideas being stolen. Anyway, it's only been a matter of hours, and it's still daylight in the

Pacific. If Czastka hasn't checked in by midnight, our time, I'll ask the Hawaiian police to send out a drone."

Hal and Lowenthal turned again as Oscar Wilde reappeared, carefully maneuvering his massive frame through the narrow gap into which Hal had dispatched him. Hal frowned, obviously having expected his deliberations to take a lot longer.

"You can't possibly have finished," Hal said.

"Indeed not," said Wilde. "But I have temporarily abandoned the detailed work to a trusted silver, who will report in due course on the precise capabilities of the murderous organism. In the meantime, given that it's nearly nine o'clock, and that rejuvenation always sharpens my appetite, I wonder if I might give you my preliminary observations over dinner? I presume that even policemen have to eat." He didn't seem entirely certain of this conclusion; his inquiring expression implied that he might be wondering whether there were some kind of intravenous feeding mechanisms concealed in the back of Hal's chair.

"There's a restaurant upstairs," said Charlotte. "We can eat there."

Oscar looked at her, raising his eyebrow just a fraction.

"Upstairs?" he queried. "I had thought of the Carnegie, or perhaps Gautier's. Quail *en croûte* was my first inspiration, but if . . ."

"The restaurant here is as good as any in the city," she assured him. "We have a first-rate synthesization service, and there's an excellent dining room."

"I can't leave my workstation," Hal said, "but if you leave a phone link open so that I can ask questions . . ."

"Of course," said Wilde. "Will *you* join us, Mr. Lowenthal?"

"Certainly," said the man from the MegaMall.

"Excellent. I should reassure you immediately, of course, that there is absolutely no need to panic regarding the possibility of a random outbreak of homicidal flowers—less need, in fact, than even I had feared. This particular weapon will never be used again, because it was designed expressly to consume the flesh of Gabriel

King. It is what the parlance of the old plague wars called a *smart agent*—far smarter, in fact, than any agent then devised. It may well qualify as the most narrowly targeted weapon in history."

Hal and Lowenthal absorbed this information silently. Even Charlotte knew enough about genetics to be astonished by it.

"Perhaps I ought also to say," Oscar went on, "that although I remain absolutely convinced that the plant's designer was Rappaccini, it appears to have been derived from a natural template that Rappaccini has never actually used—a temporarily extinct species that was recovered from a twenty-first-century seed bank by another person, and which has so far been developed for the marketplace exclusively by that person."

"Which person?" Hal asked—although Charlotte presumed that he must already have guessed.

"Me," said Oscar Wilde. "Although the finished product bears little enough resemblance to its model, the gentemplate makes it clear that the original was a globoid amaranth of the genus *Celosia*—once popularly known, my research assures me, as the cockscomb. That is as far as facts can take us. If I am to make more of the information I have gleaned, I shall have to make use of intuition—and I intuit far more effectively on a full stomach. There is nothing like good food and a bottle of fine wine to liberate the power of the imagination."

Hal Watson would undoubtedly have protested that what was required of an expert witness was scrupulous attention to fact rather than indulgence of the imagination, but he was distracted by two beeping sounds, which immediately entered into competition for his attention. While he tried to deal with both of them, a third commenced its siren song, and he was forced to begin juggling all three data streams.

"Go," he said. "I'll be listening."

"It's good to know," Wilde observed as Charlotte led her two companions toward yet another elevator, "that there are so many silvery recording angels sorting religiously through the multitudinous sins of mankind. Alas, I fear that the capacity of our fellow men for committing sins may still outstrip their best endeavors."

"Actually," Charlotte observed as she pressed the button to summon the car, "the crime rate is still going down—as it always has while the number of spy eyes and bubblebugs embedded in the walls of the world has increased."

"I spoke of *sins,* not crimes," said Wilde as they moved into the empty car. "What your electronic eyes do not see, the law may not grieve about, but the capacity for sin will lurk in the hearts and minds of men long after its expression has been banished from their public actions."

"People can do whatever they like in the privacy of their virtual environments," Charlotte retorted. "There's no sin in that. The point is that what lurks in the darker corners of their hearts and minds shouldn't—and mostly doesn't—affect the way they conduct themselves in the real world."

"If there were no sin in our adventures in imagination," Wilde said, evidently reluctant to surrender the last word even in the most trivial of arguments, "there would be no enjoyment in them. While we are as vicious at heart as we have ever been, and are encouraged to remain so by the precious freedom of virtual reality, we cannot be entirely virtuous even in the real world. The ever-presence of potential observers will, of course, make us exceedingly *careful*— but in the end, that will only serve to make all murders as intricate and ingenious as the one we are investigating. If you do not understand that, my dear Charlotte, I fear that you will not be comfortable in your chosen career."

Charlotte tried hard not to be infuriated by his condescension, but it wasn't easy. It wouldn't have been easy even if she hadn't formed the impression that Michael Lowenthal was amused by her distress. She wondered whether it might be natural that so-called Naturals would find amusement in the petty quarrels of mere mortals.

As they left the car two uniformed officers got in, one of them a sergeant in whose company Charlotte had gone through basic training.

"Any progress, Charlotte?" the sergeant asked, his inquisitive gaze sliding sideways to examine her two companions.

"Not yet, Mike," Charlotte said as breezily as she could, "but all the bloodhounds are out."

"Newshounds too," Mike murmured. "They don't know the details yet, but King's big enough to make them chase hard. Watch out for hoverflies."

Charlotte nodded, glad that she had been adamant that they ought to eat within the building. Even police headquarters couldn't be guaranteed to be 100 percent secure, but eating in any public restaurant would have been tantamount to hiring a loudhailer.

Once they were seated, Oscar Wilde decided that what his appetite demanded was tournedos béarnaise with sauté potatoes, carrots, and broccoli. He informed Lowenthal, while Charlotte was busy acknowledging other greetings from sympathetic colleagues, that he had had an unusually taxing day for one so recently restored to youth, and that the solidity of beef would serve his needs better than the delicacies of quail. He decided on a bottle of Saint Emilion to go with it—the occasion, he declared, cried out for a full-bodied wine. Lowenthal agreed to take the same dish and share the wine, but Charlotte punched out an individual order for tuna steak and salad, with water to drink.

The police restaurant's food technology was, of course, easily adequate to the task of meeting Wilde's requirements. Its beef was grown by a celebrated local tissue culture which had long rejoiced in the pet name of Baltimore Bess: a veritable mountain of muscle which was fiercely guarded by traditionalists from the strong competition offered by SAP-derived "meat." The Saint Emilion was wholly authentic, although the Bordeaux region and its immediate neighbors had been replanted from gene banks as recently as 2330, when connoisseurs had decided that the native rootstocks had suffered too much deterioration in the tachytelic phase of ecospheric deterioration which had followed the environmental degradations of the Crash.

The dispenser delivered fresh bread, still warm from the oven, and a selection of hors d'oeuvres. Charlotte took some bread but left the rest to her companions; she had never liked excessively complicated food.

Hal had been silent while they made their way to the restaurant, but as soon as Charlotte had opened a link from the table's screen he took up the theme of Wilde's observations about the murder weapon. "According to my records," he said, "no one but you has ever withdrawn specimens of this particular globoid amaranth from the bank—which implies that you must have supplied the stocks from which the weapon was developed."

"*Supplied* seems a trifle exaggerated," Wilde objected. "*My* amaranths have been on open sale for decades. Tens of thousands of people have fertile specimens growing in their walls and gardens."

"I wasn't implying that you intended to supply the raw material for a murder weapon," Hal said disingenuously. "I've set one of my silvers to collaborate with one of yours in sorting through your records. I'd be obliged if you'd keep track of them, just in case some idiosyncratic modification of yours can be traced through a particular customer to the murder weapon."

"I'll do that," Wilde promised, although his tone suggested that he didn't expect a result. Hal nodded, and his face disappeared from the screen.

"Assuming that it would be relatively easy, once the basic pattern was in place, to modify this kind of smart weapon for other targets," Michael Lowenthal put in pensively, "I assume that it would also be relatively easy to plant individually targeted booby traps in gardens and hotel rooms all over the world." Charlotte inferred that he was still pondering the possibility that King's murder was just a warning shot, and that the murderer's next target might be closer to the Inner Circle.

"It's an intriguing possibility," Wilde agreed, "although the involvement of Rappaccini suggests that booby-trapped funeral wreaths might be more likely—as well as more artistic—than booby-trapped gardens."

Lowenthal didn't react to the reference to artistry, and Charlotte stifled her own objection. Wilde had hesitated, but he obviously had more to say.

"The idea of plants which take root in animal or human flesh, consuming living bodies as they grow, is very old," the geneticist went on, "but it's a trick that no natural species ever managed to pull off. There are fungi which grow in flesh, of course, but fungi are saprophytic by nature. Flowering plants are late products of the evolution of multicelled photosynthesizers. Legend and rumor have always alleged that they flourish with unaccustomed exuberance and luxury when planted in graveyards or watered with blood, but the motif is sustained by macabre notions of aesthetic propriety rather than by observation. The person who adapted my *Celosia* to develop in such a remarkable environment did so by a complex process of hybridization, much more elaborate than anything routinely attempted by specialist engineers. He has taken genes from nematode worms and cunningly grafted them onto the *Celosia* gentemplate. That's extremely difficult to do. We're all familiar with tired old jokes about genetic engineers crossing plants and animals to make fur coats grow on trees and produce flower heads with teeth, but in actuality those kinds of chimeras are almost impossible to generate.

"The artworks which Rappaccini showed at the Great Exhibition of 2405 were certainly bizarre, but they were not nearly as ambitious as this. If he really did take on a new identity fifty or sixty years ago, he must also have taken on a new lease of intellectual and creative life. He has made inroads into realms of innovation in which no one else has dared to trespass. Michael is right to conclude that once the basic pattern was in place, targeting the weapon at a particular individual could be regarded as a secondary matter, but we should not lose sight of the fact that *this* plant was designed purely and simply for the purpose of murdering Gabriel King. Given the complexity of the modified *Celosia,* it seems almost certain to me that this plot—including the selection of its victim—must have been hatched at least half a century ago, and probably long before. My instinct also tells me that no matter how reluctant I may be to accept the fact, Rappaccini must be the actual murderer, not merely the supplier of the weapon. Its deliverer, I feel sure, is his daughter. I only wish that I could divine his *motive.*"

Wilde took a careful sip of wine after finishing this speech, but his eyes were on his companions, waiting for a reaction. Before he obtained one, however, the dispensary signaled that their main courses were now ready.

The three diners disposed of the plates which they had so far been using and took delivery of larger ones. Charlotte's meal was accommodated easily enough, but Wilde and Lowenthal took their time dividing up their vegetables. While waiting for them to catch up, Charlotte studied their faces soberly, comparing their different styles of beauty. Even in an age of inexpensive off-the-peg glamour they were both striking, but Lowenthal's beauty was more conventional, more carefully respectful of the popular ideal. Lowenthal's face might well have benefited from the assistance of a first-rate somatic artist, but she felt sure that Wilde must have designed his own features before hiring an expert technician to execute his plan. It was rare to see such flamboyant femininity in the lines of a male face. Charlotte had to admit that it not only suited Wilde particularly well but also subjected her own appreciative sensations to a unique agitation.

Charlotte kept all the usual intimate technology at home, and her sexual desires were nowadays mostly served within that context, but she had found that there was a certain *frisson* which she could only gain from eye contact with actual human beings. She did not consider herself a slave to fashion and did not care at all whether real partners were in or out just now. She had not the slightest interest in joining an aggregate household, because she could not bear the thought of sacrificing all the joyous luxuries of solitude, so she was reasonably well accustomed to the tactics of forming occasional temporary liaisons. She could not help considering such a possibility while she bathed in the slight thrill of lust awakened by Wilde's perfect features, even though she was more than half-convinced that he was a murderer whose present occupation was trying to make a fool of her.

"Can you make an antidote?" said Michael Lowenthal suddenly, as he finally finished spooning broccoli from the serving dish to his plate.

The question obviously shifted Wilde's train of thought onto a new track, and for a moment or two he looked puzzled. Then he said: "Oh, of course! You mean a *generic* antidote—one that could be used to protect anyone and everyone against the possibility of encountering an amaranth tailored to consume his own flesh. Yes, Mr. Lowenthal, I could—and so could any halfway competent doctor now that we have the fundamental *Celosia* gentemplate. A problem would arise if *another* natural species had been used as a starting point for a similar weapon, but given the complexity of the project that seems unlikely. One would, of course, have to be able to identify the individuals who might require such protection, unless one were to administer the antidote to the whole population."

Not if you were only concerned with defending a small minority, Charlotte thought. As long as the Knights of the Round Table could be protected, and the Gods made safe in their Olympian retreat, the rest of us could take our own risks. She knew as she formed the thought, however, that the judgment was unfair. What the proprietors of the MegaMall would actually be enthusiastic to do would be to put the antidote on the market as soon as their faithful newscasters had wound public alarm up to its highest pitch.

She even found time to wonder whether it was conceivable that the MegaMall might commission the murder of a high-profile target in order to stimulate the market for a product that might otherwise seem unnecessarily expensive—but she dismissed the idea as a monstrous absurdity.

"You met the man who posed as Rappaccini more than once," Charlotte said, trying to return her wandering mind to more fruitful areas of conjecture. "Did he seem to you then to be a madman—a potential murderer?"

"I must confess that I rather liked him," Wilde replied. "He had an admirable hauteur, as if he considered himself a more profound person than most of the exhibitors at the Great Exhibition, but he did not strike me as a violent or vengeful person. I dined with him several times, usually in the presence of others, and I found him to be a man of civilized taste and conversation. He appeared to like me, and we shared a taste for antiquity—particularly the nineteenth century, to which we were both linked by our names. Memory is such a feeble instrument that I really cannot remember in any detail what we discussed, but I may have some recordings in my private archives. It would be interesting, would it not, to know whether we talked about nineteenth-century literature in general, and Baudelaire in particular?"

"We'll need access to those archives," said Charlotte.

"You are more than welcome," Wilde assured her. "I'm sure that you'll find them absolutely fascinating."

"A silver would do the actual scanning, of course," she added, blushing with embarrassment over the reflex that had caused her to state the obvious.

"How sad," Wilde replied teasingly. "Artificial intelligence is admirable in so many ways, but even its so-called geniuses have never quite mastered the sense of humor, let alone a sense of style. A human eye would find so much more to appreciate in the record of my life."

"Do you remember anything *useful*?" Charlotte asked, her

voice suddenly sharp with resentment of the fact that he was making fun of her. "Anything at all which might help us to identify the parallel existence which Biasiolo must have maintained alongside his life as Rappaccini, and into which he subsequently shifted."

"Not yet," Wilde replied, taking another appreciative sip of the Saint Emilion. "I *am* trying, but it was a long time ago, and our memories were not shaped by evolution to sustain themselves over a life span of a hundred and thirty years. I have preserved my mental capacity far better than some of my peers—but not, it seems, as well as Rappaccini."

Charlotte's beltphone buzzed and she picked up the handset. "Yes, Hal," she said.

"Just thought you'd like to know," he said. "Walter Czastka called in. He's alive and well. I sent him the data Wilde's been looking over, so we should have a second take on that by morning. We have a highly probable link between the suspect and a passenger who boarded a maglev two hours after she left the Trebizond Tower. Her ticket was booked in the name of Jeanne Duval. The ID's fake and the account is a cash-fed dummy, but I've got a flock of surfers chasing every last detail down. It could be the vital break."

"Thanks," said Charlotte. Polite discretion had presumably dissuaded Hal from simply reappearing on the table's screen and interrupting their meal—unless he was using politeness as an excuse for leaving Michael Lowenthal out of the loop for a few minutes. If so, she thought, she had better be careful. Hal would, of course, have to copy Lowenthal's employers in on the results of his chase—but if it were possible, he would infinitely prefer to catch the quarry first. In a race like this, minutes might make all the difference, and the reputation of the UN police was on the line.

"We reached Walter Czastka," Charlotte informed Wilde as she picked up her fork again. "He's alive and well—and he's double-checking your work."

"You might have made contact with him," Wilde said waspishly, "but I doubt that anyone has actually *reached* Walter for half a century or more."

"You don't seem to like Walter Czastka," Charlotte observed. "A matter of professional jealousy, perhaps?"

Wilde hesitated briefly before responding, but decided to ignore the insulting implication. "I don't dislike Walter *personally,*" he said carefully. "I will admit, however, to a certain distaste for the idea that we're two of a kind, equal in our expertise. He's an able man, in his way, but he's a hack; he has neither the eye nor the heart of a true artist. While I have aspired to perfection, he has always preferred to be prolific. He will identify the *Celosia* and will doubtless inform you that it is based on a gentemplate of mine, but he will not be able to see Rappaccini's handiwork in the final product. I hope that you will not read too much into that omission."

"But Czastka must have artistic ambitions of his own," Michael Lowenthal observed. "While you've been in New York, undergoing a third rejuvenation which most people would consider premature, he's been laboring away on his private island, patiently building his personal Eden."

"Walter has Creationist ambitions, just as I have," Wilde admitted, "but that's not what you're interested in, is it? You're exploring the possibility that Walter might be the man behind Gabriel King's murder, and wondering whether I might be underestimating him. You're wondering whether he knows what I think of him— and whether, if so, he might have involved me in his criminal masterpiece merely in order to make a fool of me. You're wondering whether he might have planned this magnificent folly to show the world how absurdly wrong I have been in my estimate of his abilities. I almost wish that it were conceivable, Michael, but it is not. I'll gladly stake my reputation on it."

"Walter Czastka knew Gabriel King quite well," Lowenthal observed mildly. "They were both born in 2301, and they attended the same university. Czastka has done a great deal of work for King, on various building projects—far more than you ever did, Dr. Wilde. They seem to have been on good terms, but they've had plenty of time to generate a motive for murder. Most murders involve people who know one another well." He had obviously done some background work on this hypothesis, presumably while Charlotte had failed to engage him in conversation in Hal's office.

"I daresay that nothing I can say will affect your pursuit of this line of inquiry," said Wilde wearily, "but I assure you that it is quite sterile. Walter has not sufficient imagination to have committed this crime, even if he had a motive. I doubt that he did have a motive; Walter and Gabriel King are—or were, in the latter case—cats of a similar stripe. Like Walter, Gabriel King might have been a true artist, but like Walter, he declined the opportunity."

"What do you mean by that?" Lowenthal asked.

"A modern architect, working with thousands of subspecies of gantzing bacteria and shamirs, can raise buildings out of almost any material, shaped to almost any design," Wilde pointed out, reverting to quasi-professorial mode. "The integration of pseudo living systems to provide water and other amenities adds a further dimension of creative opportunity. A true artist could make buildings that would stand forever as monuments to contemporary creativity, but Gabriel King's main interest was always in productivity—in razing whole towns to the ground and reerecting them with the least possible effort. His business, insofar as it is creative at all, has always been the mass production of third-rate homes for second-rate people. Walter has always been the first choice to provide those third-rate homes with third-rate interior and exterior floral decorations."

"I thought the original purpose of bacterial cementation processes was to facilitate the provision of decent homes for the very poor," said Charlotte. "Gabriel King was a structural bioengineer, after all, not an architect."

"Even so," Wilde said, "I find it infinitely sad to see modern methods of construction being applied so mechanically to the mass production of housing for people who are wealthy enough not to need mass-produced housing. The building of a home, or a series of homes, ought to be part of an individual's cultivation of his own personality, not a matter of following convention—or, even worse, some briefly fashionable fad, like so-called Decivilization. Like education, making a home will one day be one of the things every man is expected to do for himself, and there will be no more Gabriel King houses with Walter Czastka subsystems."

"We can't *all* be Creationists," objected Charlotte.

"Oh, but we can, Charlotte," Wilde retorted. "We can all make every effort to be whatever we can be—even people like us, who have not Michael's inbuilt advantages."

"Even the members of the New Human Race still die in the end," said Charlotte. "Lowenthal might be able to have ten careers, or twenty, instead of a mere handful, but there are thousands of different occupations—and as you pointed out yourself, our memories are finite. The human mind can only hold so much expertise."

"I'm talking about attitudes rather than capacities," said Oscar. "The men of the past had one excuse for all their failures—man born of woman had but a short time to live, and it was full of misery—but it was a shabby excuse even then. Today, the cowardice that still inhibits us is far more shameful. There is no excuse for any man who fails to be a true artist and declines to take full responsibility for both his mind and his environment. Too many of us still aim for mediocrity and are content with its achievement—"

He would undoubtedly have continued the lecture, but Charlotte's beltphone began to buzz again. She put the handset to her ear again.

"Shit hits fan," said Hal tersely. "The worst-case scenario just kicked in."

By the time Charlotte put the handset down again Wilde and Lowenthal knew that something important had happened. Wilde was still cradling his last glass of Saint Emilion, but he wasn't drinking. He was waiting for the bad news.

"Michi Urashima's just been found dead in San Francisco," she reported. She knew that it wasn't necessary to tell either of them who Michi Urashima was. For the sake of completeness she added: "He was murdered. Same method as King."

"Michi Urashima!" Lowenthal repeated incredulously.

"I'm very sorry to hear that," said Wilde. "Michi was a better man by far than Gabriel King."

Lowenthal had snatched up his own handset by the time Wilde had finished his sentence, and had turned away to speak into it. Charlotte had no difficulty at all in deducing that Michi Urashima's was not one of the names Lowenthal's employers had feared or expected to hear in this context—although there was one item of their discussion downstairs which had pointed to a pattern into which Urashima fit as snugly as a hand into a glove.

Before his trial and imprisonment, Michi Urashima had been one of the world's foremost pioneers of "encephalic augmentation": brainfeed research. Gabriel King must have known him well. So must Jafri Biasiolo, alias Rappaccini.

On the other hand, it was difficult to imagine anyone less in tune with the MegaMall's economic and social philosophy than Urashima. Even in the earliest phase of his career, when he had been an expert in computer graphics and image simulation, widely celebrated for his contributions to synthetic cinema, he had been a political radical. If the Hardinist Cabal feared that King's assassination had been the first move in a conspiracy directed against their ownership of the world, Michi Urashima was the last person they would expect to find on the hit list.

"Not everyone would agree with you about his being a better man," Charlotte said to Wilde speculatively, "but he must, I suppose, have been of the same generation. In any case, there's no need for you to take the midnight maglev now."

"On the contrary," said Oscar. "Even if this revelation is, by

Rappaccini's reckoning, premature, I feel that he would still want me to visit the scene. This affair is still in its early stages, and if we want to witness the further phases of its unfolding we really ought to follow the script laid down for us."

"You think there will be more murders?" Charlotte asked.

"I always thought so," said Wilde. "Now, I am certain of it."

INTERMISSION TWO
A Pioneer on the Furthest Shore

As if it were caught by the surge of a fast-flowing black river, the soul of Paul Kwiatek was hurled upon its wayward course through the warp of infinity. It was outside the universe of atoms, beneath the wayward play of nuclear interaction forces, having been reabsorbed into the implicate order itself. Paul knew that his fleshy envelope must be dead and that his body must already be in its coffin, borne through the streets of Bologna on a black-draped bier—but his soul was free, miraculously inviolate.

Tossed as he was by the whim of the reckless current, Paul could see nothing of the river's shore, the Land of the Dead. Perhaps it was only his imagination which assured him that he could hear the whispering voices of the spirit legions, welcoming him with gossip as they marveled over the achievements of his life.

The guardian at the entrance to an older heaven might have stopped him at the gate, for his life had not been entirely without sin, but he had always worked in the cause of Mind and the further evolution of the human intellect. In the reckoning of cowards, he had committed crimes—crimes from whose legal consequences the agents of the MegaMall had fortunately condescended to shield him—but everything he had done he had done for the sake of increased understanding of the last and greatest of the ancient mysteries: the nature of consciousness, the fundamental phenomenon of the human mind. In any case, the heaven of tradition was now a virtual theme park owned and operated by the MegaMall, through which silver saints offered guided tours to the living; *this* was the world beyond death, the ultimate upload, the exit to eternity.

Paul knew that the flow of the river was not the flow of time, because he was now beyond the reach of time, although his consciousness had no alternative but to arrange its thoughts and feelings consecutively, preserving the illusion of duration even in a realm without any such dimension. Nor was his soul confined in any way; free of his body, it had neither width nor breadth nor depth—but consciousness had no alternative but to define itself in terms of "position" and "magnitude," and so he perceived himself as an inconsiderable atom in the flotsam of a river which fed the Sea of Souls—an atom as yet alone, but fit nevertheless to join the company of all humankind at the omega point of creation.

Paul did not fear dissolution in the ocean of the implicate order, nor did he fear annihilation at the Climacticon; he knew that he could not be lost, even in infinity. Nothing, ultimately, could be lost, no matter how many inflationary domains bubbled up from the wellspring of creation, making worlds within worlds within worlds and selecting those best fitted to be cradles of further worlds, further minds, further candidates for the ultimate upload. The surge of creativity was illimitable, possessed of no vestige of a beginning and no prospect of an end, and the surge of mind within it was irresistible in its insistence on being heard and felt. Every sensation that was ever felt, every thought that was ever framed, was gathered here into the river of intelligence, neatly bound into identities and personal histories, stories made from memory, racing upon the tide toward omega, the summation of all.

Souls bound for lesser heavens were supposed to be joyous, worshipful, and above all *grateful,* but Paul was prey to no such petty treasons. He was an explorer, whose mind was *questioning,* and he had no space within his virtual self for gladness or triumph, ecstasy or awe. He had come to see all that there was to be seen, to feel all that there was to be felt, and above all else to know all that there was to be known. His purpose was discovery: to go to the undiscovered country where multitudes had been before, but from whose bourn no traveler had yet returned; to be what multitudes would one day be, although they could not know it.

It was, of course, a virtual experience—Paul had always despised the phrase "virtual reality" as a vile oxymoron, and thought "virtual environment" misleading because it implied that a person within one had merely altered his existential wallpaper without altering himself—but that did not make it any less valuable, in Paul's reckoning. As he was fond of reminding the few friends he had left, *all* experience was virtual, because that was the very essence of Mind. The cogitative brain was a machine for generating virtual experiences of a kind that would allow the body to function in the world of things-in-themselves, but to describe the phenomenal world of things-as-perceived as the *real* world was a conceptual step too far.

Few would have agreed with him, but Paul felt perfectly entitled to put the experience of the black river on a par with his experience of the Tiber or the Po, and to deem the implicate order of the Sea of Souls as sensible as the streets of Rome and the shores of the Adriatic.

Paul had no doubt of his own effective immortality, but still he could not shake the last vestiges of his fear of death. Perhaps, if he had been able to do that, he would have been able to ride the black current to its terminus, without the necessity of a return to vulgar quiddity. As things were, however, he felt compelled to call an end to his odyssey when his IT began to send unmistakable distress calls from his not-quite-abandoned flesh.

Paul lifted the VE hood from his head and set about unsealing the special suitskin in which he had been enwrapped for thirty-six hours. He fumbled every seam, his quivering fingers seeming huge and repulsive.

When he was finally free he made no immediate attempt to raise himself into a sitting position, let alone to swing his legs from the cradle to the floor. He simply lay there, becoming reaccustomed to his lumpen body and his mere humanity. He felt utterly deflated as well as severely disoriented; it was an effort even to blink his rheumy eyes.

He could no longer remember a time when this kind of return had seemed like returning *home*. He felt as if he had been washed up on an alien shore, stranded there as a castaway in a state of utter exhaustion. There was nothing he could do, until he recovered far better possession of himself, but lie still and wait. His IT was no longer transmitting distress calls, but it was laboring under duress. Although he had not consulted a physician in some time, his personal nanotech was neither obsolete nor broken down, but while the law forbade "explicit neural cyborgization," IT could only do so much to help the brain to maintain its efficient grip on the motor nerves. Given that the whole point of a VE hood-and-suitskin was to distract the brain from its involvement with a body, it was hardly surprising that the efficiency of that grip could be compromised while a person was lost in virtual experience.

Suitskins designed for everyday use were purely organic—even supposedly state-of-the-art sexsuits and commercially augmented VE trippers were only lightly cyborgized—but the suitskin Paul had been wearing was nearly 40 percent inorganic. Fortunately, there was no law specifying the limits of explicit neural cyborgization in artificial constructions. The suitskin was as awkwardly bulky as a twenty-second-century deptank, but it carried ten times as much fibertech and fifty times as much nanotech—and every single nanosuit was a great deal sleeker than its ancient ancestors. The suitskin's power was so much greater than a deptank's, and the virtual realities to which it took its user were so much more complicated, that the difference had to be reckoned as a qualitative one rather than a merely quantitative exaggeration.

Paul thought of the suitskin as his own invention, refusing to admit that the contribution of the giants on whose shoulders he had stood while drawing up its blueprint had been significant. He also thought of it as his own personal property, although he could never have financed its construction. All the money he had ever extracted from the MegaMall in the days when he had been a pioneer, oblivious of the cautionary elements of the emerging brainfeed laws, would not have served to buy an eye and a glove, let alone a whole suit—but if ever it became an item of controversy, he would have to take sole responsibility for its possession and its use. The Secret Masters of the world were hardly likely to come forward in his defense and say: the guilt is ours, and the penalty too. He had ceased to be an officially acknowledged employee of the MegaMall on the day that Michi Urashima had been thrown to the wolves. Others had thought of it as expulsion, but Paul had thought of it as freedom. In his eyes, the augmented suitskin was *his* creation, *his* property, and *his* gateway to eternity, no matter who had fed the cash into his bank account or what elaborate chain of transfers had culminated in the final delivery.

Paul's friends occasionally took leave to inform him—as if he had asked, or cared, or needed to know—that his apparatus was simply a souped-up version of the VE kits that ordinary folk used for remote work and virtual tourism. He always denied it, pointing out that suitskins intended for the use of VE tourists and others like them were content to pretend merely to alter the worlds in which their users moved, while ostensibly leaving their sense of self unmolested. Relatively few VE suitskins were actually *designed* to alter their users' subjective experiences of their own persons as profoundly as they altered the environments through which their bodies appeared to be moving. Most of the ones which could and did were geared to produce the illusion of being some other kind of animal: a leopard stalking its prey; a dolphin in the deep; an ant in the hive. Paul's pride and joy was far more ambitious than that, and the virtual worlds in which he routinely immersed himself were stranger by far. He was an explorer of artificial universes whose physical laws were markedly different from those pertaining to our own inflationary domain, and of alien states of being as remote from the human as the digital imagination could produce.

He was always prepared to explain this, not merely to his

friends but to anyone who would listen, but no one really understood who had not done what he had done and been where he had been. Had he tried much harder, he might eventually have persuaded one or more of his friends to do that, but he never tried *too* hard. To evangelize was one thing; to share the embrace of his most intimate possession was another.

When he had finally managed to sit up, Paul reached for the plastic bottle waiting on the shelf beside the cradle, uncapped it with hands that were almost steady, and sucked at the tube. He held the glucose-rich liquid in his mouth for six or seven seconds before easing it into his esophagus. The last of the time-release capsules that he had carefully committed to his stomach before donning the suitskin had exhausted its cargo of nutrients five hours before; he and his loyal IT were both in need of the energy fix.

Another ten minutes passed while he flexed the muscles in his limbs, preparing for the arduous journey to the bathroom. An everyday sleepskin would have absorbed the secretions of his skin as easily as it absorbed all other excreta, then turned him out perfectly fresh, but the suit he had been using had only the most elementary provision of that kind. He needed a shower and a generous dusting of talcmech before he was fit to receive company.

Sometimes he wondered whether it might be better to become a total recluse, but he did not like to be called a VE addict and he knew that if he were to withdraw from all human contact it would be taken as proof that the label had not been unjustly attached to him. The idea of a permanent retreat into the suitskin's inner worlds was not altogether attractive, even though it was now practicable. Thanks to the sudden flood of wealth produced by their stake in Zaman transformation technology, the Ahasuerus Foundation had been able to put a whole fleet of new susan technologies on the market, including a DreamOn facility which promised year-round support. He had enough money to pay for his upkeep for far longer than his body and mind were likely to hold out, and his doctors had advised him that a third core-system rejuvenation was out of the question unless he wanted to start over with a tabula rasa personality. The whole point of his odysseys in exotica was, however, to undertake voyages of discovery. How could he be reckoned a true explorer unless he brought the fruits of his labor back to Earth? Whatever people might say, he was *not* a VE addict; he was a pioneer.

Even susan-becalmed dreamers were, of course, only a phone call away from their real-world neighbors, but those voluntary Endymions to whom Paul had talked on various virtual grounds had always given abundant evidence of the fact that they were entranced. When they posed as scrupulous scientific observers reporting on their findings, they never gave the impression of reliability. Paul did not want to be seen as an unreliable witness, let alone a figure of fun; his journeys into the remotest regions of virtual space were attempts to expand reality, not attempts to escape it, and in order to make that plain he had to retain the capability of wakefulness.

He set the temperature control on the shower ten degrees too low, so that the first jet of water would startle his flesh, but he held on to the knob so that he could twist it to a more comfortable setting as soon as the benign shock had worked its way through his system. After that first reminder of what manner of being he was, it became far easier to relax into what he still considered—even after all his amazing adventures—to be his true self.

By the time he had slipped into a conventional daysuit Paul was beginning to wonder if he had left himself enough time to check his mail and get something to eat, but he still had thirty minutes to spare before the appointed time for his rendezvous, and he had already taken note of the fact that his visitor's sense of timing was extraordinarily exact. Although he had known her for less than a fortnight, he felt that he knew the young woman as well as he knew anyone else in the world, and he trusted her to appear at the appointed time, neither a minute early nor a minute late.

He did not, of course, have time to reply to any of his mail, but no one who knew him even slightly would be expecting a rapid response. His meal was whole diet manna, as uncomplicated as possible, but he followed it with hot black coffee, as authentic in taste and texture as his dispensary could contrive.

While he drank the coffee he reflected that although his lifestyle might have appeared frugal to anyone who had cause to consult the record stored by the mechanical eyes which had him under observation, they would have been wrong. "Only those with extensive experience of the unreal," he murmured, "can properly appreciate the real." It was one of his favorite aphorisms; he could no longer remember from whom he had stolen it.

"That's not what most people say," the beautiful woman had observed when he had quoted the saw on the occasion of their first meeting. "Some reckon that the near perfection of virtual reality can only devalue actual experience, by proving that it is—at least in principle, and nowadays very nearly in practice—reducible to a mere string of ones and zeroes."

"That's absurd," Paul had told her. "Even if one were to ignore the hardware whose structures are animated by the digital programs, it's as grossly misleading to think of the programs *merely* as a string of ones and zeroes as it is to think of living organisms *merely* as a string of *A*s, *C*s, *G*s, and *T*s threaded on a DNA strand. In any case, how can it be a devaluation to know that *everything*, in the ultimate analysis, can be reduced to the pure and absolute beauty of abstract information?"

The beautiful woman had been as deeply impressed by his eloquence as she was by his originality. There had been a spark between them from the very first moment: a spark that was emotional as well as intellectual. The fact that he was a hundred and ninety-four years old while she could hardly be more than twenty—twenty-five at the most—was no barrier to empathy. On the contrary: the difference between them actually increased the quality of their relationship by marking out complementary roles. She had so much to learn, and he so much to teach. She had such bright eyes, such fabulous hair . . . and he had such a wealth of experience, such a wonderful elasticity of mind.

"The professions of information technology have generated many derisory nicknames over the centuries," Paul had explained to his new lover when she wondered aloud whether she ought to follow a career trajectory in Webwork, "but those of us who have a true vocation learn to bear them all with pride. I've never been ashamed to be a chipmonk, or a bytebinder, or a cyberspider. I've devoted my life to the expansion of the Web and its capabilities. It is, after all, the mind of the race. In my youth I found it tattered and torn, ripped apart by the Crash, and in my middle years I had to fight with all my might to preserve its scaffolding from the vandalistic activities of the new barbarians—but in the end, I saw the triumph of the New Order and felt free to move on to further fields, searching for the road that would lead to the ultimate upload. That's the way to true immortality, after all. No matter what the so-called New Human Race is capable of, it can only be emortal; if we're to look beyond the very possibility of death, it's to the Web that we must look in the first instance, because it's the Web that will ultimately be fused with the Universal Machine, the architect of the omega point. It's a pity that so many of the people whose souls are inextricably caught in the embrace of the Web feel compelled to belittle it with their talk, even while they enjoy the wonderful privileges of its caresses, but it seems to be human nature to take the best things in life for granted."

"Rumor has it," she had told him while inspecting his cradle and his collection of uncommon suitskins, "that the most realistic VEs of all don't require a suitskin. The illusion is produced entirely by internal nanotech while the dreamer lies unconscious in a kind of susan. It's said that the suite was never put on the market because the illusions were *too* convincing for some of its users."

"Actually, the system in question *was* made commercially available for a while," Paul had been able to tell her, "but it was withdrawn after the first half-dozen shock-induced fatalities. An overreaction, in my opinion, but typical of the way the World Government works, always turning panic into legislation. All that was required was a slight tightening of the IT safety net, but the vidveg never see that, and democracy gives the vidveg the right of campaign. I've used the relevant IT myself, but work on the software stopped when the scandal forced the product off the market, and the existing VEs aren't nearly as sophisticated as the best of those designed to run on equipment like mine. If the MegaMall ever puts it back on the market I'd certainly consider adapting my own work to that kind of system, but it would involve some heavy and exceedingly laborious work. I'm probably too old for that kind of project."

"I doubt that," she had said, with a brilliant smile. "You've worn better than any other two-hundred-year-old man I know."

He hadn't even bothered to point out that he was still six years short of his second century.

By the time the door chime sounded, Paul was entirely ready to receive his visitor. He felt perfectly at home in his flesh, and perfectly at home in his apartment.

"Why thank you," he said as she offered him a bouquet of golden flowers. "I think I have a vase, somewhere. Are they Wildes or Czastkas?"

"Wildes," she told him. "His latest release."

"Of course—I should have known. The style's unmistakable. Czastkas always look so lackluster, so very *natural*—although I suppose we'll have to give up calling things natural, now that the adjective's been turned into a noun by the new emortals."

Paul did have a vase, although it wasn't easy to find. He was not a man who liked clutter, and he kept the great majority of his possessions neatly and efficiently stored away. "My memory isn't what it used to be," he explained while he searched for it.

"It doesn't matter," she said. "You can set them in the wall if you have the right kind of plumbing."

"I don't," he replied, still searching. "In my day, picture windows and virtual murals were all the rage. Nobody wanted creepers and daisy chains covering their interior walls—even daisy chains designed by Oscar Wilde or Walter Czastka. I was at university with Czastka, you know. He was *so* intense in those days—so full of plans and schemes. A little bit crazy, but only in a good way. He was an explorer then, like me. Sometimes I wonder where all his daring went. I haven't spoken to him for decades, but he'd become exceedingly dull even then."

"It really doesn't matter about the vase," the woman told him anxiously.

"It's here *somewhere*," he said. "I really *ought* to remember where I keep it. I might have thirty or forty years in me yet, if only I can keep my mind alive and alert. My brain might be a thing of thread and patches, but as long as I can keep the forces of fossilization at bay I can keep the neural pathways intact. As long as I can look after my *mind. . . .*"

Paul realized that he was rambling. He shut up, wondering whether he could find an opportunity to ask her whether or not *she* was a Natural, engineered for such longevity that she might not ever need "rejuvenation." If so, her mind might have a thousand years to grow and learn, to refine itself by the selection of forgetfulness. He wondered whether it would really be indelicate simply to ask her—but he decided against it, for the moment. She was authentically young; *that* was what mattered. What would become of her in two or five hundred years was surely none of *his* concern.

"The apartment sloth will know where it is," he told her while he continued to move hither and yon uncertainly, "but if I ask it, I'll be giving in to erosion. Sloths never forget, but that shouldn't tempt us to rely on them too much, lest we lose the ability to remember. A *good* memory is one that's as adept in the art of forgetfulness as it is in the art of remembrance." He realized, somewhat belatedly, that he was losing the thread of his own argument—and that he still had not found the vase.

"I'll put them down here," the woman said, laying the flowers down on the table beside the food dispensary. "They'll be fine for an hour or two—longer, if necessary. You can look for the vase later, if you really want to."

"Yes, of course," Paul said, trying not to sound annoyed with himself lest she take the inference that he was also annoyed with her. He resolved to start the encounter again, and went back to greet her for a second time, in a better way.

The young woman was extraordinarily beautiful, in an age where ordinary beauty was commonplace. Her eyes sparkled, and her hair was a delight to eye and hand alike. The touch of her lips seemed to Paul's old-fashioned consciousness to be a sensation which not even the most elaborate and sensitive virtual experiences could yet contain.

"Sometimes, when I emerge into the daylit world," he told her, "I feel as if I had passed through a looking glass into a mirror world which is subtly distorted. It seems very like the one I left behind, but not quite the same. I always need the touch of a human hand or a kiss from human lips in order to be sure that I'm really *home*."

"You can be sure of that," she told him. "This is the world, and you're certainly in it."

And so he was, for a while.

By the time death came to claim him, Paul Kwiatek was deep in yet another waking dream, and it seemed to him that he was in a very different body, in a very different world. Even before the seeds began to germinate within his flesh, he was a ghost among ghosts, in a world without light, adrift on a black torrent pouring over the edge of a great cataract, falling into an infinite and empty abyss.

The memory of the kisses he had so recently shared had already been stored neatly away, ready to be forgotten. Now, like the elusive vase, they would be forever lost.

So far as most people were concerned—even others like himself—Paul Kwiatek had been a mere phantom of the information world for years. His extinction passed unnoticed by any kind of intelligence, human or artificial, and the fact of it might have remained undiscovered for months had no one found a particular reason to search for him. It was not until a dutiful silver linked his name to those of Gabriel King, Michi Urashima, and Walter Czastka that anyone thought to wonder where he actually was, or what he had actually become.

INVESTIGATION: ACT THREE
Across America

By the time she had installed herself in the maglev couchette, Charlotte was exhausted. It had been a long, eventful, and mentally taxing day. Unfortunately, her head was still seething with crowded thoughts in Brownian motion, and she knew that sleep would be out of the question without serious chemical assistance. She knew that her disinclination to avail herself of such assistance would undoubtedly punish her the next day, when she would doubtless need chemical assistance of a different kind to maintain her alertness, but that seemed to her to be the dutiful way to play it. There was plenty of work she could do while she stayed awake, even if her powers of concentration were not at their peak.

The couchette had a screen of its own, but it was situated at the foot of the bed, and Charlotte found it more comfortable by far to plug her beltphone into the bed's head and set the bookplate on the pillow while lying prone on the mattress.

At first she was content to scan data which had already been collated by Hal's silvers, but she soon grew bored with that. Now that she had elected to play the detective, she knew that she ought to be doing research of her own. She could hardly compete with Hal's private army in matters of detail, but even Hal had confessed to her once that the principal defect of his methodology was the danger of losing sight of the wood among the trees. Given that she was a legman, operating in the human world rather than the abstract realm of digitized data, she needed to think holistically, making every effort to grasp the big picture. To have any chance of doing that, however, she needed more information on the game's players. Hal had already shown her the near vacuum of data that was supposedly the man behind Rappaccini, but if her suspicions could be trusted, the real key to the mystery must be Oscar Wilde.

She had, of course, to hope that her suspicions could be trusted; if they could not, she was going to look very foolish indeed. Modern police work was conventionally confined to the kind of data sifting at which Hal Watson was a past master. Legmen were at the bottom of the hierarchy, normally confined to the quasi-janitorial labor of looking after crime scenes and making arrests. She was mildly surprised that Hal had actually consented to let her accompany Wilde, because he obviously felt that this trip to San Francisco was a wild-goose chase, and that it was of no relevance whatsoever to the investigation. She wondered whether he would have given her permission if it had not been for Lowenthal. Although he would never be able to say so out loud, Hal would be much happier if the man from MegaMall were chasing distant wild geese instead of looking over his shoulder while he did the real detective work. At any rate, Charlotte knew that she could expect no backup and no encouragement, and that her one chance of avoiding a nasty blot on her record was to prove that her instincts were correct. If she could do that, the outlandishness of her action would be forgiven—and if she were *spectacularly* successful, her efforts might actually make the UN hierarchy think again about the methodology of modern police work.

It was the work of a few moments to discover that Oscar Wilde was anything but a data vacuum. That did not surprise her—although she was slightly startled by the revelation that there was almost as much data in the Web relating to the nineteenth-century writer after whom the contemporary Oscar had been named as there was to the man himself. It took her a further fifteen minutes fully to absorb the lesson that mere mass was a highly undesirable thing when it came to translating information into understanding. By the time that quarter hour had elapsed, she had cultivated a proper appreciation for the synoptic efforts of compilers of commentaries and encyclopedists.

She tried out half a dozen points of entry into the hypertextual maze, eventually settling for the *Condensed Micropaedia of the Modern World.* From there she was able to retrieve a reasonably compacted description of the life and works of Oscar Wilde (2362–) and Oscar Fingal O'Flahertie Wills Wilde (1854–1900). When she had inwardly digested that information, she looked up Charles Baudelaire. Then she looked up Walter Czastka, then Gabriel King, and then Michi Urashima. She had been hoping for inspiration, but none came; she felt even more exhausted but even less capable of sleep.

On a whim, she looked up Michael Lowenthal. She found references to a dozen of them, none of whom could possibly be the man in the next-but-one couchette. She keyed in MegaMall, but had to go to the *Universal Dictionary* to find an entry, which merely recorded that the word was "A colloquial term for the industrial/ entertainment complex." There were no entries even in the *Universal Dictionary* for the Secret Masters, the Nine Unknown, or the Dominant Shareholders, and the entries on the Gods of Olympus and the Knights of the Round Table were carefully disingenuous. There were, however, entries in both the dictionary and the *Condensed Micropaedia* on Hardinism, each of which deigned to include a footnote on the Hardinist Cabal.

According to the micropaedia, Hardinism was the name adopted by a loose association of early twenty-first-century businessmen to dignify their assertive defense of the principle of private property against steadily increasing demand that a central planning agency administered by the United Nations should be appointed to supervise the management of the ecosphere. The name had been appropriated from an obscure twentieth-century text called *The Tragedy of the Commons,* by an agricultural economist named Garrett Hardin. There, Hardin had pointed out that in the days when English grazing land had been available for common use, it had been in the interests of every individual user to maximize his exploitation of the resource by increasing the size of his herds. The inevitable result of this rational pursuit of individual advantage had been the overgrazing and ultimate destruction of the commons. Those former English commons which had been transformed into private property by the Enclosures Act had, by contrast, been carefully protected by their owners from dereliction, because they had been calculated as valuable items of inheritance whose bounty must be guarded.

According to the footnote, the members of the consortium of multinational corporations who had masterminded the so-called Zimmerman coup, which had taken advantage of a financial crisis in the world's stock markets to obtain a stranglehold on certain key "trading derivatives" relating to staple crops, had justified their actions by citing Hardinist doctrine. Although they had left Adam Zimmerman to acquire the primary notoriety of being "the man who cornered the future" or "the man who stole the world," they had nevertheless been stuck with the nickname of the Hardinist Cabal.

Neither the dictionary nor the micropaedia had anything to say about the contemporary use of the nickname, but it did not require much imagination to see the implication of its continued currency. Whatever the truth behind the myth of the Zimmerman coup might be, its effects were still in force. If a cartel of big corporations really had acquired effective ownership of the world in the early twenty-first century, they still had it. Even the Crash could not have served to loosen their grip; indeed, the establishment of the New Reproductive System must have helped to insulate it from the main kind of disintegration to which private property had previously been subject: dissipation by distribution among multiple inheritors.

In a sense, this was not news. Everybody "knew" that the United Nations didn't really run the world, and that the MegaMall did—but the ease with which that ironically cynical doctrine was accepted and bandied about kept the awareness at a superficial level. The idea of the MegaMall was so numinous, so difficult to pin down, that it was easy to forget that in the final analysis, it really was under the control of a relatively small number of Dominant Shareholders, whose names were not generally known. Like the ingenious Rappaccini, they had slipped away into the chaotic sea of Web-held data, forging new apparent identities and abandoning old ones, hiding among the electronic multitudes.

According to Hardinist doctrine, of course, such men were the saviors of the world, who had prevented the ecosphere from falling prey to the tragedy of the commons. Presumably, they were Hardinists still, utterly convinced of the virtue as well as the necessity of their economic power—and the next generation, to whom the reins of that power would be quietly handed over, would have the opportunity to hold it in perpetuity.

Michael Lowenthal had said that he was only a humble employee, like Charlotte, but while she only worked for the World Government, he was a servant of the Secret Masters of the world. Those Secret Masters had thought it necessary to take an interest in the murder of Gabriel King, in case it might be the beginning of a process that might threaten them. Now Michi Urashima was dead too—and to judge by Michael Lowenthal's reaction, that had been both unexpected and unwelcome. If it had suggested that their initial anxieties had been unfounded, it must also have suggested a few new anxieties to take the place of the originals. With luck, Lowenthal and his associates would be as confused and frustrated at this moment in time as she was.

If Oscar Wilde really was the killer, Charlotte realized, then this whole affair was nothing more than a madman's fantasy. How grateful the Hardinist Cabal would be if that were indeed the case—or if, indeed, it turned out to be some *other* madman's fantasy! The question that still remained, however—the question which was presumably responsible for Michael Lowenthal's continued presence on the maglev—was whether there was any kind of method within the seeming madness.

If so, she wondered, what kind of method could it possibly be? What could anyone possibly achieve, or even seek to achieve, by the murders of Gabriel King and Michi Urashima?

•   •   •

Charlotte rose somewhat earlier than was her habit—the couchette was not the kind of bed which encouraged one to lie in, no matter how little sleep one had had. She immediately patched through a link to Hal Watson in order to get an update on the state of his investigations, but he wasn't at his station yet.

She decanted all the messages that he had left in store for her, and took careful note of those which seemed most significant before walking to the dining car in order to obtain a couple of manna croissants and a cup of strong coffee. She did not doubt that Michael Lowenthal would do the same as soon as he awoke, if he had not done so already; she could only hope that her estimations of significance might prove better than his.

By the time Charlotte had finished her breakfast, the train was only three hours out of San Francisco. Oscar Wilde joined her while she was sipping coffee. He was looking very neat and trim save for the fact that the unrenewed green carnation in his buttonhole was now rather bedraggled. When he saw her looking at it, he assured her that he would be able to obtain a new one soon after arrival, because one of his very first commissions had been to plan the interior decor of the San Francisco Majestic.

"Such has been the mercy of our timetable," he observed, peering through the tinted window, "that we have slept through Missouri and Kansas."

She knew what he meant. Missouri and Kansas were distinctly lacking in interesting scenery since the restabilization of the climate had made their great plains prime sites for the establishment of vast tracts of artificial photosynthetics. Nowadays, the greater part of the Midwest looked rather like sections of an infinite undulating sheet of matte black, which could easily cause offense to eyes that had been trained to love color. The SAP fields of Kansas always gave Charlotte the impression of looking at a gigantic piece of frilly and filthy corrugated cardboard. Houses and factories alike had retreated beneath the Stygian canopy, and the parts of the landscape which extended toward the horizon were so blurred as to be almost featureless.

By now, though, the maglev passengers had the more elevating scenery of Colorado to look out upon. Most of the state had been carefully reforested; apart from the city of Denver—another of the Decivilizers' favorite targets, but one they had not yet claimed—its centers of population had taken advantage of the versatility of modern building techniques to blend in with their surroundings. Chlorophyll green was infinitely easier on the human eye than SAP black, presumably because millions of years of adaptive natural selection had ensured that it would be, and the Colorado landscape seemed extraordinarily soothing. Had the hard-core Green Zealots not been so fixated on the grandiose glories of rain forest, they might have nominated this as a corner of Green Heaven. Had it been authentic wilderness, of course, it would have been mostly desert, but no one in the USNA would go so far in the cause of authenticity as to insist upon land remaining desolate; the republics of Gobi and Kalahari had a monopoly on that kind of nostalgia.

While Oscar ordered eggs duchesse for breakfast, Charlotte activated the wallscreen beside their table and summoned up the latest news. The fact of Gabriel King's death was recorded, as was the fact of Michi Urashima's, but there was nothing about the exotic circumstances. She was momentarily puzzled by the fact that no one had yet connected the two murders or latched onto the possible biohazard, but she realized that the MegaMall's interest in the affair had advantages as well as disadvantages. The MegaMall owned the casters, and until the MegaMall decided that discretion was unnecessary, the casters would keep their hoverflies on a tight rein.

"Where's Lowenthal?" she asked. "Still sleeping the sleep of the just, I suppose." She wondered briefly whether she ought perhaps to wait for the man from the MegaMall before talking to Wilde about the investigation, but figured that it was up to her, as the early bird, to go after any available worms as quickly and as cleverly as she could. Unfortunately, she wasn't at all sure how to start.

"My dear Charlotte," said Oscar, while she dithered, "you have the unmistakable manner of one who woke up far too early after working far too hard the night before."

"I couldn't sleep," she told him. "I took a couple of boosters before breakfast—once the croissants get my digestive system in gear they'll clear my head."

Wilde shook his head. "I am not normally a supporter of nature," he said. "No one who looks twenty when he is really a hundred and thirty-three can possibly be less than worshipful of the wonders of medical science—but in my experience, maintaining one's sense of equilibrium with the aid of drugs is a false economy. We must have sleep in order to dream, and we must dream in order to discharge the chaos from our thoughts, so that we may reason effectively while we are awake. Your namesake, I know, was in the habit of taking cocaine, but I always thought it implausible of Conan Doyle to suggest that it enhanced his powers of ratiocination."

Charlotte had already taken note of Oscar Wilde's date of birth while researching his background, and the fact that he had mentioned his age offered her an opportunity to ask what seemed to be a natural—if not conspicuously relevant—question. "If you're only a hundred and thirty-three," she said, "what on earth possessed you to risk a third rejuvenation? Most people that age are still planning their second."

"The risks of core-tissue rejuvenation mostly derive from the so-called Miller effect," Wilde observed equably. "In that respect, the number of rejuvenations is less significant than the absolute age of the brain. Given the limitations of cosmetic enhancement, I felt that an increased risk of losing my mind was amply compensated by the certainty of replenishing my apparent youth. I shall certainly attempt a fourth rejuvenation before I turn one hundred and eighty, and if I live to be two hundred and ten I shall probably try for the record. I could not live like Gabriel King, so miserly in mind that I allowed my body to shrivel like the legendary Tithonus."

"He didn't look so bad, until the flowers got him," Charlotte observed.

"He looked *old*," Wilde insisted. "Worse than that, he looked *contentedly* old. He had ceased to fight against the ravages of fate. He had accepted the world as it is—perhaps even, if such a horror could be imagined, had actually become *grateful* for the condition of the world."

Charlotte remembered that Wilde had not yet arrived at the Trebizond Tower when Hal had forwarded King's last words, which had carried a different implication. She did not attempt to correct him; he had turned his attention to his eggs duchesse.

It was a pity, Charlotte thought as Colorado flew past, that there was no longer a quicker way to travel between New York and San Francisco. She had an uncomfortable feeling that she might end up chasing a daisy chain of murders all around the globe, always twenty-four hours behind the breaking news—but the maglev was the fastest form of transportation within the bounds of United America, and had been since the last supersonic jet had flown four centuries before. The energy crises of the twenty-first and twenty-second centuries were ancient history now, but the inland airways were so cluttered with private flitterbugs and helicopters, and the zealots of Decivilization so enthusiastic to crusade against large areas of concrete, that the scope of commercial aviation was now reduced to intercontinental flights. Even intercontinental travelers tended to prefer the plush comfort of airships to the hectic pace of supersonics; electronic communication had so completely taken over the lifestyles and folkways of modern society that almost all business was conducted via comcon.

When the silence proved too oppressive, Charlotte began to talk again, although Wilde was still engrossed in his breakfast. "The detail is still piling up by the bucketload," she said, "but we've had no major breakthrough. We still haven't pinned down the current name and location of the woman who visited the victims or the man who used to be Rappaccini, although Hal thinks that we're getting close on both counts. Most of the new information concerns the second murder, and possible links between Urashima and King. You knew Urashima at least as well as you knew King, I suppose?"

"We met on more than one occasion," Wilde admitted, laying down his fork for a moment or two, "but it was a long time ago. We were not close friends. He was an artist, and I had the greatest respect for his work. I would have been glad to count him as a friend, had that ridiculous business of house arrest not made it virtually impossible for him to sustain and develop his social relationships."

"He was released from the terms of his house arrest and communications supervision thirteen years ago," Charlotte observed, watching for any reaction, "but he seems to have been institutionalized by the experience. Although he began to receive visitors, he never went out, and he continued to use a sim to field all his calls. The general opinion was, I believe, that he was lucky to get away with house arrest. If he hadn't been so famous, he'd have been packed off to the freezer."

"If he hadn't deserved his fame," Wilde countered, "he wouldn't have been able to do the work he did. His imprisonment was an absurd sentence for a nonsensical crime. He and his co-workers placed no one in danger but themselves."

"He was playing about with brainfeed equipment," Charlotte observed patiently. "Not just memory boxes or neural stimulators—full-scale mental cyborgization. And he didn't just endanger himself and a few close friends—he was pooling information with other illegal experimenters. Some of their experimental results made the worst effects of a screwed-up rejuve look like a slight case of aphasia."

"Of course he was pooling information," Wilde said, pausing yet again between mouthfuls. "What on earth is the point of hazardous exploration unless one makes every effort to pass on the legacy of one's discoveries? He was trying to minimize the risks by ensuring that others had no need to repeat failures."

"Have *you* ever experimented with that kind of equipment, Dr. Wilde?" Charlotte asked. She had to be vague in asking the question because she wasn't entirely sure what multitude of sins the phrase "that kind of equipment" had to cover. Like everyone else, she bandied about phrases like "psychedelic synthesizer" and "memory box," but she had little or no idea of the supposed modes of functioning of such legendary devices. Ever since the first development of artificial synapses capable of linking up human nervous systems to silicon-based electronic systems, numerous schemes had been devised for hooking up the brain to computers or adding smart nanotech to its cytoarchitecture, but almost all the experiments had gone disastrously wrong. The brain was the most complex and sensitive of all organs, and serious disruption of brain function was the one kind of disorder that twenty-fifth-century medical science was impotent to correct. The UN, presumably with the backing of the MegaMall, had forced on its member states a worldwide ban on devices for connecting brains directly to electronic apparatuses, for whatever purpose—but the main effect of the ban had been to drive a good deal of ongoing research underground. Even an expert Webwalker like Hal Watson would not have found it easy to figure out what sort of work might still be in progress and who might be involved. In a way, Charlotte thought, Michi Urashima was a much more interesting—and perhaps much more likely—murder victim than Gabriel King.

"There is nothing I value more than my genius," Wilde replied, having finished the eggs duchesse and inserted the plate into the recycling slot, "and I would never knowingly risk my clarity and agility of mind. That doesn't mean, of course, that I disapprove of anything that Michi Urashima and his associates did. They were not infants, in need of protection from themselves. Michi could not rest content with his early fascination with the simulation of experience. For him, the building of better virtual environments was only a beginning; he wanted to bring about a *genuine* expansion of the human sensorium, and authentic augmentations of the human intellect and imagination. If we are ever to make a proper interface between natural and artificial intelligence, we will need the genius of men like Michi. I am sorry that he was forced to abandon his quest, and very sorry that he is dead—but that is not what concerns us now. The question is, who killed him—and why?" While completing this speech he refilled his coffee cup, then ordered two rounds of lightly buttered white wholemeal bread, slightly salted Danish butter, and coarse-cut English marmalade.

"So it is," said Charlotte. "Did you know that Michi Urashima was at university with Gabriel King—and, for that matter, with Walter Czastka?"

"Not until Michael communicated the fact to me," he replied calmly. "I had already suggested, if you recall, that the roots of this crime must be deeply buried in the fabric of history. I immediately asked him where this remarkable institution was, and whether Rappaccini was also at the same institution of learning. He told me that it was in Wollongong, Australia, and that there is no record of Jafri Biasiolo ever having been there. If it were Oxford, or the Sorbonne, even Sapporo, it would be far easier to believe that the alma mater might be the crucial connection, of course, but it is difficult to believe that anything of any real significance can ever have occurred in Wollongong. I could believe that Walter, who is an impressively dull man, learned everything he knew in such a place, but I would not have suspected it of Michi—or even of Gabriel King. Even so, it is a very interesting coincidence." He collected his toast and began to spread the butter, evening it out so carefully that the knife in his hand might have been a sculptor's.

"*When* did Lowenthal tell you about the Wollongong connection?" Charlotte asked, although the answer was obvious. She remembered belatedly that one thing she had forgotten to check up on was the contents of Wilde's earlier conversation with Lowenthal. Now, it seemed, she had missed a second and even more significant one.

"We exchanged a few notes last night, after you had retired," Wilde explained airily.

"You *exchanged a few notes,*" Charlotte echoed ominously. "It did occur to you, I suppose, that I'm the police officer in charge of this investigation, not Lowenthal."

"Yes, it did," he admitted, "but you seemed so very intent on following up your hypothesis that I am the man responsible for these murders. Because I know full well that I am not, I felt free to ignore your efforts in order to tease a little more information out of Michael. Unfortunately, he seems to have no interest at all in the most promising line of inquiry, which derives from the interesting coincidence that both King and Rappaccini had invested heavily in Michi's specialism. Indeed, he was so uninterested in it that I suspected him of deliberately trying to steer me away from it. I presume that one of the reasons the MegaMall decided to monitor this investigation is that they did not like the idea of Hal Watson digging too deeply into the murkier aspects of Gabriel King's past—which suggests to me that in putting money into brainfeed research Gabriel was a mere delivery boy. Alas, Michael seems intent on trying to build the Wollongong connection into grounds for establishing Walter Czastka as a key suspect. He will be of little help to the investigation, I fear—but I daresay that you will not be too disheartened to hear that."

Charlotte regarded her companion speculatively, wondering how carefully his flippancy was contrived. "What other little nuggets of information did he throw your way?" she asked, keeping her voice scrupulously level, as if in imitation of his own levity.

"He showed me a copy of the second scene-of-crime tape," Wilde admitted. He was as scrupulous in distributing his marmalade as he had been with the butter.

"We're still trying to figure out where the woman went after she left Urashima," Charlotte said, to demonstrate that she had not been idle in this particular matter. "Hal's set up silvers to monitor every security camera in San Francisco. If she's still there, we'll find her in a matter of hours. If she's already gone, we ought to be able to pick up her trail by noon. She's presumably altered her appearance again in order to confuse the standard picture-search programs, but we'll check every possible match, however tentative. If she moved on quickly enough, though, she might have had time to deliver more packages."

"We must assume that she did move on," Wilde said, licking a crumb from the corner of his mouth. "You noted, of course, that my name came up in the conversation, as her presentation of the bouquet of amaranths was doubtless intended to ensure. The poem inscribed on the condolence card caused it to be repeated. I do hope that you will not read too much into that."

Charlotte blushed slightly. If he had not caused the card to be placed at the scene of the crime, could he possibly have reacted so calmly? And if he *had* placed the card there, would he have dared to react so calmly?

Reflectively, Wilde quoted in a reverent but rather theatrical whisper:

> The vilest deeds like poison weeds,
> Bloom well in prison-air;
> It is only what is good in Man
> That wastes and withers there:
> Pale Anguish keeps the heavy gate,
> And the Warder is Despair.

"*The Ballad of Reading Gaol* was, of course, the only thing my poor namesake published after the humiliation of his trial and subsequent imprisonment—which was, of course, far harsher and even more unjust than the punishment visited on Michi Urashima. Perhaps that was why Rappaccini thought the poem particularly apposite."

"What did you make of the last words he spoke?" Charlotte

asked, not wishing to waste any more time in discussing the murderer's taste in poetry."

"Could you possibly jog my memory by displaying the tape on the wallscreen here?" Wilde countered.

Charlotte shrugged. She punched out a code number to connect the table's wallscreen to UN headquarters, and sorted through the material that Hal had left for her until she found the tape. Like the one she had displayed for Oscar outside Gabriel King's apartment, it had been carefully edited from the various spy eyes and bubble-bugs which had been witness to Michi Urashima's murder. She cut to the end.

"I am," said Urashima's voice, curiously resonant by virtue of the machine's enhancement. "I was not what I am, but was not an am, and am not an am even now. I was and am a man, unless I am a man unmanned, an it both done and undone by I-T."

"Alas," said Wilde, "I have no idea what it might mean. Could you wind the tape back so that I could take another look at the woman?"

Again, Charlotte obliged him, glad of the opportunity to take a more leisurely look herself.

The similarity between the two records was almost eerie. The woman's hair was silvery blond now, but still abundant. It was arranged in a precipitate cataract of curls. The eyes were the same electric blue, but the cast of the features had been altered subtly, making her face slightly thinner and more angular. The complexion was different too. The changes were sufficient to deceive a normal picture-search program but because Charlotte *knew* that it was the same woman she could *see* that it was the same woman. There was something in the way her eyes looked steadily forward, something in her calm poise that made her seem remote, not quite in contact with the world through which she moved.

"She carries herself like an angel," murmured Oscar Wilde,

finally pushing his breakfast plate aside, "or a sphinx—with or without a secret."

There was a studied close-up, taken by the door's eye while the woman was waiting to be admitted, then an abrupt cut to an interior anteroom, where the woman's entire body could be seen. She was not tall—perhaps a meter fifty-five—and she was very slim. She was wearing a dark blue suitskin now, whose decorative folds hung comfortably upon her seemingly fragile frame. It was the kind of outfit which would not attract much attention in the street.

Like Gabriel King, Michi Urashima was visible only from behind; there was no chance to read the expression on his face as he greeted her. As before, the woman said nothing, but moved naturally into a friendly kiss of greeting before preceding her victim into an inner room beyond the reach of conventional security cameras. There was a brief sight of her which must have been obtained by a bubblebug, but it cut out almost immediately; Urashima had screened the bug. Her departure was similarly recorded by the spy eye. She seemed perfectly composed and serene.

There were more pictures to follow, showing the state of Urashima's corpse as it had eventually been discovered, and the card bearing the words of the poem penned by the original Oscar Wilde. There were long, lingering close-ups of the fatal flowers. The camera's eye moved into a black corolla as if it were venturing into the interior of a great greedy mouth, hovering around the *crux ansata* tip of the bloodred style like a moth fascinated by a flame. There was, of course, a layer of monomol film covering the organism, but its presence merely served to give the black petals a weird sheen, adding to their near supernatural quality.

Charlotte let the tape run through without comment and left the link open when it had finished, after repeating the words they had already heard. "What do you see?" she asked.

"I'm not sure. I'd like to have a closer look at the flowers. It's difficult to be sure, but I think they were subtly different from the ones which ornamented poor Gabriel's corpse."

"They are. You'll get a gentemplate in due course, but Regina Chai's counterpart in San Francisco has already noted various phenotypical differences, mostly to do with the structure of the flower. It's another modified *Celosia,* of course."

"Of course," Wilde echoed.

"The woman traveled to San Francisco on a scheduled maglev," Charlotte told him. "The card she used to buy the ticket connects to a credit account held in the name of Jeanne Duval. It's a dummy account, of course, but Hal's tracking down all the transactions that have moved through it. She didn't use the Duval account to reach New York, and she'll presumably use another to leave San Francisco."

"It might be worth setting up a search for the names Daubrun and Sabatier," Wilde suggested. "It's probably too obvious, but Jeanne Duval was one of Baudelaire's mistresses, and it's just possible that she's got the others on her list of noms de guerre."

Charlotte transmitted this information to await Hal's return. The maglev was taking them down the western side of the Sierra Nevada now, and she had to swallow air to counteract the effects of the falling pressure on her eardrums. As she did so she saw Michael Lowenthal making his way through the car, looking wide awake and ready for action.

"By the time we get to San Francisco," she said to Oscar Wilde, although she was still looking at Lowenthal, "there probably won't be anything to do except to wait for the next phone call."

"Perhaps," said Wilde. "But even if she's long gone, we'll be in the right place to follow in her footsteps. Michael! It's good to see you. We've been catching up on the news—you've doubtless been doing the same."

"I think I might be a little ahead of you," Lowenthal said, in a casual manner that had to be fake. "My associates and I think that we might have identified a third victim."

Charlotte's first reaction to Lowenthal's dramatic statement was to reach out to the common beneath the screen, intending to put in an alarm call to Hal, but Lowenthal raised a hand in what was presumably intended as a forbidding gesture.

"There's no need," he said. "Your colleagues in New York have already been informed—they're checking it out. It's possible he's simply not responding. VE addicts are even worse in that respect than Creationists."

"*Who*'s not responding?" Charlotte wanted to know.

"Paul Kwiatek."

Charlotte had never heard of Paul Kwiatek. VE addicts didn't normally fall within her sphere of concern. She immediately looked at Oscar Wilde to see what his reaction to the name might be.

The geneticist was content to raise a quizzical eyebrow while meeting Lowenthal's eye. "I had no idea that he was still alive," he said—but then he turned to Charlotte and added: "I did not know him well, and I had no reason at all to wish him dead." Then he turned back to Lowenthal and said: "He was an associate of Michi's at one time, was he not? Is that why your employers think that his lack of response to their calls may be significant?"

"He was more than an associate," the Natural said as he lowered himself into the seat beside Charlotte's. "Paul Kwiatek and Michi Urashima were at university together, at Wollongong in Australia."

"Ah yes!" said Wilde blithely. "The Wollongong connection strikes again. Given that Gabriel and Michi were there at the dawn of modern time, it can't have been too onerous a task for you to obtain the names of everyone still living who was there at the same time. Have the MegaMall's assiduous market researchers tracked down every single one of them? Is Paul Kwiatek the only one who failed to reply?"

"No," Lowenthal replied, "but his name stood out, partly because of his one-time connections with Urashima and partly because we're certain that he's at home. He might, admittedly, be so deeply immersed in some exotic virtual environment that even the most urgent summons can't get through to him—but we'll know soon enough. There are a dozen other people we haven't been able to get a reply from as yet, but there seem to be perfectly good reasons for their being unavailable."

"Who is this Kwiatek?" Charlotte demanded. "Apart from being a VE addict, I mean."

"A software engineer," Lowenthal told her. "He worked in much the same areas as Michi Urashima for some years, while they were both involved in education and entertainment. They went their separate ways when their interests diverged, becoming more . . . esoteric."

"Illegal, you mean."

"Not necessarily. Not in Kwiatek's case, anyhow. Extreme, perhaps; uncommercial, certainly—but he was never charged with any actual offense."

"So the connection between them doesn't suggest any obvious motive?" Charlotte said.

"Not *that* connection, unless Kwiatek's recent work has implications of which we're unaware. What interests *me* is the fact that they and King were at Wollongong together. That's the one solid link between all three victims."

"When you say *together*," Wilde put in, "how close a tie do you mean. Did they room together? Did they all take the same courses? Did they even graduate at the same time?"

"Well, no," said Lowenthal. "None of those, so far as we can determine—but the data's old and very scrappy. The fact remains that they were all at Wollongong during the years 2321 and 2322. You see the significance of the timing, of course."

Charlotte didn't, but dearly wished that she had when Oscar Wilde said: "You mean that Jafri Biasiolo was born in 2323."

"Yes," said Lowenthal. Then, after a moment's pregnant pause, he said: "You're a much older and wiser man than I am, Dr. Wilde, and you obviously have all kinds of insights into this affair that I don't have. This is all new to me and I'm completely out of my depth, but I've formed a hypothesis and I'd like to put it to you, if

I may. It might be stupid, and I'd like your advice before I relay it to my employers. May I?"

Flattery, thought Charlotte, will get you almost anywhere. The cynical thought could not quell the rush of resentment she felt. She, after all, was the policeman. This was *her* investigation. What monstrous injustice had determined that she had to sit here listening to the self-congratulatory ramblings of two amateurs? Why was Michael Lowenthal, agent of the Secret Masters, sucking up to her chief suspect while ignoring her completely?

"Please do," said Oscar Wilde, as smug as a cat in sole possession of a veritable lake of cream.

"Whoever is responsible for this flamboyant display has taken great care to involve you in it," Michael Lowenthal said. "He or she has also gone to some trouble to place Rappaccini's name at the very center of the investigation. You have suggested—and I agree with you—that the roots of this affair must extend into the remote past, and that it may have been more than a century in the planning. When you made the suggestion, what you seemed to have in mind was a scenario in which Jafri Biasiolo, alias Rappaccini, had decided at some point in his career to construct an entirely new identity for himself, leaving behind an electronic phantom, and that he had done this in order to prepare the way for this theatrical series of murders.

"The problem with that scenario is that it gives us no clue as to how, why, or even when Biasiolo could have formed a grievance against the two people who are so far definitely numbered among the victims. If Paul Kwiatek is, in fact, the third, that puzzle becomes even more awkward. If Kwiatek *is* the third, I think we must consider a different scenario, whereby the motive for the crime originated in Wollongong in 2321 or 2322. If that is the case, then it is possible that *every* record of Jafri Biasiolo's existence and every aspect of his subsequent career as Rappaccini might have been a contrivance aimed toward the eventual execution of this plan. If so, we should not be asking our surfers to discover who Jafri Biasiolo *became* when he vanished into thin air in 2430 or thereabouts, but to discover who the person was who created him in the first place and used him as a secondary identity for the preceding hundred years. Do you see my point, Dr. Wilde?"

"I certainly do," Wilde replied with perfect equanimity. "I fear, dear boy, that I have also anticipated your punch line—but I would not dream of depriving you of the opportunity to declaim it. There is certainly considerable virtue in your powers of imagination, and not a little in your logic, but I fear that your conclusion will not seem so compelling. Do tell us—who *is* the person that you suspect of harboring this remarkable grudge against Gabriel and Michi for more than a hundred and seventy years?"

Charlotte could see that Wilde's teasing sarcasm had had a far more devastating effect on Lowenthal's confidence than any simple appropriation of the Natural's conclusion could have had. The young man had to swallow his apprehension before saying: "Walter Czastka."

Having already heard Wilde's response to the observation that Czastka had been at Wollongong at the same time as King and Urashima, Charlotte expected another dose of scathing sarcasm—but Wilde seemed to have repented of his cruelty in setting Lowenthal up to deliver a punch line that was bound to fall flat. He leaned back, giving the appearance of a man who was thinking a matter through, reappraising everything he had previously taken for granted.

"I can see the attractions of the hypothesis," Wilde admitted finally. "Walter can be cotemporally linked to both the murdered men, and to one who might have been murdered. As an expert in creative genetics, specializing in flowering plants, he might conceivably have had the expertise necessary to run two careers instead of one, diverting all his flair and eccentricity into the work allocated to the Rappaccini pseudonym while cunningly taking credit for a flood of vulgar commercial hackwork. You have observed that I have a very low opinion of Walter, and you presume that he must have an equally low opinion of me—thus providing a possible motive for the admittedly curious determination of the murderer to involve me in the investigation.

"It would certainly be ironic if I were to insist now that Walter could not possibly be the murderer because he is so utterly dull and unimaginative, if it were to turn out in the fullness of time that he *is* the murderer, and that I had spent the greater part of my life mistakenly despising him. The possibility is so awful that I am almost moved to caution. Nevertheless, I feel obliged to stand by my earlier judgment. Walter Czastka could not have invented Rappaccini because he does not have the necessary aesthetic resources. He is not the author of this bizarre psychodrama. If I am proved wrong, I shall unhesitatingly admit that he has outplayed me magnificently, but I cannot believe that I will be proved wrong."

"Do you have an alternative hypothesis to offer?" Lowenthal demanded, carefully suppressing his ire.

"Not yet," Wilde replied. "I am obliged to wait until I discover what awaits me in San Francisco."

Charlotte was just about to say that thanks to the presumably premature discovery of Michi Urashima's body they already knew what awaited them in San Francisco, when the buzzer on her beltphone sounded. She snatched up the handset, but that was unnecessary; the table's screen was still patched through to UN police headquarters, and it was there that Hal Watson's face appeared.

"One of Rappaccini's bank accounts just became active again," Hal informed them. "A debit was put through about ten minutes ago. The credit was drawn from another account, which had nothing on deposit but which had a guarantee arrangement with the Rappaccini account."

"Never mind the technical details," Charlotte said. "What did the credit buy? Have the police at the contact point managed to get hold of the user?"

"I'm afraid not," Watson told her. "The debit was put through by a courier service. They actually got the authorization yesterday, but it's part of the conditions of their service that they guarantee delivery within a certain time and don't collect until they've actually completed the commission. We've got a picture of the woman from their spy eye, looking exactly the same as she did when she went to Urashima's apartment, but it's almost three days old. It must have been taken before the murder, immediately after she arrived in San Francisco."

Charlotte groaned softly. "What did she send, and where did she send it to?" she said.

"It was a sealed package—a broad, shallow cylinder. It was addressed to Oscar Wilde, Green Carnation Suite, Majestic Hotel, San Francisco. It's there now, awaiting his arrival."

Even though Charlotte had not quite had time to get her foot into her mouth, she felt a sinking feeling in her stomach. She turned from the screen to stare at Oscar, who shrugged his shoulders insouciantly. "I always stay in my own personalized hotel suites," he said. "Rappaccini would know that."

"We don't have the authority to open that package without your permission," Hal put in. "I could get a warrant—but it would be simpler, with your permission, to send an order to the San Francisco police right now, instructing them to inspect it immediately."

"Certainly not," Wilde replied without a moment's hesitation. "It would spoil the surprise. We'll be there in less than an hour."

Charlotte frowned deeply. "You're inhibiting the investigation," she said. "I don't think you should do that, Dr. Wilde. We need to know what's in that package. It *could* be a packet of deadly seeds, fine-tuned to your DNA."

"I do hope not," said Wilde airily. "I can't believe that it is. If Rappaccini wished to murder me he surely wouldn't treat me less generously than his other victims. If they're entitled to a fatal kiss, it would be unjust as well as unaesthetic to send my *fleurs du mal* by mail."

"In that case," Charlotte said, "it's probably just another ticket.

If we open it now, we might be able to find out where the woman's next destination is in time to stop her making her delivery."

"I cannot believe it," said the insultingly beautiful man, in his most infuriating tone. "The delayed debit was almost certainly timed to show up *after* that event. The third victim—whoever it might have been—is probably already dead. Perhaps the fourth and fifth also. No, I must insist—the package is addressed to me and I shall open it. That is what Rappaccini intended, and I am certain that he has his reasons."

"Dr. Wilde," Charlotte said, in utter exasperation, "the reasons of a murderer—or a murderer's accessory—are hardly deserving of respect. You seem to be incapable of taking this matter seriously."

"On the contrary," Wilde replied with a sigh. "I believe that I am the only one who is taking it seriously *enough*. You, dear Charlotte, seem to be unable to look beyond the mere fact that people are being killed. At least Michael has imagination enough to see that if we are to understand this strange business, we must consider hypotheses which are extraordinarily elaborate and frankly bizarre. We must take *all* the features of this flamboyant display as seriously as they are intended to be taken: the kisses, the flowers, the cards . . . everything that is calculatedly strange and superfluous. They are, after all, the details that the newscasters will focus on as soon as Michael's careful employers decide to let them off the leash. Those details hold the key to the nature and purpose of the performance.

"At any rate, whatever message is in this mysterious packet is intended for me, and I intend to take receipt of it. We will not reach our next port of call any sooner by having it opened prematurely."

"I hope you're right," said Charlotte, grimly and insincerely. She was annoyed by her utter helplessness in the face of what now seemed certain to be a series of murders quite without parallel, in this or any other century—so annoyed, in fact, that she now did not know whether to hope that Oscar Wilde would turn out to be the murderer or Walter Czastka's dupe.

• • •

When the three travelers arrived at the Majestic they found, as promised, that the mysterious package had been set upon a polished table in the reception room of the Green Carnation Suite. It was, as Hal had told them, a broad and shallow cylinder, but it was somewhat larger than the vague description had led Charlotte to expect. It was about a hundred centimeters in diameter and twenty deep. The box itself was emerald green, but it was secured by a cross of black ribbon neatly knotted in a bow.

Charlotte went straight to the table, but Oscar Wilde paused in the doorway. Michael Lowenthal, bringing up the rear of the party, had no alternative but to pause with him.

"The walls are not blooming as they should," Wilde said in a vexed tone. "The buds are browning at the edges before they have even opened—there must be a fault in the circulatory system within the walls of the hotel. I've never really trusted the Majestic; its staff have no flair for aesthetic detail."

Charlotte stared at him, making every attempt to display her exasperation. Eventually, he condescended to join her.

Charlotte was taking no chances, in case the box *did* contain dangerously illegal products of macabre genetic engineering. The policeman stationed at the door of the apartment had passed her a spray gun loaded with a polymer which, on discharge, would form itself into a bimolecular membrane and cling to anything it touched. She also had a plastic bladder of solvent ready. Her hands were gloved.

Another officer had followed them in—a uniformed inspector named Reginald Quan, who had been assigned by the local force to the Urashima murder. "You'd better let me open that with a knife," he volunteered as soon as Oscar Wilde reached out to take hold of the knot in the black ribbon which secured the box.

"It is addressed," said Wilde with heavy dignity, "to *me*."

Charlotte met Quan's eye, raising her own eyebrows as if to say: "What can we do? Let him have his way." Although the local man outranked Charlotte, she was operating under the technical authority of Hal Watson, and Quan had to defer to her. The inspector shrugged his shoulders and took a step back. Michael Lowenthal immediately moved into the gap, craning his neck to get a better view. Charlotte held the spray gun ready, her finger on the trigger.

The ribbon yielded easily to Wilde's quick fingers, and he drew it away. The lid lifted quite easily, and Wilde laid it to one side while he, Lowenthal, and Charlotte looked down at what was in the box.

It was, as Charlotte had half expected since she had first seen the shape and size of the container, a Rappaccini wreath. Its base was a very intricate tangle of dark green stalks and leaves. The stalks were thorny, the leaves slender and curly. There was an envelope in the middle of the display, and around the perimeter were thirteen black flowers like none she had ever seen before. They looked rather like black daisies—but there was something about them that struck Charlotte as being *not quite right*.

Oscar Wilde extended an inquisitive forefinger and was just about to touch one of the flowers when it moved.

"Look out!" said Michael Lowenthal and Reginald Quan, in unison.

As if the first movement had been a kind of signal, *all* the "flowers" began to move. It was a most alarming effect, and Wilde reflexively snatched back his hand as Charlotte pressed the trigger of the spray gun and let fly.

When the polymer hit them, the creatures' movements became suddenly jerky. They had been moving fairly slowly, in random directions, but now they thrashed and squirmed in obvious distress. The limbs which had mimicked sepals struggled vainly for purchase upon the thorny green rings on which they had been mounted. Now that Charlotte could count them she was able to see that each of the creatures had eight excessively hairy legs. What had seemed to be a cluster of florets was a much embellished thorax.

They were not perfectly camouflaged; it was simply that she had been expecting to see flowers, not spiders, and Charlotte's expectation had enabled them to get away with their masquerade for a few seconds. She was perversely gratified to notice that Michael Lowenthal's eagerness to get in on the act had evaporated; he had taken a big stride backward and now appeared to be awkwardly caught between conflicting desires. Now that the man from the MegaMall had a hypothesis at stake, he was desperately anxious to keep up with the data flow, but he was clearly arachnophobic. Either he had undergone some unfortunate formative experience while in the care of his foster parents or the Zaman transformation had not tidied every last vestige of deficiency from the human genome.

"Poor things," said Oscar Wilde as he watched the spiders writhe in desperate distress. "They'll asphyxiate, you know, with that awful stuff all over them."

"I may have just saved your life," observed Charlotte dryly. "Those things are probably poisonous."

"My dear Charlotte," said the geneticist tiredly, "the last human being to die of a spider bite did so more than five hundred years ago—and that was the result of a totally unexpected allergic reaction."

"It was a perfectly ordinary spider too," Charlotte retorted. "Those aren't. If this murderer can make man-eating plants, he can make deadly spiders."

"Perhaps," Wilde conceded. "But this little performance was no attempted murder. It's a work of art—presumably an exercise in symbolism."

"According to you," she said, "the two are not incompatible."

"Not even the most reckless of dramatists," said Wilde, affecting a terrible weariness, "would destroy his audience at the end of act two of a play that is clearly intended to extend over twice or three times that number. I am quite certain that I am safe from any direct threat to my well-being, at least until the final curtain falls.

I am almost certain that the same immunity will extend to anyone accompanying me on my journey of discovery. Even when the final act is done, I assume that Rappaccini will want us alive and well. He surely would not take the risk of interrupting a standing ovation and cutting short the cries of Encore!—and he surely will not want my obituary to appear before my review of his work."

While the man Gabriel King had described as a "posturing ape" was making this speech, and because he showed no inclination to do so himself, Charlotte reached out a gloved hand to pick up the sticky envelope which still sat on its dark green bed at the center of the ruined display.

The envelope had been splashed by the polymer, but it was not sealed. Although the gloves made her clumsy, Charlotte contrived to open it and to take out the piece of paper which it contained. She took what precautions she could to screen its contents from the inquisitive eyes of Lowenthal and Quan. For once, she wanted to have the advantage, if only for half a minute

It was a car-hire receipt. The invoice stated that the car in question was ready and waiting in a bay beneath the hotel, and was stamped with a warning note in garish red ink: ANY ATTEMPT TO INTERROGATE THE PROGRAMMING OF THIS VEHICLE WILL ACTIVATE A VIRUS THAT WILL DESTROY ALL THE DATA IN ITS MEMORY.

It was probably a bluff, but Charlotte had a strong suspicion that Oscar Wilde wasn't about to let her call it—and Hal still didn't have any legal authority to take over the trail of clues. He couldn't commandeer the car unless and until he could get a warrant. By that time, Charlotte suspected, the car would be en route, with Oscar Wilde in it. She had every intention of being in it with him. While there was a trail to follow, she might as well be on it—and if it transpired that Oscar Wilde was the layer of the trail as well as its follower, she wanted to be the one to arrest him.

Charlotte turned to Reginald Quan, trying hard to give the impression that everything was comfortably under control. The image of the UN police had to be preserved at all costs. "Our forensic team will have to examine these things," she said. "The biotechnics are almost certainly illicit, perhaps dangerous. Hal Watson will sort out the details."

Quan shrugged. "Going somewhere?" he inquired innocently, with a nod toward the receipt. Her attempts to screen it from his view had obviously not been entirely successful.

"Yes, we are," she said, pausing only to pass the relevant details to Hal before handing the document to its rightful owner, "and there's no time to lose."

While they took the elevator down to the car park, Hal gave Charlotte a rapid update on his most recent findings. The car-hire company had reported that they had delivered the vehicle three days earlier, and that they had no knowledge of any route or destination which might have been programmed into its systems after dispatch.

"It looks as if we're going on a mystery tour," she said to Oscar Wilde dourly.

"We've been on a mystery tour since yesterday afternoon," he pointed out. "I do hope that our next destination will be a little more interesting than the places we have so far visited."

Hal also reported that he'd launched an investigation of the account used to pay for the hire car, although it appeared that it had been set up entirely for that purpose. The initial deposit had been adequate to cover the car's expenses for three days' storage and a journey of two thousand kilometers.

"That could take you as far north as Anchorage or as far south as Guatemala," Hal pointed out unhelpfully. "I can't tell for sure how many more accounts there might be on which Rappaccini and the woman might draw, but the transfers made so far have allowed me to trace several that are held under other names; it's possible that one of them is his current name."

"What are they?" Oscar Wilde inquired.

"Samuel Cramer, Gustave Moreau, Thomas Griffiths Wainewright, and Thomas De Quincey."

Wilde sighed. "Samuel Cramer is the hero of a novella by Baudelaire," he said. "Gustave Moreau was a French painter associated with the French decadent movement. Thomas Griffiths Wainewright was a critic and murderer who was the subject of an essay by my namesake called 'Pen, Pencil and Poison'—an exercise partly inspired by Thomas De Quincey's more celebrated essay 'Murder Considered as One of the Fine Arts.' I fear that these aliases are little more than a series of jokes—decorative embellishments of the unfolding plot."

"The names don't matter," said Hal. "What matters is where the money that fed the accounts originated, and where it goes when it makes its exits. I already have surfers going through the books of Rappaccini Inc. with a fine-toothed comb. At present, the money trail seems more likely to deliver the goods than the picture searches. With luck, I'll eventually be able to find out where the man who used to use the Rappaccini name and our mysterious nonexistent woman have their basic supplies delivered—food, equipment, and so on—and when I know that, I'll know where *they* are, and what names they use when they're not using silly pseudonyms. Then we can pick them both up and charge them."

"What about this brainwave of Lowenthal's?" Charlotte asked—having reported the conjecture while the maglev was pulling into the San Francisco station. "Have you found any evidence to suggest that Czastka might have set up the Biasiolo identity?"

"Not yet," said Hal noncommittally. Charlotte guessed that Hal wasn't taking Lowenthal's hypothesis any more seriously than Wilde was. Although he was reluctant to say so, Hal was presumably still beavering away at the brainfeed link—which could easily extend from King, Urashima, and Rappaccini to Kwiatek, but not to Czastka. Or to Wilde, for that matter, Charlotte admitted to herself. Despite her aggressive question about whether he had ever used brainfeed equipment, she had found not the slightest shred of evidence that he had ever had a substantial financial or practical interest in the field.

The car which awaited them in the underground garage was roomy and powerful. Once it was free of the city's traffic-control computers it would be able to zip along the transcontinental at two hundred kilometers per hour. If they *were* headed for Alaska, Charlotte thought, they'd be there sometime around midnight. They'd need a couple of thermal suits.

Michael Lowenthal opened the door to the seat which faced the driver's control panel and politely stood aside, offering it to her—but she remembered their journey across Manhattan only too well. She shook her head, leaving him no alternative but to take the front himself while Charlotte got into the rear with Oscar Wilde.

As soon as they were all settled, Wilde activated the car's program. The car slid smoothly up the ramp and into the street.

Michael Lowenthal, who had skipped breakfast on the maglev in order to lay his beautiful hypothesis before the stern gaze of Oscar Wilde, called up a menu from the car's synthesizer and looked it over unappreciatively.

"I fear," said Wilde as he scanned the duplicate which had appeared in the panel on the back of the seat in front of him, "that we are in for a rather Spartan trip." Most hire cars only stocked manna with a choice of artificial flavorings; this one was a deluxe model, but it didn't have anything else to offer.

"The time to worry about *that*," Charlotte said tersely, "is when we reach Guadalajara." She had taken note of the fact that the car had turned southeast, heading for intersection nine of the transcontinental instead of eight. Wherever they were headed, it was not Alaska.

Lowenthal was obviously used to better fare than the car had to offer; he decided not to bother with breakfast after all.

Charlotte plugged her beltphone into the screen mounted in the back of the drive compartment and began scrolling through more data that Hal's silvers had collated while she had been otherwise occupied. The artificial geniuses had found a great many links between Gabriel King and Michi Urashima to add to the coincidence of their possible attendance at the same university—more links, in fact, than anyone could reasonably have expected, even allowing for the fact that they had been acquainted for more than a hundred and seventy years. There was, however, no clear evidence as yet that King's funding of Urashima's various exploits had been compensated by slightly larger sums paid to him by third parties who did not wish to be seen funding brainfeed research themselves.

Charlotte could see that the AI searches had only just begun to get down to the real dirt. No one whose career was as long as King's was likely to be completely clean, especially if he'd been in business, but a man in his position could keep secrets even in today's world, just as long as no one with state-of-the-art equipment actually had a reason to probe. It was only to be expected that his murder would expose a certain amount of dirty linen, but to Charlotte's admittedly naive eyes King's laundry basket seemed fuller than anyone could have expected. She began to wonder whether Lowenthal had made a mistake in starting at the beginning of the King/Urashima relationship rather than the end. Even when Michi Urashima had landed in deep trouble, it seemed, his connections with King had remained intact, but they had been hidden. King had not only funded Urashima but had helped to establish all kinds of shields to hide his work and its spin-off. Hal's silvers had only just begun to build Paul Kwiatek into the picture, but they had already uncovered some commercial links between King and Kwiatek that were as surprising in their way as the links between King and Urashima. Rappaccini's involvement with Urashima was, by contrast, beginning to seem perfectly straightforward.

Maybe all this flimflam with Wilde, Czastka, and Rappaccini is just a smoke screen, Charlotte thought. Maybe its sole purpose is to blind the silvers with superfluity, to distract us from the real pattern. But what could that pattern possibly be?

As the data tying Gabriel King to Paul Kwiatek's allegedly esoteric and uncommercial research continued to accumulate, Charlotte saw that Gabriel King had not been quite as colorless a character as Oscar Wilde had implied. Perhaps no one was who had lived a hundred and ninety-four years and had learned along the way to despise the affectations and showmanship of men like Wilde. But if King, Urashima, *and* Kwiatek had been murdered for business reasons, what could those reasons be? And who was the mysterious female assassin?

Charlotte broke in on the data stream and said: "Hal—is there any news of Kwiatek yet?"

"Any time now," he said. "They're executing the entry warrant as we speak, although the building supervisor's doing his level best to obstruct them. Protecting the privacy of his tenants, he says. What he's paid for. Any idea where you're headed yet?"

Charlotte glanced out of the window, but there was nothing to be seen now except the eight lanes of the superhighway. "Mexico City, for now," she said. "Exactly how far toward it we'll go—or how much further beyond it—is anyone's guess. Is there any sign of the woman traveling south out of San Francisco?"

"No match yet," Hal admitted. "As I said, the money trail's looking better than the picture trail, for the moment. Hold on . . . they're in Kwiatek's apartment now. No sign of him, unless he's in the cradle. . . ."

Charlotte looked up. Michael Lowenthal was peering through the gap between the headrest of his seat and the drive compartment. Oscar Wilde seemed equally rapt, although his posture was as languid as ever.

"Yes," said Hal, evidently dividing himself between two conversations. "In the cradle. That's confirmed. Kwiatek's dead—same method. We already have a fourth name that may have to be added to the list, but it's going to take time to get investigators out to the place where he's supposed to be. Same pattern—no response even to top-priority calls."

"Who?" said Lowenthal.

"Magnus Teidemann—the ecologist. Graduated from the University of Wollongong in 2322, with Czastka—a year ahead of King, Urashima, and Kwiatek. He's in the field, working on some kind of biodiversity project; he hasn't checked in with his base for a week. Not particularly unusual, they say, but. . . ."

"If he's dead too," Lowenthal opined, "Wollongong has *got* to be the crucial link."

"*If* he's dead," Charlotte echoed. "There are other links binding King to Urashima and to Kwiatek. If it's just the three of them, the motive might have arisen a lot later than 2322. Let's face it, no one but a madman would formulate a murder plan that would take so long to come to fruition. If you have a powerful desire to kill someone, you don't wait a hundred and seventy years, until they're practically at death's door, before you implement it."

"Czastka called in his report on the first murder weapon," Hal put in. "It confirms Wilde's in every respect but one."

"Which one?" Charlotte wanted to know.

"He can't see any evidence of a link to Rappaccini."

"That fault is in Walter's sight, not in the evidence," Wilde was quick to say.

"Even so," said Hal, "the only name mentioned in Czastka's report is Wilde's—because he's the only one known to have worked with the basic *Celosia* gentemplate. Czastka's still on standby. I'll send him the data on Urashima's killer—and Kwiatek's when we have it."

"Did you ask him about being at Wollongong with King and Urashima?" Charlotte wanted to know.

"Of course I did. He says that he doesn't remember anything about events that long ago. He supposes that he must have known King, given that some of their courses overlapped, but he has no memory of ever having met Michi Urashima."

"He would say that, wouldn't he?" murmured Michael Lowenthal.

"Got to go," said Hal, breaking the connection.

Oscar Wilde immediately began tapping out a phone number

on the comcon set in the back of Lowenthal's seat.

"Who are you calling?" Charlotte demanded.

"Walter Czastka, of course," Oscar replied with his customary equanimity.

"You can't do that!" Lowenthal exclaimed. Charlotte was glad that he'd beaten her to it, because she knew exactly what Wilde's reply would be.

"Of course I can," said Wilde. "We're old acquaintances, after all. If he's involved with this business, I'm the best person to find out how and why—I know his little ways." By the time he had finished speaking, it was a dead issue. The call had gone through and had been answered.

Charlotte could see the image on Wilde's screen even though she was invisible to the camera that was relaying Wilde's image to Czastka. She knew immediately that the face must be that of the flesh-and-blood Czastka, not his dutiful sloth. No one would ever have programmed so much wizened world-weariness into a simulacrum.

"Hello, Walter," said Wilde.

Czastka peered at the caller without the least flicker of recognition. He looked very old—far older than King or Urashima—and distinctly unwell. His skin was discolored and taut about the facial muscles. Charlotte could not imagine that he had ever been a handsome man, and he had obviously decided that it was unnecessary to compromise with the expectations of others by having his face touched up by cosmetic engineers. In a world where almost everyone was good-looking, unmarked by the worst ravages of time and circumstance, Walter Czastka was an obvious anomaly. There was nothing actually ugly or monstrous about him, however. To Charlotte, he simply seemed ancient and depressed. His eyes were a curious faded yellow color, and his stare had a rather disconcerting quality.

"Yes?" he said.

"Don't you know me, Walter?" asked Wilde, in genuine surprise.

For a moment, Czastka simply looked exasperated, but then his stare changed as enlightenment dawned.

"Oscar Wilde!" he said, his tone redolent with awe. "My God, you look well. I didn't look like that after *my* second rejuvenation . . . but you already had . . . how could you need a third so soon?"

Oddly enough, Oscar Wilde did not swell with pride in reaction to this display of naked envy. It seemed to Charlotte that Wilde's anxiety about Czastka's condition outweighed his pride in his own. This surprised her a little, and she wondered what motives Wilde might have for feigning such a response.

"Need," Wilde murmured, "is a relative thing. I'm sorry, Walter—I didn't mean to startle you. In my mind's eye, you see, I *always* look like this."

"You'll have to be brief, Oscar," said Czastka curtly. "I'm expecting the UN police to call back—ever since they got past my AI defenses they've been relentless. Someone's using flowers to murder people. I've given them one report, but they want more. People like that *always* want more. I should have known better than to respond to the first call, I suppose. Terrible nuisance."

Charlotte noticed that Czastka had dutifully avoided mentioning to Oscar Wilde the fact that he'd been obliged to mention Wilde's name in his report on the lethal flowers. Czastka did not seem to relish the idea of a long conversation with his old acquaintance.

"The police can break in on us if they want to, Walter," said Oscar gently. "They showed the *Celosia* gentemplate to me too. I came to one conclusion that you apparently failed to reach."

"And what was that?" Czastka asked sharply. Charlotte knew that Hal Watson wouldn't want Wilde putting ideas into Czastka's head, but she was powerless to prevent it.

"It seemed obvious to me that Rappaccini had designed them," said Oscar. "Do you remember Rappaccini?"

"Of course I remember him," snapped Czastka. "I'm not senile, you know. Specialized in funeral wreaths—a silly affectation, I always thought. Haven't heard of him in years, though—I thought he'd retired on the proceeds. I daresay you know him much better than I do. You were birds of a feather, I always thought. It was your *Celosia,* wasn't it? What makes you think that Rappaccini had anything to do with it?"

Charlotte didn't need to make a mental note of the fact that Czastka considered Wilde and Rappaccini to be *birds of a feather*.

"How's your ecosphere coming along, Walter?" asked Oscar softly. Charlotte frowned at the change of subject.

Czastka didn't answer the question. "What do you *want,* Oscar?" he asked rudely. "I'm busy. If you want to slander Rappaccini to the UN police, go ahead, but don't involve me. I told them all I know—about the plant, about everything. I just want to be left alone. If this is going to carry on, I'm going to disconnect permanently. If anyone wants to talk to me, they can get the boat from Kauai."

Charlotte wondered when Czastka had last been rejuvenated. He looked as if his second rejuvenation had somehow failed to take—as if he were degenerating rapidly. He looked as if he couldn't possibly have long to live, and he looked as if he knew it.

"I'm sorry, Walter," said Oscar soothingly, "but I do need to talk to you. We have a problem here, and it affects us both. It affects us generally, and specifically. Genetic art may have come a long way since the protests at the Great Exhibition, but there's still a lot of latent animosity to the kind of work we do, and the Green Zealots won't need much encouragement to put us back on their hate list. Neither of us wants to go back to the days when we had to argue about our licenses, and had petty officials demanding to look over our shoulders while we worked. When the police release the full details of this case there's going to be a lot of adverse publicity, and it's going to hurt us. That's the general issue. More specifically, there's a great deal of confusion about who planned these murders and why. I'm in a car with Sergeant Charlotte Holmes of the UN police and a man named Michael Lowenthal, who represents certain commercial interests. We all have our various theories about the affair, and I think you're entitled to be copied in on them. To be brutally frank, I think Rappaccini is behind the murders, Charlotte thinks I'm behind them, and Michael thinks *you're* the guilty party—so it really is in your interest to help us sort things out."

"Me!" said Czastka. If his outrage wasn't genuine, it was the best imitation Charlotte had ever seen. She only wished that Michael Lowenthal could see it. "Why on earth would I want to kill Gabriel King or Michi Urashima?"

"And Paul Kwiatek," Wilde added. "Maybe Magnus Teidemann too. Nobody knows, Walter—but if this goes on, you might soon be the only survivor of that select band of famous men who graduated from Wollongong University in the early 2320s."

Czastka's face had a curious ocherous pallor as he stared at his interlocutor. Charlotte noted that Czastka's eyes had narrowed, but she couldn't tell whether he was alarmed, suspicious, or merely impatient.

"I don't remember *anything* about those days," Czastka said stubbornly. "Nobody does. It was too long ago. I hardly knew Kwiatek. I never knew any of them, really—not even King. I've had some dealings with his companies, just as I've had some dealings with Rappaccini Inc., but I haven't set eyes on King for fifty years, and I haven't seen Rappaccini since the Great Exhibition. I've seen Urashima's work and I heard about the wireheading scandals, but that's *all*. Leave me alone, Oscar, and tell the police to leave me alone too. You know perfectly well that I couldn't kill anyone— and I don't know anything about Rappaccini that you don't already know."

"What about his daughter?" said Wilde quickly.

If he intended to catch the other man by surprise it didn't work. Czastka's stare was stony and speculative, with more than a hint of melancholy. "What daughter?" he said. "I never met a daughter.

Not that I remember. It was all a long time ago. I can't remember anything at all. Leave me alone, Oscar, please."

So saying, the old man cut the connection.

Charlotte could see that Oscar Wilde was both puzzled and disappointed by the other man's reaction.

"That was a mistake, wasn't it?" she said, unable to resist the temptation to take him down a peg. "Did you really think he'd rather talk to you than to us? He doesn't even *like* you. You should have left him to Hal—you've upset him now, maybe so badly that he won't even take Hal's calls, and you didn't learn anything at all."

"Perhaps not," Oscar agreed. "I certainly didn't expect him to freeze up like that. On the other hand. . . ." He trailed off, evidently uncertain as to what kind of balancing factor he ought to add.

"Have you changed your mind about the possibility of Czastka having set up the Biasiolo/Rappaccini identity?" Charlotte asked Michael Lowenthal.

"I don't know," said Lowenthal guardedly. "But I do wish you hadn't told him about my suspicions, Dr. Wilde, however absurd you may think them."

"I'm sorry," Wilde said, still taken aback by the nature of Czastka's response to his call. "But if he *were* our stylish murderer, why would he react so churlishly to my inquiries? Surely he'd have made better preparation than *that*."

"Would he?" Lowenthal parried.

Hal's face reappeared on Charlotte's screen. "I just got notification of your little conversation, Dr. Wilde," he said. "What on earth do you think you're playing at? I tried to ring Czastka, and I got that bloody sloth again, telling me that he's unavailable, even though I know he's sitting right there at his antique desk!"

"I couldn't stop him!" Charlotte complained.

"It wasn't Charlotte's fault," Wilde obligingly added—although she could see that the intervention didn't improve Hal's mood at all.

"Well," Hal said, "you'd better pray that this won't cost us time and effort. You might care to know that the money trail is getting clearer by the minute. Some of Rappaccini's pseudonymous bank accounts have been used over the years to purchase massive quantities of materials that were delivered for collection to the island of Kauai—that's in Hawaii."

"So the man behind Rappaccini must live on Kauai," Charlotte deduced, trying to remember the context in which she had heard the place name mentioned not ten minutes before. She could tell from the way that Michael Lowenthal had reacted to the name that *he* remembered—and as soon as she had mentally reviewed that observation, she remembered too. It was too late to say anything; Hal was already speaking again.

"Not necessarily," he was saying. "The supplies were collected by boat. There are fifty or sixty islets west and south of Kauai, some natural but most artificial. Over half of them are leased to Creationists for experiments in the construction of artificial ecosystems. Oscar Wilde's private island is half an ocean away in Micronesia."

"But Walter Czastka's isn't," said Michael Lowenthal with evident satisfaction.

"That's right," said Hal. "All the supplies that Czastka purchases in his own name are forwarded from Kauai, by the same boat that forwarded the equipment purchased by the pseudonymous accounts we've just connected to Rappaccini Inc. Perhaps, Mr. Lowenthal, your wild hypothesis isn't as wild as it first seemed."

A Mind at the End of Its Tether

ichi Urashima was having trouble with time again. He had lost all sense of it and couldn't remember what day it was, or what year, or how many times he had grown young and then old again. None of that would have been of much significance had he not had the vague impression that there was something he ought to be doing, some important project that needed attention. He could not remember whether or not he was still forbidden to leave his house, or whether or not there was anywhere else he might want to be.

When he asked what year it was, the silken voice of his household sloth dutifully informed him that it was 2495, but Michi could not remember whether 2495 was the present or the past, so he could not tell whether or not he had suffered an existential slippage. There was no point in asking the sloth whether or not he had lost his mind, because the sloth was too stupid to know.

Although he had lost touch with himself, Michi still had command of vast treasures of factual information. He knew, for instance, that sloths were called sloths because the Tupi word for the three-toed sloth was AI, and AI had stood for artificial idiot or artificial imbecile ever since the concept of artificial intelligence had been subdivided. A sloth could not possibly judge whether or not he had lost his mind; for that he would have needed a silver. Silvers were called silver because the chemical symbol for silver was Ag, which stood for artificial genius. There was no popular shorthand for "artificial individual of average intelligence" because the obvious acronym sounded like a strangled scream. Because AP had been claimed by artificial photosynthesis—LAP for liquid, SAP for solid—there was no such thing as a mere artificial person, and an

acronymic rendering of artificial mind would have been too con-
fusing by half.

Actually, Michi thought, the attempt to possess an artificial
mind of his very own had indeed led him into dire confusion.

"I am," he said, and giggled. "I am an AM, or am not an AM,
or am caught like a half-living cat between the two. Perhaps I was
an AM, and am no longer, or was not but now am, or would be if
only I could think straight, like an AM. Perhaps, on the other hand,
I am no longer an AM, and am no longer, but am merely an it, held
together by IT."

He sat in his armchair and breathed deeply: in, out; in, out; in,
out. Slowly but surely, his sense of self came together again, and
his sense of temporal location returned. His IT was probably
stretched to the limit, but he was not yet an it. Precarious though
his grip on reality was, the Miller effect still had not obliterated him
from the community of human minds.

Morgan Miller must have been a kindred spirit, he thought. The
first man ever to beat the Hayflick limit and discover a viable technology of longevity, and his reward for taking such infinite pains
over the project had been two bullets in the back. Unfortunately—
as Miller had understood, although his assassins had not—the
method had worked far too well. It was so utterly irresistible in
renewing the body that it wiped out the mind. Even internal nanotech did that eventually, but at least it gave a man time to breathe,
time to play, time to work, time to be . . . and time, in the end, to
lose himself.

"I am," he said again. "I am Michi still, at least for a little while.
Do I have any appointments today?"

"Yes," said the sloth. Before Michi could rephrase the question,
he remembered. Yes, indeed—today, he had an appointment.

"Oh yes," he said aloud. "I am, I am, I definitely am."

He reached up his hand to caress his skull, running his fingertips over the numerous sockets which sat above the main sites of
his implanted electrodes. He wondered whether he ought to put on

a wig, or a hooded suitskin. Did *she* wear a wig, or a hooded suit-skin? Could that luscious hair really be rooted in her skull? Maybe, maybe not. He would find out. But in the meantime—to obscure or not to obscure?

He decided not. She was fascinated by what he was, what he had been; why try to hide it? A martyr should wear his stigmata proudly, unafraid to display them. They were, alas, mere relics of the past, but they were the remnants of a glorious endeavor.

Michi still wondered, sometimes, whether he ought to make one more attempt to break through to the unknown. If he were to flush out all his IT and douse the sockets so as to flood the under-lying electrodes with neurostimulators, the neurons further beneath would resume the business of forging new connections, further extending the synaptic tangles which already bound the contacts to every part of his brain. The removal of his IT would condemn him to death, of course, but he was dying anyway. Suppose he could trade a few months of not knowing what day it was for just *one moment* of enlightenment, one flash of inspiration, one revelatory proof that everything he had tried to achieve *was* possible, *was* within the grasp of contemporary humankind, if only people were willing to try, to take the risk.

Just *suppose* . . .

It would be his triumph, and his alone. Official sources of finance had bailed out on him a hundred years ago, and he had been forbidden to call for further volunteers. The funds channeled from the Pharaohs of Capitalism by way of Gabriel King and his fellow buccaneers had dried up fifty years ago. The private backers had held out a little longer, but the law had built walls around him to keep their funds out. Like Kwiatek, he had been left high and dry—but Kwiatek had at least avoided the indignity of a show trial and subsequent house arrest. If Kwiatek eventually ended up in susan, it wouldn't be the law that had put him there; he would go of his own accord, unbranded and uncondemned.

"I was the only one prepared to go *all the way*," Michi said aloud. "If they hadn't abandoned me, I might even have got to where I wanted to be. Do you hear me?"

"Yes," said the sloth, as pedantically terse as ever.

"How long is it before my visitor's due?" Michi demanded, determined to make the stupid machine do a little work to justify its keep.

"Thirty seconds," replied the conscientious machine. Doubtless, in some abstract and ideal sense, it was absolutely right—but even as it spoke, the door chime sounded.

The woman was early.

"Let her in," said Michi, levering himself up from his armchair, hoping as he did so that he would not lose himself again before she left.

"I'm sorry," Michi said to the young woman as they lay in bed together. "I've grown unused to visitors of any kind, let alone lovers. All the old skills. . . ."

"I understand," the woman said very gently. "Fifty years of solitary confinement is a very harsh penalty to pay for trying to push back the frontiers of human understanding."

"Most people thought of it as getting off lightly," Michi said morosely. "They don't realize. There are millions of people in the world who spend days on end—weeks on end if they're VE addicts—cocooned in their apartments, and there are millions who routinely protect their privacy by filtering all their electronic communications through clever sims. They don't know the true value of the power of choice, which allows them to break the pattern anytime they wish. They don't understand how demeaning it is to be forbidden the use of credit, of the most elementary privacy screening. Everybody nowadays thinks that they're under observation, but they don't really know what it means to have ever attentive eyes trained so intensively on the minutiae of one's everyday life."

"I can't pretend to know how it feels to be withdrawn from

human society for fifty years, after having lived in it for over a hundred," the young woman told him as she eased herself from his embrace and reached for her suitskin, "but I *have* spent a good deal of my own brief life in enforced solitude. I've learned very quickly to appreciate the worth of being in the world."

"Part of the problem," Michi observed, grateful for the opportunity to mumble on, hoping thereby to cover his embarrassment, "is the ongoing debate about the susan long-termers. They're the ones whose punishments attract all the public attention. Everybody carps about the unreasonableness of the jurists of the past, who just wanted to get supposedly dangerous individuals off the streets during their own lifetimes and didn't care about the ethical problems they were handing down to their descendants. House arrest is seen as a more reasonable alternative—but communication control ensures that the victims don't have a voice. When the sentence ended . . . I was a hundred and eighty-three years old, and I hadn't talked face-to-face with anyone for fifty years. Most of my former acquaintances were dead, and most of the rest had forgotten me. Even the ones who had stood by me and helped me as best they could, had to impersonalize the communication process. The ones who wanted to carry forward my work—the ones who *did* carry it forward, insofar as the law allowed them to, had to do so without any input from me—I wasn't even allowed to *help*. By the time it ended, it was impossible to pick up the fifty-year-old threads, and there was no hope of changing everything back again. The only *real* relationships I've been able to form in the last thirteen years have been new ones, but so many of the authentically young seem to think of me as some kind of monster or demon . . . sometimes I feel like the Minotaur made by Daedalus, lost in the labyrinth of Minos."

Michi knew that he should not be running on and on in this ridiculous manner, but he couldn't help himself. He had lost the knack of conversation as well as the knack of making love. His social skills had atrophied.

Had he gone to the freezer he'd have emerged into an altered

world, but this wasn't the twentieth century; the pace of technological change was much less fierce than it had been at its peak. He
could have adapted readily enough—but actually having to *live* the
fifty years of his sentence, aging at a normal rate, had turned him
into an *old man* in every sense of the word: a social and sexual
incompetent, hovering on the brink of mental incompetence.

It would probably be best for everyone, he thought, if he were
to flush out his IT and stick his head into a bath of neurostimulators—or perhaps to attempt a third rejuve, disregarding the 90 percent probability that the Miller effect would wipe his mental slate
clean.

"The time will come," the young woman assured him as she
adjusted her suitskin and ran her fingers lightly through her hair,
"when you will be recognized as a great man. When brain-
cyborgization technology is finally perfected, you'll be remembered
as a bold pioneer, tragically frustrated by the enemies of progress.
You *are* a great man, and there are people in the world who know
it now."

"I'm not a great man," he told her uncomfortably. "I never
pretended to be. I never did anything for the benefit of future generations. It was all for my own self-gratification. The people whose
brains were wrecked were the victims of *my* ambition. No matter
how resentful I may become about my punishment, I have to remember that I *was* guilty."

As he spoke, reflex lifted his wrinkled hand and passed it over
the hairless dome of his skull, the gnarled fingers dancing on the
sockets embedded in the bone as if they were dancing on a keyboard. The continued presence of the sockets was oddly reassuring,
despite their uselessness. While they were there, he could never
entirely forget who and what he was. Those who had set out to
punish him had not dared to remove the apparatus lest they kill
him in the process. His neurons had forged too many synapses with
the compound electrodes; it was no longer possible to say with any
exactitude where he ended and the brainfeed apparatus began.

"You *are* a great man," the woman insisted, her eyes flashing with uncanny brilliance. Michi lowered his hand. "One day, we *will* be able to make productive use of encephalic augmentation. Then, no matter how long each of us may live, there will be no limit to what we might become. Evolution will be the prerogative of the individual."

If only, Michi thought.

When the cruel sentence had first been passed upon him, revoking the prerogative of future individual evolution, Michi had thought that the sockets would be his greatest asset. He knew a thousand combinations whose stimulation created pleasure—and he did think of it as a primal process of *creation*—and a thousand patterns of varying intensity which made inner music of the ebb and flow of elemental ecstasy. He had been a connoisseur of fundamental self-stimulation, then. The superficial mock experiences available in commercial virtual environments had been of no interest to him at all, and he had taken leave to despise them. What arguments he and Kwiatek had had! He had been arrogant enough to think that nothing that the people of the real world could do to him could hurt him so long as he had power over his own inner being. He had thought himself complete as well as competent.

Fifty years had been more than long enough to reduce pleasure and ecstasy to tedium and mechanism, and to inform him how woefully incomplete he was. Long before the further growth of his new synapses had spoiled the messages with noise, they had lost their intrinsic existential value.

That had been the worst punishment of all.

Once, Michi had thought that the fear of robotization by cyborgization was a mere phantom of the frightened imagination, a grotesque bugbear unworthy of the anxiety of serious men. In those days, he had been convinced that the so-called Robot Assassins were mere lunatics. Now, he was not so sure . . . and yet, the flatteries heaped upon him by this remarkable young woman were anything but unwelcome. The knowledge that there were still a precious few among the newest generation who counted him a hero was very precious.

The woman was probably not a Natural; in two hundred years' time she would run into the crucial limitation of nanotechnological repair exactly as his own generation had. There must, however, be Naturals who thought as she did, who would carry his memory into the fourth millennium—perhaps even to the fifth if the limited research in encephalic augmentation that was still permitted eventually solved the problem of forgetfulness without eroding the capacity for empathy. . . .

"I don't have much time, Michi," the woman told him. "I'll have to go."

"Of course," he said, hauling himself from the bed into an upright position, ignoring her pantomimed protest.

"Don't get up," she said when she realized how determined he was. "Please—stay where you are. I'll let myself out."

"Will you come again?" he asked, although he wasn't entirely sure that he wanted to risk another possible humiliation.

"Yes," she said. "I promise."

For some reason, he couldn't even begin to believe her—and it was that, rather than the mere instruction, which made him sink back onto the bed and wait, supine, until he was sure that she had left the house.

When he finally managed to rouse himself, Michi went back into the outer room, without bothering to put his own suitskin on. He slumped upon the settee, drained and dejected, staring at the golden flowers that the woman had brought for him and mounted in his wall.

They were garden flowers, but they were products of modern genetic art rather than ancient selective breeding. According to the young woman, they were one of Oscar Wilde's designs—but for some reason he could not quite fathom, they reminded Michi of the kind of flowers one might put in a funeral wreath.

He wished that he had not lost his grip on the artistry of actual life. Like the soft caresses of data suits and the visual illusions of virtual reality, the rewards of ordinary sensation now seemed to him so remote from *authentic* intimacy as to be utterly worthless. In his first youth, which had all but disappeared into the oblivion of forgetfulness, he had devoted a great deal of time to the enhancement of the visual illusions deployed by VE technology. Even in his second youth, he had contrived to devote a certain amount of attention to the lucrative businesses of VE education and VE entertainment, but by then he had been determined to become a pioneer of experiential augmentation, and he had succeeded in that mission to the extent of becoming an outlaw. In doing so, he had lost his appetite for the ordinary. Perhaps that was why he seemed to be perpetually on the brink of losing his unfortunately ordinary mind.

The young woman was right, of course—all true pioneers so far outstripped the ambitions of their contemporaries that they were condemned to perdition for their bravery—but she could not know the true cost of his abandonment of the phenomenal world, any more than she could know the real effect of his long imprisonment.

"One day," Michi had actually said to the judge who had pronounced sentence upon him from the conventional safety of a virtual courtroom, "the world will despise the kind of cowardice whose representative you are. Michi Urashima, the men of the future will say, was demonized by those too dull to see that he was the seed of the Afterman. Those future men will not be prisoners within their own skulls, rotting in the dungeons of their incompetent wetware. The crude paths which I have hacked out will be built by future generations into the roads of freedom. Our children's children will live forever, and they will wear the crowns of Emperors of Experience: crowns of silicon which will give them the memories they will need, the calculative capacities they will need, and all the ecstasies that they will not be ashamed to demand. Our children's children will be properly equipped for eternal life."

Even now, he was certain that he had been right—but still he was forced to count the cost of his martyrdom.

Michi was wise enough to understand the kinds of fear which his experiments had inspired in those who condemned him. He knew now that there was real cause for anxiety in their nightmarish visions of people made into robotic puppets by external brainfeed equipment, either by operant conditioning or straightforward usurpation of the command links to the nervous system. He had responded to those fears in the same speech, appropriating the defense offered by the pioneers of the Genetic Revolution. "All technologies can be used for evil ends as well as good ones," he had said, "but willful ignorance is no protection. Biotechnology provided the means for hideous wars, but it also provided the defenses which prevented their devastations from becoming permanent and freed humankind from the oppressions of the Old Reproductive System. What we require, as we face a future of limitless opportunity, is not blind fear and denial but a clear-sighted sense of responsibility, and the means to undo all the evils of oppression—including the oppressions of our imperfect evolutionary heritage." That too had been true—but it had not been sufficient then to lay the fears of others to rest, and it was not sufficient now to quell his own anxieties.

The simple fact was that he had not, in the end, succeeded in freeing himself from the oppressions of his imperfect evolutionary heritage. His purpose had been to add to the sum of human freedom by increasing the power which individual consciousness had over its own recalcitrant wetware, and he had indeed added to that sum, but his own freedom had been lost, and not merely by imprisonment. He had never been intimidated by the fears of those who believed that brainfeed equipment would provide new technologies of enslavement and new technologies of punishment, preferring to concentrate his own efforts on the pursuit of empowerment and pleasure—but in the end, he had lost more than he had expected, and gained less than he had hoped.

Whatever the woman said, and whatever she believed, he was what he was, and it was not *enough*.

In the hope of shaking himself out of his lachrymose mood, Michi stood up and went to the wall fitting in which the young woman had placed the golden flowers.

He noticed for the first time that there was a card nestling within the bouquet—and the observation reminded him yet again of the vague impression he had formed of the bouquet's kinship to a funeral wreath.

Michi reached out to read what was written on the card, and saw with a slight shock that it bore the "signature" of Rappaccini Inc.—but it did not seem to be a condolence card. The legend on the card was a poem, or part of a poem. The corporation was evidently attempting to broaden its commercial scope, albeit somewhat enigmatically.

The words read:

> Yet each man kills the thing he loves,
> By each let this be heard,
> Some do it with a bitter look,
> Some with a flattering word.
> The coward does it with a kiss,
> The brave man with a sword!"

Why on earth, Michi wondered, had the woman selected such a peculiar message? Was she suggesting that *he* had killed the things he loved? If so, she was more closely in tune with his morbid mood than any indication she had given in word or gesture. Had it been so obvious, the first time he accepted her kiss, that he was a coward? Had she known all along that she would find him impotent? Had the few flattering words he had contrived to produce, in poor recompense for hers, wounded her with their feebleness?

He replaced the card, cursing himself for his folly in searching for hidden meanings. It was, he vaguely recalled, a very old poem;

she must have chosen it because it was a time-honored classic, more beautiful in its antiquity than in its sentiment.

"Who wrote these words?" he asked his dutiful sloth, reciting them for the benefit of the machine. The sloth had no answer in its own memory, of course, but it had wit enough to consult the reference sources available on the Web.

"Oscar Wilde," it replied, after a few moments' pause.

Michi was astonished until he remembered that there had been more Oscar Wildes in the world than one. The coincidence of names must have been what inspired the young woman to pick this particular card.

A whole bouquet of Oscar Wildes! he thought. Well, better that than a whole bouquet of Walter Czastkas. He remembered that he had known Walter Czastka when the old bore was still in the full flush of youth, although Kwiatek had known him better. They had all been pioneers in those days, but they had all been as stupid as sloths, too young by far to realize that one cannot be a pioneer until one has mastered what has gone before. That had not stopped them hatching all manner of mad schemes, of course. Even Czastka! What was it that he had found which had seemed to him the making of a new era? He had sucked Kwiatek into it, and others too.

Why, Michi thought, with sudden astonishment, that must have been the very first time that I became an outlaw, and I cannot even remember what I did, or why. Who would have thought it? Paul was an outlaw through and through, even then—and that rascal King too, already well on his way to becoming a sly lackey of the MegaMall. But what on earth can stolid Walter Czastka have found that turned him around so completely, if only for a moment? What was it that he tried to do, that seemed so daring and so desperate?

For a moment, as he touched the petals of the golden flowers, Michi almost remembered—but it had all taken place too long ago. He was a different man now, or a different half-man.

"I am," he murmured. "I was not what I am, but was not an am, and am not an am even now. I was and am a man, unless I am

a man unmanned, an it both done and undone by IT." He spelled
out the final acronym, pronouncing it "eye tee."

Then he laughed. What could it possibly matter now what deliciously illicit assistance he and Kwiatek had rendered to Walter
Czastka at the dawn of all their histories?

He could not know, of course, that he had already begun to die
because of it.

The Heights and the Depths

I t may be just coincidence, of course," Hal Watson said, referring to the possible connection between Walter Czastka and Rappaccini that had been exposed by his indefatigable silver surfers. "The supplies could have been delivered to a different island—the boatmaster doesn't keep electronically available records—so they may have been intended for a rival exercise in Creationism. Even if we could prove that Czastka *is* more intimately linked to Rappaccini than other appearances suggest, the only hard evidence linking Rappaccini to the murders is the fact that the woman is drawing money from bank accounts fed by income generated by the corporations which seem to be his. She's the one we have to identify and locate before we can proceed any further."

"I disagree," said Oscar Wilde, before Charlotte could reply. "Given that the flowers are victim-specific, their *designer* must be regarded as the actual murderer. The woman is delivering them, but she may not have been aware that they were lethal until news broke of Gabriel King's death—and even now she may not be certain that she was responsible, unless the news tapes have publicized the manner of his death."

"They haven't," Michael Lowenthal put in. "Those dogs won't be let off the leash until the early evening news. After that, it'll be a free-for-all."

"I'm sure the UN will be very grateful for your employers' discretion," Charlotte said sourly. She turned away slightly as she said it, embarrassed by her own temerity.

There was nothing visible through the window but a concrete blur speckled with racing vehicles. She had to squint slightly in order to refocus her eyes on the rim of jet-black SAP systems that topped the superhighway's sound-muffling walls. It was an inner sensation of deceleration rather than any visual cue which told her that the hire car's driver was responding to an instruction in its secret programming. It was changing lanes, moving to the inside. As the vehicle slowed and Charlotte's eyes adjusted, the blur of uncertainty began to resolve itself into a much clearer image. The road markings appeared out of the sun-blazed chaos of the surface, and the other cars on the road became discrete and distinct.

If only the case could be clarified as easily, she thought, peering into the distance in the hope of seeing a road sign that would tell her which intersection they were approaching. Belatedly, she regretted having left the driver's monitor to Lowenthal. Had he not been turned around, maintaining his position as best he could within the four-way conversation, he would have been able to obtain the car's exact location at the stab of a button.

"The person we have to identify and locate with all possible expedition," Oscar Wilde went on, overriding the comments which had interrupted his flow, "is the man behind Rappaccini Inc.—and with all due respect to Michael's reasoning and the evidential fruit provided by its pursuit, I still can't believe that Walter Czastka is that man. If Jafri Biasiolo never actually existed, who was the man who appeared at the Great Exhibition and discussed matters of technique and aesthetics with such evident authority? Whose face appears in the records dutifully assembled by Hal's inquisitive silvers?"

"A well-briefed actor," said Michael Lowenthal. "Hired to secure the illusion that Rappaccini had a real existence—and then removed from the scene, having done his work. You shouldn't have told Czastka that he was a suspect, Dr. Wilde. Until you did that, he must have thought that his plan was working perfectly. He must have assumed that he was the only expert witness the police had called upon."

"Even though he had summoned me to the Trebizond Tower and simultaneously made himself unavailable for immediate consultation?" Wilde queried. "I think not. The *real* Rappaccini may be involving Walter in his affair with the same scrupulous ingenuity that he is applying to my own involvement—but if so, he clearly cannot expect that either of us will actually be arrested and charged. My part is that of an interested witness. Walter's—"

"Czastka has a much stronger link to the victims," Lowenthal insisted stubbornly. "He has to be reckoned the most likely suspect."

"Not at all," Wilde insisted. "If this matter of the supplies is not a red herring, the most likely hypothesis is that the elusive Rappaccini is hiding out in exactly the location one would expect of a genetic engineer: in the Creationist archipelago."

"It doesn't matter who the *most likely* suspect is," Hal Watson informed them both sharply. "We have to pursue *all* the relevant lines of inquiry, and we have to intercept the woman before she does any more damage, even if she's only a dupe. The boatmaster will be questioned as soon as we can get through to him, and I'll be sure to check the leases on all the islands south and west of Kauai. It's just a matter of time. We still have a better than even chance of putting the whole jigsaw together before the early evening news turns the inquiry into a circus."

Charlotte winced as the car suddenly lurched, throwing her sideways to jostle Oscar Wilde. They had left the transcontinental superhighway at the intersection—she still did not know which one—and had already made a second turn, taking it off the subsidiary highway. The car was now climbing steeply into the hills, along a road which did not seem to have been properly maintained.

Having missed the sign at the intersection, Charlotte's first response to this realization was to crane her neck to look back at the valley they were leaving behind, trying to figure out where they might be. The nature of the terrain suggested that they must have passed the Los Angeles junction, but she couldn't tell whether they were south of the Salton Sea. She had only the vaguest knowledge of the West Coast, and wasn't even sure what state they were in.

This had been a densely populated region in the distant past, but southern California had suffered worse than any other region of the old USA during the ancient plague wars. The so-called Second Plague War—whose obsolete title still lingered, even though modern historians no longer recognized the distinctions made by near-contemporary commentators—had made its grisly debut in Hollywood, which had been widely perceived as the ultimate symbol of twenty-first-century vanity, privilege, and conspicuous consumption. The rumor had been put about that the terrorists who had launched that particular team of viruses had been seeking revenge on the supposed beneficiaries of the "First Plague War," who had allegedly launched it with the aim of wiping out the economic underclasses of the developed world.

If any of that was true, the "second war" had misfired badly. As in all wars, and plague wars more than any other kind, the poor had sustained far more casualties than the rich. Although the proximity of medical resources and the relative efficiency of emergency measures had helped to keep death rates down in the cities, the response in many rural areas to the emergence of the first cases had been a mass exodus of refugees. Most of those who had survived had never returned, preferring to relocate to more promising land. Three-quarters of the ghost towns of the Sierra Madre were ghost towns still, even after three hundred years.

Charlotte knew that the car hadn't been on the road long enough to have got to the Sierra Madre, but these lesser hills seemed just as bleak, and the same pattern of response to the plague wars must have been duplicated here. Now that Hal had removed his image from the screen in order to concentrate on his Herculean labors, Charlotte took the opportunity to call up an annotated map of the region onto the screen in front of her. She summoned a blinking light to show her the car's position, but the datum provided no obvious clue as to where it might be headed or why. The names of several small towns—all flagged as uninhabited—were scattered along their present route, but Charlotte wasn't surprised that she was unable to recognize any of them.

"The region up ahead seems to be wasteland," she told Lowenthal and Wilde, vaguely hoping that one of them might be better able to guess where they were being taken.

"She's right," Lowenthal confirmed, addressing himself to Wilde yet again, as if she were merely a hanger-on. "Nobody lives up here—and I mean *nobody*. The work of repairing the effects of the ecocatastrophe hasn't even begun, even though we're practically in LA's backyard. Nothing grows here except lichens and the odd stalk of grass. The land's never been officially reclaimed, not even for wilderness. It's just rock and dust. The names on the map are just distant memories."

"*Something* must be up there," Wilde said, shifting uncomfortably as the car took another corner with unreasonable haste. "Rappaccini wouldn't bring us up here if there were nothing to see. If there were no real reason for this expedition he might as well have left us kicking our heels at the Majestic, or your headquarters in New York. Perhaps it's the fact that no one ever comes here which recommended it to him as one of the bases of his secret operations."

"But none of these ghost towns is cable-connected to the Web," Charlotte objected, drawing her finger across the screen in an arc.

"Which might be reckoned a considerable advantage by anyone intent on hiding," Wilde pointed out.

It was easy enough for Charlotte to follow the line of thought. Land as derelict as this might be a *very* good place to hide. A man living up here would not be entirely deaf and blind, provided that he had equipment to receive information broadcast by comsat, but he could be effectively invisible as long as he made no long-distance purchases or person-to-person contacts. If he always kept a roof over his head during daylight hours he would go unnoticed even by surveillance satellites.

●   ●   ●

The hire car had been designed for highway travel, and its speed had slowed considerably when it first began to follow the winding road up into the foothills of the mountain range, but its AI did not seem to have mastered the art of mountain climbing. Although the road surface was getting worse and the bends were becoming sharper and more frequent, the car still seemed to be making haste. As she was forced to sway yet again Charlotte cursed the AI driver for not being sloth enough, although it could not have had wit enough to qualify as a silver, but she assumed that she was being oversensitive. A driver's prime directive was to ensure the safety of its passengers.

The map disappeared from Charlotte's screen, replaced by a list which Hal Watson had posted there.

"There are twenty-seven names here," Hal said. "So far as we can ascertain, it's a complete list of living men and women who attended the University of Wollongong while King, Urashima, Kwiatek, and Czastka were also in attendance. We've now contacted all of them but one—Magnus Teidemann—so we're fairly certain that any other bodies that turn up will break the pattern."

Michael Lowenthal patched the list through to his own screen, but no sooner had he set it up than his beltphone buzzed. Rather than displace the list, he picked up his handset and put the mike to his ear.

"What!" he said—not very loudly, but with sufficient emphasis to command the attention of his companions.

"What is it?" Charlotte asked—but she had to wait until Lowenthal had lowered the handset again. When he turned in his seat, it was Oscar Wilde that he transfixed with his triumphant gaze.

"I asked my employers to check the record of Jafri Biasiolo's DNA against Walter Czastka's," Michael Lowenthal said proudly, peering back through the gap between the headrests.

"And were they identical?" asked Oscar Wilde, raising a quizzical eyebrow.

"No," said Lowenthal, "they weren't identical." Charlotte

wondered why, in that case, he looked so immensely pleased with himself—but he had only paused for effect. "The comparison gave much the same initial estimate of similarity as the comparison between Biasiolo's and the woman's—forty-some percent. Closer analysis of key subsections, however, suggests a consanguinity of fifty percent, blurred by substantial deep-somatic engineering."

"I'm not sure that lends any support to your hypothesis," said Wilde. "Indeed, it suggests—"

Lowenthal didn't let him finish. "That's not all," he said. "When they uncovered the link between Czastka and Biasiolo, they immediately compared Walter Czastka's DNA profile with the record Regina Chai obtained from Gabriel King's bedroom. The overlap's no better than random. Consanguinity zero!"

"But how can that be?" Charlotte complained. "If Czastka and Biasiolo are close relatives, and the woman is Biasiolo's daughter . . ."

"She's not!" Lowenthal was quick to say triumphantly. "The only way that Czastka and the woman could each have fifty percent of Biasiolo's genes without being significantly consanguineous themselves is by being his parents. She's not Rappaccini's daughter at all: she's his *mother!*—and Walter Czastka's his father!"

"Congratulations," said Oscar Wilde dryly. "You seem to have found me guilty of an illegitimate inference—and you doubtless feel that if one of my inferences is defective, the rest might be equally mistaken. But you seem to be overlooking the true significance of the finding—"

"Wait a second," Charlotte interrupted. "This doesn't make sense. It's perfectly plausible that Walter Czastka had made a sperm deposit while he was still in his teens, but he certainly couldn't have applied for a withdrawal only two or three years later! We're not talking about the Dark Ages here, or the aftermath of the Crash. People of his generation *never* exercised their right of reproduction when they were in their twenties—it's only in very special circumstances that they exercise them even now, while they're still alive."

"If Czastka had made any *formal* application," Lowenthal agreed, not in the least confounded by her argument, "then his name would be included in Biasiolo's record. Obviously, he didn't— but he was training as a geneticist, and he must have had privileged access to a Helier hatchery. He must have substituted his own sperm for a donation which had been legitimately drawn from the bank. He wouldn't have been the first hatchery tech to do that, nor the first to have got away with it."

"But it doesn't help your hypothesis that Czastka is the designer behind Rappaccini Inc.," Charlotte pointed out. "Your original contention was that Biasiolo was a mere phantom, invented by Czastka for the purpose of establishing a separate identity under which he could undertake various clandestine endeavors."

"That's true," Lowenthal agreed. "It's now established that Biasiolo *is* a real person, not a ghost—but he's Walter Czastka's *son*. Doesn't that put Czastka behind Rappaccini Inc.?"

"But if your scenario is accurate," Charlotte objected, constructing the argument as she spoke, "he'd never know it—Biasiolo, I mean. I suppose Czastka might have kept track of a substitute donation, if he'd made one, but he could hardly tell the foster parents about it, could he? What he did—according to you—was a criminal offense. He could never *tell* Biasiolo that he was his biological father."

"You're still missing—," Oscar Wilde said.

Michael Lowenthal didn't let him finish; for once, he was fully engaged with Charlotte. "He could never *tell* anyone," the man from the MegaMall said, in answer to her quibble, "but that doesn't mean that nobody knew what he'd done. Maybe it wasn't his own idea. Maybe it was some kind of challenge, some kind of initiation into a secret society. He was a student, after all—and so were Gabriel King, Michi Urashima, and Paul Kwiatek. Maybe they *all* knew. Maybe—"

"I fear that your flair for melodrama is getting out of hand, Michael," said Wilde impatiently, firmly reclaiming center stage.

"As Charlotte says, we're not talking about the Dark Ages—but we *are* talking about the past. It isn't in the least surprising that an authentically young woman might have undergone sufficient genetic engineering to reduce an actual consanguinity of fifty percent to an apparent overlap of forty-one, but it's *not* plausible that two closely related old men should be that much less similar, unless something very odd had happened. As for this secret-society initiation, it's the stuff of ancient romance—and it provides no explanation of the timing of the murders. If Walter were Biasiolo's father, how could the revelation hurt Walter *now*? Even if everyone who knew it then still remembered it nearly a hundred and seventy years later, why should any of them attach any importance to it?"

The list of names that Hal had posted on Charlotte's screen disappeared, to be replaced by his face. He didn't look pleased—presumably because he felt that he ought to have been the one to discover the link between Biasiolo and Walter Czastka.

"I hate to break in on such a fevered discussion," he said, "but I just checked the DNA trace Regina Chai recovered against the record of one Maria Inacio, listed in Jafri Biasiolo's birth record as his biological mother. The same record says, 'Father Unknown'—a statement whose significance has only just become apparent to me. The trace recovered from King's apartment is indeed similar to Inacio's, and might have been identical were it not for the differentiating effect of the younger woman's genetic engineering. As I told you before, though, it doesn't match the record of any *living* person. According to the register, Maria Inacio was born in 2303 and she died in 2342."

"So she can't be our murderer," Charlotte said.

"Nor can she be Jafri Biasiolo's mother," Oscar Wilde was quick to put in. "Not, at least, if Michael's new version of events is correct. If Walter or anyone else had merely substituted his own sperm for a donation drawn from the bank, it would have been used to fertilize an ovum which had come from the same bank, which could not—at least under normal circumstances—have been freshly deposited there by an eighteen-year-old girl."

"If Jafri Biasiolo had been conceived in a Helier hatchery," Hal Watson said, completing his own revelatory bombshell with evident satisfaction, "the record would have said, 'Father Unrecorded.' Perhaps my silver should have picked the discrepancy up on first inspection, but it had no reason to attribute any significance to the datum. Jafri Biasiolo was the product of a late abortion; he wasn't introduced to a Helier womb until he was three months short of delivery. Maria Inacio must have been immune to the endemic chiasmatic transformers—and probably never knew it, until her doctor told her that the strange growth in her abdomen wasn't a tumor. Her own fosterers must have belonged to an antinanotech cult of some kind; there was one active in Australia at the time whose members called themselves Naturals; had they not selected themselves for rapid extinction, we might have needed a different label for the likes of Mr. Lowenthal."

"So all this stuff about substitute donations is rubbish," Charlotte said, to make sure she had it straight. "You're saying that Walter Czastka impregnated the girl by means of everyday sexual intercourse—intercourse which neither he nor she had the slightest reason to think capable of producing a pregnancy."

"Given that the record says, 'Father Unknown,' " Hal said, "we can probably assume that neither Czastka nor Biasiolo ever knew of the relationship Mr. Lowenthal's eager investigators have now brought to light. Given that it *has* been brought to light, I suppose someone ought to tell Walter Czastka—except, of course, that he's not answering his phone just now because Dr. Wilde offended him. I'm not entirely happy about merely reporting it to his sim."

"But they *must* know!" Lowenthal protested. "How else can we begin to make sense of all these connections?"

"*One* of them must know," Oscar Wilde agreed, his voice animated by a sudden fervor. "I owe you an apology, Michael—your hypothesis, although mistaken in detail, has indeed paved the way to the crucial enlightenment. Walter can know nothing of all this—

but Rappaccini must know *everything*. We have had the vital connection set before us for several hours, but have not realized its significance! Walter is . . . am I mistaken, or is the sloth driving this vehicle becoming *extremely* reckless in its speed around these bends?''

Charlotte had not bothered to look out of the windows for some time, having become accustomed to the swaying of the vehicle. Now that she did, it seemed to her that Oscar Wilde was understating the case.

Because AI drivers were programmed to the highest safety standards, everyone fell into the habit of trusting them absolutely, but the road on which they were traveling was undoubtedly far too rough and curvaceous to warrant progress at their present velocity. There was no guardrail on their right-hand side, and the scree slope fell away precipitously.

Charlotte remembered the message warning them not to interrogate the driver's programming. Like Lowenthal and Wilde, she had automatically assumed that this was merely a device to protect the secrecy of their destination—but what if it were not? What if such an interrogation would have revealed that the driver's safety programming had been carefully and illegally stripped away? She banished Hal's image from her screen and flicked the switch connecting the comcon to the driver. She typed a rapid instruction to the machine, ordering it to moderate the vehicle's speed.

There was no immediate response.

She slid her swipecard into the comcon's confirmation slot and invoked the full authority of the United Nations to back up her instruction. The only effect was that a printed message appeared on the screen: INCREASED SPEED NECESSITATED BY PROXIMITY OF PURSUING VEHICLE.

Charlotte blinked, then tapped in an instruction to open a viewpoint in the rear of the cabin. She and Oscar Wilde turned together to look through it, their heads almost touching as they converged.

The vehicle behind them was not an ordinary car. It was smaller, squarer, and looked as if it were heavily armored. It appeared, in fact, to be some kind of military vehicle. It was also far closer to their rear end than safety regulations permitted. Charlotte knew that it must have an AI driver, because its windscreen was quite opaque, but the sloth in question had obviously been programmed in frank defiance of the law.

"It's trying to force us off the road!" said Charlotte, hardly able to believe her eyes. In all her years in the police force she had never encountered anything so outrageous.

Her beltphone buzzed, and she lifted it from its holster reflexively, her eyes still fixed on the pursuing vehicle and her cheek less than a centimeter away from Oscar Wilde's uncannily beautiful face.

"Hal!" she cried. "Someone's trying to kill us!"

"What?" said Hal, his voice as incredulous as her own.

"There's some kind of jeep trying to smash into us from behind!"

The car carrying Charlotte and Wilde swept around a bend, and the resultant lurch bounced their heads together. It was not a bad bump, but the combination of surprise and pain made Charlotte cry out.

"Charlotte!" said Hal, his incredulity replaced by alarm. "What's happening?"

Charlotte had to make an effort to force her train of thought onward through the barrier that pain had erected. She wanted to shout instructions to the people who would by now be monitoring their situation through the car's sensors. "Scramble a helicopter!" she wanted to scream. "Send a software bomb! Get us the hell out of here!"

As she straightened up again she looked out of the side window at the drop which awaited them if their driver were to be careless enough to let a wheel slide over the edge.

It was a *very* long drop.

Michael Lowenthal let loose an inarticulate cry of anguish, as befit a potential emortal who was staring death in the face for the first time.

Charlotte gave voice to a wordless cry of her own as they soared around another bend, even sharper than its predecessors. She turned back to the rear viewport, clutching her throbbing head as she did so. She felt a sudden instinctive pulse of hope that the pursuing vehicle might not make it around the bend.

Alas, the jeep did make it. It fell back eight or ten meters in so doing, and Charlotte felt her heart surge as she wondered whether some preventative signal had got through—but then there was a curious rattling noise at the rear end of their own vehicle.

"Hal!" she cried again. "They're shooting at us, Hal! They've got a gun!"

"Charlotte!" came the reply. "I've got visual patched through from a sat! I've got . . . *corruption and corrosion!*"

Charlotte had never heard Hal use such words before, except in their uninflected and strictly literal forms. Had she been able to find words herself she would have delved even deeper in search of more profound expletives.

They had just taken yet another bend. This time, the pursuing vehicle failed to make the turn—in fact, it seemed to keep going straight ahead: straight over the edge and into empty air.

For almost a second it seemed to hang there, like some absurd toon character in a synthemovie, who would not start to feel the effects of gravity until he became conscious of being unsupported.

Then, with a peculiar gracefulness, the jeep began to fall.

It tumbled over and over as it fell, and when it finally hit the rocky slope two hundred meters below, it exploded like a bomb, sending shards in all directions.

The sloth driving the hire car had applied the brakes the instant that the threat of a damaging collision was removed from the viewport, but it had done so judiciously so as to minimize the risk of skidding.

"Hal," said Charlotte tremulously, "I think you just got another data trail to follow." It was, she felt, a very feeble attempt at humor. By now—assuming that this absurdly tilted patch of crumpled wasteland lay within their jurisdiction—the California Highway Patrol's best silvers would have identified the rogue vehicle, and they would already be tracking down its owner and programmer.

Charlotte shut her eyes and breathed deeply, while the pain in her head ebbed slowly away.

When she opened her eyes again, Oscar Wilde had converted his side window into a mirror, and he was inspecting his own head very carefully. There was a noticeable bluish bump just above the right eyebrow. She could not find it in her heart to regret the temporary damage done to his outrageous good looks, although he obviously felt differently about it.

"What do you make of *that*?" she asked him.

"I can only hope that it was simply another vignette in the unfolding psychodrama," he said grimly. "Perhaps Rappaccini feared that the journey might be a trifle boring, and laid on a measured dose of excitement."

She stared at him for a few seconds. "You mean," she said slowly, "that the person who hired *this* car also hired *that* one—as a *practical joke*!"

Oscar shrugged his shoulders, turning back again to his pained inspection of the damage done to his temple.

"He might be right," said Hal, over the phone link. "The information's coming through now. The jeep was hired at the same time as the car, although the fee came from an account I hadn't yet connected to Rappaccini. The local police have no reason to think that anyone was aboard, although they'll send a crew out to check the debris. It wasn't carrying a gun—that rattling sound you heard was produced by your own car's AI."

Charlotte was speechless.

"Are you all okay?" Hal inquired solicitously.

"Physically, we're fine," Michael Lowenthal replied. Given that he had not bruised his own head, his entitlement to speak on behalf of his companions seemed a trifle dubious to Charlotte.

"That's good," said Hal, his voice reverting instantly to its normal businesslike tone. "I've just got some more data in from Bologna, if you want to look at any of it."

"Bologna?" said Charlotte.

"It's where Kwiatek was killed," Lowenthal informed her.

"We've got another picture of the woman," Hal said. "We're fairly certain that she flew to New York on an intercontinental flight from Rome. Do you want to see the tape?"

"Not really," said Charlotte, who was still profoundly shaken by the fake attack—although she was quick enough to add: "Not yet, I mean. Where was she before Bologna?"

"Darkest Africa, we think—visiting Magnus Teidemann. His death is still to be confirmed, but we're not optimistic. Are you sure you don't want the Kwiatek data?"

"Was there a calling card with Kwiatek's body?" Oscar Wilde put in, shutting his own eyes as if to blank out the image of the bruise.

"I'll check the tapes," Hal said. "Give me a couple of minutes."

"There's no hurry, Inspector," Lowenthal said, exchanging a sympathetic glance with the shaken Charlotte. "I think we'd all benefit from a moment's pause."

"Did you look at the list I put up?" Hal asked, evidently seeing no necessity for any such pause. It wasn't entirely clear whether he was addressing Lowenthal or Charlotte.

"I saw it," Charlotte said wearily. "Was there something significant I should have taken note of?" She knew that she ought not to end sentences with prepositions, but thought that the stress of the situation made the infelicity forgivable.

"Maybe not," Hal replied. "But I thought Mr. Lowenthal's eye might have been caught by one of the addresses."

The list reappeared yet again, on all three of the seatscreens. Hal had obviously decided that he would follow his agenda no matter what. This time, Charlotte's eye was immediately drawn to the word *Kauai*. One Stuart McCandless, ex-chancellor of the University of Oceania, had retired to the island. He had graduated from the University of Wollongong in 2322.

"Can you connect him to Czastka or Biasiolo?" Lowenthal said.

"Is he answering his phone?" asked Charlotte. "If so, it might be helpful to find out what he remembers about his student days."

"He's alive and well," Hal said. "He says that he still meets up with Czastka occasionally, when Czastka's on Kauai, but not for some months. He never met Biasiolo and he doesn't know anything about Rappaccini. He doesn't remember anything significant about Walter Czastka's university career."

While this catalogue of negatives was in transmission, Charlotte glanced out of the side window again as the car swung—slowly and carefully—around a bend.

The road was no longer poised above the sheer slope, and she realized that they were coming into one of the ghost towns whose names were still recorded on the map, in spite of the fact that no one had lived in them for centuries.

The car came to a standstill.

The ancient stone buildings that were all that now remained of the town had been weathered by dust storms, but they still retained the sharp angles which proudly proclaimed their status as human artifacts. The land around them was quite dead, seemingly incapable of growing so much as a blade of grass. It was every bit as desolate as an unspoiled lunar landscape, but the shadowy scars of human habitation still lay upon it.

The sun was reddening against the peacock blue background, and the shadows it cast were lengthening toward the east.

"What now?" Charlotte said to Oscar Wilde. "Do we start looking for another body?"

Before they had time to get out of the car, the screens in front of them blanked out. While Charlotte was still wondering what the interruption signified, the car's sloth relayed a message in flamboyant red letters.

It said: WELCOME, OSCAR: THE PLAY WILL COMMENCE IN TEN MINUTES. THE PLAYHOUSE IS BENEATH THE BUILDING TO YOUR RIGHT.

"Play?" said Charlotte bitterly. "Have we come all this way just to see a *play*? Hal was right—I should never have left New York."

"I'm sorry that your decision has caused you some inconvenience," said Wilde as he opened the door and climbed out into the sultry heat of the deepening evening, "but I will confess that I'm glad you both decided to come with me. In spite of the entertainment laid on for us as we climbed the mountainside, the journey would have been infinitely more tedious had I been forced to take it alone. I suspect that whatever experience awaits us will benefit from being shared. Do you carry a supply of transmitter eyes in that belt you're wearing, Charlotte?"

"Of course I do," she said as she moved to the rear of the car to inspect the place where bullets had seemed to strike it. Hal was, inevitably, absolutely right. There were no marks at all. The sound of the shots had been manufactured by the hire car's sloth, to intensify the fear its passengers felt. The sloth was, of course, far too stupid to be held responsible, but Charlotte cursed it anyway, along with its still-mysterious programmer.

All very amusing for you, she thought, but we could have been killed if we'd gone off the road, and we could have died of fright. When we catch up with you . . .

"I suggest that you place a few transmitters about your person," Wilde said to her, his own equanimity seemingly restored. "You too, Michael. I only have a bubblebug, incapable of live transmission—but I'll mount it on my forehead, so that I may preserve the moment for my own future reference."

Charlotte turned to stare at the building to their right. It did not look in the least like a theater. To judge by its display window—empty now of glass, and shutterless—it must once have been a primitive general store. It was roofless now and seemed to be nothing more than a gutted shell.

"Why bring us out here to the middle of nowhere?" she demanded angrily. "If it's just a tape, why didn't he just run it in a theater in San Francisco—or New York?" As she spoke, she planted two electronic eyes on her own head, one above each eyebrow. One of them had power enough to transmit a signal to the car, provided that nothing substantial got in the way, and the car's power system would hopefully boost the signal sufficiently for it to be picked up by a relay sat and copied all the way to Hal Watson's lair. Whether Hal would bother to watch the transmission as it came in she had no idea, but she took the trouble to give him notice of its imminent arrival.

The notice proved to be premature. Oscar Wilde had already located a downward-leading flight of stone steps inside the derelict building. It was obvious almost as soon as they had begun the descent—with Charlotte planting head-high nanolights every six or seven steps to illuminate their passage—that it had been hollowed out using bacterial deconstructors far more modern than the building itself. By the time they reached the foot of the flight, Charlotte knew that there must be several meters of solid rock separating her from the car. Her transmitter eye was useless, except as a recording device; no signal could reach the car's sloth.

At the bottom of the stairway there was a very solid door made from some kind of synthetic organic material. It had neither handle nor visible lock, but as soon as Wilde touched it with his fingertips it swung inward.

"All doors in the world of theater open to Oscar Wilde," Michael Lowenthal muttered sarcastically.

Beyond the doorway was a well of impenetrable shadow. Charlotte automatically reached up to the wall inside the doorway, placing another nanolight there, but the darkness seemed to soak up its luminance quite effortlessly, and it showed her nothing but a few square centimeters of matte black wall. The moment Wilde took a tentative step forward, however, a small spotlight winked on, picking out a two-seater sofa upholstered in black, set a few feet away from them.

"Very considerate," said Oscar dryly. "Had you not been here, dear Charlotte, I would have been obliged to distribute myself in a conspicuously languid fashion. As things are, one of us will be obliged to stand."

"I'll stand," said Lowenthal. "I've been sitting down too long." Charlotte had to imagine the expression that must have been on his face as he looked at the sofa. There was no dust on it, but it was conspicuously cheap as well as very old. No modern MegaMall outlet would have stocked anything so tawdry.

"Shall we?" said Wilde. He invited Charlotte to move ahead of him, and she did, although she moved a little hesitantly through the darkness, unable to see the floor beneath her feet. There was an interval of five or six seconds after they were seated, and then the spotlight winked out.

Charlotte could not suppress a small gasp of alarm as they were plunged into a darkness which would have been absolute had it not been for the single nanolight she had set beside the door, which now shone like a single distant star in an infinite void.

When light returned, it was very cleverly directed away from them; Charlotte quickly realized that she could not make out Oscar Wilde's form, nor the contours of her own body. It was as if she had become a disembodied viewpoint, like a tiny bubblebug, looking out upon a world from which her physical presence had been erased.

She seemed to be ten or twelve meters away from the event which unfolded before her eyes, but she knew well enough that the distance—like the event itself—was an illusion. Cinematic holograms of the kind to which Michi Urashima had devoted his skills before turning to more dangerous toys were adepts in the seductive art of sensory deception.

The illusory event did not seem to be a "play" at all, according to Charlotte's reckoning, but merely a dance, performed solo. The hologrammatic dancer was a young woman. Charlotte had no difficulty at all in recognizing her, because her bronzed features were made up to duplicate the appearance that the image's living model had presented to Michi Urashima's spy eyes. Her hair was different, though; it was now long, straight, and jet-black. Her costume was different too and did not seem to be the conventional artifice of a suitskin. The dancer's bare flesh was ungenerously draped with soft, sleek, and translucent chiffons of many colors, secured at various strategic points of her lissome form by glittering gem-faced catches.

The music to which she danced—lithely and lasciviously—was raw and primitive, generated by virtual drums and reedy pipes.

"Salome," whispered Oscar Wilde.

"What?" said Lowenthal uncomprehendingly. "I don't—"

"Later!" was Wilde's swift response to that. "Hush now—watch!"

Two days ago the name would have meant absolutely nothing to Charlotte, but thanks to the background reading she had done in the maglev couchette, she now knew that Oscar Wilde—the *original* Oscar Wilde—had written a play called *Salomé*. She had taken sufficient note of it to recall that he had written it in French, because it had been too calculatedly lewd to be licensed for the nineteenth-century English stage. She had also pressed the support key which had informed her that Salome was the name attached by legend to the daughter of Herodias, wife of King Herod of Judea, who was mentioned in two of the gospels of the New Testament, the holy book of the Christian religion.

Forearmed by this knowledge, Charlotte thought that she understood what it was that she was to watch—and now assumed that the dance would indeed turn into a play of sorts.

Her ready understanding made her feel rather smug, even though she still had no idea what the purpose of this display could possibly be. For the first time since leaving New York, Charlotte did not feel that she was trailing hopelessly in the wake of the better-informed counterpart dispatched by the Secret Masters to keep track of her investigation. She assumed that she was at least as well prepared as Michael Lowenthal for whatever coups de théâtre were to follow.

As the nonexistent woman, isolated in an apparently infinite cage of darkness, swayed and gyrated to the beat of ancient drums, the first impression Charlotte received was one of utter artlessness and a pitiful lack of sophistication. Modern dance, which had all the artifice of contemporary biotechnology as a key resource, was infinitely smoother and more complicated. But this performance, she knew, was three times an artifact. The image of the dancer was produced by the technology of the twenty-fifth century, but what was being offered to her eyes was a nineteenth-century vision of the first century before the conventional calendrical century count began. This was a half-primitive representation of the genuinely primitive: an ancient fantasy recapitulated as a fantasy of a different kind, contained by a medium which was no less fantastic, in its own marvelous fashion.

In the nineteenth century, Charlotte knew—and thought that she had at least *begun* to grasp—there had been something called pornography, which had to be distinguished from art, although there had been some people who considered that much art was merely pornography with pretensions and others who felt that at least some pornography was art which dared not speak its name. Nowadays, in a world where most sexual intercourse took place between individuals and clever machinery, while most of the remainder was consciencelessly promiscuous, the idea of pornography had become quaint and antique. To nineteenth-century eyes, the programming of any modern person's intimate technology would have been bound to seem pornographic, but everyone—in spite of what Oscar Wilde had said about a sense of sin being somehow necessary to sexual pleasure—now accepted that in the realm of private fantasy nothing was perverse and nothing was taboo.

Charlotte understood, therefore—and was proud of herself for being able to understand—that part of the point of this performance was that one had to try to see it from several different viewpoints: from the viewpoint of some legendary petty ruler of the early Iron Age; from the viewpoint of would-be aesthetes and their rival moralists of the late Iron Age; and from the viewpoint of a double rejuvenate of the middle period of the Genetic Revolution.

After a moment's hesitation, she added two more hypothetical viewpoints: the viewpoint of an authentically young citizen of the late-twenty-fifth-century United States of North America; and the viewpoint of a nanotech recording device whose function was to preserve for future reference the sensory experiences of lives which were continually outstripping the resources of inbuilt memory.

With all this to take into account, she thought, the sight of Salome dancing should have been far more interesting that it actually was. In spite of all that she knew, Charlotte simply could not place herself, imaginatively, in the shoes of one of Herod's courtiers, nor the shoes of one of the original Oscar Wilde's gentleman friends, nor even the shoes of whatever strange individual had manufactured the mercurially virtual Rappaccini. She doubted that anyone of her era could have done better—not even the flesh-and-blood Oscar Wilde who sat invisibly but not quite intangibly beside her.

Charlotte found the steps of the dance trite and inexpressive; to her it seemed neither stimulating nor instructive, nor even quaintly amusing. The gradual removal of the dancer's seven veils was merely a laborious way of counting down to a climax that was already expected. And still there was nothing to suggest a *purpose* for the charade—unless, as she had earlier suspected, all of this was mere distraction, intended to divert attention away from the true substance of the crime and to confuse the investigations being carried out by Hal's silvers.

If this is mere mockery, she thought, Wilde might soon change his mind about being glad that Lowenthal and I chose to accompany him. If all this is just another joke intended to tease him, he might prefer to have kept it to himself. As soon as Lowenthal and I decant our bubblebugs, this will be public property—and when the MegaMall gives the go-ahead to the casters, it will be all over the news.

No sooner had she formulated the thought, however, than she realized that she might have got it backward. Perhaps the whole point of the summons to Gabriel King's appointment, the wreath at the San Francisco Majestic, and the car chase through the mountains had been to make Wilde's involvement in this matter *newsworthy*. Perhaps the mystery and melodrama were intended solely to create audience interest in a rough-and-ready artwork which had little enough interest of its own. Perhaps the real intended audience of this play was the vidveg, who would need Wilde as an interpreter. Under ordinary circumstances, the vidveg would not have found it at all interesting, but if it were aired on the news, as an appendix to the tale of three—perhaps four—lurid murders, it would command an eager audience of billions.

Was that what its author craved? Was it conceivable that all of this, including the murders, was a *publicity stunt*?

Salome was almost naked now, and the few encrustations she preserved upon her body were intended to heighten rather than to conceal, but Charlotte could summon up neither any vestige of emotional response nor any twinge of moral panic. All she could sense within herself was a precautionary tension, because she knew that at any moment Salome was likely to acquire a mute partner for her mesmerized capering.

The dancer *did* look as if she were mesmerized, Charlotte noted. She looked as if she were lost in some kind of dream, not really aware of who she was or what she was doing. Charlotte remembered that the young woman had given a similar impression during the brief glimpse of her which Gabriel King's cameras had caught. Was that significant—and if so, of what?

The dance slowed and finally stopped.

Without speaking, Salome stood with bowed head for a few moments—and then she reached out into the shadows which crowded around her, and brought out of the darkness a silver platter, on which there rested the decapitated head of a man. She plucked the head from its resting place, entwining her delicate fingers in its hair.

The salver disappeared, dissolved into the shadow.

Charlotte was not in the least surprised. She was quite ready for the move. Nevertheless, she flinched. The virtual head—which she knew to be a synthesized illusion—looked more startlingly horrid than a real head would have done, by virtue of the artistry which had gone into the design of its agonized expression and the bloodiness of the crudely severed neck.

She recognized the face which the virtual head wore: it was Gabriel King's.

The dance began again.

How differently, Charlotte wondered, was Oscar Wilde seeing this ridiculous scene? Could he see it as something daring, something monstrous, something clever? Would he be able to sigh with satisfaction, in that irritating way of his, when the performance was over, and claim that Rappaccini was a genius of many disparate talents? If he could, she thought, it would surely be pure affectation: an assertion of the virtual reality which he wore as a costume, by courtesy of the genius of cosmetic engineers. She felt certain that Michael Lowenthal would have as low an opinion of this vulgar theatricality as she had, even though he would not have anticipated the arrival of the severed head and probably would not know even now that it was supposed to be the head of Christ's precursor, John the Baptist.

The macabre dance began to seem even more mechanical. The

woman appeared to be unaware—or at least uncaring—of the fact that she was supposedly brandishing a severed head. She moved its face close to her own and then extended her arms again, all the while maintaining the same distant and dreamy expression.

Charlotte began to grow impatient—but then her attention was caught again. Subtly, almost imperceptibly, the features of the severed head had changed. Now it was no longer the head of Gabriel King; it had acquired an Oriental cast. Charlotte recognized Michi Urashima and suddenly became interested again, eager for any hint of further change. She was fully aware of the necessity of capturing every detail of the sequence—if it were indeed to be a sequence—with her recording devices, so she fixed her own gaze steadfastly upon the horrid head.

She had seen no picture of Paul Kwiatek as yet, so she could only infer that the third appearance presented by the luckless Baptist was his, and she became even more intent when the third set of features began to blur and shift. This, she thought, was a countdown of a rather different kind, in which the number and nature of the steps might well be crucial to the development of her investigation.

She felt a surge of triumph as she realized that this revelation, if nothing else, might vindicate her determination to accompany Oscar Wilde on his strange expedition.

She did not recognize the fourth face, but she was confident that the bubblebug set above her right eye would record it well enough for computer-aided recognition. If Hal's investigations could be trusted, it was almost certainly the ecologist Magnus Teidemann.

How many more, she wondered, would there be?

The fifth face was darker than the fourth—naturally dark, she thought, not cosmetically melanized. Men of King and Urashima's generation rarely played games with skin color, even when they had recourse to cosmetic engineers to make them handsomer. She did not recognize this man either.

She recognized the sixth face, though. She had seen it on a screen within the last few hours, looking considerably older and more ragged than its manifestation here but unmistakably the same. It was Walter Czastka.

Charlotte remembered belatedly that Oscar Wilde had been about to say something about Czastka's role in this affair when he had been interrupted by sudden anxiety about the speed of the hire car. Had he been about to confound Michael Lowenthal with the judgment that Czastka, far from being the murderer, must have been marked down as a victim? Could this be taken as proof that Czastka was not, after all, the man behind Rappaccini, but merely one more of Rappaccini's chosen victims? Or might it simply be one more joke, one more bluff?

She tried to pull herself together. The real significance of this revelation, surely, was that if Walter Czastka had been marked down as a victim, he might yet be saved—as might the mysterious fifth man. Czastka, at least, had been alive not much more than an hour ago, even though he had stopped answering his phone as soon as Oscar Wilde had talked to him.

There was no seventh face. Salome slowed in her paces, faced the sofa where Oscar and Charlotte sat watching, and took her bow.

Then the lights came on.

Charlotte had assumed that the performance was over, and its object attained, but she was wrong. What she had so far witnessed was merely a prelude.

The lights which sprang into dazzling life brought a new illusion, infinitely more spectacular than the last. Charlotte had attended numerous theatrical displays employing clever holographic techniques, and knew well enough how a black-walled space which comprised in reality no more than a few hundred cubic meters could be made to seem far greater, but she had never seen a virtual space as vast and as ornate as this.

Here was the palace in which Salome had danced, transfigured

by the phantasmagoric imagination of some later artist: a crazily
vaulted ceiling higher than that in any reconstructed medieval ca-
thedral, with elaborate stained-glass windows in mad profusion,
offering all manner of fantastic scenes. Here was a polished floor
three times the size of a sports field, with a crowd of onlookers that
must have numbered tens of thousands. There was no sense at all
of this being an actual *place:* it was an edifice born of nightmarish
dreams, whose awesome and impossible dimensions weighed down
upon a mere observer, reducing Charlotte in her own mind's eye to
horrific insignificance.

Men like Gabriel King called their quasi-organic nanotech con-
structors shamirs, after the magical entity which had helped Solomon build his temple when his laborers had been forbidden the use
of conventional tools, but this was the first time Charlotte had seen
an edifice worthy of the labor of fabulous mythical creatures.

Salome, having bowed to the three visitors from the future who
had watched her dance at far closer range than any of the fictitious
multitude, turned around to bow to another watcher: to the biblical
king of Judea, Herod, seated on his throne.

Charlotte could not remember whether Herod had been Salome's father or merely her stepfather, but she was certain that he
had been one or the other. She was certain too that there had never
been a throne like this one in the entire history of empires and
kingdoms. None but the most vainglorious of emperors could even
have imagined it; and none of them could have ordered it built. It
was huge and golden, hideously overburdened with silks and jew-
els: an appalling monstrosity of avaricious self-indulgence. It was,
Charlotte knew, intended to appall, to constitute an offense to any
taste or sense of proportion.

All of this was a calculated insult to the delicacy of effective
illusion. It was a parody of grandiosity, an exercise in profusion for
profusion's sake. And yet, she understood the kind of technological
sophistication that must have been required to produce this. She
knew how much more difficult it was to produce such a fabulous

extravaganza than it would have been to produce something which would have seemed possible and likely, on any scale.

"Do you like it?" asked the man on the throne: the *king* on the throne, who had even drawn himself three times life-size, as a bloated, overdressed grotesque.

Herod's body, even had it been reduced to a natural scale, was like nothing any longer to be seen in a world which had banished obesity four hundred years before—but the face, had it only been leaner, would have been the face which Jafri Biasiolo, alias Rappaccini, had worn in the three photographs which Hal Watson had shown to Oscar, Lowenthal, and herself the day before.

But we know that she's not his daughter, Charlotte thought. She's supposed to be his mother now!

Charlotte felt Oscar Wilde's hand take up her wrist and squeeze it. He was still invisible to her, as she was to herself, although the glorious light of the illusory palace surrounded them. "Tread carefully," Wilde whispered, his lips no more than a centimeter from her ear. "This simulation may be programmed to tell us everything, if only we can question it cunningly enough."

Herod/Rappaccini burst into mocking laughter. The sim's tumultuous flesh heaved and seethed with it: "Do you think that I have merely human ears, my dear Oscar? You can hardly see yourselves, I know, but you are not hidden from me. Your friends are charming, Oscar, but neither the woman nor the man is one of *us*. They are of an age which has forgotten and erased its past. They are neither revenants nor artists."

AI or not, thought Charlotte, it's still mad. As absolutely and irredeemably insane as the man whose simulacrum it is. She wondered whether she might be in mortal danger, if the man beside her really was the secret designer of all of this: Rappaccini's creator and puppet master.

"Gustave Moreau might have approved," Wilde said offhandedly, "but he always tended to become dispirited and leave his work half-done. His vision always outpaced his capacity for detail. Michi Ur-ashima would not have been satisfied so easily even when he was a VE technician, although I detect his early handiwork in some of the effects. Did Gabriel King supply the artificial organisms which hollowed out this Aladdin's cave, perchance?"

"He did," answered the gargantuan Rappaccini, squirming in his uncomfortable seat like a huge painted slug. "I have made art with his sadly utilitarian instruments. I have taken some trouble, as you have seen, to weave the work of all my victims into the tapestry of their destruction." The sim was obviously a high-grade silver rather than a sluggish sloth, but it was making preprogrammed speeches rather than responding with any real intelligence to Wilde's provocations.

"It's overdone," said Oscar Wilde with insultingly mild contempt. "Grotesquely overdone and more than a little chaotic. As a show of apparent madness, it's too excessive to be anything but pretense. Can we not talk as one civilized man to another, Jafri, since that is what we are?"

Rappaccini smiled. "That is why I wanted you here, my dear Oscar," he said. "Only you could suspect me of cold rationality in the midst of all this. But you understand civilization far too well to wear its gifts unthinkingly. You may be the only man in the world who understands the world's decadence, but you cannot hide that understanding from me, or deny it to my face. Have the patient bureaucrats of the United Nations police force discovered my true name yet?"

"Jafri Biasiolo?" Wilde queried. "Is that what you mean by your *true* name? I doubt it. Even Rappaccini is truer than that. Half a dozen other pseudonyms have come to light—but I doubt that we have found the *true* one yet. Would you care to tell us what it is?"

"Not Herod," said the sim. "Be sure of that, at least."

"It's only a matter of time, as you must know," Charlotte put in, unable to resist the temptation. "By the time we get back to the car, it might be all over."

The sim turned its bloodshot eyes upon her, and she could not help but shrink before the baleful stare.

"The final act has yet to be played," Rappaccini told her. "Even the penultimate phase of the drama has not yet reached its fatal climax. You may already know all of my true names, but you might still have difficulty in identifying the one which I presently use as my own, for reasons which dear Oscar will readily understand." The sardonic gaze moved again, to meet Wilde's invisible stare. "You will thank me for this evasiveness, Oscar—an element of surprise is indispensable to the enjoyment of any unfolding drama. You would never have forgiven me had I not been just that little bit *too* clever for you."

"The car chase was entirely gratuitous," said Oscar. "A jarring note of modernism in a performance which might otherwise have had the benefit of consistency, if not of coherency. I cannot concede that manifestation of cleverness."

"Consistency is the hallmark of a narrow mind," replied the sim, seemingly unworried by the criticism.

"If you wanted to kill six men," said Oscar Wilde, in a pensive tone which rather suggested that he was talking to himself rather than the AI, "why did you wait until they were almost dead? I cannot understand the *timing* of your performance. At any time in the last seventy years fate might have cheated you. Had you waited another month, you might well have been too late to find Walter Czastka alive."

"You underestimate the tenacity of men like these," Biasiolo-as-Herod replied. "You think they are ready for death because they have ceased to live, but longevity has ingrained its habits deeply in the flesh. Without me to help them, they might have protracted their misery for many years yet—even dear, sad Walter. But I am nothing if not loyal, nothing if not affectionate to those most deserving of my tenderness. I bring them not merely death but glorious transfiguration—'Mortality, Behold and Fear! What a change of flesh is here!' But even you, Oscar, can never have read Beaumont . . . the point is, dear Oscar, that the mere *fact* of death is not the central motif here. Did you think me capable of pursuing mere revenge? It is the *manner* of a man's death which is all-important in our day and age, is it not? Have we not rediscovered all the ancient joys of mourning, and all the awesome propriety of solemn ceremony and dark symbolism?

"Wreaths are not enough for the likes of us, Oscar—not even wreaths which are spiders in disguise. The death of death itself is upon us, and how shall we celebrate that, save by making a new and better compact with the grim reaper? Murder is almost extinct—but it should not be, and cannot be, and *must* not be. Murder must be rehabilitated, Oscar, made romantic and flamboyant, made gorgeous and excessive, made glamorous and hideous and larger than life. What have my six victims left to do but set an example to their younger brethren? Who is more fitted than I to appoint himself their deliverer, their ennobler, the proclaimer of their fame— and who more fitted than my beloved daughter to serve as my instrument?"

"But she's not—," Michael Lowenthal began—and Charlotte suddenly realized what should have been plain even as they sat in the car, distractedly arguing possibilities.

"She's a clone!" whispered Charlotte fiercely.

"I fear, my friend," said Wilde, loudly overriding their brief exchange, "that this performance might not make the impact that you intend. If you hope for sympathy from me, and find none, what can you expect from the world at large? Perhaps you pretend too hard to madness. If the world thinks you merely mad, they will see neither motive nor artistry in anything you may have done. For myself, I do not deny that you have intrigued me, but I have always been an unnaturally generous man. My attention is easy to capture—my approval is less so. So far, Dr. Rappaccini, I have yet to see the merit in your murders or your absurd distractions, not because they seem too clever but because they seem so stupid."

The hologrammatic sim of Rappaccini smiled again. "You will

repent that cruelty, Oscar," he said. "You must, for you are already committed, already exposed, already known to me. Your hands are bound; the privilege of disapproval was surrendered when you chose the truth of your name. You must judge me as a true liar, Oscar Wilde, and no trick of the mind or the pen can reduce what I have done to mere deception. No matter how hard you resist, I will convince you. You know in your heart that what surrounds you now is no mere rock, rough-hewn and polished for delusion's sake. You know in your heart that this marvelous appearance is real, and the hidden reality a mere nothing. This is no cocoon of hollowed stone; it is my palace. Hear me, Oscar: you will see the finest rock of all before the end."

Wilde did not reply to that immediately; Charlotte could imagine the frown of vexation which must lie upon his forehead.

"Your representations are deceptive, King Herod," she said. "Your dancing stepdaughter showed us Gabriel King's head first and foremost, but Kwiatek died before him, and I suspect that Magnus Teidemann was probably dead even before Kwiatek. It was optimistic too—we have already warned your fifth and sixth intended victims, and we intend to save them both."

Herod turned back to face her. She had not been able to deduce, so far, exactly how high a grade of artificial intelligence its animating silver had, but she hoped that it might be less clever than it seemed. It was responsive, to be sure, but much of what it said consisted of scripted speeches fairly loosely connected to the reactive remarks which prefaced them. She was not optimistic about the prospect of provoking it to reveal anything authentically useful, nor did she expect any explicit confirmation of her guess that Magnus Teidemann was indeed a victim, but she felt obliged to try.

"All six will go to their appointed doom whatever you do," the sim told her. "You do not understand what is happening here. You and your companion must look to Oscar to provide what explanations he can. If he does not understand yet, he will understand soon enough."

Charlotte noted that the sim did not use her name, even though Wilde had addressed her by her first name as they had entered; that made her feel slightly better, because it was a welcome reminder to her that the abilities of the mercurial Rappaccini were not, after all, supernatural. All this was mere artifice, albeit of Byzantine complexity. She wanted to get out now, to transmit a tape of this encounter to Hal Watson so that he could identify the fifth face—but she hesitated.

"What can these men possibly have done to you?" she asked, trying to sound contemptuous although there was no earthly point in it. "What unites them in your hatred?"

"I do not hate them at all," replied the sim, "and the link that unites them in my affections is not recorded in that silly Web built by cyberspiders to trap the essence of human experience." The image was no longer looking at her, but at Oscar Wilde. She suspected that it had somehow received the cue for another programmed speech, which it was determined to direct to the intended recipient. "I have done what I have done," the AI continued, steadfastly following its programming, "because it was absurd and unthinkable and comical. Lies have been banished from the world for far too long, and the time has come for us not merely to tell them, but to live them also. It is by no means easy to work against the grain of synthetic wood, but we must try. All this is for you, dear Oscar— the last and best gift you will ever receive."

"I think I could have done without it," said Oscar, not quite as coldly as before. "In any case, this is not my birthday. I repeat—I cannot fathom your *timing*."

"Oh, but it *is* your birthday," countered the fatuous creature on the ridiculous throne. "And you look simply *fabulous*."

And with that, darkness fell.

The gloom would have been absolute and impenetrable were it not for a single tiny pinprick of light which shone behind them, marking the door through which they had entered the underworld.

INTERMISSION FOUR

A Teacher and His Pupil

Stuart McCandless walked along the beach on the southern shore of Kauai east of Puolo Point, patiently awaiting the restoration of his subjective equilibrium. His IT had already taken charge of his heart, and his pituitary monitors would ensure that his endocrine system would soon be finely tuned and perfectly balanced, but within the gap that separated state of being from state of mind there was still a considerable margin of unease.

Stuart adjusted the brim of his hat to take better account of the angle of the afternoon sun and stared out over the quiet Pacific, fixing his eyes on the distant horizon. Although he knew that there were countless smaller islands out there, hidden by the subtle curvature of the earth, it was easy enough to imagine that the ocean went on forever, unsullied by the dabblings of the so-called continental engineers and their Creationist clients. One day, he supposed, the Hawaiian archipelago would be so extensively augmented that there would be islet eyesores by the score visible in every direction, but he counted himself fortunate to have lived in an era of relative stability, when the most ingenious efforts of the world's environmental revisionists had been directed to the repair of the damage done to the natural islands by the Greenhouse Crisis and the ecocatastrophic Crash.

The sight of the seemingly infinite sea calmed him, as it always had done, and helped him to feel that his true self had been restored to him. Ever since childhood, Stuart had been claustrophobic. He had consulted therapists of half a dozen different kinds, but their analyses and practical advice had never had the least impact on the problem. Before his second rejuve, while it still seemed that brain-feed research might yield results, he had taken as keen an interest as any nonspecialist could in the painful advance of neurophysiological science and technology, but he had waited in vain for a product that might cure him of his unwanted delicacy.

There were, of course, worse afflictions that a man might be condemned to live with for a hundred and ninety-four years, but Stuart had never been able to take comfort from that fact. His situation would not have been so bad if he had only been required to avoid such close confinement as that associated with elevators and whole-body VE apparatuses; that would have been a definite inconvenience, but not a crippling handicap. The real problem was the slow unease which crept upon him by day whenever he was confined to his house. It was not something that caused him any acute pain, and it never threw him into a panic attack no matter how long the pressure was sustained, but its very slightness was annoying. It was like an insidious internal tickling, whose effect grew by degrees until its psychological effect was out of all proportion to its sensational marginality.

In order to maintain his sense of equilibrium, he had to get out into the open for an hour or more at least once a day. That was one of the reasons why he lived on Kauai, where the air was always warm enough and rarely too hot for comfort, and where the stars were clearly visible at night in order that they might emphasize the limitlessness of the universe. That was also why he lived close to the beach, where the land met the huge and seemingly infinite sea. He had always loved beaches. All the most significant encounters in his life had taken place on beaches.

Ever since his second full rejuve, his claustrophobia seemed to be more easily aggravated than it had been before. The repair work which the nanotech shock-troops had carried out within his brain seemed to him to have increased the magnitude of the innate flaw in his makeup, if only slightly. Nowadays, it required only the merest disturbance of his routines to set him on edge and to cause the inexorable closing-in of his walls to proceed just a little bit faster.

When Inspector Watson of the UN police had called to tell him that he might be on the hit list of a mad murderer, it had not mattered in the least that the assertion was patently absurd; it had unsettled him nevertheless.

He had been angry, of course—especially when he discovered what had led Watson to contact him. "Are you calling *everyone* who was at Wollongong in 2322?" he demanded.

"Yes," Watson had replied, as if there were nothing even slightly unreasonable about the policy. "Everyone who's still alive."

"You can't possibly think that this lunatic intends to murder everybody who happened to be at university with him!"

"That's not the point," the policeman had told him, as if *he* were the one who was being obtuse. "Until we know more about his motive, we have no idea how he's selecting out his victims. All we know for sure is that the people killed so far were all at Wollongong in that year. Until we know exactly what links Gabriel King, Michi Urashima, Magnus Teidemann, and Paul Kwiatek, we can't figure out which of their contemporaries might have to be added to the list. One of the reasons we're contacting everybody is the hope that somebody who was there at the time might be able to identify the connection for us. Can you think of any such connection, Professor McCandless?"

"Don't be ridiculous," Stuart had said. "It was more than a hundred and seventy years ago. Nobody can remember that far back—and it's preposterous to think that anyone might start killing people in 2495 because of something that happened in 2322."

"The person actually delivering the fatal blow seems to be a much younger person," Watson had admitted. "We're having trouble tracking her movements because she keeps changing her appearance. I'm posting three images now—please look at them very carefully, Professor McCandless, and tell me if you recognize this person. Please bear in mind that if she is known to you, she will have confronted you with an appearance as subtly different from these as they are from one another."

"That's even more ridiculous," Stuart had told him, becoming even angrier. "Every woman nowadays aspires to one or other of the conventional ideals of beauty, Inspector, and every one has access to the technologies which allow her to secure it. As a university administrator, I've been in contact with young people all my life, and I must have known thousands of young women who sculpted their faces along those general lines. This is a small island, and there can only be a few hundred authentically young women resident here, but at least half of them could pass for one of these three if she put her mind and cosmetic skills to work on the problem. The same is true of any woman who's just undergone a first rejuve."

Watson had tried to assure him that it wasn't true, and that if he would only look carefully enough he would be able to discern certain distinguishing features, but Stuart hadn't had the time to waste. As a university administrator, he'd long grown used to seeing young people in quantity, as a kind of undifferentiated mass. Their academic records varied, but in person they were merely segments of an infinite crowd. Things were different now, of course; since retiring from administrative work to concentrate on research he no longer saw young people at all, except for Julia—but that only proved the point. Julia could have made herself look like the woman in Watson's pictures with no difficulty at all, and there was nothing unusual about Julia.

Even so, he had looked up the four victims named by the policeman, to jog his memory as to who they were and what their accomplishments had been. He had also taken a second look at the pictures, just in case he could discern something meaningful therein.

There wasn't anything meaningful. They could have been anyone. They could even have been Julia.

Stuart knew that he had to put the whole matter out of his mind now and concentrate his mind on the sea, and on infinity—but it wasn't easy. The puzzle was too intriguing. What could possibly link Gabriel King the demolition man, Michi Urashima the brainfeed buccaneer, Magnus Teidemann the econut, and Paul Kwiatek the software engineer turned VE veg?

Stuart had known them all by reputation, although he hadn't previously realized that they had all been at Wollongong at the same time, and he'd needed the encyclopedia to remind him of *exactly* what they were famous for. He must, presumably, have been aware of their simultaneous presence at the university way back in the 2320s, but the memory of the coincidence had faded long ago. Their subsequent careers had diverged as widely as those of any four individuals picked at random, and it was difficult to imagine why anyone might want all four of them dead—especially when one considered that Urashima and Kwiatek were half-dead already. There was, it seemed, a young woman involved—perhaps more than one, if Inspector Watson was incorrect in his estimation that the three pictures were all representations of the same woman— but that didn't offer any clue as to the connection. It was difficult to imagine a crime of passion involving Urashima or Kwiatek, and it seemed that the only thing about which Teidemann was capable of being passionate was his hypothetical Mother Goddess. King was surely the only one who had it in him to attract the wrath of a jealous lover, if one could believe in a lover jealous enough to kill.

Stuart *could* believe in a lover jealous enough to kill, because he knew that jealousy—like claustrophobia—was one of those soul afflictions with which nanotechnology had never quite come to grips. He could not, however, believe in a lover jealous enough to kill four times over, picking out victims who were all approaching two hundred years old. Who in the world could possibly be jealous of a man whose brain had exploded in a chaotic mess of superfluous neural connections? Or a man who had almost lost contact even with simulations of the real world, preferring expeditions into the remoter reaches of perverted perception?

"I knew I'd find you here."

The voice cut through Stuart's ruminations like a knife, and he felt his heart lurch as he started—but by the time he turned, he was in control of himself.

"Julia!" he said. "You shouldn't creep up on a man when he's just been told that he might be about to be murdered. Not a man of my age, at any rate. I'm fragile."

Her vivid green eyes seemed to be laughing, although her beautiful mouth was only slightly curved into a quizzical smile. The sultry breeze drifting from the sea was barely sufficient to stir her red-gold hair, but the hairs were so fine that her tresses shifted like the surface of the patient sea. Her hair had always seemed to Stuart to have a life of its own. "Murdered?" she echoed. "Why would anyone want to murder you?"

"They wouldn't," he answered. "They couldn't possibly. But someone, it seems, has a grudge against selected Wollongong alumni of my particular vintage. The UN police are actually calling everyone who was there at that time, fishing for a motive. And you needn't feel complacent about it—they're circulating a description of a murder suspect who's almost as beautiful as you. If you were to change the color of your hair and eyes, and apply a little synthetic flesh to the contours of your cheeks . . . you should be grateful that I know you so well and that I'm not in the least paranoid. A lesser man might have given your name to the police, and you'd be under arrest by now."

"I doubt that," Julia said, coming forward to take him by the arm and turning him so that he could walk back to the house with her. "They'd have to find me first, then catch me."

"It's a small island," he pointed out, "and there's nowhere to run or hide."

"It's big enough," she assured him. "I brought you some flowers, by the way. I put them in your living room. It's a new design, by Oscar Wilde."

"I can't quite understand your fondness for that man's work," Stuart confessed. "He's a nineteenth-century man, insofar as he's a historian at all. Not one of *us*." By *us* he meant specialists in the twenty-second century: the most eventful era in human history, when history itself had trembled on the brink of extinction; the era of the great plague, the Crash, the New Reproductive System, and the nanotech revolution.

"He designs beautiful flowers," Julia said. "He's an artist. There are very few true artists in the world."

"But he's not *original,*" Stuart said. "It's all recapitulation and recomplication."

"All human life is recapitulation and recomplication," she said, with the casual confidence of unfalsified youth.

"No, it's not," he assured her. "There are genuine ends and authentic beginnings. Conrad Helier was a *true* artist. He put an end to the old world and forged a new one. He designed the womb which ultimately gave birth to the New Human Race. He, not Eveline Hywood, was the original designer of the fundamental fabric of the alternative ecosphere—the stuff she tried to pass off as alien life after his death. You can't compare a mere flower designer to a man like that."

"According to the best evidence available," Julia said gently, "Conrad Helier only designed one of the chiasmatic transformers, and his was only the first artificial womb to be mass-produced—at best, a tiny recomplication of designs that were being produced in some profusion. The time had come to put an end to so-called natural childbirth, and it would have ended anyhow. When historians put the bloody knife in Helier's hand, it's as much a matter of scapegoating as anything else. He's the heroic villain appointed to the role, but he was just an instrument of causal process. As for Hywood's fake alien life, it was her foster son who actually worked out most of the key applications: LSP, SAP systems, shamirs, and so on. In any case, you can't call that kind of utilitarian endeavor *Art*. Art is essentially superfluous, and that's why it's so necessary to *human* existence."

"Nothing is historically superfluous," Stuart told her sternly. "Nothing is outside the causal process by which the world is made and remade. Art is merely an expression of that process, no matter what individual artists may think." It was a serious argument, but not in the sense that their disagreement might come between them as a hurdle or a moat. He and Julia had an understanding which allowed them to debate points of intellectual nicety without being divided. That, in Stuart's view, was what friendship amounted to— and in spite of the difference in their ages, he and Julia were the firmest of friends. The rapport between them went far beyond their common interest in the study of history.

"Even the art of murder?" Julia asked lightly.

"If murder were not an expression of historical causality," Stuart insisted, "it would have to be considered devoid of artistry, even by the most daring interpreter."

Stuart had always considered himself a daring interpreter. His ambition had always been to understand the whole of human history and the whole of the human world: to hold it entirely in his mind's eye, as if it were a vast panorama in which every element stood in its proper relation to every other element, a huge seamless whole whose horizons held the promise of infinity. In a way, he had to reckon himself a failure, because he knew well enough that there was a great deal which he did *not* understand, and never would understand, but he could forgive himself that inadequacy—which was, of course, an inadequacy which he shared with all other living men—because he had at least made the effort. He had never allowed himself to be intellectually *confined* in the way that men like Urashima and Teidemann had.

"You must understand that you too will fail to grasp the whole," he had told Julia when she had first come to him as his pupil. "Everyone fails, but there is no shame in failure, provided that you have set your sights widely enough. The human condition has its limitations, and always will have. Even if the genetic engineers are right in claiming that they have at last brought the human race to the very threshold of emortality, and even if the prophets of man/machine symbiosis are right in saying that the fallibility of human memory can be compensated by appropriate augmentation of the brain, there will still be limitations of understanding. A man may live forever, and remember everything, and still understand hardly anything. It is as easy—perhaps easier—to breed a race of immortal fools as a race of mental giants. The majority of men have always made fools of themselves, and the vidveg will undoubtedly continue to do so, however long they live and whatever ingenious devices may one day be connected by artificial synapses to the substance of their souls."

Julia had listened to such speeches very dutifully, in the beginning, and that had pleased him immensely—but their friendship was not based in anything as shallow as adulation. He was not in love with her; erotic orthodoxy had long ago begun to bore him, and he had never felt the least impulse to reinvest in it when the many and various unorthodoxies with which he had briefly experimented had similarly begun to pall. In fact, since becoming young for the third time Stuart had experienced a dramatic loss of libido which he had not the slightest interest in repairing. He felt—he *understood*—that there might be advantages in being old, to one who was as cerebrally inclined as he. Nor was he particularly flattered by Julia's attentiveness; he had been an educator for so very many years that he drank up the respect of pupils by sheer force of habit, not tasting it at all. If she had been more to him than a mere sounding board, which reflected his thoughts in a pleasing manner, he could not have felt as close to her as he did. He valued her disagreement as much as her agreement now; he loved to exchange ideas with her. He needed someone like her, who would not merely listen to his ideas but challenge them, playing white to his black in an endless game of intellectual chess.

Ideas were healthier when they were challenged; kept inside, in the dark and secret theater of the mind, protected from exposure, they did not flourish half so well. If ideas were to grow—and thus give birth to understanding—they must be let out, and tested.

"Will you stay for dinner?" he asked his companion. "We can eat on the veranda, if you wish. It's going to be a beautiful evening."

"Of course," she said. "But I don't know how long I can stay afterward. There's something I have to do—I have to go to one of the other islands."

"Which one?" he asked reflexively.

"One of the new ones. I have to visit a Creationist."

"Why? I didn't think they encouraged visitors." When it became clear that she did not intend to answer the question, he carried on. "You'll have to be careful—you must have heard the rumors about dinosaurs and giant spiders, and the jokes about the Island of Dr. Moreau. How long will you be away?"

"I don't know," she said. "It depends."

It occurred to Stuart that Walter Czastka was a Creationist, and that Walter Czastka had been at the University of Wollongong in 2322—and that he had once walked on a beach with him, much as he was walking with Julia now, discussing some project that Walter had dreamed up. Walter had wanted his help . . . but Stuart could no longer remember exactly what it was that Walter had wanted from him, or whether or not he had obliged.

It was on the tip of his tongue to ask Julia whether it was Walter Czastka that she intended to visit, and what she could possibly want with a man like him, but he suppressed the impulse. It would probably seem like prying motivated by jealousy.

"I'm glad that I retired here," he said, glancing briefly upward in the direction of the blazing sun, then more languorously downward at the glints that its light imparted to the crests of the lazy waves. "The heat suits me, now that I'm growing old for the final time, and I can't see the twenty-sixth century creeping up on me. There was never any but the most rudimentary agriculture here, you know, not even in the Colonial Era. The volcanoes are tame now, of course, and the bigger islands in the group were badly affected by the population movements following the plague wars, but Kauai's seen less change than almost any other place on the earth's surface since the beginning of the twenty-second century."

"But it's not the same, even so," Julia pointed out. "Every time you step indoors, it must be obvious that you're living in the present—and you're entirely a product of the present. There were no men of your antiquity in the twenty-second century."

"Granted," he said. "But still, I'd far rather live beside the blue sea than the green, and I could never be content in a valley between SAP black hills. I can still remember the days before the green seas and black hills, you know; I think my memory has held up better than most, in spite of the unease of illusory déjà vu. Sometimes I'm half-convinced that I've known you before, in the long-gone days of my first youth . . . but I understand how these tricks of the mind work. In these days of cosmetic engineering, when everyone is beautiful, it's easy to recognize in the woman one sees today some or all of the women one knew many years before, who are simply phantoms imprinted on the vanishing horizon of remembrance. . . ."

He trailed off because they had reached the threshold of his home: a place at which he always hesitated.

Although he could not bring himself to entertain the thought, let alone believe it, Stuart McCandless was fated to die very soon.

It was likely that nothing could have saved him—certainly not a better memory. What he took for an illusion of similarity was indeed an illusion, because he had recently been shown a better likeness of his darling Julia than ancient memory could possibly have preserved, and had not recognized it.

Sometimes victims collaborate in their own murders, even when they have been warned of danger—and why should they not, if they believe that murder and art are mere expressions of historical process, deft feints, and thrusts of causality?

If idiosyncrasy, madness, and genius are no more than tiny waves on a great sullen tide of irresistible causality, even a man forewarned can hardly be expected to defy their force. Stuart McCandless certainly did nothing to avoid his fate, even when the second and far more explicit warning arrived. He simply could not imagine that his pupil could be anything but what she seemed or anyone but who she pretended to be. He was old, and he was complacent. He knew that he was fated to die, but he carried in his consciousness that remarkable will to survive that refuses to recognize death even while it stares death in the face. Nor was he a fool; he was probably as knowledgeable a historian as there was in the world, and as wise a lover.

If those who tried to warn him had been able to explain to him exactly *why* he was being murdered, he would have laughed aloud in flagrant disbelief. Like the vidveg he affected to despise, and in spite of his claustrophobia, he was a man whose imaginative horizons were narrower than he knew or could ever have admitted to himself.

From Land to Sea

T he sun was setting by the time Charlotte and her companions emerged into the open; it remained visible solely because its decline had taken it into the cleft of a gap between two spiry crags.

The car had gone.

Charlotte felt her hand tighten around the bubblebugs which she had carefully removed from their stations above her eyebrows. She had been holding them at the ready, anxious to plug them into the car's systems so that their data could be decanted and relayed back to Hal Watson.

She murmured a curse. Michael Lowenthal's exclamation of distress was even louder—and the man from the MegaMall immediately reached for his handset, moving to one side to call for assistance.

Charlotte took out her beltphone and tried to send a signal, although the charge indicator suggested that the battery no longer had enough muscle to reach a relay station or a convenient comsat. Nothing happened. She muttered another curse beneath her breath, and then she turned back to Oscar Wilde.

"I should have . . . ," she began—but she trailed off when she realized that she didn't know exactly what she should have done, or even what she might have done.

"Don't worry," said Wilde. "I doubt that Rappaccini brought us up here simply to abandon us. I suspect that a vehicle of some kind will be along very shortly to carry us on our way."

"Where to?" she asked, unable to keep the asperity out of her voice.

"I don't know for certain," he said, "but I would hazard a guess that our route will be westward. We might have one more port of call en route, but our final destination will surely be the island where Walter Czastka is playing God. He is to be the final victim, and his death is presumably intended to form the climactic scene of this perfervid drama."

"We have to warn him," said Charlotte. "And we have to identify the fifth man too. If the car were here. . . ."

"Walter has already had a warning of sorts," said Oscar ruminatively. "If Hal has been able to contact him with the news that he may be Rappaccini's father. . . ." He left the sentence dangling.

"Let's hope it's not too late to tell him that we now have clear evidence of Rappaccini's intention to kill him," said Charlotte, "and let's hope the fifth man is still alive when we get a chance to find out who he is. He may be dead already, of course, like Kwiatek and Teidemann. Your ghoulish friend displayed his victims in the order in which their bodies were discovered, not the order in which they were killed."

"He was never my friend," Oscar objected, seemingly more than a little disturbed by what he had just witnessed, "and I am not at all sure that I can approve of his determination to involve me in all this."

"You should have challenged him about Czastka," Michael Lowenthal put in, having despaired of making his own call heard. "You should have told him that we've discovered that Czastka's his father."

"It was only a sim," Wilde reminded him. "It could not have been startled or tricked into telling us anything it was not primed to tell us. In any case, if the DNA evidence *can* be trusted, Rappaccini must already know that Walter is his father, even if Walter has not the slightest idea that Rappaccini is his son. As Charlotte pointed out, Rappaccini knew enough to create a modified clone of his mother—a very special stepdaughter—and he must have done so with his present purpose in mind. We must concentrate our attention on the questions I *did* ask, especially the one to which I received two different but equally enigmatic answers."

"Timing," said Charlotte, to show that she was now able to keep up. "The sim said that it *is* your birthday—by which it must mean your third rejuvenation. Is *that* what triggered this bizarre charade?"

"That was the second response," Wilde pointed out. "It required a repetition of the cue to elicit it, it was markedly different in tone from the other speeches delivered by the sim, and it was the last thing it said before shutting down. The comment had all the hallmarks of an afterthought—a belated addition to the program. Rappaccini must have known for years *approximately* when I would attempt my third rejuve, but he can only have known the exact date of my release from the hospital for eight or ten weeks—three months at the most. The real answer to the question must somehow be contained in the earlier and much more circuitous speech."

"How much of that did you actually understand?" she asked him. "I recognized the characters, but a lot of what the Herod effigy said went over my head."

"I understood most of the references," Oscar said, "if only because so many of them were to works by my ancient namesake—but the meaning hidden between the lines was by no means obvious even to me. There *was* meaning in it, though—meaning that I am intended to divine, given time. The setting was, of course, an elaboration of one of Gustave Moreau's paintings of Salome's dance, and Rappaccini's Herod made several oblique references to Wilde's essays, including 'The Decay of Lying' and 'Pen, Pencil and Poison.' "

Charlotte knew that she had heard the second title before, and was very eager to show that she was still at least one step ahead of Michael Lowenthal. "That's the one which refers to the Wainewright character Hal listed among Rappaccini's other pseudonyms," she said.

"That's right. My namesake argued there, not without a certain macabre levity, that the fact that Wainewright had been a forger and a murderer should not blind critics to the virtues of his work as a literary scholar. Indeed, the essay suggests that Wainewright's fondness for subtle murder—he was apparently a poisoner of some dexterity and skill—might be regarded as evidence of his wholeness as a person, and might provide better grounds for critical praise than his admittedly second-rate writings. The argument is not as original as it may seem—as I mentioned when the name first came up, De Quincey had earlier written an essay called 'Murder Considered as One of the Fine Arts.' The relevance of the argument to the present case is abundantly clear, I think; Rappaccini obviously regards his murders as phases in the construction of a work of art and considers them at least as estimable as his ingenious funeral wreaths. He is asking me—although I doubt that he can seriously expect me to comply—to look at them admiringly, in the same light."

Charlotte was tempted to observe that Wilde had seemed hitherto to be complying with some enthusiasm, but she could see that there was more to come and felt obliged to give explanation priority over sarcasm. "What else?" she asked, instead.

"In 'The Decay of Lying,' my namesake laments the dominance of realism in the artwork of his own day. He argues—again, rather flippantly—that there is no virtue at all in fidelity of representation, and that the glory of art lies in its unfettered inventiveness. Art, he argues, should not endeavor to be truthful or useful, nor should it limit itself to the kinds of petty deception which are committed by vulgar everyday liars—salesmen and politicians. He proposes that art should lie with all the extravagance and grandiosity of which the human imagination is capable. That is why Rappaccini asked me to judge him as a true liar. But the word *decay* is also very significant, and you will doubtless recall that the simulation said that I, of all people, should understand the world's decadence. That, I think, is a subtler—"

He broke off as Charlotte suddenly turned away, looking up into the sky. While Oscar had been speaking, his words had gradually been overlaid by another sound, whose clamor was by now too insistent to be ignored. Its monotonous drone threatened to drown him out entirely.

"There!" she said, pointing at a dark blur only half-emerged from the dazzling face of the sun. It was descending rapidly toward them, growing hugely as it did so.

The approaching craft was a light aircraft, whose engines were even now switching to the vertical mode so that it could land helicopter-fashion. Charlotte followed Wilde and Lowenthal as they hurried into the shelter of the building from which they had come, in order to give the machine space to land.

The plane was, of course, pilotless—and the first thing Charlotte saw as she hurried to the passenger cabin was a message displayed on its one and only screen which said: ANY ATTEMPT TO INTERROGATE THE PROGRAMMING OF THIS VEHICLE WILL ACTIVATE A VIRUS THAT WILL DESTROY THE DATA IN QUESTION.

She had expected that and was sufficiently glad to have access to an adequately powerful comcon. For the moment she did not care exactly where the machine might be headed. While Oscar Wilde and Michael Lowenthal climbed in behind her she plugged her beltphone into the comcon and deposited her bubblebugs in the decoder.

As soon as the doors were closed, the plane began to rise into the air.

"Hal," said Charlotte as soon as the connection was made. "Sorry to be out of touch. Vital data coming in—crazy message from Biasiolo, alias Rappaccini, delivered by sim. It's conclusive proof of Rappaccini's involvement. Pick out the face of the fifth victim and identify it for me. Send an urgent warning to Walter Czastka. And tell us what course this damn plane is following, if you can track it from orbit."

Hal Watson acknowledged the incoming information, but paused only briefly before saying: "I'm sure all this is very interesting, but I've closed the file on Jafri Biasiolo, alias Rappaccini, alias Gustave Moreau. We're now concentrating all our efforts on the woman. We assume that she's a modified clone of Maria Inacio, illegally and secretly created by Biasiolo before his death."

"Death!" Charlotte echoed, dumbfounded by the news. "When? How?"

Unfortunately, Hal was busy decanting the data from her bubblebug and didn't reply immediately. There was a long, frustrating pause. Wilde and Lowenthal were waiting just as raptly as she was.

Charlotte filled in time by looking around the cabin. The airplane was a small one, built to carry a maximum of four passengers. Again, Lowenthal had been left to play odd man out. Behind the second row of seats there was a curtained section, but the curtains were drawn back, allowing her to see the four bunks it contained. That implied that they were in for a long flight—and the plane's engine seemed distinctly fainthearted. They were traveling no faster than they had on the maglev or the transcontinental superhighway.

"Hal!" she said as soon as her colleague's image appeared on the inset screen. "What do you mean, you've *closed the file*? The tape is proof of Rappaccini's involvement."

"He's *dead*, Charlotte," Hal repeated, calmly emphasizing the crucial word. "He's been dead all along. I found the new identity he took up after his rejuvenation, with the aid of a much-changed appearance, as soon as I'd cut through the obfuscations in the leases pertaining to the artificial islands in the vicinity of Kauai. Actually, he'd established half a dozen fake identities under various pseudonyms, but the one he appears to have used for everyday purposes is the late Gustave Moreau. As Moreau, Biasiolo leased an islet west of Kauai; he's been Walter Czastka's nearest neighbor for the last forty years. He's spent most of the last quarter century on the islet, never leaving it for more than three or four weeks at a time. According to the official records, he was alone there, but we now presume that he was taking advantage of the quarantine gifted to all Creationists in order to bring up his mother's clone. All of this was carefully obscured, of course, but it was just a matter of digging down. We've touched bottom now—everything's in place except the location and arrest of the woman."

"The late Gustave Moreau," Charlotte repeated, glancing sideways at Oscar Wilde. It had been Wilde, she remembered, who had said that the Moreau name was just part of a series of jokes, not worth taking seriously—but that was before they had seen the "play" whose stage set was based on a painting by the original Gustave Moreau. Was it possible, she wondered, that Biasiolo/Rappaccini/Moreau had gone out of his way to involve Wilde in this comedy simply because he, like Wilde, had taken the name of a nineteenth-century artist fascinated by the legend of Salome?

"That's right," Hal replied patiently. "Gustave Moreau, alias Rappaccini, alias Jafri Biasiolo, died six weeks ago in Honolulu. The precise details of his conception might be lost in the mists of obscurity, but every detail of his death was scrupulously recorded before the body was released. According to the boatmaster who handled Moreau's supplies, the corpse was shipped back to the islet—where the mysterious foster daughter presumably took delivery of it. There's no doubt that the dead man *was* Biasiolo; I'd have found the DNA match if I'd only thought to check Biasiolo's record against the register of the dead as well as the living. It was the same error of omission I initially made with the woman's DNA, delaying her identification as an Inacio clone.

"The comcon links to Moreau's island haven't been closed down, but there's no one answering at present. The boatmaster says that he's been shipping equipment and bales of collapsed LSP from the islet to Kauai for over a year, every time he's made a supply drop. According to him, there's virtually nothing left on the islet except for the ecosystem which Moreau built—and, presumably, his grave. The UN will send a team in to examine and record the ecosystem. Under normal circumstances it would probably take three months or so to put the people together and another three before they finished the job, but in view of the biohazard aspect of the case I've put Regina Chai in charge and I've asked her to make all possible speed. She and her team will be there before the end of the week."

"But Biasiolo's still *responsible* for all this, isn't he?" Charlotte protested, again glancing sideways at Oscar Wilde. Wilde was staring upward with an expression of annoyance on his face which strongly implied that he was mentally kicking himself for failing to deduce that it was Rappaccini's death which had determined the timing of this remarkable posthumous crime. "He must have set it all up before he died. The woman is obviously implicated, but what we just saw in that cellar must have been put in place years ago—and it must have taken years to build up, if what you say about Biasiolo never leaving the islet for more than a month at a time is true."

"Agreed," said Hal. "But we can't charge a dead man. *She's* the one we want—the one we need. The evening news broke the full story of the sequence of murders—the story so far, at any rate. I don't know how much the MegaMall will hold back, but now that they know for sure that this isn't aimed at them, however obliquely, I suspect they'll just sit back and enjoy the show along with everybody else. The news tapes haven't identified the killer, of course, but they know what's going on. By now there'll be a whole swarm of hoverflies heading for Kauai and Biasiolo's island."

Charlotte turned to look at Michael Lowenthal, who did indeed have the air of a man who had decided to sit back, even if the remainder of the show afforded him little enjoyment. His face was a picture of misery—presumably because even he had now been forced to accept that Walter Czastka was not the guilty party. Given that the assassination of Gabriel King had not been aimed at the MegaMall he must now be regretting that he had ever become involved in the investigation at all.

"You haven't picked her up yet," Charlotte said, slowly realizing that it wasn't over yet. "You don't even know where she is."

"We think we know where she's going," Hal replied. "She's headed for Walter Czastka's island."

"Not *directly*!" Charlotte said, her voice suddenly insistent. "Look at the tape, Hal! There's a fifth intended victim—one she's set out to hit before she gets to Czastka. His face is on the tape!"

"*If* the tape has any significance," Hal replied with reflexive skepticism. "It looks to me like a shoddy version of the dance of the seven veils!" He obviously had it set up on one of his screens, and he was playing it through.

Charlotte didn't bother to congratulate him on his perspicacity. "Fast-forward to the severed head!" she said urgently. "Track the changes!"

"I don't think he'll be able to reach her before we do," Oscar Wilde said softly. "As slow as this glorified giant hoverfly is, I suspect that we've been given the fastest available track to the climax of the psychodrama. That's the way it's been planned, at any rate. Whoever the fifth man is, he's probably already dead—perhaps for some time. I understand now why the simulacrum said that we might have difficulty identifying the true name among the false, for reasons which I would understand. He must have thought of Moreau as his *true* name, by then—but he knew that the coincidence would make me assume that it was a mere pseudonym. There must be more hints hidden in the tape. I must talk to Walter again, if I can only get through."

"The fifth face is Stuart McCandless," said Hal suddenly. "We already had him in the frame as a possible victim. We've spoken to him once and shown him pictures of the woman, so he's been warned already. I'm trying to get through to him again now—his house AI says that he's out walking. It's sent out a summoner. Oh, and your plane's heading is a few degrees south of due west—dead on course for Kauai."

This, at least, was one datum of which Charlotte was already aware; the blood red sun was slipping inexorably toward the horizon almost dead ahead of them, and its last rays would soon be teasing the surface of the ocean.

"I'll try to get through to McCandless again," Hal said. "I'll alert the local police as well—and I'll picture-search everyone who's arrived on the island since our busy murderess left San Francisco."

Charlotte's fingers were still resting on the rim of the keyboard, claiming it for her own, but Oscar Wilde put his hand on top of hers, gently insistent. "I *have* to call Walter," he said. "Hal will take care of McCandless."

Charlotte let Wilde take control of the comcon, although she felt, uncomfortably, that she should not be allowing her authority to slip away so easily. She, after all, was still the investigating officer. Oscar Wilde was only a witness. She no longer thought he was a murderer, but that didn't affect the fact that *he* was the one who should only be along for the ride, if he had any entitlement to be here at all.

Wilde's call was fielded by a sim, which looked considerably healthier than the real Walter Czastka.

"This is Oscar Wilde," said the geneticist. "I need to talk to Walter. It's extremely urgent."

"I'm not taking any calls at present," said the simulacrum flatly.

"Don't be ridiculous, Walter," said Wilde impatiently. "I know you're listening in. I know that the police have told you exactly what's going on, even if you haven't had the courtesy to acknowledge it. This is no time to go into a sulk. We have to talk."

The sim flickered, and its image was replaced by Czastka's actual face. "What do you *want*, Oscar?" he said, his voice taut with aggravation. "This is nothing to do with you."

"I'm afraid that you're a player in this game whether you like it or not, Walter," Wilde said soothingly. "I know it's a nuisance, but we really do have to try to figure out why your natural son and next-door neighbor intends to kill you."

"I'm not in any danger and I don't need protection," said Walter in a monotone that was as replete with stubbornness as it was with weariness. "There's no one else on the island, and no one has been here. No one can land here without the house systems knowing about it. I can seal all the doors and windows if I need to. I'm perfectly safe and I don't need any assistance. I never heard of anyone called Jafri Biasiolo and I never had the slightest suspicion that I had fathered a child, let alone the lunatic on the next island over. I can't think of any reason why he or anyone else should want to murder me." It sounded to Charlotte like a rehearsed speech—one that he had probably recited more than once to the UN police. It also sounded to Charlotte like a pack of lies: a refusal to cooperate, or even to acknowledge the problem, whose pigheadedness would not have been out of place in the fake personality of a low-grade sloth.

"I don't think Rappaccini's motive is conventional, Walter," said Wilde, "but the six intended victims of his murderous sequence certainly weren't chosen at random. There must be *some* kind of connection linking you to King, Urashima, Kwiatek, Teidemann, and McCandless, and it must be something that happened when you were all at Wollongong. It must have to do with the circumstances in which you fathered a child with Maria Inacio."

Charlotte noted that Walter Czastka looked astonishingly pale. His eyes were unblinking, his features set firm.

"As I told your friends, Oscar," Czastka said in a voice devoid of all emotion, "*I don't remember.* Nobody remembers what they were doing a hundred and seventy years ago. *Nobody.* I have no memory of ever having met Maria Inacio. None."

Lies, thought Charlotte. He knows everything—but he's determined not to let us in on the secret. It won't work. Everything will come out, and everyone will know. Now that Rappaccini has recruited the vidveg as well as Wilde, everyone will be interested. That's what Rappaccini intended.

"I'm not sure that I can believe that, Walter," said Wilde, treading very softly indeed. "We forget almost everything, but we can always remember the things which matter most, if we try hard enough. This is something which matters, Walter. It matters now, and it mattered then. Are you certain that you don't know the woman whose picture they showed you—the Inacio clone? The others all seemed to know her—perhaps you've met her too? She seems to have been born and raised on the island next to yours—perhaps you met her in Kauai."

"I *can't*." The word was delivered with such sudden bitterness and flaring anguish that Charlotte flinched.

Wilde didn't react to the unexpected outburst. "What about you and Gustave Moreau, Walter?" he asked soothingly. "You obviously didn't know that Moreau was Rappaccini, let alone that he was your son, but how did you get on with him as a neighbor? Was there some special hostility between you? Why did you describe him as a lunatic just now?"

"I've hardly ever *seen* Moreau," said Czastka, his annoyance almost incandescent. "His island may be nearer to mine than any other, but it's still way over the horizon. I may have bumped into him on Kauai a couple of times, but I never said more than half a dozen words to him. He has a reputation for eccentricity among the islanders, but so does every Creationist. I shouldn't have echoed the opinion of the ignorant by calling him a lunatic just because I've got sick of hearing the jokes—*you'd* probably appreciate the humor in them, but I never have. The Island of Dr. Moreau—get it? You've probably even *read* the damn thing. We all keep ourselves to ourselves out here—surely you understand *that*. All I want to do is to *keep myself to myself*. Do you get the message, Oscar? I don't want protection from the UN police and I certainly don't want *you* interfering in my business. *I just want to be left alone*."

There was a brief silence while Oscar Wilde paused for thought.

"Do you *want* to die, Walter?" he asked finally. It was not an aggressive question, and the inflection suggested that it was not rhetorical.

"No," said Czastka sourly. "I want to live forever, like you. I want to be young again, like you. But if I do die, I don't want flowers by Rappaccini at my funeral, and I don't want anything of yours. If I do die, I want all the flowers to be *mine*. Is that clear?"

"Given that he must have known for a long time what you never did—that he was your biological son—why should Rappaccini have hated you?" Wilde asked, trying as hard as he could to make the question seem innocuous, although it was obviously anything but.

"I don't know," Walter Czastka said resentfully. "*I* don't hate anyone. It's not in my nature to hate. It's not supposed to be in anyone's nature anymore, is it? Didn't we leave the era of hatred behind after the Crash, when Conrad Helier and PicoCon saved the world with the New Reproductive System and dirt-cheap longevity? We don't hate one another anymore because we don't expect other people to love us, and we don't feel slighted when they don't. This is the Era of Courtesy, the Era of Common Sense, when *all* emotion is mere histrionic display. I was born a little too early to adapt myself fully to its requirements, but you and Rappaccini always seemed to me to have mastered the art completely. I don't even hate *you*, Oscar. I don't hate you, I don't hate Rappaccini, I don't hate Gustave Moreau, and I certainly don't expect any of *you* to hate *me*. You don't hate me, do you, Oscar? You might despise me, but you don't hate me. You wouldn't want to kill me—why should you take the trouble, when you think I'm hardly alive to begin with? Why should *anyone* take the trouble?"

The heat of Czastka's bitterness had faded while he spoke, its near incandescence cooling into ashen SAP black, but Charlotte couldn't begin to figure out why the Creationist had felt the need to say all that.

"I think we're on our way to see you, Walter," said Oscar Wilde placidly. "I don't know how long it will take us to get there—quite some time, I expect, given the stately progress we're making at present. I hope everything will be all right when we get there. We can talk then."

"Damn you, Oscar Wilde," said the old man. "I don't want you on my island. You stay away, do you hear? I don't want to talk to you. I've said everything I have to say. You stay away from me. *Stay away!*" He broke the connection without waiting for any response.

Oscar turned sideways to look at Charlotte. His face looked slightly sinister in the dim light of the helicopter's cabin.

"He knows," he said. "He may not understand exactly why Rappaccini wants to kill him, but he knows what's behind it. The strange thing is that although he doesn't care at all about the possibility of being murdered, there's still something he *does* care about. I think I understand, now, what Rappaccini has done, and maybe even why he's done it—but only in broad terms. There's still a devil somewhere in the detail. Maybe if I can talk to McCandless. He lives on Kauai; he must know Walter and Rappaccini, alias Moreau. He may even have made up some of the jokes that Walter found so strangely objectionable—after all, there can't be many people on Kauai familiar with the work of H. G. Wells."

"Why don't you let me do this one?" Charlotte asked as politely as she could. "I *am* supposed to be the detective, after all."

Wilde's answering smile was very faint. The cabin lights had come up automatically as darkness had fallen, but they seemed somewhat lacking in power, like the plane itself.

"Please do," he said as infuriatingly as ever. Despite what Walter Czastka had said about the Era of Courtesy and the obsolescence of hatred, it wasn't too difficult for Charlotte to imagine that a man like Oscar Wilde might be hated—or that a man like Oscar Wilde might be capable of hate.

It didn't take as long as Charlotte had expected to get through to the ex-vice-chancellor. Hal had obviously been at his most brisk and businesslike. As she had also expected, Stuart McCandless was not answering his phone in person, but this time there was no need for begging or blustering. She simply fed his sim her authority codes and it summoned him to the comcon without delay.

"Yes?" he said, his dark face peering at her with slightly peevish surprise. He would be able to see that she was in a vehicle of some kind, but he wouldn't necessarily be able to identify it as a plane. "I'm still going through the data you people dumped into my system, although I'm sure that it's quite unnecessary. It's going to take some time to look at it all. I promised that I'd get back to you as soon as I could—this isn't helping."

"I'm Sergeant Charlotte Holmes, UN police, Professor Mc-Candless," she said. "I'm in an airplane which has apparently been programmed by Gustave Moreau, alias Rappaccini. He seems intent on providing my companion, Oscar Wilde, with a good seat from which to observe this unfolding melodrama. We're heading out into the ocean from the American coast. We don't know what destination has been filed, but we may well be heading your way, and I'm afraid that the killer might get there ahead of us. Have you ever met Moreau?"

"Once or twice. I know very little about him, except for the jokes that people tell. To the best of my knowledge, I've never seen his alleged foster daughter on Kauai, and I certainly can't imagine that he or she could have anything against me." McCandless's voice was by no means as bitter as Walter Czastka's, but he did seem petulantly resentful. He plainly did not believe that anyone might be trying to kill him, in spite of the fact that the only thing the four known victims had in common was an item of biography that he shared.

"Have you remembered anything about your time at Wollongong that might link you to the four dead men and Walter Czastka?" Charlotte demanded, desperate to get something from the interview to justify the fact that she had placed the call in Wilde's stead. "Anything at all?"

McCandless shook his head reflexively but vigorously. "I've already answered these questions," he said irritably. "I've tried—"

"But you've looked at the tapes of the girl who visited Gabriel King and Michi Urashima, haven't you? Are you certain that you'd be able to recognize her if she altered her disguise yet again?"

"I'd be able to study your tapes more closely if you'd allow me time to do it, Sergeant Holmes," McCandless snapped back. "I'm looking at them now, but quite frankly, in these days of ever-changing appearances it's almost impossible to recognize *anyone* except people one knows intimately. I don't know whether the person in those pictures is twenty years old or a hundred. I've had dozens of students who were similar enough to be able to duplicate her appearance with a little effort—perhaps hundreds. I've a guest here with me now who would only need a little elementary remodeling to resemble any one of a hundred people I see on TV every day—and your suspect could do exactly the same."

For the second time within a quarter of an hour Charlotte felt Oscar Wilde's hand fall upon hers, exercising significant pressure. This time it was quite unnecessary. The moment the meaning of McCandless's words had become clear she had felt a veritable chill in her blood. She was already trying to work out how best to phrase the next statement in such a way as not to seem crazy.

"How well do you know this *visitor*, Professor McCandless?" she asked, astonished by the evenness of her tone.

"Oh, there's not the slightest need to worry," McCandless replied airily. "I've known her for years. Her name is Julia Herold. I've just told your colleague in New York all about her—I'm sure he's checking her out, and equally sure that he'll find everything in perfect order."

"Could you ask her to come to the phone?" asked Charlotte. She looked sideways at Oscar Wilde, certain that he would share the agony of her helplessness. Even Michael Lowenthal was paying attention again, leaning avidly between the seats so that he could see the image on the screen.

"Yes, of course—she's here now," McCandless replied. He turned away, saying, "Julia?" Moments later he moved aside, surrendering his place in front of the camera to a young woman, apparently in her early twenties. The young woman stared into the camera with beguiling frankness. As McCandless had said, she could have altered her face, with the aid of subtle cosmetic resculpturing, to duplicate the features of any of a hundred female newscasters and show hosts. She could also be the woman Charlotte had seen in the tapes—but there was no single point of absolute similarity, and nothing that would have tipped off a superficial scan search. Her abundant hair was golden red and very carefully sculptured; it could easily have been a wig. Her eyes were a vivid green, but the color could easily have been a bimolecular overlay. Charlotte knew that Hal must be moving heaven and earth in the hope of finding one point of absolute proof that he could take back to the smug idiot who could not comprehend what danger he was in—but she knew too that Hal must know that he was already too late to save McCandless. The local police must be on their way to the house, but Charlotte had no idea how long it would take them to arrive, and there was no way to protect McCandless from infection.

"I'm sorry to disturb you, Miss Herold," said Charlotte slowly. "As you presumably know, we're investigating a series of rather bizarre murders, and it's very difficult to determine what information may be relevant."

"I understand," said the woman calmly. She seemed utterly unperturbed by the situation, and Charlotte couldn't help remembering Wilde's suggestion that she might not have the slightest idea of the effect that her kisses were having on her victims.

Charlotte felt a strange pricking sensation at the back of her neck. It's her, she thought. I'm actually talking to the killer—so what on earth do I say? She remembered, uncomfortably, how she had felt very nearly the same about Oscar Wilde, in eerily similar circumstances.

"Have you seen the news this evening?" Charlotte asked.

"Yes, I have," Julia Herold replied. "But as I told your colleague, I never met Gabriel King or Michi Urashima, and I've never been to New York or San Francisco, let alone Italy or central Africa."

She's playing with us, Charlotte thought. She's deliberately tantalizing us. She has McCandless in the palm of her hand and there's no way we can save him—but she'll never get away with it. Not this time. She can't make another move without our knowing about it.

"May I talk to Dr. McCandless again?" she asked dully.

They switched places again. Charlotte wanted to say, "Whatever you do, don't kiss her!" but she knew how very stupid it would sound.

"Professor McCandless," she said uncomfortably, "we think that something might have happened when you were a student yourself. Something that links you, however tenuously, with Gabriel King, Michi Urashima, Paul Kwiatek, Magnus Teidemann, and Walter Czastka. We need to know what it was. We understand how difficult it is to remember, but . . ."

"I didn't know them all," McCandless said, controlling his irritation. "I've set a silver to check back through my own records, trying to turn something up. I've always kept good records—if there's anything at all, it will be there. I hardly know Walter, even though he lives less than a couple of hundred kilometers away across the water. He keeps himself to himself, as Moreau does. The others I know only by repute. I didn't even remember that I was contemporary with Urashima or Teidemann until your people jogged my memory. There were thousands of students at the university, even then. We didn't even graduate in the same year—I've established that much. We were never together, unless. . . ."

"Unless what, Dr. McCandless?" said Charlotte quickly.

The dark brow was furrowed and the eyes were glazed as the man reached for some fleeting, fugitive memory. "There was a time with Walter . . . at the beach . . ." Then, instantly, the face became hard and stern again. "No," he said firmly. "I really can't remember anything solid. If you want my help, you must let me go back to the documents—but I'm certain that it's just a coincidence that I was at Wollongong at the same time as the men who've been murdered."

Charlotte saw a slender hand descend reassuringly upon Stuart McCandless's shoulder, and she saw him take it in his own, thankfully. She knew that there was no point in asking what it was that he had half remembered. He couldn't believe that it was important, and he couldn't remember exactly what had taken place. He was shutting her out.

It's happening now, she thought, before our very eyes. She's going to kill him within the next few minutes, if she hasn't already. And we can't do a thing to stop her—but we can surely stop her before she gets to Walter Czastka. This is the last.

"Professor McCandless," she said. "I have reason to believe that you're in mortal danger. I have to advise you to isolate yourself completely—and I mean *completely*. Please send Miss Herold away—*and do it now*. Whatever you believe or don't believe, I beg you not to have any further physical contact with her. I have no doubt at all that your life is at stake."

"Oh, don't be so stupid," McCandless retorted testily. "I know how the mind of a policeman works, but I have a far better understanding of my present situation than you do, Sergeant Holmes. I can give you my absolute assurance that I'm in no danger whatsoever. Now, please may I get on with the work which your colleague asked me to do?"

"Yes," she said numbly. "I'm sorry." She let him break the connection; she didn't feel that she could do it herself. She found the futility of her attempted intervention appalling.

When the screen went blank, Charlotte turned to Oscar Wilde and said: "He's already dead, isn't he? He doesn't know it yet, but he's infected. Nothing we could have done would have stopped it."

"The seeds may well be taking root in his flesh as we speak," Wilde agreed. "If Julia Herold is the Inacio clone—and I say *if*, because it is still conceivable that she is not, although neither of us dares to believe it—then Professor McCandless had secured his own doom before you or Hal Watson had any reason to contact him."

"What was it that he started to say, I wonder?" she whispered. "Why did he stop and blank it out?"

"Something that came to mind in spite of his resistance," Wilde said. "Something he didn't really *want* to remember. Something, perhaps, that Walter remembers too, if only he dared admit it. . . ."

" 'There was a time with Walter at the beach,' " Michael Lowenthal quoted speculatively. "Assuming that he didn't mean a tree, he must have been referring to something that happened at a beach. Maybe that's where Czastka met Maria Inacio—maybe it's where they *all* met Maria Inacio. A party, do you think? Six drunken students, who hardly knew one another . . . ?"

"That *might* make sense," Oscar Wilde conceded thoughtfully. "If Rappaccini had reason to think that any one of them might have been his biological father, and that Walter was merely the unlucky one. . . ."

Charlotte felt that duty required more urgent action from her than joining in with speculative games. She called Hal. "Julia Herold," she said shortly. "Have you tied her in with Moreau yet? She *has* to be the killer."

"I've no proof yet," Hal replied impatiently. "The records say that she's a student at the University of Hawaii. She lives on Kauai. Although McCandless is retired from administration, he still does research—he's a historian, specializing in the twenty-second century. That's Herold's main area of interest too. According to the official record, Herold's been on Kauai all along—but I'm double-checking everything, and there's a distinct possibility that the woman is a masquerader, not really Herold at all. If there's disinformation in there, the seams will come apart in a matter of minutes, but it'll be too late to save McCandless."

"She's the one," said Charlotte. "Whatever the superficial data flow says, she's been halfway around the world in the last few days, killing people all the way. It's all in place, Hal—everything except the reason. You've got to stop her from leaving the island. Whatever else happens, you mustn't let her get to Czastka."

"I've already taken care of *that*," said Hal. "Even if she's exactly who she says she is, she's going nowhere tonight. Every exit is blocked, right down to the last rowboat—I can assure you of that."

"Who's Julia Herold's father?" Oscar Wilde put in. "Whose child is she supposed to be?"

"Both egg and sperm were taken from the banks, according to the records," said Hal. "Both donors are long dead. I can give you a list of the coparents who filed the application to foster, if you like—there are six names on the form. I haven't had time to talk to any of them, but I'm still checking to make sure that their Julia Herold and the woman with McCandless are the same. It might all be irrelevant."

"Who are the biological parents supposed to have been?"

"The sperm was logged in the name of Lothar Kjeldsen, born 2225, died 2317. The ovum is annotated 'Deposited c.2100, Mother Unregistered.' That's not surprising—when the sterility plague hit hard, scientists were stripping healthy ova from every uninfected womb they could locate, including embryos. No duplicate pairing registered, no other posthumous offspring registered to either parent. Nothing significant."

"You're right," Wilde conceded readily. "If the killer is merely masquerading as Julia Herold for the sake of temporary convenience, we should return our attention to *her* origins. If my memory serves me right, Dr. Chai's original report concerning the DNA traces recovered from Gabriel King's apartment implied that the evidence of somatic engineering was unusual—idiosyncratic was the word she used, I think."

"Regina was being typically cautious," Hal said. "DNA traces recovered from crime scenes always show some effects of somatic engineering, but it's usually straightforwardly cosmetic. The Inacio clone has had orthodox cosmetic treatment, but that's by no means all. After due consideration, Regina now thinks that the engineering was more fundamental than somatic tinkering. She also says that no matter how unlikely it sounds, the differences obscuring the Biasiolo/Czastka consanguinity almost certainly resulted from embryonic engineering, not from subsequent somatic modification."

"That was something that bothered me before," Wilde said. "I couldn't believe that there'd been any considerable somatic modification to a child born in 2323—but the alternative is even more astonishing. How did Maria Inacio die?"

"She drowned, in Honolulu. The records say that it was *presumed* accidental, which means that whoever conducted the inquest thought there was a possibility that it was suicide. I'm not sure where this is taking us, Dr. Wilde, and I have whole panels lighting up on me here—I'll have to cut you off."

The screen immediately went blank yet again.

"In the story, Rappaccini's daughter was raised among poisons," Wilde murmured. "She acquired her immunities—but we do things differently nowadays. Rappaccini worked on her embryo to provide her immunities, whatever they are. If he'd duplicated a Zaman transformation, Regina Chai would have spotted the rip-off, but if it was his own variation on the theme, inspired by a different basal template if not actually developed from it. . . ."

"It won't help her when we catch her," Charlotte put in ominously. "And we *will* catch her—she can't get away from Kauai. With Biasiolo dead, she'll have to stand alone in court. Even if she pleads insanity, she's likely to go into the freezer for a very long time. Even the most rabid antisusanists are unlikely to rally to her defense. At the end of the day, there are some people who simply can't be allowed to pollute the world the rest of us live in. If Biasiolo *did* build the corruption into her genes, that makes her all the more dangerous."

"That's the weakest point of the whole argument," Wilde said. "Rappaccini would never have let this happen if he thought that his mother-daughter would have to bear the full weight of the law's vengeance. And you're wrong about her not being able to get away from Kauai. She *will* get to Walter. I don't know how, but she will—even if she has to swim."

The "condolence card" among the flowers that had been found in Paul Kwiatek's apartment read:

> *Cette vie est un hôpital où chaque malade est possédé du désir de changer de lit. Celui-ci voudrait souffrir en face du poêle, et celui-là croit qu'il quérirait à côté de la fenêtre.*

"This life is a hospital," Oscar Wilde translated, squinting slightly at the words displayed on the screen, "where each sick man is possessed by the desire to change his bed. This one yearns to suffer by the stove, that one believes that he would get better by the window."

"What's that supposed to mean?" Charlotte demanded. Hal Watson's computers had already identified the text as the opening passage of a prose poem by Baudelaire entitled—in English—"Anywhere out of the World."

"It means," said Wilde, "that everyone in the world is ill at ease, or believes himself to be misfortunate. It means that no man can help thinking that if only he were in someone else's situation, he would feel much better. If I remember correctly, the piece extends as a hypothetical dialogue between the poet and his uncommunicative soul, in which the poet interrogates his inner being as to where, exactly, he might find his own fulfillment. The soul replies, at long last, with the words which supply the poem with its title."

Charlotte scrolled down a little way. "It says here," she remarked, "that the title was taken from the works of Edgar Allan Poe, which Charles Baudelaire had translated into French."

"What exceedingly dutiful programs your colleague has!" said

Wilde sarcastically. "Does it, perhaps, also observe that 'Anywhere out of the World' was Jean Des Esseintes's favorite among Baudelaire's prose poems?"

"No," she said. "But I can get a readout on this Jean Des Esseintes if it would help."

"It wouldn't," Oscar assured her.

"Look," said Charlotte, carefully letting her annoyance show. "Does all of this stuff mean something, or not? Because if it doesn't, I think I'd like to get some sleep. We're still a long way from Hawaii, but it's midsummer and dawn will probably break before we get to Czastka's island—and I really don't see the point in waiting up for news of Stuart McCandless. The fool wouldn't listen. . . ."

"So fate will doubtless take its course," Wilde finished for her. "And yes, *all* of this means something, if only to Rappaccini. Whether it will help *us* to discover what it means is a different matter. If your interest is confined to the possibility of interrupting the unfolding tragedy before it reaches its end, and the probability of making an arrest, I fear that any tentative explanation I can offer will seem irrelevant."

Charlotte felt that she was being subtly insulted, or at least cunningly challenged. Despite the fact that she had done little for the last thirty-six hours but sit in vehicles, she felt physically exhausted and direly in need of rest. On the other hand, she hated to think that Wilde might be treating her with thinly veiled contempt.

"If you have *any* kind of explanation," she said, "I really would be glad to hear it."

"So would I," said Michael Lowenthal. "The other one seems even weirder than that one, even though it's in English." He meant the legend on the condolence card found in Magnus Teidemann's tent—which they had inspected first, because it had been in English.

Oscar Wilde nodded, with a faint smile which somehow contrived to suggest that he had intended both of them to reply in exactly that fashion.

"As the UN's dutiful silver observed," Wilde said, "the card left with Teidemann's body carried lines abstracted from a poem called 'Athanasia,' which is one of my namesake's finest. The poem as a whole speaks—symbolically, of course—of the discovery of a seed closed 'in the wasted hollow' of the hand of a mummy exhumed from an Egyptian pyramid. The seed, when sown, produces 'a wondrous snow of starry blossoms' which outshines all other flowers in the eyes of the insects and the birds. Unlike ourselves, who 'live beneath Time's wasting sovereignty' the miraculous plant is 'a child of eternity.'

"I think we must look for that text's significance in terms of a series of inversions. Rappaccini's flowers are, of course, more often black than white, and their function is to emphasize that the wasting sovereignty of time still extends over those who once hoped to find themselves ranked among the first fragile children of eternity. When the victims of this crime were born, you see, the great majority of people were only just awakening to the fact that the nanotech escalator had stalled: that serial rejuvenation could not and would not preserve human life forever, and that the extra years bought by any future suite were extremely unlikely to carry its users into an era when further extensions would be routinely available. By the time that Rappaccini was born, it was virtually taken for granted that the quest for human emortality would have to make a new beginning. It was necessary to go back to the drawing board, in more ways than one."

"We don't know for sure, as yet, that the Zaman transformation will be any more effective in beating the Miller effect than core-tissue rejuve," Michael Lowenthal modestly pointed out. "We hope—"

"That's precisely my point," said Oscar Wilde. "You hope. The generations of the twenty-second and twenty-third centuries *hoped*. Even men born at the very dawn of the twenty-fourth, in 2301, still *hoped*, although they became aware eventually that their hopes had been ill-founded because their nanotech idols couldn't beat the Mil-

ler effect. Rappaccini and I, on the other hand, belonged to generations whose members *knew* from the beginning—as the men of
the nineteenth and twentieth centuries had known—that eventual
extinction of the personality was inevitable. We grew up knowing
that our own makers, and their makers before them, had made a
mistake. They had contentedly put all their eggs into the basket of
nanotechnology, trusting that even if the escalator effect did not
carry them all the way to true emortality it would surely carry their
children. That unwarranted trust, Michael, could easily be seen as
a kind of betrayal. I have forgiven my own foster parents, although
I think that Charlotte may one day find it a great deal more difficult
to forgive hers—and however paradoxical it may sound, it may be
that Jafri Biasiolo might have found it even more difficult to forgive
the still-mysterious circumstances of his own conception."

"That's nonsense," said Lowenthal sharply. "Even if Maria Inacio was raped by Walter Czastka and five others—"

"Actually," Wilde interrupted him, "I prefer your earlier hypothesis to the gang-rape scenario—the one you formed when you
still presumed that Biasiolo had been conceived in the orthodox
manner, and were thinking in terms of dares, challenges, and ini-
tiations to student secret societies. Until we have better reason to
do so, however, I think we should resist the temptation to jump to
conclusions which are nasty *or* silly. I can assure you that what I
have said is *not* nonsense. There *was* a point in history when it was
abruptly realized that our whole approach to the problem of emortality had been seriously misled, and that the commercial monopoly
established by the men who had begun to think of themselves as
the Gods of Olympus had cost us dear. Professor McCandless, if
he is still alive, would doubtless be able to tell you that the Ahasuerus Foundation continued to plough a lone furrow throughout
the era of PicoCon's economic dominance, refusing to admit that
nanotechnological techniques of rejuvenation were ever anything
more than superficial. If others had followed the example of their
funding policies, the Zaman transformation—or something very

like it—might have been available at least a century before your conception."

"A hundred and thirty-four years ago," Charlotte murmured. Oscar Wilde ignored her.

"What is incontrovertible," the geneticist said in a more level tone, "is that Jafri Biasiolo, alias Rappaccini, alias Gustave Moreau, devoted his life to the design and manufacture of funeral wreaths—and whatever else this series of murders may be, it is Rappaccini's own funeral wreath. All its gaudy display, including the invitation sent to me, is explicable in those terms, and *only* in those terms. Rappaccini has supplied materials to so many funerals that he must have decided a long time ago that *he* could never be satisfied by any mere parade through the streets of a city, however grandiose. He wanted a funeral to outdo every other funeral in the history of humankind—and we are part and parcel of its ceremony. These condolence cards are not addressed to his victims—they are leaves from his own Book of Lamentations, and must be understood in that light."

"I can't believe it," said Michael Lowenthal, shaking his head. "It's too ridiculous." Wilde's remark about refraining from jumping to silly conclusions had obviously needled him.

"Maybe it is ridiculous," said Charlotte, "but it's no more so than the crimes themselves. Go on, Dr. Wilde—*Oscar.*"

Wilde beamed, welcoming her belated concession. Then he relaxed back into his seat and half closed his eyes, as if preparing himself to deliver a long speech—which, Charlotte realized, was exactly what he intended to do.

"It may seem unduly narcissistic," Oscar Wilde began, "but I wonder whether the most fruitful approach to the puzzle might be to unpack the question of why Rappaccini chose me to be its expert witness. The Herod sim informed us that it was because I was better placed than anyone else to understand the world's decadence. The quotations reproduced on the condolence cards are taken from works identified in their own day as 'decadent,' but it is not ancient history per se that is the focus of attention here. It's the *repetition* of history: the resonance implied by Jafri Biasiolo's performances as Rappaccini and Gustave Moreau, and my own performance as my ancient namesake.

"According to the tape which you kindly showed me, Gabriel King described me as a 'posturing ape,' and you probably took some slight pleasure in the implied insult. The description is, however, perfectly accurate, provided one assumes that *ape* is a derivative of a verb meaning to imitate rather than a reference to an extinct animal. I am, indeed, an imitation; my whole existence is a pose—but the original Oscar Wilde was a poseur himself, and ironic echoes of my performance extend through my own work and through his. Once, when someone complained that my namesake had criticized a fellow artist for stealing an idea when he was an inveterate thief himself, he observed that he could never look upon a gorgeous flower with four petals without wanting to produce a counterpart with five, but could not see the point of a lesser artist laboring to produce one with only three. You will understand why that analogy has always been particularly dear to me—but there are other echoes more vital still.

"In the first Oscar Wilde's excellent novel, *The Picture of Dorian Gray*, the eponymous antihero makes a diabolical bargain, exchanging fates with a portrait of himself, with the consequence that the image in the picture is marred by all the afflictions of age and dissolution while the real Dorian remains perpetually young. In the nineteenth century, of course, the story of Dorian Gray was the stuff of which dreams were made: the purest of fantasies. We live in a different era now, but you and I, dear Charlotte, have been caught on the cusp between two ages. We can indeed renew our youth—once, twice, or thrice—but in the end, the sin of aging will catch up with us. It still remains to be proven whether Michael's New Human Race is really capable of enduring forever, but the glorious vision is in place again: the ultimate hope is there to be treasured.

"Like me, Charlotte, you will doubtless do what you may to make the best of the life you have. I am living proof of the fact that even our kind may set aside much of the burden with which ugliness, disease, and the aging process afflicted us in days of old. We are corruptible, but we also have the means to set aside corruption, to reassert in spite of all the ravages of time and malady the image which we would like to have of ourselves. I daresay that you will play your part bravely and make the best of what is, after all, a golden opportunity for achievement and satisfaction. Perhaps, even as you watch the progress of such contemporaries as Michael, you will never experience a single moment's anguish at the thought that you are a mere betwixt-and-between, becalmed halfway between mortality and authentic emortality. Perhaps, though, you will not find it impossible to find a grain of sympathy for Rappaccini's obsession with death and its commemoration. In designing a funeral for himself that would surpass all the funerals of the past in its ludicrous self-indulgence and mawkish extravagance, he must also have had it in mind that there would soon come a time when funerals would lose their aura of inevitability, occurring only in the wake of rare and unexpected accidents."

"But I still don't see—," Charlotte began.

Oscar Wilde silenced her with an imperious wave of his delicate hand. "Please don't interrupt," he said. "I realize that you may well find this boring as well as incomprehensible, but I am trying hard to arrange my own thoughts in order, and I hope you might allow me to bore and confuse you a little while longer. Even if you fail, in the end, to make sense of what I have to say, you will be no worse off than you are now."

"I wasn't—," Charlotte protested, but stopped as he pursed his perfect lips. She felt a perverse pulse of lust as his gleaming eyes bade her be silent.

"The nineteenth-century writers who were called decadent,"

Wilde continued, "saw themselves as products of a culture in ter-minal decay. They likened their own era to the days of the declining Roman Empire, when the great city's grandeur gradually ebbed away, and its possessions were overrun by barbarians. According to this way of thinking, the aristocracy of all-conquering Rome had grown effete and self-indulgent, so utterly enervated by luxury that its members could find stimulation only in orgiastic excess. By the same token, the decadents asserted, the ruling classes of nineteenth-century Europe had been corrupted by comfort, to the extent that anyone cursed with the abnormal sensitivity of an artistic temper-ament must bear the yoke of a terrible ennui, which could only be opposed by sensual and imaginative excess.

"An entire way of life, according to the decadents, was damned and doomed to collapse; all that remained for men of genius to do was mock the meaninglessness of conformity and enjoy the self-destructive exultation of moral and artistic defiance. Many of them died of excess, poisoned by absinthe and ether, rotted in body and in mind by syphilis—but they were, of course, absolutely right. Theirs *was* a decadent culture, absurdly distracted by its luxuries and vanities, unwittingly lurching toward its historical terminus. The next two hundred years saw wars, famines, and catastrophes on an unprecedented scale, in which billions of people died, al-though the hectic increase in human population was not halted until the descent of the final plague: the plague of sterility. The comforts of the nineteenth century—hygiene, medicine, international trade—were the direct progenitors of the feverish ecocatastrophe whose crisis was the Crash. Throughout the twentieth century the petty deceivers of politics maintained their ruthless grip upon the fettered imagination of the vast majority of humankind, ensuring that few men had the vision to understand what was happening, and even fewer had the capacity to care. Addicted to their luxuries as they were, even terror could not give them adequate foresight. Blindly, stupidly, madly, they laid the world to waste and used all the good intentions of their marvelous technology to pave themselves a road to hell.

"What a waste it all was!"

Wilde paused again, but only for effect. This time, it wasn't Charlotte who made haste to interrupt him.

"You can't compare the present era to the one that preceded the Crash, Dr. Wilde," said Michael Lowenthal, the agent of the MegaMall. "There's no prospect whatsoever of another ecocatastrophe. Everything is under control now."

"Exactly so," said Wilde. "The old world ended with a bang and a whimper. Ours will not. Ours is far more likely to end in Hardinist stasis, in perfect order, with *everything under control.*"

"That's not what I meant, and you know it!" Lowenthal protested. "The masters of the MegaMall *like* change. They *need* change. Change is what keeps the marketplace healthy. There has to be demand. There has to be innovation. There has to be growth. There has to be progress. But . . ."

"But it all has to be *managed,*" Oscar Wilde finished for him. "It has to be measured and orderly. Change is good but chaos is evil. Growth is good but excess must be stifled. There are still those among us who cannot agree. Few of them are authentic revolutionaries—even the most extreme Green Zealots and Decivilizers, like the Eliminators and Robot Assassins before them, probably ought to be reckoned clowns and jesters rather than serious anarchists— but they still desire to make their dissenting voices heard. I think you will agree that whatever the outcome of this comedy may be, Rappaccini will certainly succeed in being heard. When dawn breaks, five men will be dead and a sixth will be under sentence of execution. A vast swarm of helicopters and hoverflies will be headed for Walter Czastka's island, avid to watch the denouement of the drama at close quarters. Can Walter be saved? Can the woman be apprehended? What has been done, and how, and why? Above all else: *why?*

"Perhaps, when all is said and done, the question *is* the answer; perhaps the sole purpose of every move in this remarkable play is to force us to recognize that it is, indeed, play. At any rate, my friends, we are no longer an audience of three: tomorrow, we will merely be the avant-garde of an audience of billions. Tomorrow, everyone will listen, even if hardly anyone will actually understand, while Rappaccini informs us, in the most grandiosely bizarre way he can contrive, that our culture too has reached its terminus, and that it is on the brink of being interred forever, mourned for a while, and then forgotten."

"It's nonsense!" Michael Lowenthal protested. "Everything worthwhile will be preserved. Everything!"

"But you and those like you, Michael, will be the ones who decide what is worthwhile," Wilde pointed out. "Even if men like Rappaccini and I were to agree with you, we should still feel the need to mourn the loss of the superfluous. What Rappaccini is trying to make us understand, I suppose, is the horror of a Hardinist world of carefully stewarded property, inhabited entirely by the *old*. That might, after all, be the ultimate consequence of the Zaman transformation. Children have already become rare on the surface of the earth; they will eventually become as nearly extinct as those obscure species which are never decanted from the ark banks except to supply the demands of zoos.

"Whatever might happen on Mars, or in the circumlunar colonies, Earth will presumably remain what it has already become: the MegaMall-dominated Empire of the Old. In time, maturation will ensure that it becomes the Empire of the Eternal. Some form of that empire is the heart's desire of every thinking man and the ambition of every practical scientist—even those, like me, who stand condemned as the last generation of the envious—but its emergence is bound to cause us anxiety and fear. The death of death is a prospect we ought to celebrate, but it is also a prospect we ought to approach with solemn concern. Who better to remind us of that than Rappaccini, the master of commemoration, the monopolist of wreaths?"

Charlotte suddenly realized that Wilde was deliberately understating the case. He was waiting for someone else to take the next step in the sequence, lest it be thought that he understood a little *too* well what the man he called Rappaccini wanted to achieve.

"He's murdering people," she said, taking it upon herself to fill the gap. "He's murdering *old men*. He's not just making an aesthetic statement; he's writing an ad for the philosophy of Elimination. That's how some of the vidveg are going to read this crazy business, at any rate—and I, for one, think that he always intended them to read it that way. His sim said as much, when it said that murder mustn't be allowed to become extinct."

Oscar Wilde smiled wryly. "He did indeed," he admitted.

"And is that the way *you* were supposed to read it?" Charlotte followed up. "Is that part of the interpretation that you were supposed to put to the world on his behalf?"

"I don't know," he answered frankly. "But I am, as you have cleverly observed, reluctant to go so far in my approval."

"So you don't agree with him, then?" Michael Lowenthal put in. "When all the fancy rhetoric is set aside, you agree with *us*." Charlotte knew that the implied collective was the masters of the MegaMall, not Lowenthal and herself.

"I do share Rappaccini's anxieties," Wilde replied, "but I don't think the threat is as overwhelming as he seems to think. I don't believe that the old men will ever take over the world *completely*, no matter how few they are or how long they live, or how clever they are in sustaining their claim to own the earth. I can't believe that a world in which death has been virtually abolished will be a world full of Walter Czastkas. I may, of course, be prejudiced by vanity, but I think that such a world could and should be a world full of Oscar Wildes. I'm even prepared to concede that the world will probably get by perfectly adequately even if I'm half wrong, and men like me are forced by circumstance to live alongside men like Walter.

"The spark of authentic youth *can* be maintained, if it's properly nurtured. The victory of ennui isn't inevitable. When we really can transform every human egg cell so as to equip it for eternal physical youth, at least some of those children—hopefully the greater number—will discover ways to adapt themselves to that condition by cultivating eternal *mental* youth. My way of trying to anticipate that is, I will admit, primitive and rough-hewn, but I am here to help prepare the way for those who come after me: the true children of our race; the eternal children; the first authentically *human* beings."

"That's all very well," Charlotte said, "but it's Rappaccini, not you, who's going to be world-famous tomorrow, at least for a while. Others may be more sympathetic to the violent aspects of his message than you are."

"Undoubtedly," said Wilde.

"On the other hand," said Michael Lowenthal, "the great majority will be horrified and sickened by the whole thing."

"I'm a police officer," said Charlotte sourly. "I'll be dealing with the troublesome minority."

"That was another thing the decadents helped to demonstrate, or at least to reemphasize," Oscar Wilde observed, stifling a yawn. "Human beings are strangely attracted to the horrific and the sick. We have been careful in this guilt-ridden age of dogged reparation to invent a multitude of virtual realities which serve and pander to that darker side of our nature, but we have no guarantee that it can be safely and permanently confined in that way. With or without Rappaccini's bold example, we might well be overdue for a new wave of Eliminator activity or a new cult of *hashishins*. VEs have done sterling work in displacing our baser selves, but the impulse to sin is not something that can be entirely satisfied by vicarious fulfillment. As our indefatigable murderess has demonstrated, actual sexual intercourse is coming back into fashion. Can violence be far behind?"

Charlotte turned to look out of the viewport beside her, lifting her head to stare at the patient stars. I'm a police officer, she repeated in the privacy of her own thoughts. If he's right, it's me, not him or Michael Lowenthal, who'll bear the brunt of it. It might have been a symptom of her own exhaustion, but she couldn't bring herself to believe that Wilde might be wrong, even about the likelihood of Julia Herold evading all Hal's traps. She no longer had any faith at all in the ability of the UN and the MegaMall to prevent the late Jafri Biasiolo, alias Rappaccini, alias Gustave Moreau, from bringing this affair to the conclusion which he had predetermined, or from making as deep an impression upon memory and history as he had always intended.

A Failed God and His Creation

Whenever Walter Czastka attempted to focus his attention on the practical questions which still required settlement, they slipped away. He could not confront them without first confronting the sheer enormity of the fact, unkindly revealed to him by the UN's hapless investigators, that *Jafri Biasiolo was his son.*

He had, of course, always known that he *had* a son, but he had never made any attempt to find out what name the boy had been given following his perfectly orthodox birth. It would have been very foolish of him to make any such inquiry, given that it would have been compounding a criminal act, whose commission had been carefully covered up by calculatedly bad record keeping—but that had not been the real reason for his refusal to investigate.

The truth was, Walter admitted to himself at long last, that he simply had not cared enough. Once the experiment had been rudely taken out of his hands, he had forsaken all interest in it. The authorities had taken over, and the young Walter had reacted in a way that had been typical of the young Walter; he had resentfully washed his hands of the whole affair. The fact that he had escaped punishment for his alleged misdeed had made things worse rather than better; it had been the *local* authorities which had stepped in, undertaking in their wisdom to keep the "problem" confined, to enter the child into the records in a calculatedly and deceptively economical fashion: to pretend, in essence, that the whole thing had never happened, and to demand—on pain of punishment—that he should do likewise.

Presumably they had done that for the child's sake, but all that the young Walter had seen was a brutal minimization of his heroic effort, a casual refusal to see it as anything important, anything meaningful, anything worth recording. And his own direly youthful reaction had been: So be it; if that's what you think, you're welcome to it. You want pretense, I'll pretend—and I'll never try to change the world again. From now on, the world can rot.

He saw, now that he was forced to see, that it had been a petty and childish reaction—but he had been no more than a child.

Perhaps, he thought, pettiness was something he had not entirely grown out of, even now. What had become of his once-grand ambitions, his once-fervent lust to be a pioneer? He had followed through with his threat, and had let the world's corruption alone, leaving it to fester. He had pretended, as the supposedly generous authorities pretended, that he had done nothing, and that nothing had been the right thing to do.

Now, at the age of a hundred and ninety-four, he had nothing to look back on but that determined pretense. Apart from the single experiment that had produced Jafri Biasiolo—which had to be recognized, in retrospect, as a failure—had he ever even tried to pioneer anything worth pioneering? He had tried . . . but *what* had he tried, and how hard?

He had abandoned all thought of human engineering and had turned instead to the engineering of pretty flowers. He had thought himself accomplished in that safe and lucrative field, and he had been successful. Had he really been outdone by those who came after him: Oscar Wilde and his unacknowledged son? Had he somehow consented to be upstaged by a clown and a designer of funeral wreaths?

Surely not. And yet . . .

Had he been allowed to follow his experiment through, Walter thought, his career path would have been very different, and his life too—but it had been taken from him in too brutal a fashion. The unborn child had been transferred to a Helier womb, and its transference undocumented, so that no one referring to the bare record of the child's birth would see at once that he was anything but an ordinary product of the New Reproductive System.

The "local authorities" who had discovered what he had done had died off one by one, but the young men who had helped him out, in their various mostly trivial ways, had not. Like him, they had gone unpunished; like him, they had probably pushed the memory of their involvement to the very backs of their minds and might even have contrived to forget it entirely. Only three of them had known the whole story, and not one of them knew the names of *all* the others who had helped him. Maria Inacio was the only one who could have listed all five names and coupled them to his. Clearly, she had—but the only person to whom she had revealed the names was her son.

Her presumably beloved son.

Her presumably *uniquely* beloved son. Or was that presuming too much, given that the world of 2323 had changed so drastically since the days when all women had been born like Maria Inacio, capable of conception and parturition?

There was no reason, of course, why Maria Inacio or any of his accomplices should ever have spoken publicly of what they knew. None of them could have won any credit by revealing that they had been part of such a wild endeavor. It was in no one's interest belatedly to add into the record that which had been carefully excluded therefrom—not even Jafri Biasiolo's. Now, Biasiolo had gone to his grave and had taken King, Urashima, Kwiatek, and Teidemann with him. That only left McCandless, and McCandless did not even know that the other four had been involved. Even if McCandless were spared, or had been spared long enough to tell the police what he knew, he would be unable to connect himself to Urashima or Kwiatek. The most he might remember—and even that would require a prodigious feat of memory—was that Walter might have mentioned King's interest, and Teidemann's, while the two of them had walked along that lonely beach discussing a little favor which McCandless might do in order to help Walter keep a secret.

The secret was safe now. Or was it? There was one other person who might—perhaps must—have heard from Biasiolo's lips the names of those involved and the nature of his scheme: the woman who was carrying out Rappaccini's scheme.

And that too was a mystery.

"What, exactly, is my murder intended to achieve?" Walter murmured aloud. "What, if anything, is it intended to demonstrate?"

Saying it aloud did not help. There was no answer waiting in the wings for an audible prompt.

All of it, Walter thought, is beyond understanding. If I were to wrestle with the puzzle for a hundred years, I would not get close to a solution.

He sat on his bed and stared into the depths of an empty suitcase. He had opened it with the intention of filling it with everything he needed and fleeing the island, but the plan had spontaneously aborted within ten seconds of its launch. It had taken him no longer than that to realize that he had nothing whatsoever to put in the case. The world had changed while he had lived in it. When he had been a young man, people really had packed luggage when they needed to travel; suitskins and household dispensers had not been as clever in the early twenty-third century as they were in the late twenty-fourth, and utilitarian possessions had not been so easily interchangeable. Information technology had been almost as clever, but people's attitudes to its instrumentality had been far more cautious; even people with nothing to hide had routinely kept data bubbled up, and had carried self-contained machines wherever they went in order to access and process the bubbles. In those days, the notion of "personal property" had meant far more than it seemed to mean now.

Walter realized belatedly that there would have been no point in filling the case even if there had been anything to put into it. No matter what the UN police said, he was not going to leave. There was no need, because there was nothing left to be afraid of—not even the threat of murder.

"After all," he murmured, "I am guilty of *something*. No matter how long I have lived, and no matter how much time I have wasted, I am still the man who found Maria Inacio, still the man who tried to grasp that single slender reed of opportunity . . . and failed."

He wondered whether there might be grounds for perverse gratitude in the fact that his unnatural son had somehow found in that unique circumstance a motive for murder. He could not fathom that motive, and it was too late now to repair the omission of a lifetime and make the attempt to *communicate* with his son, but at least he knew now that his son had not been as neglectful of their relationship as he. The fact that his son, having discovered the circumstances of his birth, had decided to murder his father and all of his father's accomplices was surely proof that the matter of paternity was not irrelevant to him, and could therefore be construed as a compliment of sorts.

That, at any rate, was surely what Oscar Wilde would have said.

"Damn him to hell," Walter murmured—meaning Oscar Wilde, not Jafri Biasiolo, alias Rappaccini.

The profoundest mystery of all, of course, was why Jafri Biasiolo, having learned from Maria Inacio the identity of his father and the circumstances of his birth, had done nothing for so long. Had he postponed his "revenge"—if "revenge" it was—until he himself was dead merely in order to avoid punishment? If so, he was worse than a coward, because his agent undoubtedly *would* be caught and would suffer his punishment in his stead.

It made no sense.

Walter left the bedroom and ordered a bowl of tomato soup from the dispenser in the living room. He ordered it sharp and strong, and he began to sip it while it was still too hot, blistering his upper palate. He carried on regardless, forcing the liquid down without any supplementation by bread or manna. He contemplated chasing the soup with a couple of double vodkas, but there was a difference between the stubborn recognition that he ought to eat and mere folly. In any case, the benign machines which had colonized his stomach would not let him get drunk unless he first sent messengers to rewrite their code—and that would take hours.

He tried yet again to drag his mind back to the matter in hand. Why should his son want to kill him? Because he—the son—felt abandoned? Because the experiment had failed? Because his mother had asked him to? But why should Maria Inacio want him dead, when she had been a willing partner in the escapade? Why should she want all those who had helped to set it up to be killed along with him, when not one of them had hurt her in any way? And if Maria or her son *had* wanted to take revenge, why had they waited so long? Why *now*, when there was so little life left in any of their intended victims? If Moreau had lived thirty or forty years longer—as he certainly would have, had the experiment not failed so ignominiously—there would probably have been no one left for him to murder. Only luck had preserved all five of the people who had given Walter the resources with which to work, a place to hide his experimental subject, and the alibis he had needed to keep his endeavors secret. Only luck had preserved him long enough to outlive his son—if his current state of body and mind could be thought of as "preservation."

Perhaps that was what Moreau resented: the fact that Walter and his five accomplices had all outlived him, when the whole point of his creation was that *he* was supposed to outlive *them*. Perhaps, if he had been a better artist, a better Creationist, he would not have failed. Perhaps that was what his forsaken son had been unable to forgive him. Perhaps that was why his forsaken son had said to himself: when I die, you must come with me, for it was your failure that determined the necessity of my death. That almost made sense. Could it also begin to make sense of the fact that the instrument of the son's murderous intent was a replicate of his mother?

The game of God, Walter reflected, must have been the only one he had wanted to play when he was young and devoid of pretense. Perhaps, when he had been forced to put that game aside, he had put aside playfulness itself. Perhaps, thereafter, he had presented to the world at large the perfect image of a man who was down-to-earth and matter-of-fact. Everyone thought of him as a realist: a man of method, a hardheaded person without any illusions about himself or anything else. He had lived that pretense for nearly two hundred years—unless, of course, it was no pretense at all, and he really was down-to-earth and matter-of-fact, hard of head and hard of heart, incapable of play.

Walter remembered the Great Exhibition held in Sydney in 2405, when he had seen the work exhibited by Oscar Wilde and Rappaccini and said to himself: These idle egotists can only play; they have not the capacity for real work. They are vulgar showmen whose only real talent is for attracting attention. Even their names are jokes. They are the froth on the great tide of biotechnics, whose gleam and glitter will adorn the moment while the real power of the surge will come from honest, clear-sighted laborers like myself. I am the one who has the intelligence and the foresight to play the game of God as it was meant to be played.

In the ninety years that had passed since the days of the Great Exhibition, Walter had gradually come to understand the frailty of that hope. Here, on his Pacific atoll, he was the unchallenged lord of all he surveyed, with none to stay his hand or resist his edict, and yet . . .

He had set out to build a Garden of Eden, but the Tree of Knowledge was not here, nor even the Tree of the Knowledge of Good and Evil. When he was dead—which would presumably be fairly soon, whether or not Gustave Moreau's murderous scheme could be interrupted—people would be able to visit his island, and say: "Yes, this is Walter's work."

If they were generous of spirit, they might say: "Look at the sense of order, the cleanness of line, the careful simplicity. No wild extravagance for Walter, no illusions. Method, neatness, economy— those were always Walter's watchwords."

And if they were not so generous?

"Dull, dull, dull."

In the quiet arena of his mind, Walter could almost hear the voices which would deliver that deadly verdict. Oscar Wilde would state it much more elaborately, of course, while waving his pale left hand in a dismissive arc. Few people would pay any attention to Oscar—people never did pay attention to mere caricatures—and no one would ever believe for a second that he, dear Walter, would care a fig what Oscar Wilde might think of his work, but the majority opinion was not the important one.

"What do *I* think?" Walter asked himself, knowing that that was the real heart of the matter. "Now that it's all coming out, now that it can't be kept inside anymore, what do I think? What have I made of my life and my work, and how does it compare with what I might have made? That's the thing that has to be decided."

It sounded so simple, but it wasn't. There were far too many awkward questions, and far too little time to hunt for the answers he should have found a hundred and seventy years before.

The hour of Rappaccini's judgment—the judgment of the reckless father by the resentful son—was at hand. Whether he were here or elsewhere, Walter thought, there was nowhere left for him to run. If fools like Oscar Wilde were not so foolish after all, there was nowhere left where he might even stand and fight.

Eden Approached from the East

C harlotte woke with a start, jolted out of a fugitive dream by a sudden flash of light. Behind the tiny plane, in the east, the dawn was breaking; a fleeting sequence of reflections had diverted a ray of golden light from the tip of the wing to the viewport beside her head and then to the strip of chrome around the forward port.

Ahead of her, in the west, the sky was still dark blue and ominous, but the stars were already fading into the backcloth of the day. Charlotte roused herself and craned her neck to look out of the viewport at her side. Beneath the plane, the sea was becoming visible as fugitive rays of silvery light caught the tops of lazy waves.

In these latitudes, the sea was relatively unpolluted by the vast amount of synthetic photosynthetic substances pumped out from such artificial islands as those which crowded the Timor Sea. By day it was stubbornly blue, although its eventual conquest by the Stygian darkness of Liquid Artificial Photosynthesis was probably inevitable. Even now, this region of the ocean could not be thought of as an authentic marine wilderness; the post-Crash restocking of the waters had been too careful and too selective. The so-called seven seas were really a single vast system, which was already half-gentled by the hand of man. The continental engineers, despite the implications of their name, had better control of evolution's womb than extinction's rack.

Even the wrathful volcanoes that had created the Hawaiian islands were now quite tame, sufficiently manipulable that they could be forced to yield upon demand the little virgin territories which the likes of Walter Czastka and Gustave Moreau had rented for their experiments in Creation.

Charlotte felt her eyes growing heavy again; although she had slept, she still felt drained by the efforts and displacements of the previous day. She found, somewhat to her distress, that her memory of the rambling arguments which Oscar Wilde had laid before her was already becoming vague. She knew that she had to pull herself together in order to be ready for the final act of the drama, and she tried to do it. Reflexively, she rubbed the surface of her suitskin, her hand traveling from her shoulder to her thigh by way of her ribs. The smart fabric needed no such stimulation in order to continue its patient work of absorption and renewal, but the touch had some psychological utility. When she had stretched the muscles in her arms and legs she could imagine her internal technology springing back to life, priming her metabolism for the long day to come.

She turned to the seat in which Oscar Wilde had placed himself when they boarded the plane, but it was empty. So was the seat that Michael Lowenthal had occupied. They had both retired to the bunks to make themselves more comfortable while they rested.

She saw that her beltphone was still plugged into the aircraft's comcon, and that text was parading across the screen, presumably at the command of Hal Watson's fingertips.

"Hal?" she said. "I'm awake."

"Good morning, Sergeant," came the prompt reply. "I was about to wake you. You've certainly taken your time about it, but you're only twenty minutes from Kauai now, and your autopilot has requested a landing slot—although there's nothing for you to do there."

Because she was slightly befuddled by sleep, it took Charlotte a second or two to work out what he meant by the last remark.

"McCandless is dead!" she said finally.

"Quite dead," Hal replied. "The local police—who were, of course, on standby all night while a host of spy eyes kept watch on him—had him removed to an intensive care unit as soon as he showed signs of illness, but there was absolutely nothing to be done for him. The biotechnologists inspecting the organisms which killed the previous victims haven't yet come up with the kind of general antidote that Wilde talked about, although they've promised it by noon. That leaves us with no chance at all of getting it out to you in time to save Walter Czastka, if he is indeed the next intended victim."

Charlotte was much quicker to see the implications of that remark.

"They didn't get her, did they?" she said.

"No, they didn't."

Charlotte knew that she ought at least to feign astonishment and outrage, but all she actually felt was a sense of bitter resignation.

"How?" she asked dully. "How could they possibly fail to intercept her?"

"She'd already left the house when the local police first got there," said Hal dispiritedly. "That was long before McCandless began to show signs of distress. He told them she'd gone for a moonlight swim, and still refused to believe that she wasn't exactly what she seemed to be. There were mechanical eyes set to follow her, of course, mounted on hoverflies and flitterbugs—but as soon as they entered the water they were mopped up by a shoal of electronic fish. By the time they were replaced by more robust entities she was beyond the scope of their location faculties. The flying eyes watching avidly for her to surface couldn't possibly have missed her, so we must infer that she had a breathing apparatus secreted offshore and some kind of mechanized transport."

"A submarine?" said Charlotte incredulously.

"We'd have detected anything as big as that," said Hal. "More likely a simple towing device of some kind."

"But we know where she's going, don't we?" Charlotte said. "When she comes out of the water again on Walter Czastka's island, we should be able to stop her from reaching him. In any case, *he* knows how dangerous she is, even if McCandless didn't."

"He certainly *knows*," Hal agreed. "The thing is—does he

care? I can't get a peep out of him. His sim is stonewalling all communications. If he knows why she's after him, he certainly isn't going to tell us—and I've trawled every remaining record relating to Maria Inacio, however obliquely. There's no clue as to what might have happened to her. She probably never said a word to anyone—except, we must presume, Jafri Biasiolo. The Kauai police have dispatched four helicopters to wait for her, but Czastka's sim has forbidden them permission to land. They're prepared to remain airborne until they actually catch sight of her—at which point his permission becomes irrelevant, because they'll be pursuing a fugitive."

"What about me?" Charlotte asked urgently. "Can I get there in time?"

"Who can tell? There'll be a helicopter ready for you and Lowenthal when you land, and there's also a machine awaiting Oscar Wilde, although he may prefer to make use of the police vehicle if you and Lowenthal are willing to take him along. Notionally, the whole operation is under my command—which, in effect, puts you in immediate control as my proxy. I'm hoping that if Biasiolo really has set things up to provide a ringside seat for Wilde, the woman won't proceed to stage six until you and he arrive. In theory, of course, Wilde will be unable to land unless Czastka relents and gives him permission, but he's probably not as enthusiastic to stick to the letter of the law as the commander at Kanai.

"In case you haven't noticed, by the way, you're surrounded by caster 'flies. So are the copters from Kauai. For every flitterbug we've got on Czastka's island, the news tapes probably have a dozen. The whole of the morning news, bar fifteen seconds of other headlines, was given over to the five murders, described in the minutest detail. Having identified the text on the first condolence card, they're headlining it Flowers of Evil—except for that crank French station which is still trying to maintain the purity of the native tongue. As soon as we failed to apprehend the woman on Kauai the MegaMall took the gloves off—however this works out, we're not going to look good. In fact, we're going to look very, very bad. If she were to succeed in killing Czastka too. . . ."

"Have you considered evacuating him?"

"Of course I have—but I can't do it against his will. He's sealed himself in. If I ordered the helicopters to land and seize him, I'd look even more stupid than I already do if they couldn't actually get to him to execute the order. He really does seem to be intent on securing his own destruction. He may not actually want to die, but he's perversely determined not to be saved."

"As he said before, all he actually needs to do is to keep the house sealed," Charlotte pointed out. "If we can't get in, neither can she. He must know that—he's perfectly safe, as long as he doesn't open the door to her, unless she has an atom bomb as well as a submarine. If all she has is nanotech, it's his against hers—and his ought to win, given that they have the home-ground advantage."

"It all sounds so simple, put like that," Hal agreed. Charlotte could tell that he had no more confidence in the calculation than she had. All the evidence said that the woman had no chance at all of getting to Czastka, but even Hal couldn't quite believe that Rappaccini's grand plan was going to fizzle out into a soggy anticlimax.

"We located the real Julia Herold, by the way," Hal continued. "She's a dead ringer for the fake. She really was on Kauai while the Inacio clone was making her way around the world—and, for that matter, while her double was carefully forging a relationship with Stuart McCandless in her name. She spends a *lot* of time in VE, and she's rather careless about security of her sims and systems. If you want more details, I've downloaded everything to the copter that's waiting on Kauai—and to the machine in front of you, although you won't have time to look at it before you land. It's all in place: every detail of the woman's journey; every dollar of the money trail. It's a magnificent job of case building, although no one will ever believe that, given that we failed to apprehend the killer on Kauai."

Charlotte wished that she were capable of feeling more sympathy for Hal's plight, but she still had her own to worry about—and she was distracted by the fact that Michael Lowenthal had just risen from his bunk. The emissary from Olympus climbed into the seat formerly occupied by Oscar Wilde and said: "What's new?"

Charlotte took a deep breath and began to tell him.

"This is the text on the condolence card the woman left at McCandless's house," Charlotte told Michael Lowenthal, displaying the words on the screen.

> Farewell, happy fields,
> Where joy forever dwells! Hail, horrors! hail,
> Infernal world! and thou, profoundest Hell,
> Receive thy new possessor, one who brings
> A mind not to be changed by place or time.
> The mind is its own place, and in itself
> Can make a Heaven of Hell, a Hell of Heaven.

"Very apt," said Lowenthal dryly. "Should we wake Dr. Wilde, do you think, and plead with him for an interpretation?" It was a rhetorical question.

"It's from *Paradise Lost*," Charlotte said.

"John Milton," Lowenthal was quick to say, avid to seize a rarely accessible corner of the intellectual high ground. "Not the nineteenth century. Earlier."

"The seventeenth," said a muffled voice from the rear. "Written then, allegedly, to 'justify the ways of God to men'—but by the nineteenth, some had begun to adjudge that Milton had been of the Devil's party without knowing it and had made a hero of Satan and a villain of God in spite of his own intention. Which passage is it, exactly, that Rappaccini has taken the trouble to quote?"

Charlotte was tempted to tell Wilde to come forward and read it for himself, but did not want to be churlish. She read it aloud.

"It hardly needs interpretation," Wilde observed—not altogether accurately, if Michael Lowenthal's expression could be taken as a guide. Charlotte understood what Wilde meant, though. The words could be read as a valedictory speech by Rappaccini/Moreau: a warning, a threat, and a statement of intent.

"When this is all over," Lowenthal said to the still-invisible Wilde, "you can write a book about it—and then we'll see how many of the world's busy citizens have the time and inclination to download it to their screens."

"Soon," said Wilde, "*all* the world's children will have the time—and I hope that they will also have the inclination. I suspect that their fascination with the artistry of death will be all the greater because death will be, for them, a matter of aesthetic choice. When everyone has the opportunity to extend life indefinitely, the determination to cling onto it for the sake of stubbornness alone will inevitably come to seem absurd. Some will choose to die; those who do not will feel obliged to make something of their lives. I hope, Michael, that you will take your place in the latter company."

By the time he had finished this speech, Wilde had slipped into the seat behind Lowenthal—the one which the man from the MegaMall had occupied the previous evening. Glancing back and forth from one to the other, Charlotte decided that although there was nothing to choose between them on the grounds of physical perfection, Wilde had emerged more rapidly from sleep to claim the fullest advantage of his brightness and beauty. The authentically young man who now sat beside her was still afflicted by the temporary stigmata of frustration and mental weariness.

"You seem to have slept well, Oscar," Charlotte said.

"I usually do, my dear," he said. "You'll probably find, as you get older—especially at those times when you replenish your youth without losing the wisdom of maturity—that deep sleep will come more easily."

"We've all had the biofeedback training," Lowenthal said dismissively. "We all know the drill."

Charlotte felt a sudden surge of anxiety about the appearance of her own face. She altered the lateral viewport to full reflection and studied her lax features and bleary eyes with considerable alarm. The face she wore was not entirely the gift of nature; she had had all the conventional manipulations in infancy, but she had always refused to be excessively pernickety about matters of beauty, preferring to retain a hint of naturalness on the grounds that it gave her *character* and *individuality*. Oscar Wilde had all of that *and* phenomenal beauty, and he was a hundred and thirty-three years old. Somehow, it didn't seem quite fair. She worked her facial muscles feverishly, recalling the elementary exercises that everyone learned at school and almost everyone neglected thereafter. Then she straightened her hair.

Oscar Wilde looked politely away as she did so, tutting over the condition of the fading green carnation which still protruded from the false collar of his suitskin.

As Charlotte took stock of the reward of her efforts she noticed the faint wrinkles which were just becoming apparent in the corners of her eyes. She knew that they could be removed easily enough by the most elementary tissue manipulation, and she would not have given them a second thought two days before, but now they served as a reminder of the biological clock that was ticking away inside her: the clock that would need to be reset when she was eighty or ninety years old, and again when she turned a hundred and fifty . . . and then would wind down forever, because her brain would be unable to renew itself a third time without wiping clean the mind within.

For Michael Lowenthal, she knew, it would be different. No one, least of all Lowenthal himself, knew as yet exactly how different it would be, but there was reason to believe that he might live for three or four hundred years without needing any kind of nano-tech restructuring, and reason to hope that he might go on for a further half-millennium, and on and on. . . .

Barring accidents, suicide, and murder.

But who would be the suicides and murderers, in a world of

beautiful ancients? Who would kill or choose to die, if they could live forever?

"The mind is its own place," Charlotte quoted silently, "and in itself can make a Heaven of Hell, a Hell of Heaven." She passed a hand across her face, as if to wipe away the tried laxity of the muscles and the embryonic wrinkles. Fifty or sixty years to rejuve number one, she told herself, and no point yet in counting.

By the time she switched the viewport back to transparency, the island toward which they had been headed was below them, and their plane was descending toward the trees, preparing to alter the orientation of its engines so that it could complete its descent in helicopter fashion.

Like all the Hawaiian islands, Kauai had been blighted by the eco-catastrophes of the twenty-first century and the fallout from the plague wars. Most of its ecosystems had been stripped down almost to the prokaryot level, but it was small enough to have been comprehensively rehabilitated. The biodiversity loss had been enormous, and the current genetic variety of the island was probably only a few percent of what it had been in pre-Crash days, but the painstaking work done by natural selection in the cause of diversification was beginning to bear fruit on a prolific scale. The trees over which the aircraft passed while making for the landing field almost qualified as authentic wilderness.

Charlotte checked the equipment in her belt, making dutiful preparations for the dash from one vehicle to another. She had already invited Oscar Wilde to accompany her rather than taking the helicopter chartered by the late Gustave Moreau, but he had declined the offer. She was not displeased by the thought of putting a little distance between herself and one of her annoying companions—although, had she been given a choice, she would have kept Wilde and banished Lowenthal.

As soon as they had set down at the heliport, Charlotte opened the cockpit door and leapt down to the blue plastic apron. Michael

Lowenthal made haste to follow her, but Wilde had perforce to take his time. Uniformed officers hurried toward her, directing her to a police helicopter that was waiting less than a hundred meters away. Its official markings were a delight to Charlotte's eyes, holding as they did the impression of authority. From now on, she told herself, she would no longer be a passenger but a determined pursuer: an active instrument of justice.

One of the local men tried to tell her that there was no need for her to join the dragnet, and that she could watch it all on screens, but there was no way she was going to be turned aside now. She strode toward the police helicopter very purposefully, brushing off the attentions of the Kauai men as if they were buzzing flies, and Michael Lowenthal trotted along in her wake, barely keeping pace with her in spite of the fact that his stride was longer.

"You can strand him here if you want to," Lowenthal said, jerking his head in the direction of Oscar Wilde, who was walking to another, somewhat smaller, machine. "He needs clearance for takeoff. You could ground him for the duration."

"Hal could," Charlotte corrected him as she climbed into the helicopter, taking note of the numerous flitterbugs clinging to the hull. "I'm just a sergeant. In any case, he might come in useful. Why don't *you* take the opportunity to drop out? Your employers surely can't think that they have any particular cause for concern—and they can watch the whole thing through the flying eyes."

"I talked to them last night," Lowenthal told her. "They want me to stay with it. They're still anxious—and that's as much your fault as anyone's. All that stuff about advertising for a new generation of Eliminators. They've probably had their own PR teams working through the night, figuring out the best way to spin the story once the final shot's been fired."

The helicopter lifted as soon as they were both strapped in. The automatic pilot had been programmed to take them to Czastka's island without delay. Charlotte reached into the equipment locker under the seat and brought forth a handgun. She loaded it and checked the mechanism before clipping it to her belt.

"Do you think you'll have a chance to use that?" Lowenthal asked. Charlotte noticed that the interpolation of the words *a chance* put a distinct spin on the question.

"It would be within the regulations," Charlotte answered tautly. "I couldn't even be rude to her when I spoke to her at McCandless's house, but now the proof's in place I'm entitled to employ any practical measure which may be necessary to apprehend her. Don't worry—the bullets are certified nonlethal. They're loaded with knock-out drops. We're the police, remember."

"Have you ever fired one before?" he asked curiously. "Outside a VE, I mean."

She chose to ignore the question rather than answer it—as honesty would have forced her to do—in the negative.

The copter was traveling at a speed which was only a little greater than that attained by their previous conveyance, but they remained so low that their progress seemed far more rapid. The sea was the deep sapphire blue color renowned in ancient tradition, modestly reflecting the clarity of the cloudless morning sky. The waves, aided by the onrushing downdraft of their blades, carved the roiling water into all manner of curious shapes.

High in the sky above them a silver airship was making its stately progress from Honolulu to Yokohama, but the other police helicopters, dispatched before their arrival on Kauai, were out of sight beyond the horizon. Oscar Wilde's charter craft was half a kilometer behind them, but it was keeping pace.

Like their previous craft, the helicopter had only one comcon. Charlotte tuned in to a broadcast news report. There were pictures of Gabriel King's skeleton, neatly entwined with winding stems bearing black flowers in horrid profusion. They had not come from Rex Carnevon—they were obviously taken from Regina Chai's footage. Given that Hal would not have released them, they must have been forwarded by somebody he had been obliged to copy in on the investigation: Michael Lowenthal's employers. The tape had been reedited so that the camera lingered lasciviously over its appreciation of the horrid spectacle.

The King tape was swiftly followed by footage of Michi Urashima's similarly embellished skeleton. The AI voice-over was already speculating, in that irritatingly insinuating fashion that AI voice-overs always had, that the UN police had been caught napping by the murderous tourist. The word *negligence* was not actually mentioned, but the tone of the coverage suggested that it would not be long delayed in the wings. Charlotte was tempted to purge the skin of the craft of the news-tape eyes that had hitched a ride thereon, but there was no point. There would be hundreds more flying under their own power.

Charlotte knew that although the information which had passed back and forth between Hal and herself would have been routinely cloaked, it could be uncloaked easily enough if anyone cared to take the trouble. Although the conversation she, Wilde, and Lowenthal had conducted in the restaurant at the UN complex was probably safe from retrospective eavesdroppers, very little they had said to one another since boarding the maglev would be irrecoverable. Their conversational exchanges after they had quit the car in the hills near the Mexican border would all be contained on the bubblebug tapes she had relayed back to Hal Watson—and, of course, to Michael Lowenthal's employers.

It was anyone's guess, now, what the casters might think worth broadcasting if the climax of the chase proved to be sufficiently melodramatic to pull in a big audience. By now, even skyballs might be turning their inquisitive downward gaze in the direction of Walter Czastka's proto-Eden; the privacy which the genetic engineer so passionately desired to conserve was about to be rudely shattered. But then what? How would the tentative attention of the vidveg be captured—and how would it be secured?

She wondered whether it would be necessary to use the gun—and what effect it would have on her career, her image, and her self-regard if the entire world were to watch her shoot down an uncommonly beautiful unarmed woman, albeit with a certified non-lethal dart.

The newscast flickered as the comcon signaled that a call was incoming from the helicopter trailing in their wake.

"What is it, Oscar?" Charlotte said.

"I tried to call Walter," said Wilde. "This is what I got." His own face was immediately replaced by that of Walter Czastka's silver-animated sim.

"Damn you, Oscar Wilde," the sim said, apparently without having bothered with any conventional identification or polite preliminary. "Damn you and Rappaccini to the darkest oblivion imaginable."

"That's not very nice, Walter," Wilde's voice countered, although the image on screen was still the sim's. "We have a responsibility to our AI slaves not to use them in this tawdry way. They can be pleasant on our behalf, but we shouldn't require them to be insulting. It isn't worthy of us."

"Damn you, Oscar Wilde," the sim repeated. "Damn you and Rappaccini to the darkest oblivion imaginable."

"Nor should we lock the poor things into tight loops," the Wildean voice-over added. "It's a particularly cruel form of imprisonment."

"Damn you, Oscar Wilde," said the sim yet again. "Damn you and Rappaccini to the darkest oblivion imaginable."

It was obviously programmed to make that response to anything and everything that Wilde might say. Charlotte cut off the tape and punched out Czastka's phone code herself.

"Dr. Czastka," she said when the sim appeared, "this is Sergeant Charlotte Holmes of the UN police. I need to speak to you urgently."

"Damn you, Oscar Wilde," replied the sim stubbornly. "Damn you and Rappaccini to the darkest oblivion imaginable."

Charlotte restored the link to Wilde's helicopter. His face had creased into an anxious frown. "I have a horrible suspicion," Wilde said, "that we might already be too late."

Charlotte looked at the comcon's timer. They were still thirteen minutes away from their estimated time of arrival at the island. She punched in another code, connecting herself to the commander of the task force whose hovering copters had surrounded the island.

"What's happening?" she demanded.

"No sign of her yet," the answer came back. "She can't possibly have landed without being seen. If anything happens, Sergeant, you'll be the first to know, as per New York's orders." The local man did not seem particularly pleased by the fact that he had orders to check all his moves with a mere sergeant. The fact that she was from New York probably added an extra hint of insult to the tacit injury.

"What do you mean, *too late*?" she said to Wilde, having cut back to him yet again. "If he were dead, it could only be suicide. His phone sim may be the stupidest obsolete sloth still in use, but there must be silver-level smarts somewhere in his systems. If he were actually dead, they'd override the sloth. We've put the whole island on full alert!"

"Even if he is not dead," Wilde said stubbornly, "we may still be too late. That is what Rappaccini intends."

There was nothing to do but wait and see, so Charlotte sat back in her seat and stared down at the agitated waves, letting the minutes tick by. Michael Lowenthal did not attempt to engage her in conversation.

They were still two minutes short of their ETA when the voice of the local commander came back on-line. "We have visual contact with the woman," he said. "Relaying now."

When the picture on the copter's screen cleared, it showed a female figure in a humpbacked suitskin walking out of the sea, looking for all the world as if she were enjoying a leisurely stroll after a few minutes in the water.

"We're going in," said the commander.

"Not *yet!*" said Charlotte. "We're coming in now! Don't set down until I do. Leave her to me." She was not entirely sure why she had told him to wait, but she was acutely aware of the responsibility of enacting Hal Watson's authority—and it was, after all, *her* investigation too.

Charlotte watched raptly as the woman who looked like Julia Herold paused at the high-tide line and began detaching the hump on her suitskin, which presumably contained a built-in paralung. The camera eye zoomed in, not because it was refocusing but because the helicopter carrying it was moving closer. Obedient to Charlotte's order, however, the machine did not complete its touch-down, hovering a meter or so above the sand. Over the voice link, Charlotte could hear the sound of loudhailer-magnified voices instructing the woman to stand still.

The woman did not seem to see the slowly settling helicopters or hear the loudhailers. She pushed back the hood of her suitskin and shook loose her long tresses. Her hair had changed color again; it was now a gloriously full red-gold, which seemed luminously alive as it caught the rays of the rising sun. The assassin knelt beside the discarded augmentation of her suitskin, removing something from a pocket. She made no attempt to move from the spot where she had been instructed to remain, but she swiftly unwrapped whatever it was that had been bound up with the paralung in the bimolecular membrane.

"What's she doing?" Charlotte murmured as her own copter nudged its way into a gap in the surrounding ring.

"I don't know," Michael Lowenthal answered.

Over the voice link they could still hear the officer who had spoken to them. He was instructing her to desist from whatever she was doing and raise her hands above her head.

Charlotte's copter settled on the sand, thirty meters closer to the woman's position than any of the others, and Charlotte threw open the door. She stepped down onto the beach, conscious of the fact that hundreds of flying eyes would now be focused on her.

Suddenly the air around the red-haired woman was filled by a haze of what looked like smoke. As she came back to an erect position, the haze dispersed.

"Artificial spores," Michael Lowenthal guessed. He was still in the copter, but he had moved to Charlotte's seat in order to get a better view. "Millions of them—she knew she'd never get to kiss Czastka, so she's casting them adrift on the wind."

"Where's Czastka?" Charlotte shouted, turning up the mike on her beltphone in the hope that the task-force commander might still be able to hear her—but the thrum of the slowing helicopter blades was still too loud to allow her to be heard. She hoped that the Creationist was still inside, his walls sealed tight against any form of biological invasion.

Charlotte took three steps toward the young woman, then raised her gun, holding it in both hands, and pointed it. The noise of the copters was fading fast, and she was certain that she would be heard if she shouted.

"Raise your hands!" she yelled.

The woman was standing perfectly still now, but she had to turn through ninety degrees to face Charlotte. The expression on her face was unreadable, and Charlotte was not at all sure that the woman could see her, let alone hear her—but as she turned she meekly raised her hands high above her head. By the time her bright green eyes met Charlotte's, she was still, impassive, and seemingly harmless.

Charlotte felt a wave of thankfulness sweep through her tense frame. She took her left hand off the stock of the gun and beckoned to the woman.

"Come to me!" she instructed. "Slowly, now."

From the corners of her eyes Charlotte could see uniformed men dismounting from the other helicopters, but they simply stepped down to the ground, watching and waiting. The sound of the copter blades was a mere hum by now, but Charlotte's ears had been numbed by the cacophony, and she was not sure how loud the sound was. She could hear the distant whine of Oscar Wilde's copter, though. It had turned to circle the beach rather than coming in to land.

The woman showed not the slightest sign of obeying Charlotte's last order. She stood where she was, unmoving. Her arms were still upraised in a gesture of surrender, but the gesture suddenly seemed to Charlotte to be slightly mocking. The murderess had apparently done what she came to do, and had accepted that it was all over—but she did not seem to be in any hurry to place herself in custody and climb aboard the helicopter that would ferry her to judgment.

"Come this way!" Charlotte repeated, shouting in case the woman had not been able to hear the first command. "Walk toward the helicopter, slowly." She lifted the handset from her beltphone and spoke into it. "Better get your men back into the copters," she said to the task-force commander. "The stuff she's released is probably harmless to anyone but Czastka, but there's no point in taking risks. When we get back to Kauai, everyone goes through decontamination."

"As you wish, *Sergeant,*" said the officer sourly.

The woman still had not moved. She stood statue-still, looking up into the brilliant blue sky. It seemed that Charlotte had no alternative but to go to her.

Charlotte replaced the handset of her beltphone and took two steps forward, saying: "My name is Detective Sergeant Charlotte Holmes of the UN police. I'm arresting you on suspicion—"

She was interrupted by a cry of alarm from the helicopter that had settled on the far side of the woman's position. The uniformed men had been obediently climbing back aboard, but the last one had paused and turned—and now he was pointing, apparently at the two women.

"Look out!" he cried.

Charlotte's right hand tensed about the handle of the gun, and her left moved back to support it. Her forefinger curled around the trigger—but the red-haired woman hadn't moved a muscle, and there was no evident threat. Charlotte heard a strange squawking sound emanating from the region of her hip and realized that someone was trying to attract her attention by shouting over the voice link to her handset. She lowered her left hand again, rather uncertainly, and plucked the handset from its holster. "It's okay," she said impatiently. "She has no weapon. It's all under control."

"Look behind you!" screeched the unrecognizable voice, still trying to shout at her although the volume control on the beltphone was automatically compensating. *Corruption and corrosion, woman, look behind you!"*

Uncomprehendingly, Charlotte looked behind her.

Gliding toward her from the vivid brightness of the climbing sun was a broad black shadow. At first she could judge neither its breadth nor its exact shape, but as it swooped down upon her the truth became abundantly and monstrously clear.

She could not believe the evidence of her eyes. She knew full well that what she was seeing was impossible, and her mind stubbornly refused to accept the truth of what she saw. She understood, as her unbelief stupefied and froze her, why the voice had been trying so hard to achieve an appropriate level of amplification. In addition to the need to warn her that she was in danger, there had been a need to express shock, horror, and sheer terror.

It was a bird—but it was a bird like none which had ever taken to the skies of Earth in the entire evolutionary history of flight. Its wingspan was larger than the reach of the helicopter blades that were already spinning again as the automatic pilots prepared for flight. Its vast wings were black, but they glinted like the wings of starlings; their pinion feathers somehow reminded Charlotte of scimitars and samurai swords. Its enormous and horrible head was naked, like a vulture's, and its eyes were the size of basketballs; they were crimson in color, but as they caught the sunlight it seemed that they were all aglow with a sulphurous inner light.

The creature's raptorial beak was fully agape, and it cried out as it swept over her head. Its call was a terrible inhuman shriek, which put Charlotte in mind of the wailing of the damned in some ancient mythical hell. She felt as if she had been frozen in place, like a pillar of salt, to await her doom as that terrible beak closed upon her tender flesh—but the beak passed her by, and the huge claws too. Their talons were aimed at the other woman: Rappaccini's unnatural daughter.

Charlotte's momentary petrifaction came to an end. Even as she perceived that she was not the target of the monster's dive, panic took hold of her and threw her aside like a rag doll. She had no time to realign and fire her gun, nor even to think about realigning and firing it. Her reflexes rudely cast her down, tumbling her ig-nominiously onto the silvery sand.

Rappaccini's daughter, if that were indeed what she deemed herself to be, did not change her position in the slightest. Her hands were still lifted high into the air. Her eyes were unconcerned, apparently entranced.

Charlotte understood now—how obvious it was, *now!*—that the meek raising of those arms had not been a gesture of surrender at all; the woman had merely been making preparations for the arrival of her appalling rescuer. Charlotte twisted her body so that she could watch, but her limbs still hugged the ground, as if they were trying to bury into the warm and welcoming sand.

And this is going out live to half the population of the world! Charlotte thought. What a way to win a ratings war!

As though with an ease induced by long and patient practice, the woman who had been Rappaccini's murderous instrument in-terlaced the fingers of both her hands with the reaching talons of the huge bird and was lifted instantly from her feet.

Charlotte was still conscious of the fact that what she was see-ing was, according to all the most reliable authorities, quite impos-sible. No bird could lift an adult human being from the ground, and rumors of eagles of old which had been able to lift children and sheep were confidently judged by historians and naturalists to have been wildly exaggerated. No bird which had ever been shaped by natural selection to fly above the surface of the earth could lift such a weight in addition to its own. But how much did this monstrosity weigh? More than a helicopter, and as much as the aircraft which Rappaccini had provided to fly Charlotte and her two companions to Kauai? Its metabolism must be highly unorthodox, or it would not be able to take off—but it was gliding now, and any man-made glider of similar dimension could have carried several passengers. It *was* possible, because it was happening. Somehow, it was possible.

The bird was already climbing again, soaring on the thermal which rose from the warm morning sea. It beat its fabulous night black wings with extravagant majesty—once, twice, and again—but then it banked and circled around into the dazzling halo of brilliance which surrounded the tropical sun, whence its awesome dive had come. A moment later, as Charlotte shielded her eyes, it flew out of the fire again, like a phoenix reborn.

Charlotte reached up her free hand to take the one which Michael Lowenthal was extending to her, having appeared as if by magic at her side. Her right hand returned the dart gun to its clasp as she was raised to her feet.

"Best get back if we intend to chase it," he said.

He let go of her hand and she had to hurry along behind him, stumbling in the soft surface. The other helicopters were already taking off, the sound of their many blades escalating into a hideous roar.

"She didn't get Czastka!" Lowenthal shouted as he stopped by the copter's landing rail, letting Charlotte pass him before shoving her from behind to help her into the cabin.

Didn't she? Charlotte wondered, not bothering to speak the words aloud. She did what she came to do—that much is certain.

Once the helicopter was off the ground and its cabin was sealed, the background noise became bearable again—and Oscar Wilde was already clamoring for the attention of the machine's comcon. Charlotte took his call.

"He told us what would happen!" Wilde lamented. "He told us—and I failed to hear it!"

"What?" she said. "*Who* told us?"

"Rappaccini! The simulacrum costumed as Herod said, 'This is no cocoon of hollowed stone; it is my palace. Hear me, Oscar: you will see the finest roc of all before the end.' I heard it as r-o-c-k, but he meant r-o-c all the time. A cheap trick, but when Michael's friends release the tape of Herod's performance, everyone who hears it will wonder why it never occurred to us. We are being made to look foolish, Charlotte—and we have only one opportunity left to redeem ourselves."

"She can't get away," Charlotte said grimly. "I don't know how far or fast that thing can fly, but we can fly further, and maybe even faster. She is *not* going to get away."

"I don't think she's even trying," said Wilde, with a sigh. "She's merely leading us to the much-joked-about Island of Dr. Moreau, so that we may cast our wondering eyes upon her father's demi-paradise: his Creation."

Charlotte's heart was no longer pounding quite so hard, and she forced herself to relax into the seat. She glanced out of the viewport at Walter Czastka's island, already dwindling to a green diamond rimmed with silver and set on a bed of royal blue.

"We've got to warn Czastka," she said. "We have to tell him not to unseal his locks."

"That's not necessary," said Oscar Wilde. "He has a TV set. If he's taking any notice of anything, he must have seen the woman release the spores—but he will not fall into the trap that claimed us. He knows, as I think he always knew, what form the final murder was always intended to take."

"What do you mean?" Charlotte asked.

"I mean that we failed to anticipate the last ironic twist and turn of Rappaccini's plot. It's not Walter those spores are after—

it's his ecosphere. The woman didn't come here to murder Walter, but to murder his world. But what will poor Walter be, when his entire Creation is gone? Or should the question be: What has he become during these last forty years, while it was taking shape? Did you not see, Charlotte? Did you not see what lay beyond the palms fringing the beach?"

Charlotte remembered, vaguely, that as her helicopter had come in to land she had looked briefly sideways, scanning the trees which stood guard on the margin of the island's vegetation. She recalled a blurred impression of lush ferny undergrowth nestled about the boles of palmlike trees. She half remembered an extensive patchwork of vivid green, flecked with darker colors: crimsons, purples, and blues deep enough to be almost black—but nothing distinct. She had looked, but she had not *observed*. Her attention had been fixed on the woman and the rival helicopters; she had not spared a moment's thought for Walter Czastka's exercise in petty godhood.

"I didn't notice anything in particular," she told Oscar Wilde.

"Nothing can stop them," Oscar said, his voice reduced almost to a whisper. "Each murderer is one hundred percent specific to its victim. Walter's own body is safe inside the house, but that's not what Walter cares about . . . it's not what Walter *is*. What you didn't even notice, *in particular*, was Walter Czastka. It was all that was left of him, the sum total of his life's achievement. Rappaccini's instruments will devour and digest his ecosphere—every last molecule of it—and in doing so will devour Walter more absolutely than they could ever have done by transforming his flesh. I doubt that he can or will be thankful for the fact that he's already past caring, and that the spores are carrion-feeders consuming something that had never properly come to life."

For the first time, Charlotte realized, Oscar Wilde was genuinely horrified. The infuriating equanimity which had hardly been rippled by his first sight of Gabriel King's hideously embellished skeleton, or anything else they had seen in their travels, had at last been moved to empathetic outrage. The thought that *this* kind of murder might be visited upon a fellow human being—a fellow Creationist—had finally cracked his composure.

For the first time, Oscar was identifying with one of Rappaccini's victims—ironically enough, with the one who had most aroused his contempt. He was finally seeing Rappaccini as a great criminal as well as a mediocre artist.

"Why do you say that Czastka's miniecosphere had *never properly come to life*?" Charlotte asked.

"Did you really see nothing?" he countered. "Did you really not see what kind of demi-Eden Walter Czastka had been endeavoring to build? Perhaps that is the most damning indictment of all. Were you to visit my island in Micronesia, even under such stressful circumstances . . ."

As Wilde left the sentence dangling, Charlotte tried once again to remember what she might have glimpsed—in addition to helicopters—from the corners of her eyes while she confronted the red-haired woman on the beach. There had been trees, bushes, flowers—but no animals. Nothing remarkable. Nothing which had called attention to itself. Even so, given the strength of the competition from the items which *had* grabbed and held her gaze, was that in any way remarkable?

While she was trying to remember, Wilde's fingers stabbed at the console in front of him. No sooner had she admitted defeat than the image she could not summon to mind was displayed for her—by courtesy, she supposed, of the cameras attached to one of the hovering helicopters.

There were, as she had vaguely observed, tall palm trees bordering the beach. Within their picket line was a complex array of broad-leaved bushes, lavishly decorated with brightly colored flowers. Charlotte could not tell a rhododendron from a magnolia, but the flowers seemed to her to be very nicely shaped as well as capacious. The bushes were not gathered into hedges, but they were planted in such a way as to form curving lines, which mapped out a circular maze interrupted by dozens of elliptical gardens, where other flowers grew on pyramidal mounds, their contrasted colors swirling around one another in carefully contrived patterns. It was impossible to see much detail from the camera's vantage point, but the overall effect seemed to Charlotte to be not unpleasing. She actually formed that phrase in her mind before realizing that it concealed a barb.

Walter Czastka's Eden was *not unpleasing*. Its elements were *very nicely shaped*. The whole vast expanse was neat and delicately coordinated, colorful, and clever, but ultimately lifeless. Perhaps, Charlotte thought, Walter Czastka had never seen his work from such a distance and altitude. Perhaps it all seemed very different at ground level. Perhaps, if one could only see the fine detail, the meticulous workmanship, the delicacy of each individual flower. . . .

"I can't judge it," she said to Oscar Wilde. "I'm not qualified."

"I am," Wilde told her, with all the assurance of perfect arrogance. "So was Rappaccini. What a miserably enfeebled Arcadia poor Walter had built! Immature and incomplete though it undoubtedly was, its limitations were painfully conspicuous. Had you only had time to stand and stare, you would have seen—and even you, dear Charlotte, would have *known* that you had seen—the work of a hack. A hack, admittedly, who was trying to exceed his own potential, but the work of a hack nevertheless. Had you my eyes, you would see plainly enough even in this snapshot the work of a man who had not even the imagination of blind and stupid nature. Skills honed by a hundred years and more of careful practice had been exercised on that isle, but the result was mere kitsch."

"That's not fair," Charlotte said. "You don't know what he was trying to achieve, or what he would have achieved, given time."

"No," said Oscar, "it's not *fair*—but neither is artistry. I know now why Walter tried to keep me away. I understand the message which he engraved upon the minuscule soul of his nearest and dearest simulacrum. But Rappaccini had seen it! Rappaccini must have kept careful watch on Walter for more than half a lifetime, ever since his mother took the trouble to tell him what and who he was. How disappointed he must have been in his Creator!"

"Creator?" Charlotte queried.

"But of course! What is the subject of this melodrama, if not Creation? Unless Walter cares to tell us, or Rappaccini has left a record, I doubt that we shall ever know the intimate details, but I cannot believe that Maria Inacio's pregnancy was an accident or the result of a rape. Hal blithely assumed that she could never have known that she was immune to the endemic chiasmatic transformers until she became pregnant, and perhaps he was right—but when did she *first* become pregnant, and who did she tell? If we suppose that her first pregnancy was surreptitiously terminated, we may also suppose that she might then have come to seem, in the eyes of an ambitious but desperately naive Creationist, a unique resource. Suppose, for a moment, that the plagues which sterilized the human race had never occurred and never forced the universalization of ectogenesis. Had the chiasmatic transformers not ravaged all the wombs that Mother Nature had provided, what other kinds of transformers might have been sent forth in their stead?"

"You're saying that Walter Czastka used Maria Inacio in some kind of clandestine experiment in human genetic engineering—that he used her as an incubator for a modified embryo that he'd never have got permission to grow in an artificial womb?"

"It was 2322," Oscar Wilde reminded her, "more than eighty years before the Great Exhibition. The limitations of indwelling nanotech had come to light, but work to put something in its place had hardly begun in earnest. The Green Zealots were in their heyday, and the Robot Assassins were not yet a spent force. The opportunity for daring was there—but so was the need for secrecy. We know that Jafri Biasiolo had been subjected to considerable genetic manipulation that was idiosyncratic in nature and unusual in extent. Who could or would have done that but Walter? Who else but he could have removed ova from her womb, fertilized them with his own sperm, then set about remaking them? Who else but he could have selected out the best of the transformed embryos and reimplanted it within her womb?

"I don't know how the other five were involved, but each of them must have contributed something to the project, even if some or all were ignorant of the contributions made by the others. Perhaps one of them was responsible for Maria Inacio's first pregnancy, while another assisted in its termination. Perhaps one was Walter's accomplice in the laboratory, while another played some part in having the second embryo removed to a Helier womb. Perhaps one was to have provided safe accommodation for the pregnant mother when she could no longer be seen in public. There are a thousand different scenarios I could imagine . . . but the one salient point is that Jafri Biasiolo did not think of Walter Czastka as his *father*. He thought of him as his *Creator!* In all of this, he has engaged himself with Walter the Creator—and in preparing to obliterate all the products of Walter's Creationist ambition, he also took it upon himself to obliterate all those named by Maria Inacio as accomplices in the exploitation of her unexpectedly fertile womb."

"You certainly have an extraordinarily vivid imagination, Dr. Wilde," Charlotte murmured. Her policeman's conscience had already reminded her that there was not a shred of hard evidence to support any of it, but she could see that it had to be true in its essentials.

"Yes, Charlotte, I certainly have," he said, casually accepting the compliment. "Walter Czastka, alas, has not. He had the seed of the gift, but he lost it—or killed it. He let it shrivel within his soul, out of shame, or guilt, or fear, or petty regret. Though his heart still beats within his withered frame, he has already begun to rot. Rappaccini's worms are feeding on his carcass."

"But what was he trying to do with Maria Inacio?" Charlotte asked.

"The one thing worth attempting, at that time and in that context," Wilde said, with a heavy sigh. "Walter must already have known, even though the rest of the world was only just beginning to realize and had not yet openly admitted, that the nanotech escalator had stalled. Human emortality could not be attained by means of nanotech and superficial somatic engineering; it required genetic engineering in embryo. What Walter attempted was a transformation of the kind that was not perfected for a further century and more: a Zaman transformation. Alas, its effects were purely cosmetic; Jafri Biasiolo retained the appearance of dignified maturity longer than his contemporaries, but he remained as mortal as they. He must have known soon after the Great Exhibition that he was little different from other men."

"And that's why Rappaccini decided to kill Czastka and all his accomplices? Because they *failed*?" Charlotte was incredulous. That seemed to her like monstrous ingratitude.

"I doubt that it was as simple as that. Rappaccini was too sensible and sensitive a man to condemn a fellow scientist for an experiment that produced a negative result. Perhaps he decided to kill his Creator and all the accomplices in his Creation because, having failed in their bold attempt to be midwives of a new era, *they gave up*. Perhaps Rappaccini the scientist and Rappaccini the artist could forgive them their failure, but not their repentance. Perhaps he hoped that his Creator might return to the true path, and in the end despaired. On the other hand, he may simply have decided that he had been a closely kept secret for far too long, and that he ought to be remembered for what he truly was: a unique man, and a unique artist. Perhaps he became determined to shout from the rooftops that which Walter and his coconspirators were so determined to keep quiet, by way of compensation for his own betrayal. By the time the casters have unraveled the thread of this plot, everyone in the world will know what Jafri Biasiolo was, and what he made of himself."

By the time that Gustave Moreau's green-clad island came in view, Charlotte had placed a bubblebug on her forehead in preparation for the landing. Hal Watson would be able to use it as an eye as long as she stayed within a few hundred meters of the copter. Given that Moreau's island was more or less identical in size and shape to Walter Czastka's, it seemed unlikely that she would have to stray beyond that limit.

The flight of the giant bird had now become slightly drunken, although it was still gliding. Every slight adjustment of its wings seemed exaggerated, and it was losing height inexorably. Huge though it was, the weight of an adult human being and the instability induced by her awkward position were making it difficult for the monster to complete its task. Charlotte wondered whether the creature had sufficient strength left to make a successful landfall.

It was clear to Charlotte that the woman's murders must have been planned in such a way as to lay a trail, and that it was Moreau's island, not Czastka's, that had always been the end point of that trail. Thanks to the special provision which Moreau had made for Oscar Wilde, she and Lowenthal had been able to follow the trail's most scenic route and had arrived at the appointed destination ahead of any other actual persons—but every news service in the world must have scrambled every available flying eye by now.

It wasn't every day that the vidveg had the chance to see a police helicopter chase come unstuck because a roc had abducted a beautiful female serial killer.

Nor did Charlotte need Oscar Wilde to tell her that she was about to attend an exhibition: an exhibition which was presumably designed to put the so-called Great Exhibition of 2405 to shame. Most of the exhibits, she suspected, would be illegal—which was one reason why the exhibitor had chosen this peculiarly flamboyant method of issuing invitations. Moreau's roc had already demonstrated that he was a genetic engineer of genius—perhaps the greatest genetic engineer the world had ever known—but its function was merely to attract attention. In her own way, the "daughter" that Moreau had produced by cloning his mother and then modifying her genome in as-yet-unspecified ways was equally astonishing, and Charlotte assumed that the island would be abundantly stocked with similar miracles.

Moreau was clearly a man for whom the impossible was merely routine, and the miraculous that which could confidently be scheduled for the week after next. He was also a man whose *real* work had been kept secret for a century and more, while he had been content to restrict his public dealings to the design and supply of funeral wreaths.

Charlotte watched the bird summon up the last vestiges of its strength for its landing maneuver. It banked to the left, its wings curving to catch the air; then the gargantuan limbs flapped once, twice, and thrice as the creature fell toward the silver strand where the waves were breaking over Dr. Moreau's island.

Charlotte's helicopter followed, then Oscar Wilde's. The five copters from Kauai were still in attendance, but they had already received orders to keep their cabins sealed after landing lest their occupants become vectors of unknown biocontamination. Charlotte had already reconciled herself to the prospect of a period in quarantine.

The copter's safety-minded silver pilot gave the beached roc a wide berth, putting Charlotte and Lowenthal down a full sixty meters from the point where the woman had been dropped. The fugitive had already picked herself up and had disappeared into the trees which fringed the beach.

Charlotte unplugged her beltphone from the helicopter's comcon without bothering to sign off, and put the handset in its holster. Hal would be able to see what was going on, but she didn't want him babbling in her ear. It had fallen to her to make the final arrest, with the world looking on, and she didn't want it to look as if she were merely a marionette, dancing to New York's tune.

She did not attempt to approach the roc, although she took a long look at the chimerical creature before turning to follow the red-haired woman. The bird peered back at her dolefully from one unnaturally large and bloodily crimson eye; the other was hidden by the bulk of its naked head. It did not look so horrid onow that it seemed helpless. It looked mournful, and rather tragic.

Michael Lowenthal came abreast of her as she paused, and Oscar Wilde was already running across the sand to join the two of them.

"You shouldn't have got out," she said to Wilde as lightly as she could. "You'll have to be quarantined now."

"You know perfectly well, dear Charlotte," Wilde replied, not quite breathlessly, "that I could not possibly be content to watch the final act of the comedy through an artificial eye mounted on the brow of a police officer."

"It's a comedy now, is it?" said Lowenthal sourly. "I can't quite see the joke."

"It is," Wilde intoned, puffing himself up with false dignity, "a *divine* comedy. If we can read it rightly, all of modern life's metaphysical frame will be shown to us here: our land of darkness, our purgatory, our paradise."

Charlotte and her two companions walked side by side to the place where Moreau's murderous agent had disappeared, keeping a wary eye on the roc while they did so. The bird made no move toward them; its wings were still outstretched, and it seemed to be in considerable distress. It must have been created, Charlotte realized, merely in order to make that single flight; it had served its purpose and might never fly again. As she glanced back for the last time before moving into the trees, Charlotte saw the bloody eyes eclipsed by wrinkled lids.

"Will it die?" she asked of Oscar Wilde.

"I hope not," he replied. "It would be unfortunate were such a magnificent creation to lose its life in the interests of a mere coup de théâtre. On the other hand, one cannot push back the limits of the possible without sacrifice—and Rappaccini has shown little sign of compunction in that regard."

Together, they moved into the forest.

●　　　●　　　●

Charlotte found herself leading the way along a narrow grassy pathway, which had the appearance of an accident of nature but which must in fact have been designed with the utmost care. As Charlotte looked from side to side the whole scene seemed remarkably focused, clear and sharp in every detail. It seemed that every leaf on every tree had been not merely designed but *arranged* with excessive scrupulousness.

There were no mock palms here. This forest was very different from any that Charlotte had ever seen before. The trunk of every tree had grown into the shape of something else, as finely wrought in bronze-barked wood as any sculpture. No two were exactly alike: here was the image of a dragon rampant, here a mermaid, here a trilobite, and here a shaggy faun. Many were the images of beasts which natural selection had designed to walk on four legs, but all of them stood upright here, rearing back to extend their forelimbs, separately or entwined, high into the air. These upraised forelimbs provided bases for spreading crowns of many different colors: all the greens and coppery browns of Ancient Nature; all the purples, golds, and blues that Ancient Nature had never quite mastered; even the graphite black of Solid Artificial Photosynthetic systems. Some few of the crowns extended from an entire host of limbs rather than a single pair, originating from the maws of krakens or the stalks of hydras.

The animals whose shapes were reproduced by the trunks of the trees all had open eyes, which seemed to look at Charlotte no matter where she was in relation to them. Although she knew that they were all quite blind, she could not help feeling discomfited by their seeming curiosity.

Her own curiosity, however, was more than equal to theirs.

Every tree of the forest was in flower, and every flower was as bizarre as the plant which bore it. All possible colors were manifest in the blossoms, but there was a noticeable preponderance of reds and blacks. Butterflies and hummingbirds moved ceaselessly through the branches, each one wearing its own coat of many colors, and the tips of the branches moved as if stirred by a breeze, reaching out toward these visitors, seemingly yearning to touch their tiny faces.

There was no wind; the branches moved by their own volition, according to their own mute purposes.

Charlotte could see electronic hoverflies mingling with Gustave Moreau's insects, and ponderous flitterbugs jostling for position with the tinier hummingbirds. No predators came to harass them, although there were larger birds concealed by the foliage, audible as they moved from branch to branch and occasionally visible in brief flashes of vivid coloration.

Charlotte knew that much of what she saw was manifestly illegal. Creationists were restricted by all manner of arcane regulations in the engineering of insects and birds, lest their inventions should stray to pollute the artwork of other engineers or to intermingle with the more extensive ecosystems of the world at large. Most Creationists undoubtedly took some liberties to which they were not theoretically entitled—even Walter Czastka had probably been guilty of that, no matter how dull his efforts had seemed to Oscar Wilde—but Charlotte had no doubt that when the final accounting of Gustave Moreau's felonies and misdemeanors was complete, he would turn out to have been the most prolific as well as the most versatile criminal who had ever lived upon the surface of the earth.

All of this would be destroyed, of course—as Moreau must have known when he had planned it and while he built it. He had given birth to an extraordinary fantasy, fully aware that it would be ephemeral; but instead of leaving it to the scrupulously scientific attentions of a UN inspection team—who would have filed their records away and left them moldering in some quiet corner of the Webworld—he had found a way to *command* that rapt attention be paid to it by every man, woman, and child in the world. Only thus, he must have decided, could due recognition be given to his

awesome genius: his talent as an artist and engineer, and his ingenuity as a social commentator.

Had the designer of this alien ecosphere, Charlotte wondered,
dared to hope that his contemporaries might recognize and reckon
him a true Creationist, to be set as far above the petty laws of
humankind as the obsolete gods of old had once been set? Had he
dared to believe that even the vidveg might condone what he had
done, once they saw it in all its glory?

No, she concluded. Even Rappaccini/Moreau could not have
credited the vidveg with that much imagination.

Charlotte soon perceived that Moreau's creative fecundity had
not been content with birds and insects. There were monkeys in the
trees too: monkeys which did not hide or flee from the invaders of
their private paradise, but came instead to peep out at them from
the gaudy crowns and stare with patient curiosity at their visitors.

The monkeys were not huge; none was more than a meter from
top to toe, and all had the slender bodies of gibbons and lorises—
but they had the wizened faces of old men. Nor was that appearance
merely the generic resemblance which had once been manifest in
the faces of certain long-extinct New World monkeys; these faces
were *actual* human faces, writ small. Charlotte recognized a family
of Czastkas, a pair of Teidemanns, an assortment of Kings and Urashimas—but there were dozens to which she could not put names.
Perhaps they too had been contemporaries of Walter Czastka at
Wollongong, or perhaps their lives had been entangled with his in
other ways. Perhaps some were still living—and perhaps the chain
of murders would have had far more links had more provisionally
selected targets survived to the ripe old age of a hundred and ninety-
four.

The eyes set in these surrounding faces, which now increased
in number with Charlotte's every stride, were neither blind nor utterly stupid; nor was she prepared to invoke her habitual notions
of impossibility to set a limit on the intelligence which lurked behind them. It seemed entirely likely that they might break out into

cacophonous speech at any moment, and just as probable that one appointed spokesman might lower itself to the path ahead of her and offer her a formal welcome.

Posturing apes, she thought, remembering Gabriel King's verdict.

Charlotte swallowed air, unsuccessfully trying to remove a lump of unease from her throat. She tried to ignore the staring eyes of the monkeys in order to concentrate on the gorgeous blossoms which framed their faces. They all seemed unnaturally large and bright, and every one presented a great fan or bell of petals and sepals, surrounding a complex network of stamens and compound styles. There was no way that she could begin to take in their awesome profusion and variety. She felt that her senses were quite overloaded—and not merely her sense of sight, for the moist atmosphere was a riot of perfumes, while the murmurous humming of insect wings improvised a subtle symphony.

Is it truly beautiful? Charlotte asked herself as she studied the sculpted trees which stared at her with their myriad illusory eyes, their hectic crowns, and their luminous flowers. Or is it all fabulously mad?

She did not need to consult Oscar Wilde; she knew his intellectual methods by now.

It *was* truly beautiful, she admitted, and fabulously mad too— and having admitted it, she let the tide of her appreciation run riot. It was more beautiful than anything she had ever seen or ever hoped to see. It was more beautiful and more intoxicating than anything *anyone* had ever seen or hoped to see. It was infinitely more beautiful than the ghostly echoes of Ancient Nature which modern men called wilderness. It was infinitely more beautiful and infinitely less sane than Ancient Nature itself, even in all its pre-Crash glory, could ever have been.

All this, even Charlotte's unschooled eyes could see, was the work of a *young* man. However many years Rappaccini/Moreau had lived, however many he had spent in glorious isolation in the midst of all this strange fecundity, he had never grown old and never grown wise. All this was Folly: unashamed and unapologetic Folly. This was not the work of a man grown mournful in forgetfulness, obsessed with the pursuit of a vanishing past; this was the work of a man whose only thought was of the future: of novelty, of ambition, of progress. Perhaps Walter Czastka's illegal experiment had not been such an abject failure after all; perhaps the transformation it had wrought had merely been subtler than its designer had intended.

This was Moreau's island—*morrow's* island—but the child that had been father to the man who became Moreau had itself been fathered, and created. Perhaps this ought to be reckoned Walter Czastka's Eden too, at least as much as the one into which he had poured the futile labor of his dotage.

Charlotte no longer needed the advice of Oscar Wilde's interpretations. Whatever resonances of the distant past might have evaded her youthful ignorance, she felt that she understood the present heart of the little world which surrounded her, and the kind of soul which hovered invisibly in every molecular skein of it all.

Yes, it was truly beautiful, and fabulous and mad—but the truth, the beauty, the fabulousness, and the madness were the work of a true Creationist.

In the heart of Moreau's island, Charlotte expected to find a house, but there was no house there. Once, no doubt, there had been a dwelling place on the site—a laboratory and a workshop, a palace and a forge, a refuge and a hatchery—but all of that had been banished now, buried underground if not actually dismantled.

Now, there was only a mausoleum.

Charlotte knew that Moreau had died in Honolulu, but she also recalled that his body had been returned to the island, where someone with no official existence must have taken delivery of it and laid it in this tomb. Charlotte assumed that it would not be allowed to remain here, but it was here now: the mortal centerpiece of Moreau's Creation.

It was a very large tomb, hewn from a white marble whose austerity stood in imperious contrast to the fabulous forest around it. There was nothing overelaborate about its formation, although it was tastefully decorated. It bore neither cross nor carven angel, but on the plain white flank which loomed above its pediment a text was inscribed. It read:

SPLEEN

Je suis comme le roi d'un pays pluvieux,
Riche, mais impuissant, jeune et pourtant très-vieux,
Qui, de ses précepteurs méprisant les courbettes,
S'ennuie avec ses chiens comme avec d'autres bêtes.
Rien ne peut l'égayer, ni gibier, ni faucon,
Ni son peuple mourant en face du balcon.
Du bouffon favori la grotesque ballade
Ne distrait plus le front de ce cruel malade;
Son lit fleurdelisé se transforme en tombeau,
Et les dames d'atour, pour qui tout prince est beau,
Ne savent plus trouver d'impudique toilette
Pour tirer un souris de ce jeune squelette.
Le savant qui lui fait de l'or n'a jamais pu
De son être extirper l'élément corrompu,
Et dans ces bains de sang qui des Romains nous
    viennent,
Et dont sur leurs vieux jours les puissants se
    souviennent,
Il n'a su réchauffer ce cadavre hébété
Où coule au lieu de sang l'eau verte du Léthé.

"Baudelaire?" Charlotte asked of Oscar Wilde.

"Of course," he replied. "Would you like me to translate?"

"If you would."

"It runs approximately thus," he said.

"I am like the monarch of a rain-soaked realm,

"Rich but powerless, young but perhaps too old,

"Who, despising the sycophancy of his teachers,

"Is as sick of his dogs as of all other beasts.

"Nothing can enliven him, neither prey, nor predator,

"Nor deaths displayed before his balcony.

"The satirical ballads of his appointed fool

"No longer soothe the frown of his cruel malady;

"His flower-decked couch is transformed into a tomb,

"And the courtesans for whom every prince is handsome,

"Can no longer find attire sufficiently immodest,

"To force this youthful skeleton to smile.

"The maker of alchemical gold has never contrived

"To extirpate elementary corruption from his own being,

"And in those baths of blood which the Romans left to us,

"Which powerful men recall in the days of their old age,

"He has failed to renew the warmth of that dazed cadaver

"Where runs instead of blood the green water of forgetfulness."

"Spleen, I assume, does not here refer to the common or garden organ of that name?" said Michael Lowenthal.

"It does not," Wilde confirmed. "Its meaning here is one that was rendered obsolete by the modern medical theories which replaced the ancient lore of bodily humors. Spleen was the aggravated form of the decadents' ennui: a bitter world-weariness, a sullenly wrathful resentment of the essential dullness of existence."

"Is that, do you suppose, what drove him to make all this?" Charlotte asked.

"I doubt it. This paradise was not born of bitterness or resentment, although the trail of murders that paved our way with bad intentions must have been. The poem is a commentary on the art-

ist's final approach to death, not on his life as a whole. Spleen was
what Moreau fought with all his might to resist, although he knew
that he could not live forever, and that it would claim him in the
end. Like us, dear Charlotte, he was delivered by history to the very
threshold of true emortality, and yet was fated not to live in the
Promised Land. How he must have resented the fading of the faculties which had produced *all this*! How he must have hated the
knowledge that his creative powers were ebbing away! How wrathful he must have become, to see his fate mirrored in the faces and
careers of all those who had a hand in his own Creation. While the
true emortals emerge from the womb of biotechnical artifice, today
and tomorrow—and tomorrow and tomorrow and tomorrow—
they can no longer care who their fathers are or might have been,
for they are designed by men like gods, from common chromosomal
clay." He looked at Michael Lowenthal as he pronounced the final
sentence—but Michael Lowenthal looked away rather than meet
the geneticist's accusing stare.

Charlotte looked around, wondering where the red-haired
woman might be—and wondering, now, exactly *what* the red-
haired woman might be. She was a clone of Maria Inacio, and yet
not *quite* a clone. Some of her genes had been modified by engineering while she was still an ovum—just as some of her son/fa-
ther's genes had been modified by the young Walter Czastka. She,
like her own Creator, had been designed by a man trying to become
like a god, from common chromosomal clay—but Gustave Moreau
must have done everything within his power to surpass Walter
Czastka in that regard. The woman must surely be a Natural, in the
limited sense that Michael Lowenthal was, but how much more had
Moreau tried to make of her?

Charlotte remembered some words that Moreau, as Herod, had
quoted at Oscar Wilde, teasing him with the charge that even he
could not have encountered them before: "Mortality, Behold and
Fear! What a change of flesh is here!" But the woman was a multiple murderess; when the law took its course, her career would

surely be subject to a demolition as comprehensive and as brutal as the one to which this exotic demi-Eden would be subject.

Charlotte knew, as she framed that thought, that it might not be quite as simple as that. Oscar Wilde, for one, would fight for the preservation of Moreau's island—and how many allies would he find among the millions of watchers who were waiting for her to locate and arrest her suspect? How many allies might the lovely murderess find, even in a world where death was regarded with such intense loathing and fascination?

While Michael Lowenthal was still making shift to avoid Oscar Wilde's stare, Charlotte moved away from them to make a tour of the massive mausoleum.

It required only half a dozen steps to bring her quarry into view. The fugitive was sitting on the pediment on the further side of the tomb, facing a crowd of leaping lions and prancing unicorns, vaulting hippogriffs and rearing cobras, all of them hewn in living wood beneath a roof of rainbows. Hundreds of man-faced monkeys were solemnly observing the scene.

The woman was quite still, and her vivid green eyes, which matched the color of the foliage of one particular tree which stood directly before her, were staring vacuously into space. It was as if she could not even see the fantastic host which paraded itself before her. Her arms were slightly spread, the palms of her hands upturned, each balancing a different object—but it was not her hands which drew Charlotte's gaze.

The woman was quite bald, and her skull was studded with silver contact points.

The hair that the woman had worn throughout her murderous odyssey lay like stranded seaweed upon the white marble between her feet—but its strands were still stirring like stately ripples in a quiet pond, and wherever it caught a shaft of sunlight it glittered, showing all its myriad colors in rapid sequence, from polished silver through amber gold and flaming red to burnt sienna and raven black.

The stars in the hairless skull glistened too, in the reflected light of the sun. Charlotte could hardly help but be reminded of the cruder decorations which Michi Urashima had accumulated on his own skull, but she knew that these must be different. Urashima was a self-made man, who had found his true vocation late in life. This person had been born to her heritage; her brain had been designed to be fed, and not with any ordinary nourishment.

In the woman's left hand lay a single flower: a gorgeously gilded rose. In her right hand she held a scroll of parchment, neatly rolled and tied with blue ribbon.

Oscar Wilde stepped past Charlotte and picked up the gilded rose. He placed it carefully in the mock buttonhole formed by the false collar of his suitskin. He had discarded his green carnation.

Charlotte stooped and reached out to touch the mass of "hair" which lay upon the marble. It moved in response to her touch, but not to recoil or flee. The ripples in its surface became waves, and its strands coiled like a nest of impossibly slender and improbably numerous snakes. It had more mass than she had thought likely. Quelling her instinctive revulsion, Charlotte picked it up and let its strands wrap themselves around her wrists and fingers, as if in grateful affection. She could not help but marvel at the awesome complexity and vivacity of its myriad threads.

"What is it?" Michael Lowenthal asked, his tone suspended somewhere between fear and fascination.

"I don't know what to call it," Charlotte said. "I daresay that the scroll will tell us."

"I can only guess at its nature," said Oscar Wilde, "but I imagine that we shall discover that it is the murderer's real accomplice. *That*, I suspect, is Rappaccini's daughter, and the woman of flesh and blood is its mere instrument. Those Medusan locks presumably comprise the virtual individual which has moved this Innocent Eve hither and yon throughout the world, fascinating her appointed victims and luring them to the acceptance of her fatal kisses. Perhaps we should think of it as the ultimate femme fatale: vengeful fury appointed by Rappaccini to settle all his earthly accounts."

Charlotte saw Lowenthal's face turn suddenly pallid, and wondered why she had not reacted in the same way.

"And we thought the flowers posed a biohazard!" he said—
we, in this instance, being a grander company by far than the one comprised by his immediate neighbors. "Imagine what *that* could do!"

"Only to those primed for its convenience," Wilde observed—
and then his own expression shifted. Mindful of the number of the eyes that were watching and the ears that would overhear, he hesitated for a second or more—but he was not a cautious man by nature. "And your ever dutiful employers already know, do they not, *exactly* what machines like this could do? Is it not part and parcel of their careful stewardship to keep such monstrosities in their place, locked away in the vaults beneath their infinite emporium where everything unfit for the marketplace is stored?"

Charlotte observed, however, that Wilde made no reference to the probable ultimate source of the income which had fed the less orthodox researches of Michi Urashima and Paul Kwiatek.

"She's got away *again,* hasn't she?" Charlotte murmured.

"I suspect that when your Court of Judgment eventually sits," Oscar Wilde agreed, "that cyborg creature you hold in your hand will be the only guilty party that can legitimately be summoned to appear before it. Alas for the justice which requires to be seen in order to be properly done, I doubt that it has any consciousness or conscience that can be sensibly held to account or punished. The evil that Rappaccini did may have lived after him for a little while, but everything that might have been punished for his sins was interred with his bones."

Charlotte let out her breath, unaware that she had been holding it. The exhalation turned into a long, deep sigh that sounded exactly like one of Oscar Wilde's. She looked up into the little tent of blue sky above the mausoleum, which marked the clearing in which they were standing.

The sky was full of flying eyes which sparkled like crystal dust in the sun's kindly light.

Charlotte knew that the words which they were speaking could be heard by millions of people all over the world and would in time be relayed to billions. The real Court of Judgment was here and now, and any verdict which the three of them chose to return would probably stick.

"It's over," Charlotte said quietly. "Punishment is neither here nor there. It's just a matter of counting the cost." She looked at Michael Lowenthal as she spoke, even though the people he represented were experts on prices rather than costs.

"It was still murder," was all that Lowenthal could find to say.

"Of course it was," said Oscar Wilde. "It was a *perfect* murder—perhaps the only perfect murder the world has seen, as yet."

Happily Ever After

I n Hal Watson's crowded workroom in the bowels of the UN building in New York—whose upper stories were already decaying to ash and dust—Sergeant Charlotte Holmes faced her superior officer with all the calm and confidence she could muster.

"Walter Czastka died of natural causes," Hal told her. "The death certificate makes conventional reference to general neuronal failure, which usually means that the nanotech patchwork holding the hindbrain together couldn't maintain the feedback loops necessary to sustain motor function."

"Usually?" Charlotte queried.

"Regina says that the wastage in Czastka's brain was more extensive than usual, and more evident in the cerebrum."

"What does that imply?"

"In Regina's words: 'If you set aside all the jargon, he just gave up on himself and faded out.' There's no hard evidence in his own files to prove that in 2322 he carried out a series of illegal genetic manipulations on egg cells which had been taken from Maria Inacio's unexpectedly active womb and fertilized by his own spermatozoa, but I've dipped into the private files of those officers of Wollongong University who could have been involved in hushing it up. There's more than enough buried there to support Wilde's conjectures. I'm still excavating it, but all bureaucrats tend to be careful in the maintenance of their private records, however fast and loose they play with official documents. Given that Czastka's death wasn't suspicious, there's no need for us to publish our findings, but I've found sufficient confirmation of the factual allegations contained in Moreau's scroll to be sure that they're true."

"Information which, being good bureaucrats, we'll naturally

commit to our own records, for the edification of future excava-
tors," Charlotte said.

Hal didn't rise to that. "I have hard evidence of the peripheral
involvement of at least twelve others in Czastka's experiment. All
of them, including the murder victims, are commemorated in the
faces of the monkeys on Moreau's island; none are still alive. That's
not to say that it was an organized conspiracy; Czastka appears to
have recruited them as and when he needed them, and it's probable
that none of them knew exactly how many others were involved,
or how. The scroll left behind by Gustave Moreau is based on hear-
say, of course, but it confirms that Maria Inacio knew more than
anyone else—except Walter himself—about the progress of the experiment and the subsequent cover-up. Moreau's account of what
she told him confirms the private notes made by the dean of Walter's faculty and the assistant registrar who arranged the transfer
of the embryo from her womb to the artificial one.

"There's no detailed map of the transformations that Walter
carried out on the embryo formed from the ovum he took from
Inacio's womb and combined with his own sperm, but he was definitely trying to engineer it for longevity. It's explicitly stated that
he worked at several of the key loci to which Zaman later applied
his own transformations. We'll never know how close he came to
succeeding, but he would have been *extremely* lucky to hit on the
right substitutions first time out, without the benefit of the prepar-
atory animal work that Zaman and his peers were able to do."

"If he'd succeeded," Charlotte observed, "we might now be
attributing the New Human Race to the Czastka transformation."

"But he didn't."

"The photographs of Jafri Biasiolo in different phases of his
career as Rappaccini that you showed Wilde when I first brought
him in suggest that what Czastka did must have had *some* effect,"
Charlotte reminded him. "If he'd carried on—if he'd kept track of
Biasiolo and tried again—it would have been hard going, but he

might have given us the New Human Race fifty or sixty years earlier than Ali Zaman."

"If he'd carried on in the 2320s," Hal opined, "he'd have ended up like Michi Urashima: a sacrifice to the forces of convention. He'd have ended up in the freezer, while the masters of the MegaMall divided the work up into manageable packets and made sure the transformations were properly tested on animals before they started work on dismantling the legal restraints. They'd have been right to do it. These things have to be *properly managed*. We're not living in the twentieth century."

"The spin-off from Michi Urashima's pioneering efforts wasn't properly managed, though," Charlotte pointed out. "Not the bits that Rappaccini took it upon himself to carry forward, at any rate."

"From now on," Hal judged, "they will be."

"Does the scroll explain why Moreau did it?" Charlotte asked curiously. She was still harboring the faint hope that Oscar Wilde might have got it completely wrong and that Moreau's madness had not been quite as divine as Wilde insisted.

"It does include some teasing comments about the ethics of scientific research, and a slighting reference to the quality of Walter Czastka's artistry, but there's no detailed explanation of Moreau's motives. He seems to have decided to carry the final solution to the mystery to his grave—unless, of course, he had such perfect trust in Wilde's skills as a detective that he was content to leave that side of the matter to him. Fortunately, I'm not required to include speculations as to motive in my own report."

"The news tapes won't be content with that," Charlotte observed wryly. "The vidveg always want to know *why*."

"The news-tape mongers won't give a damn what we say or don't say, so long as they have the charismatic Dr. Wilde to supply all the lurid fantasies they need, and a few more besides."

"What about the court?" Charlotte asked.

"It won't get to court," Hal told her. "Once the psychologists and neurophysiologists have completed their reports, all charges against the woman will be dropped. There's no doubt that she wasn't in control of her own actions; she doesn't even have any memory of what happened. She's the Robot Assassins' worst nightmare—but however reckless Moreau may have been in other respects, he certainly did his best to make sure that his chief pawn came through it all. It seems that she'll make a full recovery."

"She'll simply walk free, then?"

"Not exactly. She'll be quietly given into the custody of the Secret Masters of the MegaMall. Not as a prisoner, of course, but as a valued employee. They'll pay her whatever salary she requires in exchange for her full cooperation. There's a great deal they can learn from her, or so they hope. It's dangerous knowledge—but it'll be even more dangerous if others decide to follow in Moreau's footsteps and we don't have the means to prevent them."

Charlotte thought about that for a few moments. In the long run, the entire Moreau affair might come to be seen as mere window dressing for the proof that it *was* possible to make brainfeed equipment that would turn humans into mere robots. That knowledge would now be entrusted to the Hardinist Cabal—but were they safe custodians? And if not them, then who? She realized that the repercussions of this remarkable series of incidents would extend over centuries—and that she, Charlotte Holmes, had been privileged to see the whole drama unfold from the best seat in the house.

If only she had been able to play a more active part. . . .

"Walter Czastka could have offered his talent and his enterprise to the Ahasuerus Foundation," Charlotte pointed out when she had decided that she needed more time to mull over the other matter. "If he didn't want to set himself so far outside the mainstream of scientific research, he could at least have given *them* what he had and pointed their people in the right direction. Instead, he decided to cultivate his and everyone else's gardens: not merely to make flowers, but to make flowers to make money. Not only did he refuse to become an Ali Zaman, he even refused to become an Oscar Wilde. Not, apparently, the kind of role model that young Jafri was looking for when Maria Inacio turned up on his doorstep claiming to be his mother and volunteering to tell him everything."

"We don't have to speculate," Hal reminded her.

"No," she admitted, "but it's difficult to avoid it, isn't it? The fact that his mother went and drowned herself—deliberately or not—can't have helped young Jafri to come to terms with his inheritance. It did make him unique, though. From that moment on, he must have been very conscious of the fact that there was nobody else in the world quite like him. I can imagine how it might have preyed on his mind. Whom the gods destroy, they first make mad, according to Euripides."

"That's a terrible habit you've picked up from Wilde," Hal complained, referring to her use of the classical quotation.

"If, by *the gods,* one means the vicissitudes of chance and circumstance," Charlotte went on unrepentantly, "then we all stand on the brink of destruction: every one of us who is not a Natural. Some of us are two hundred years old, others merely twenty, but we're all doomed. Oscar Wilde thinks I ought to be even more fiercely resentful of that fact than he is, because my foster parents actually had the choice of going for the more expensive option and paying for my admission to the New Human Race. Wilde's parents didn't—and whatever Jafri Biasiolo chose to think, neither did his. Perhaps it's just youth that prevents me from plumbing the depths of disappointment that claimed both Wilde and his good friend Rappaccini. Perhaps, in due course, the news of my destruction will actually come home to me. Tell me, Hal—how mad are you? And how long will your sanity last, while we two grow old in a world where the gradually increasing majority of our contemporaries stay young?"

"We're policemen," Hal reminded her. "We're the ones who are supposed to help keep the mad ones in check. Rappaccini and Wilde haven't done us any favors there."

"We're policemen," Charlotte agreed. "We're the ones who are supposed to make sure that the Gustave Moreaus and Michi Urashimas of this world keep their follies at home and their sins in virtual reality. But are we doing the world any favors?"

"I think so," Hal answered without hesitation.

"It's a living, I suppose," she conceded. "It'll keep us occupied until we die, if we want it to. But Oscar Wilde was right about something else too. I won't want to be a policeman all my life. Life's too short, you see, for the likes of us."

"You can't win them all," said Hal philosophically, "no matter how closely you rub shoulders with the biggest winners there are. You have to play the hand you're dealt by fate, as cleverly as you can."

"That's exactly what Jafri Biasiolo must have thought," said Charlotte, determined to have the last word, "and I suppose that's exactly what he did, in his own peculiar fashion."

Having completed his report, Michael Lowenthal looked anxiously around the virtual conference room, trying to measure the response. There were thirteen men and women whose representative sims were arranged about the illusory table, seven of whom he did not yet know by name. Their images were as obsessively minimalist as the "room" in which they were gathered; they looked perfectly human and perfectly ordinary, except for a slight gloss that might have been a reflection of the light that bounced up at them from the polished tabletop.

According to those elements of the Hidden Archive which had so far been opened to Michael's inquiries, there had been a time when the Secret Masters had donned all manner of gaudy raiment in order to conduct their board meetings. They had delighted in appearing to one another as gods and demons, monsters and mirror-men, and they had met at the summits of virtual peaks higher by far than the meager mountains of Earth's crumpled crust—but that had been in the early days of their power. Now they dressed more fittingly, not out of humility but to emphasize that their assemblies were straightforwardly utilitarian, merely a matter of business.

Virtual environments were now the arena of all the most cherished dreams of humankind—every impossible adventure, every bizarre fetish, every body of knowledge, every shameful desire—but the Dominant Shareholders liked to remember that virtual space was first and foremost the repository of the world's wealth. It was where *money* was, and it was where stewardship of the earth was exercised with scrupulous care. Michael knew that this imagistic room was more securely cloaked than any other in all the world, whether bedded in the hardware of the UN police or the so-called World Government. Whatever was said here remained here, consigned to the abyssal core of the Hidden Archive—but those who met here did not think of it as the conference chamber of the Secret Masters, the Gods of Olympus, or the Hardinist Cabal. It was merely a place where businessmen could meet and consider matters of mutual concern. It was just a room with bare walls and a rectangular table, devoid of all unnecessary ostentation, except a little extra polish.

"Thank you, Michael," said the chairman. "All things considered, you did a good job. If you hadn't taken the decision to follow Wilde, the police would certainly have tried—and might have contrived—to keep a little more from us than they actually did. It would have been annoying, to say the least, if we hadn't been able to secure the equipment in that ingenious theater for our exclusive use. There are tricks we can actually *use* in that setup. They're trivial tricks by comparison with what we'll eventually learn from the girl and her lovely hair, but trivial tricks are often the most rewarding, in purely commercial terms."

"I wish the distractions had worked a little better," Michael said, feeling that it was safe, in view of the chairman's generosity, to indulge in a little judicious self-criticism. "I can't help feeling that if only I'd framed my reckless hypotheses a little more cleverly, I might have persuaded Wilde to fall for one or other of them. He *is* a sucker for a good story, and it might have been better if he hadn't been quite so accurate in his subsequent guesses."

"Wilde's a fool," opined a white-haired man who must have been two hundred and twenty if he were a day. "It doesn't matter how accurate he is—no one will ever take his opinions seriously."

"Rightly so, Mr. Hart," observed a female of equal apparent antiquity. "People know full well that it's men like him who invent disparaging terms like *vidveg,* and they're absolutely right to feel insulted. They're correct in their estimation of him as a vain, patronizing poseur. Nobody watching the final act of that farce live identified with him—they all identified with the policewoman. We don't have to put any substantial amount of spin on the commercial résumés; she's already the star, and her act only needs a little cleaning up. Wilde will come across as a spokesman for a lunatic and a lunatic himself; the only people who'll listen to what he says are people who are out on a limb anyway—irrelevant people. The show can't work against us, in the short run or the long. There'll be no substantial comeback about the extirpation. The vast majority will thank us, as they always do."

How was it possible, Michael wondered, to be so old and yet so calm? Why were these people immune to the kinds of resentments which Jafri Biasiolo and Oscar Wilde had stored up against the undying inheritors of Earth?

It was, he realized, people like Oscar Wilde who made up such disparaging epithets as "MegaMall." It was people like Oscar Wilde who charged the people whose duty and vocation it was to run the world with being hidebound monsters of greed, incapable of any but quantitative reckoning. In fact, only people like those gathered around this conference table could properly understand the *quality* of life. By virtue of that understanding, they were neither afraid to die nor resentful of their appointed heirs.

"We were right to let it go all the way," another dutiful soul put in. "It would have been a pity to put a stop to it fifty years ago. The obsessive secrecy of true madmen is a great asset to the sane;

it allows us to be discreet and eclectic in releasing the products of their creativity. It would be a terribly dull world if we always had to take the oddballs out before they did their most interesting work, just because the ripples might spread too fast and too far.''

"But we'll have to keep a closer eye on Wilde, from now on,'' another and more ominous voice put in.

"It's hardly worth it, surely,'' said Michael, so relaxed by now that he did not even feel that he was taking a risk in issuing the mild contradiction. "He'll be dead soon enough, won't he?''

In the Green Carnation Suite of the New York Majestic, Oscar Wilde stood before a full-length mirror, carefully inspecting every detail of his face. He caressed the flawless flesh with sensitive fingertips, rejoicing in its gloss.

"Ivory and rose leaves,'' he murmured. The sound of his voice, lower in pitch and more musical than he remembered it, gave him an exquisite thrill.

He repeated the phrase reverently, as though it were a magical incantation: "Ivory and rose leaves.''

Oscar had never been afraid of vanity. He was a man ready and willing to address his own reflection in the most admiring terms, provided only that it remained full of youth and perfect in its symmetry. Whenever it grew old, as it had three times over, it lost its capacity to inspire admiration and became a mocking reminder of the hazards which he and all men of his obsolescent kind still faced: decay, senescence, decomposition.

"One hundred and thirty-three years old,'' he said softly. "One hundred and thirty-three years old, and young again. Age cannot wither, nor custom stale. . . .''

He reached out to pluck a green carnation from the wall beside the mirror. It was one of only half a dozen in full bloom, and he twirled it between his delicate fingers, admiring it with as much satisfaction as he admired his own image.

The flower was a trivial creation, only a little more elegant than the variety which the horticulturalists of old had wrought without the aid of genetic engineering, but it had been a necessary endeavor. It was a joke, of course, but a very serious joke. The never-ending games which Oscar played in consequence of his name were no mere matter of public relations. His identification with the ideas and ideals of his alter ego had long ago become a deep-seated obsession as well as a mischievous fetish. He was not afraid to acknowledge that fact, nor to take pride in it. He had always felt that life, if it were to be lived to the full in modern conditions, required a definite style and aesthetic shape: a constant flow of delicate ironies, tensions, and innovations; a *cause*. Perhaps, as Charlotte Holmes and Michael Lowenthal clearly believed, his own cause was hardly less mad than poor Rappaccini's—but then again, perhaps all causes that had the power to change the world were bound to be reckoned mad until they bore sweet fruit.

He placed the flower in the mock buttonhole of his neatly tailored SAP black suitskin. Black was, he thought, the perfect background for a green carnation—and a room full of green carnations was the perfect background for a man in black.

Oscar was fully aware of the debt of gratitude which he owed to his wallflowers. Furnishing hotel interiors was vulgar hackwork unbefitting a real artist, but a real artist had to make a living, and the commonplaceness of such commissions could always be slightly offset by such flourishes of unorthodoxy as having it written into every contract that one suite of rooms should be fitted with green carnations instead of the more fashionable roses and amaranths and should always be available for his exclusive use.

His clients did not mind in the least his making such demands; they were, after all, paying for his fashionability rather than his technical dexterity, and he could not have been nearly so fashionable were it not for his extravagantly extrovert eccentricity. There were now hotels in thirty-six cities which could provide him with a distinctive pied-à-terre, and he felt entirely justified in thinking of the green carnation suites as his homes away from home.

His real home, of course, was the island which he had leased for his experiments in Creation.

Oscar half turned one way and then the other, shrugging his shoulders to make sure that the false jacket extruded by his suitskin hung perfectly upon his remodeled body. He had renewed his entire wardrobe since his rejuvenation; it had been absolutely necessary that he should—how could a man feel a tangible pulse of joy at finding himself full of youth unless he acted the part with total conviction?

"Clothes maketh the man," he murmured, "or, if the man is clever enough to be self-made, must at least refrain from unmaking him." He did not have to make a note to remember the remark; even in his inner sanctum the bubblebugs were active around the clock. They would stay that way until the first signs of aging began to show again upon his face and in the timbre of his voice.

Oscar felt that he, unlike most men of his age, had conscientiously adapted his ideas to the reality of twenty-fifth-century life. He had discarded outdated notions of privacy in favor of making a perfect record of his beautiful life. For this reason, if for no other, he was determined to be content with nothing less than sartorial perfection. This evening was, after all, to be the auspicious occasion of his reemergence into the social world. His involvement in the Rappaccini affair, and the quarantine which he had been forced to endure thereafter, had delayed his new debut but had also made certain that it would be even more dazzling than he had ever dared to hope. He was famous now, and would be for at least a quarter of an hour as the clock of history made revolution after revolution. He was profoundly glad that fame had descended upon him at exactly the right moment, while he looked his best for what would almost certainly be the last time.

"It is only shallow people," he informed his reflection, confident in the knowledge that it would be an appreciative audience, "who do not judge by appearances. Adonis, perfection is thine."

He bathed in the luxury of his own narcissism, admiring his

gray eyes, his soft lips, his pearly white teeth. He savored the complexity of his emotions as he contemplated his beauty and his ambitions. There was a warm glow of gratitude and relief—tinged with
admiration—for the artistry of the somatic engineers who had restored his body to its excellent state.

"You're a fool, Oscar," a friend had said to him when he had
confessed his intention to chance a third rejuvenation. "You had
twenty years of wear still left in your last body when you turned it
in, and you've at least twenty left in this one. Only a fool would
take the risk."

Oscar had often been called a fool. Most of the people he knew
probably thought that his entire lifestyle was nothing but foolish-
ness. He was immune to such criticism. He knew full well that when
he was called a fool the people who used the word meant it in its
common or garden sense, but he always heard it as a more dignified
reference.

"Certainly I am a Fool," he had replied more than once. "I am
an unfettering Feste, court jester to the Biotechnic Aristocracy, the
Touchstone which tests the metal of the Golden Age. I am one of
those who is privileged to whisper in the ears of the modern multitude the fateful words: 'Remember that thou art the last of mortal
men!' I am the harbinger of Eternal Youth. I am proud to be a
Fool."

Beneath the gratitude and the relief which he felt upon finding
himself young again, however, were sterner feelings. He knew well
enough that the tissue replenishments had only made a beginning
for him. He had been provided with the raw material of youth, but
it still remained for him to complete the work of art by dressing his
new body, animating it, and providing the soul and the intelligence
which would put its youth to work. The genius of medicine had
painted a portrait of Adonis, but it would be his own task to *be*
Adonis: to live extravagantly, perfectly, and beautifully. There were
deeper regrets too; had he not been so anxious to make the most
of his celebrity, he would have been in mourning, not so much for

Rappaccini but for Rappaccini's Creation, condemned by the UN as poisonous and erased from the face of the Pacific.

Oscar did not doubt for a moment, as his greedy eyes devoured the glory of his reflection, that he would be equal to the immediate task before him. He had never been the kind of habit-dominated man who renewed his appearance only to remain confined by a straitjacket which his earlier way of life had made for him. He was no crass businessman, apt to fall back into the same old routines at the first opportunity, wearing a new face as if it were merely a mask laid over the old. Nor was he the kind of man who would go to the opposite extreme, reverting to the habits and follies of first youthfulness, playing the sportsman or the rake as though there were nothing to do with the gift of youth except recycle the same stereotyped errors. He was a man properly equipped, in heart and in mind, for serial rejuvenation. There would be time, later, for him to prove himself equal to the less immediate task of making sure that the example of Rappaccini's reckless inventiveness did not go entirely to waste. There would even be time for him to become a murderer, if he decided that the cause of Art demanded it.

He closed his eyes for one last lingering moment while he savored the pleasures of anticipation. He pretended that the moment was an infinite one, in which a man might lose himself in the ecstasy of a chosen dream.

Such was the power of his imagination that he did indeed win a moment's suspension of the oppressive curse of Time: a moment of true and total freedom which promised to last . . . certainly not forever, and certainly not long *enough,* but at least for a little while.

He knew that it was up to him to use that little while as fully as he could, not merely here in the great wide world whose eyes were yet upon him and whose ears were eager for his every epigram and aphorism, but also in his private island covert: his garden; his folly; his *Creation.* Would the world ever see his like again, once he was gone? He was, of course, an imitation, but he was an imitation which had outshone its original. The first Oscar Wilde would have approved of that, just as he would have approved of the fact that in the company of Charlotte Holmes, he had reduced her to the role of a mere Watson, while he himself had played the master of deduction.

If only there were time enough, Oscar thought, to be a thousand men instead of one or two. What a wonder I might have made of myself, had my youth been truly eternal!